JOCKEY GIRL

JOCKEY GIRL

SHELLEY PETERSON

DUNDURN
TORONTO

Copy editor: Maryan Gibson
Design: BJ Weckerle
Cover Design: Courtney Horner
Cover image: © Dave Landry Photo
Illustrations: © Marybeth Drake
Printer: Webcom

Library and Archives Canada Cataloguing in Publication

Peterson, Shelley, 1952-, author
    Jockey girl / Shelley Peterson.

Issued in print and electronic formats.

ISBN 978-1-4597-3434-0 (paperback).--ISBN 978-1-4597-3435-7 (pdf).-- ISBN 978-1-4597-3436-4 (epub)

I. Title.

PS8581.E8417J63 2015   jC813'.54   C2015-905600-4
                                                 C2015-905601-2

1   2   3   4   5   20   19   18   17   16

 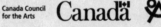

We acknowledge the support of the **Canada Council for the Arts** and the **Ontario Arts Council** for our publishing program. We also acknowledge the financial support of the **Government of Canada** through the **Canada Book Fund** and **Livres Canada Books**, and the **Government of Ontario** through the **Ontario Book Publishing Tax Credit** and the **Ontario Media Development Corporation**.

Care has been taken to trace the ownership of copyright material used in this book. The author and the publisher welcome any information enabling them to rectify any references or credits in subsequent editions.

— *J. Kirk Howard, President*

The publisher is not responsible for websites or their content unless they are owned by the publisher.

Printed and bound in Canada.

VISIT US AT

Dundurn.com | @dundurnpress | Facebook.com/dundurnpress | Pinterest.com/dundurnpress

Dundurn
3 Church Street, Suite 500
Toronto, Ontario, Canada
M5E 1M2

To those who find the
courage to move forward,
who choose not to remain mired
in the disappointments of the past.

The Caledon Horse Race

"Riders up!"

Evangeline Gibb swallowed hard. *We shouldn't be here*, she thought. If her father had any idea....

Today was the eleventh of June, the day of the Caledon Horse Race. The biggest event in town. It'd seemed like it would never arrive. But here it was, with a bright blue sky and a slight breeze sent from above to relieve the climbing temperature.

Evie took the reins in her left hand and prepared to mount the nervous black horse she'd renamed Kazzam. He was the smallest horse entered — at fifteen hands, barely taller than a pony — but he was fit and muscled and ready to run.

Kazzam pawed the ground and shook his head. He flattened his ears and pranced with anticipation, then shook his silky, short black mane impatiently. Every time she almost got her foot in the stirrup he moved away. "Settle down, Mister Racehorse," she cooed as she scratched his withers and again tried to climb on, again without success. "You're making me look stupid."

Kazzam stopped skittering for a split second and Evie seized the opportunity. She slipped her left boot into the stirrup and scrambled up into the saddle with speed, if not grace. "Thanks for your help," she muttered.

Evie sat as quietly as she could, waiting for Kazzam, and for herself, to calm down. His body trembled underneath her as she stroked his neck. "You're the fastest horse here and we're going to prove it." Electricity coursed through his tensed muscles and into her hands and legs.

All around them, fired-up horses snorted and jigged and jogged. Riders in multicoloured shirts controlled their mounts with grim faces, shouting out competitive jibes to one another. Evie tried to keep her distance, at least out of kicking range. She wondered if this was what it was like to be in the eye of a storm. She shivered in spite of the heat.

Folks had travelled for miles to cheer for their favourites, and the old wooden stands were packed with chattering people in bright summer clothes. The air virtually vibrated with noise and suspense.

Evie had drawn slot seven. There'd been fourteen riders lined up at the registration desk to enter, and she was the only female. And at sixteen, the youngest by five or ten years.

This is such a bad idea. If her father found out what she was doing, he'd skin her alive. But ... the prize money. One thousand dollars plus ten percent of the purse. It could add up to a lot of money. Money that Evie needed to find her mother.

At the thought, a tingle of excitement travelled up her arms and ended with a *ping* in her chest. Her mother. Angela. She might be alive, after all.

Evie tightened her legs as Kazzam reared, lifting both front hooves high off the ground. She reached forward and stroked his gleaming black neck. She loved how the sunlight made his coat look almost purple. "Take it easy, boy. It won't be long."

She sure hoped that was true. Horses and riders were gathered at the starting gate, and everyone, human and equine alike, was getting tenser by the second. If she was going to follow through with her plan and not lose her nerve, this race had better start soon.

"Daddy buy you a pony, little girl?"

Evie looked up to see a smirking man on a tall, tucked-up Thoroughbred. He looked like a professional jockey in his red-and-purple racing silks with matching cap and saddle cloth. She glanced around. *Is he talking to me?*

"Yes, you, freckle-face red ponytail." He laughed a forced *hahaha*, and checked with the man beside him.

His friend was riding a horse that could have been a twin to his own. This man wore blue-and-green silks. "Hey!" he guffawed. "Get a look at the headgear on baby's pony!"

Evie had customized Kazzam's bridle with a face guard to hide his distinctive, heart-shaped white star, and she'd done a half-decent sewing job. Kazzam liked it just fine.

"The kiddie race was last week!" the man in blue and green continued, as though he hadn't made his point.

Evie thought she should respond. "Nice horses." She didn't add, *I hope they like looking at my horse's butt*.

A third man, clad in bright yellow, trotted over to join his friends. It seemed he had news. "There's a registration problem."

Evie blushed and pretended not to listen. She hoped that the problem had nothing to do with her fake name or her "borrowed" horse.

"Crap." The man wearing red-and-purple silks frowned. "This horse is ready to run."

"How's the betting?" blue-and-green asked.

"Flying Pan's the odds-on favourite."

Blue-and-green scoffed. "Out of the Flying Pan into the fire?"

Purple-and-red laughed his *hahaha* and said, "He'll be back in the dust with pony-girl here." He gestured at Evie dismissively. The three men snickered.

Evie lifted an eyebrow slightly. They didn't know anything and were about to find out.

In the last couple of minutes the crowd had become restless. One section started stamping in unison. Evie was worried. If the race was delayed much longer, there'd be trouble.

The public-address system abruptly transmitted high-pitched feedback at full volume, startling the horses. Red-and-purple's horse bucked and the man was tossed off. He landed on his feet, but when he finally managed to remount the terrified horse, he whipped him hard.

Evie didn't like that at all. This beating was totally unproductive. If you don't react within a couple of seconds, a horse has no idea what he did wrong. Now his beautiful Thoroughbred was confused and rattled.

Under her breath she said, "Daddy buy you a new one," in the same condescending tone that he'd used earlier to her.

"Eat my dust, kid!" Red-and-purple seethed.

Evie had not meant him to hear her, and was frightened by the intensity of the man's anger. She moved farther away and frowned: this could escalate into something bad. She was saved by yet another screech from the loudspeakers.

"Ladies and gentlemen!" blared the speakers. "The tenth annual Caledon Horse Race is about to begin!"

The stands rumbled as people jumped to their feet. Applause exploded, resonating like thunder. It looked to

Evie as though a thousand colourful ants were swarming all over the wooden seats. Maybe the heat was getting to her. Or maybe the adrenalin. She hoped the latter.

"Riders, bring your horses to the post."

Evie couldn't breathe, but there was no turning back now. With a slight squeeze of her calves, she asked Kazzam to move forward. Step by step they walked to their slot in the seventh stall. Once in, the rear door shut behind them with a metallic click like a popgun.

Evie's heart thudded loudly in her ears, deafening her. The daylight was suddenly way too bright, and her muscles felt limp. Time stretched like warm toffee. Was she about to die of a heart attack? Was that even possible at sixteen?

Some of the other riders were having trouble getting their mounts into their posts, but Kazzam stood still, waiting for his gate to open.

Evie hugged his neck. She closed her eyes and quietly whispered a little prayer. "Dear Lord of creatures great and small, please please please help Kazzam run fast today. Give his feet wings, and if he wins I promise to be good for the rest of my life. Amen." Kazzam flicked his delicately pointed ears and nickered as if he understood.

Evie opened her eyes. Somewhere down the blurred row of horses on her right, the rear door clanked shut behind the last horse.

The bell rang and the gates flew open. "And they're off!"

Kazzam didn't move.

Evie watched thirteen horses surge out of the starting gate and tear down the track in a dense cloud of dust.

It was a spectacular sight.

Evie waited. She desperately longed to urge him to run, but knew well the fate of the jockeys who'd kicked him on.

Three long seconds later, Kazzam jolted forward in a giant leap that lifted Evie up into the air with only his mane in her hands. With a huge effort and a whole lot of luck, she landed in the saddle and held on to the racing animal like a scared monkey. Her stirrups were lost and the reins were out of reach. Her helmet had slipped over her eyes. It was impossible to see anything except the ground beneath her, and it was moving awfully fast.

Kazzam thundered on. Evie bent her head down and used his neck to push her helmet back so she could see. Dust. Dust was all she could see. *Don't panic*, she told herself. *Kazzam knows where his feet go*. Seconds passed before a solid form emerged from the hazy cloud ahead. The rump of a horse.

They were catching up rapidly, but her legs were tiring just as fast. She needed the stirrups. Even one would help. She felt for the left one blindly with her foot as Kazzam sped past the horse running last and came up on the outside of another. *Bingo!* The left stirrup. She cast about on her right side, located the other, and slid in her boot. Still no reins, but things were much improved.

Kazzam ran smoothly. He felt eager as they passed three more horses on the outside. But there was trouble just ahead — a traffic jam with half a dozen animals running as a herd, tight to the inside of the track. She needed reins to get around them.

She grabbed his mane with her right fist and crept her left hand farther and farther up his mane all the way to his ears until she was finally able to clutch the flapping reins. She forced herself to breathe. *Steady on*. Now she was ready to ride.

Evie and Kazzam veered to the outside of the group. She felt him accelerate as they sailed past, down the stretch. She smiled and almost laughed out loud. She loved his crazy power! But Kazzam had more speed in him yet.

They were closing the distance to the two front-runners. Kazzam moved inside and Evie looked for an opening. Kazzam began to crowd the horses from behind to create a space for himself, but Evie second-guessed him. She pulled him back to go around. Just as Kazzam slowed, three from the group they'd just passed galloped by on their right and overtook them all.

Evie could feel the tension explode in Kazzam's body.

His ears flattened. Jamming her heels down in case of a buck, she let the reins go slack, crouched forward on his back and kept still. As soon as she gave him his head, Kazzam circled wide around the former leaders on the outside and then made a charge to catch the three horses that had just passed. The wind of their speed forced tears down Evie's cheeks as they narrowed the gap. She sat as small as she could and let her horse run. The rumps of the three ahead got bigger and bigger. Through the dust she noticed the silks. Purple and red, blue and green, and bright yellow. Her tormentors were running as a team, three abreast.

Her horse was flying. Evie couldn't fathom how fast. *This* was the speed she'd been waiting for. She was riding an avalanche! A tsunami! A runaway train!

Time slowed in her imagination. It seemed as though the purple-and-red and blue-and-green and yellow silks on her left were running on the spot. They disappeared behind her. The three perfect Os of the surprised men's gaping mouths became imprinted in her mind as she looked ahead at clear track. Kazzam was the one making dust now.

The little horse's strides got longer and longer. His neck stretched further and further. The only noise Evie heard was Kazzam's steady breathing in rhythm with his front hooves as they hit the track. She felt lighter than air as they passed the finish line riding dead centre down the middle of the empty track.

"Whoa, boy." Evie pulled on his reins. On he galloped. Kazzam wasn't finished his race. "Steady, boy!" She wondered how much more he had to prove.

Evie looked back to see the second, third, and fourth horses finish together. They were far behind. She guessed that Kazzam had won by ten horse-lengths. Maybe more.

Kazzam began to listen to Evie as they got to the turn. He slowed a little and then slowed some more, but he was so fit and keen that he threw a happy buck up in the air. Evie laughed and crowed. "We did it, Kazzam! We won!" She stood up in the stirrups and shot a fist into the air.

They trotted back to the finish line, waving to the cheering crowds. She'd never felt so good. All these people were witnesses to Kazzam's upset victory. *You respect this tough little horse now,* she thought. *And you think I'm worth something, too.* Evie took a mental snapshot of the moment so she could remember it for the rest of her life.

Her elation was cut short by a group of people who came running onto the track with cameras. They motioned eagerly for her to come closer.

Evie hadn't expected this. She thought fast. She'd love to disappear into thin air but had no choice if she wanted to get the prize money. She pasted a big smile on her face and hoped the dust and streaks of sweat and tears would disguise her face. She trotted Kazzam over and let them snap away.

"How long have you been riding?" asked a young-looking unshaven man, who she assumed was a reporter.

Before she could answer, several others crowded around. "Is this your horse?"

"Who's your trainer?"

"What's Kazzam's breeding?"

"Is this your first race?"

"Where do you live?"

Evie was tongue-tied. She had no idea how to answer the questions without giving away her identity and getting herself in big trouble.

With perfect timing once again, the speakers blared.

"Attention, folks! We have a winner. Young Molly Peebles riding Kazzam. They won by a record *eight* lengths!"

The crowd erupted again into cheers and hoots and stamping feet. Evie thought they'd won by more, but she wasn't about to complain.

"She's the youngest person to win in the ten years we've held the race. Molly takes away one thousand dollars in prize money, *plus* five hundred and eighty dollars as her share of the purse! She's a lucky, lucky girl!"

A stout man in a Homburg hat stepped forward. He wore old-fashioned English country clothes with a plaid vest. Evie imagined that he thought it hid his fat belly. He waved a large white envelope high in the air and turned around to show it to the crowd in the stands.

The announcer introduced him, bellowing over the sound system, "Cast your eyes over to the track, folks. You'll recognize Murray Planno, our esteemed judge — he's a racing steward at Woodbine Race Track. He'll now present our winner with the prize money."

Murray Planno took his cue. He pivoted on his heel and handed Evie the envelope with a grand flourish. "Well done, Molly Peebles. The little lady on the little black horse!" he said loudly. "Nicely done!"

Evie continued to smile broadly. She accepted the envelope and nodded her thanks, while her eyes searched for the best way to get out of the park, away from all the questions. She spotted an opening.

"Molly!" called a photographer. "I need one with you holding the envelope!"

"Molly!" called another. "I'd like to get your story for the *Orangeville Banner*!"

"Molly!"

"Molly!"

"Molly!"

They were closing in.

Evie stuffed the big envelope into her waistband. She cupped an ear with one hand and shook her head, pretending she couldn't hear their questions over the din of the crowd. "Let's go, Kazzam," she whispered, and squeezed her calves together with purpose.

Kazzam leaped forward into a canter. Evie guided him toward the stands, waving and mouthing thank-yous to the appreciative audience. She and Kazzam had given them a show and now the show was over. Almost.

She pulled on Kazzam's reins and sat back, asking the horse to rear straight up in the air. He did, and she held him in the pose for as long as he was steady, and then released the pressure so he'd drop his front feet to the ground. As soon as his hooves touched down, he galloped through the hole in the crowd, past the entrance gates, and directly toward the gravel road behind the stands.

Exit, stage right.

2

Yolanda

The morning began to heat up as Evie and Kazzam trotted toward home. They took a shortcut down a lane beside a stone barn, which had been built into the hill more than a century ago. Evie liked these old Ontario "bank barns," because the thick stone walls kept the inside cool all summer and held the heat of the animals in the winter. Evie thought that horses seemed more content in them than in modern barns.

She glanced behind herself. No sign of the dented black sedan that had tailed them from the fairgrounds. She and Kazzam had ducked off the road and trespassed through the fields to avoid it. She hoped that they'd lost it for good.

She slowed the little black racehorse to a walk as they neared the gravel road. He really needed cooling down. They must get back to Maple Mills Stables before anyone noticed Kazzam was gone, but there was no rush, Evie thought. He wouldn't be missed until noon.

Kazzam's real name was No Justice, and no justice was exactly how it felt to be misunderstood and underrated. She and Kazzam shared those labels. Too bad today's success had to be kept secret. Evie snorted. How she'd love to look her father in the eye and say, "We won!" But she couldn't. And wouldn't. He was terrifying. Her own personal bogeyman.

Her father could go from smiling to white rage in two seconds. Worse, she was never exactly sure what would cause his anger or how he would react. He was able to reduce her to jelly with a whisper.

It had always been like that. When Evie was eight, she had a paint pony named Chiquita. She loved her with all her heart, and used to climb on her bareback in the field and go for little jaunts when nobody was around. Her father disapproved. One day, he caught her at it. Without saying a word, he grabbed Chiquita by her halter and began to beat her with a whip. The pony was frantic. Evie begged him to stop. It didn't make sense. He should punish *her*, not the pony. It was *her* fault, not Chiquita's. Her pleas fell on deaf ears.

Grayson Gibb knew that the most effective way to make his point was to hurt the animals Evie loved. She never rode Chiquita again without permission, but she also never trusted her father again. He baffled her. He made her wary. He'd taught her a lesson that day. There was only one way to survive, and that was to keep quiet and as far away from him as possible.

And then, there was her stepmother. Evie sighed in frustration. Paulina was much less complicated but totally irritating. Evie was eight years old when Paulina had moved to Maple Mills with her daughter, Beatrice, and made it very clear that Beatrice was the princess of the house, not Evie. Simply put, Paulina and Evie had never gotten along.

The birth of their brother, Jordie, had helped a little because it tied the family together — Evie was Grayson's kid, Beatrice was Paulina's kid, and Jordie was both. It also helped that Jordie was such a nice kid. Aside from Jordie, Evie's family life was a mess. She shook her head to erase the images of her unpredictable father and selfish step-mother. Anyway, that was old news.

The *new* news was that she'd totally embarrassed her-self at school. Actually, "embarrassed" didn't cover it a fraction, thought Evie. Try "mortified." She blushed deep red just thinking about it.

It had all started when her friend Amelia told her that Mark Sellers liked her. So she asked him to a party. He told Evie that he couldn't go and then said snarky things about her to Amelia, who thought they were funny and posted them on her Facebook wall. It was awful. Really awful.

When Evie read how everybody, even her so-called best friends Cassie, Hilary, and Rebecca, *plus* kids at other schools, jumped on the bandwagon, she panicked and hurled her cellphone from the school bus window into the Credit River in Cheltenham. She didn't want to know how crazy they thought she was to imagine that Mark, a really popular guy, would want anything to do with her.

Immediately, she'd rued her impulsive reaction. If she could've leaped into the river after her cell, she would've. Now she had no phone, no connection with school, and no way to know what was going on. She couldn't even check Facebook, because she wasn't allowed to use the computer at home. Worst of all, she had no idea if she had any friends left. Evie's face twisted with regret as she pictured her phone at the bottom of the deep, fast-flowing river. *Too late now*, she thought.

Whatever, the fact remained that Mark Sellers had made it impossible for her to return to school. *Jerk*.

Evie allowed herself to wallow a bit. It'd be nice to have a mother at a time like this. Someone whose shoulder she could cry on. A loving mother who would help her figure out what to do.

She patted Kazzam's neck as they walked along the country road. "You are the only good thing in my life."

Kazzam, a.k.a. No Justice, was a Thoroughbred of impeccable breeding and great speed, a descendant of some of the great sires. But he also had a problem. Twice he'd bucked jockeys off in a race, and twice was once too many. His future was now in question. But Evie loved Kazzam *because* of his problems, not in spite of them. It was like they recognized each other as misfits. He was a kindred spirit. She couldn't explain it any other way.

He had spunk, and Evie admired that. He held his head with pride and he strutted like a champ. Of the thirty horses on the farm, it was Kazzam who caught Evie's eye. She stroked his neck again as they ambled along.

Six months earlier, Kazzam kicked a groom across the aisle of the barn. The groom howled in anger and grabbed a broom to smack the horse. Something in Kazzam's eye alerted her that the broom would only escalate to war, so she stepped between it and the horse and stopped the blow by grabbing the broom. The groom begged her not to report him. Evie assured him that she would not.

That was the day she'd nicknamed him Kazzam, because it was like they'd made a magical connection. From that moment on, Kazzam looked at her as his friend. He allowed her to handle him easily, unlike any other person.

After that incident, the exercise riders were only too happy to let her bathe him and cool him down after workouts. And she'd never forget the first time she got on his back. Never had she dreamed of such athleticism, such muscular tension. Even at an easy walk, she could feel his power!

Then, on June 1, her sixteenth birthday, several events coincided, causing a plan of action to form in her head. Her association with Kazzam became serious.

Firstly, that day he dumped a jockey at the starting gate for the second time in a stakes race, causing him to be banned from racing by the Ontario Jockey Club. His training schedule was immediately discontinued.

Secondly, she noticed a poster advertising the Caledon Horse Race at McCarron's feed store, with a thousand-dollar prize. Come one, come all, it read. Register at the gate.

Thirdly, later that very same day, their housekeeper, Sella, delivered a very special birthday card to her. It was from an aunt she'd never known.

Until the moment she read the brief note written in her great-aunt Mary's scrawling hand, she'd believed what her father had told her all her life — that her mother was dead.

Evie knew the words of the note by heart:

Dearest Evangeline,

I wish you a very happy birthday. Sweet sixteen already! How the time has flown. Your mother always tells me how very proud she is of you. Please send me a picture! I'm sure you're a beautiful girl, since you were such a beautiful baby, and so much like Angela.

With much love, in hopes that this card will get to you,
your great-aunt Mary

Aunt Mary had written that Angela *tells* her, not *told* her how proud she is of her daughter. And that Evie's mother *is* proud of her, not *was*. Present tense, not past!

Immediately, Evie had called the number that was on the bottom of the card. It had a Toronto area code. Aunt Mary instantly invited Evie to come for a visit. And she said she could lead her to Angela. Evie was thrilled.

She'd run to her father to tell him, expecting him to be happy to get rid of her for a weekend, but he'd shut her down. He'd called Aunt Mary "an interfering old trouble-making bat," adding that she was "deranged and delusional." According to Grayson Gibb, any relative of Angela's was mentally ill.

To tell the truth, Evie *had* considered this possibility. She'd heard nothing good about her mother's side of the family. Ever. Could Aunt Mary be in denial, unable to accept the fact of Angela's death? Or could she be trying to cause trouble, like her father said?

Evie resolved to cast caution to the wind. Aunt Mary sounded very nice and perfectly sane. The way Evie saw the situation, she had nothing to lose and everything to gain. All she needed was the money to get herself to Toronto.

That's where Kazzam came in, and the Caledon race.

That same night, on the evening of her sixteenth birthday, she'd started taking Kazzam out on the practice track, late, when nobody saw. She couldn't ask for advice. Nobody must know what she was doing. So she'd watched how the experts did it and copied them as best she could.

And they'd won! Evie sat up in the saddle and straightened her shoulders with a full inhalation. Winning the Caledon Horse Race sure felt good. The money in Evie's pocket felt good, too. She patted the large envelope to be sure it was still there. If her mother, Angela, was alive, Evie would find her, starting with a visit to Aunt Mary in Toronto. Kazzam had done his part already. And nobody would ever know.

A familiar voice broke into her reverie.

"Hey, Evie!"

She emerged from her daydreams and looked around.

The waving arm of Yolanda Schmits protruded from the open window of a royal-blue truck hauling a royal-blue horse trailer with the white lettering "Maple Mills Stables."

Evie waved back. "Hey, Yoyo!" Yolanda had worked at Maple Mills ever since Evie could remember. She'd run away from home at fifteen and had worked at the track until she'd got the job with them.

"Need a lift? I got the rig safety-checked this morning and I'm heading home."

"Great!" The truck's air conditioning was a nice thought, and Kazzam would probably appreciate a ride back.

Yolanda stepped out and opened the back ramp of the trailer, while Evie slid to the ground and removed Kazzam's saddle. Yolanda took it from her and put it in the tack section.

Evie led the tired horse onto the trailer, slid the bridle over his ears, and let him spit out the bit. Kazzam licked his mouth and rubbed his forehead on her arm.

"You're a great horse. Nobody can say otherwise now." Evie clipped on the halter, scratched his ears, and then gave his neck a hug. "See you at home." His watchful right eye followed her out.

Once Evie had lifted the ramp and fastened the clamps, they were on their way.

"*Soo*, what are you doing so far from the farm?" asked Yolanda, casually looking her over.

Evie removed her helmet and shook out her sweaty, long red hair. "Thought I'd take No Justice for a hack. He never gets out."

Yolanda made a *phuh* noise with her lips. "Only because he's the spookiest horse on the planet."

"Not always."

Yolanda raised an eyebrow. "He never dumps you and races home. That's why the jocks hate you."

"Lucky me, I guess."

"Okay, Evie. Truth time. You're a mess. You were racing." It wasn't a question.

Evie didn't answer.

"You want clues? Grimy streaks down your face. Dust and dirt all over your clothes." Yolanda shot her another sideways glance. "I won't tell anybody. You know I won't. The truth, Evie. The Caledon Horse Race."

The old black sedan came up fast, passing on their left and spraying gravel. Evie ducked in time. He would've caught up to them for sure if Yolanda hadn't picked them up. Evie pulled some McDonald's napkins from the glove compartment and worked at removing the dirt from her freckled face.

"You think a spit bath will help?"

Evie pursed her lips and said nothing. It would be much better for Yolanda if she didn't know. That way she wouldn't be an accomplice if Evie was caught.

"I was listening to the Erin station while I was waiting at the garage. Heard the Caledon Race. The whole thing."

"Oh?" Evie pretended innocence. "Who won?"

"A sixteen-year-old girl named Molly Peebles. Riding a small black horse. It's all over the news." Yolanda glanced at Evie for a reaction. "They say she's deaf."

Deaf? Evie found a brush in the console and started the job of disentangling her matted hair. "Really."

"Go ahead and admit it." Yolanda's voice was serious. "Everybody and his brother is wondering about

Molly Peebles. It's a big mystery. A curiosity. Hard to keep it secret for long."

"I can trust you, Yoyo. I know I can. But I don't want to get you in trouble."

"Like it would be the first time?" Yolanda snorted.

Evie was sorely tempted to tell her all about it. In fact, she was bursting to share the thrills and all the details, from sneaking Kazzam out of the field early that morning to eluding the reporters. The shaky start. Losing her stirrups. Catching up. Crossing the finish line first.

But this was bigger than just racing her father's horse without permission. Evie was about to run away from home. If Yolanda knew anything about it, she'd lose her job.

Up ahead, the old black sedan sat idling on the side of the road. Evie pretended to be busy looking through some imaginary papers on her lap and snuck a peek as they drove past. The driver, a man, was on his cellphone, and he was definitely one of the reporters. The one with the scruffy chin. She watched through the side mirror as he pulled out and followed them.

"Okay," said Yolanda. "Why do you care who that is?"

"I don't."

Yolanda sighed. "You're such a bad liar."

They drove in silence as they turned onto the side road and travelled along the white, four-board horse-fences that enclosed the pristine pastures of Maple Mills Stables. At the entrance, they waited while the big white gates, activated by the remote on the dash, slowly opened.

Evie saw in the side mirror that the black sedan was right behind them.

"Do you want to talk to this guy?" asked Yolanda.

"Not really."

"Okay, then. I'll deal with him." Yolanda stopped the rig halfway through the entrance and approached the reporter's car window.

"May I help you?" she asked. Her voice was pleasant.

Evie couldn't hear what the man said.

"I have no idea if he's available, Mr. Reynolds."

Again Evie could hear only a mumbled response, but then the man got out of his car and Evie heard him clearly. "I'm working on a story. A soft story, a good news story about a girl and her horse." He edged closer to the window of the horse trailer. Evie got worried. If he caught a glimpse of the dirt-caked black racehorse, she'd be busted for sure.

She decided to take a risk. She checked the mirror to be sure her face was acceptably clean, then jumped out and strode around to face Yoyo and the reporter. "What *is* the delay, Yolanda?" She tossed her head and tried to mimic her stepmother's impatient, spoiled tone. She thought she got the faux society accent just right.

Yoyo's eyes widened.

Close up, Evie assessed the reporter as decent-looking and youngish, with grey eyes and floppy dark hair. He held out his hand for her to shake. "Chet Reynolds. I'm —"

Evie ignored his hand, and spoke to Yolanda. "We're already late." Then, as if it was an afterthought, she asked the reporter, "Do you have an appointment with anyone?"

"No, but I have a few ques—"

"Then I suggest you call before you come back." She handed him one of the Maple Mills Racing Stables cards that were kept in the console of the truck. Evie aped the fake smile her stepmother used when dismissing staff. "Come, Yolanda." Evie tossed her head again for good measure and got back in the truck.

Her heart rate was elevated, but her mission was accomplished. The reporter backed his car out onto the road and departed.

Yolanda climbed in and drove through. The gates swung shut behind them. "Scary imitation."

Evie laughed in a burst of release. "Don't worry. I'm still me."

They slowly drove up the long lane edged with maple trees and white horse-fences. Elegant Thoroughbred horses grazed and relaxed in the trimmed paddocks.

"That guy won't disappear so easily," warned Yolanda. "I can feel trouble coming."

"Like it would be the first time," joked Evie.

Yolanda didn't smile. "You better be careful. Paulina would love you to screw up, and your father is having no luck with his horses. He's in a bad mood. You know it."

Nothing could take the joy out of Evie more quickly than the thought of Grayson Gibb. She slumped as she gazed out the truck window. "Was he always so horrible?"

Yolanda answered thoughtfully. "He was okay when I first came to work here. Charming, actually. People always think that when they meet him. I always hear how handsome and charming my boss is."

"So what happened?"

"Hard to know. He's a control freak. And a tough boss." She sniffed. "Cross him and you're fired. But the staff thought he got even worse after your mother got sick."

"Do you remember her?" Evie asked.

Yolanda shot her a sideways glance. "Angela? Of course. We all loved her. She was smart and friendly, and pretty, too. She was good to us. Grayson Gibb couldn't help what happened to her. I think he tried. It drove him nuts."

"What *did* happen to her?"

"I don't know. She got sick and then she was gone."

That was all anybody ever said about her mother, Evie thought. "Standard line. I wish I could remember her."

"You were so small. Sella was great, but you wanted your mother. I felt so bad for you." Yolanda's voice wavered. "Look, Angela just disappeared one day. A few weeks later we were told she was dead." She gripped the wheel. "It happened so quickly. We were all shocked."

"Didn't she talk to *anybody* about what was going on? While she was sick? Somebody must know!"

"Mr. Gibb controlled access. Nobody in, nobody out. Angela was isolated. He made a firewall around her."

Evie felt very sad for her mother, sick and alone. She had only a few fleeting impressions of a loving smile and comforting warmth. And laughter. Lots of laughter. Evie's stomach tightened as she realized that laughter was missing entirely in her house now. It sounded like a small thing but it was big, she thought. The sound of laughter could fill any house, big or small, with joy, and without it, a house was empty.

She hoped she'd been a good child, perhaps a bit of sunshine in her mother's life. But maybe she'd been a wilful, rotten child, like her father said.

"Funny thing is, he thinks he has better luck controlling his second wife." Yolanda smiled wryly.

Before Evie could ask what she meant, Paulina Gibb herself appeared, riding her favourite show hunter in a lesson with Kerry Goodham, her most recent and most handsome coach.

The grass in the jumping paddock was impeccably mown and the jumps were freshly painted and well maintained. Paulina's horse was named Lord Percy. He was a glossy, elegant dark bay with a thin white blaze on his face.

They were jumping a course with ten obstacles set up at a height of a metre ten. They did it with ease — relaxed and steady, and getting all their distances and leads.

Paulina looked great on him, Evie had to admit, with her smart black blouse, well-cut tan breeches, and black boots. Her dark hair was tucked up into her riding helmet and she rode like she knew what she was doing.

Kerry Goodham was short and compact. He was probably in his late twenties, Evie guessed, and neatly dressed in tan breeches, polished brown boots, and a dark green golf shirt. His blond hair was cut long over his ears, and his white teeth flashed in his tanned face.

Paulina's white teeth flashed back at him.

Evie watched this scene objectively as they passed. Even though she cringed every time she was near the woman, Paulina really was right out of a Ralph Lauren ad.

Evie's mind went back to her mother. "Odd that you didn't know what was happening. I mean, you were here."

Yolanda paused for a second. "I was a teenager, and scared of Mr. Gibb. I didn't dare defy his orders." Yolanda reached out and patted Evie's shoulder. "I know one thing. She loved you more than the world itself."

Evie lifted her chin defensively. "Dad doesn't have anything good to say about her."

"Don't let him get to you, girl. He loved her, too, before. Angela was a fine woman. Seriously fine."

"Did you see her leave?" Evie asked. She wanted to picture it, to imagine that day.

"No. It was my day off. But I was told there was a big fuss at the house, cops and all, and lots of yelling."

"Cops? Yelling?" This was new. "About what?"

"I don't know. We were all forbidden to talk about it. Forbidden to mention Angela's name. Then she was gone. Time passed, as I said, and we were told she'd died."

"I wish I knew more."

"I promise, I don't know anything except what I've just told you. I'd tell you if I did."

The rig approached the long, white racing stables with royal-blue Dutch doors at every stall and a matching blue roof. It had been designed with a walking porch along both sides, which gave each stall shade in the summer when the top doors were open, and shelter from the wind in the winter. The gardeners had planted red flowers along the path and hung red geraniums at the entrance and at each post of the porch.

Yolanda stopped the truck at the stable entrance She looked directly at Evie. "I know you raced today, Evie. And won. I'm proud of you for that, but what I don't know is why you think you can get away with it." She spoke with concern. "You're playing with fire. Call me when you need me. Trust me, you will."

3

Maple Mills

There was truth in Yolanda's warning, Evie thought as she stepped down from the truck. After dropping the ramp, she ducked through the side door of the trailer and stood beside her horse. She rubbed Kazzam's face and ears as she fought tears, confused and uncertain.

Evie backed the black horse off. He stood still while she raised the ramp back into place and attached the clips. She waved to Yolanda, who nodded with a worried frown on her face and drove the rig away.

"I hope I'm doing the right thing, Kazzam," Evie whispered, stroking his neck. "Let's go to the barn. I'll give you a nice bath and a bran mash."

In response, Kazzam nuzzled her arm with his nose. He watched her with his big brown eyes, and she gazed back, recognizing that he'd given her his trust over everyone else.

Evie led the horse into the airy, cool stable. The ceiling fans twirled slowly overhead as Kazzam's hooves clip-clopped over the cobblestones. She walked him into the wash stall, turned him around to face the aisle, then ran the water until it was warm. With soap and a rubber scrubbing glove, Evie washed and massaged every inch of the black horse, from behind his ears to his ankles, and from his nose to the tip of his tail.

He stood quietly, relaxed and enjoying the attention. He particularly liked having his back massaged, so Evie continued working on it. Kazzam's head dropped. He yawned and licked his lips.

She hosed him down with warm water until his coat squeaked, scraped off the excess water, and rubbed his legs down with diluted liniment. She should've poulticed his legs and wrapped them, but then it would've been too obvious that he'd raced.

"Are you ready for your bran mash?"

He looked at her through half-closed eyes. Evie smiled. She traced the white heart on his forehead lovingly. "And then an afternoon nap in your clean stall?"

At the same instant, Evie and Kazzam heard brisk horse and human footsteps approaching. Les Merton, the stable manager, came up leading the pride of the stable, Thymetofly. "There's No Justice. I wondered."

Evie stiffened. "Is it turn-in time already?" she asked innocently. "I thought I'd give him a bath."

"This horse is not a toy, Evie. I've told you before. It's your father's orders. You should not be handling him."

"We get along," she said, quietly exhaling. *Phew*. He hadn't noticed him missing until now. And nobody had seen him dirty with sweat and dust except Yolanda.

"Yes, you do get along, Evie. But he kicks without warning and bucks people off." Les looked stern. "Don't let him fool you. He's dangerous."

Evie nodded. "I understand."

"Handle any other horse, Evie. Ride any of the others, but No Justice? He's finished." Les continued along the aisle with Thymetofly, shaking his head. The grooms began to bring in horses from their morning turnout, and the barn became filled with chatter and the clatter of shod hooves. The quiet moments that Evie and Kazzam had shared were over.

Evie unclipped the cross-ties from his halter and led Kazzam to his stall. If he was going to get his mash, she'd have to do it before anybody asked questions. Each horse had a special diet for its particular workload, and nobody tampered with the feed schedule. Of course, nobody knew Kazzam had been in a race, either.

She hurried into the feed room and mixed a scoop of bran with hot water and stirred in some sweet feed and extra molasses, with carrots as a bonus. When nobody was looking she sidled into Kazzam's stall and dumped it into his bowl.

Kazzam had it half finished when a menacing voice startled her. "What do you think you're doing?"

Her father. She looked up at the tall, neatly dressed, dark-haired man with chiselled features. His eyes squinted into slits. She remembered Chiquita and the whip and put herself between her father and Kazzam.

Grayson Gibb was a man who smiled with his mouth but not his eyes. In spite of his imposing manner, he had a high-pitched voice. When angry, he didn't yell, he whispered and sort of growled. Like Clint Eastwood, or Christopher Walken with a hint of Willem Dafoe from the old movies. It was downright frightening.

He wasn't smiling now. "Les told me you were here. Get out of that stall this minute."

"Hi, Dad," said Evie. She tried to appear calm.

"I said *get out*. Are you deaf?"

Deaf again. Evie suppressed a nervous giggle as she stepped out of the stall. She stood in front of Kazzam's feed bowl to hide the mash from her father's prying eyes.

"Wipe that stupid grin off your face."

She forced herself to meet his eyes.

"You've defied my orders. Never, ever, go near this animal again."

"I know, Dad. I'm sorry. But he's gentle with me."

"Just who do you think you are?" Grayson Gibb glared down at her from his full height. His whispery, yet harsh voice echoed through the stables. "You think you have the magic touch? That you're better than all my grooms and jockeys?" He sneered at her and turned on his heel. "Get out of my sight."

Evie stood still, listening to her father's retreating footsteps. Her stomach ached as if she'd been punched.

Kazzam nickered. She put her hand through the bars and rubbed his forehead. "Get a good rest, boy. You deserve it."

Evie walked out of the stable with her eyes down. All the staff had heard her father's demeaning words.

She slouched up the winding walkway to the big house, downcast. The white colonial mansion with its gracious verandas had been built on a gentle rise to catch the sun from east to west. The lawns and gardens were immaculate, with large shade trees — maples, for which Maple Mills was named — adding grace and coolness to the wide expanses of green. It was welcoming and hospitable, belying the nature of the family that lived within its walls. At least that's what Evie thought.

Now she had another worry besides her father finding out about the race. She'd defied his direct orders to stay away from Kazzam, and she'd been caught. Would he take it out on the horse, like he did Chiquita, to make his point?

Just last February one of the young racehorses had refused to get on the old trailer used to teach them how to load. Evie and a young groom had tried every trick in the book, from patience to bribery to subtle urging with a broom. Grayson showed up and told them to get it done. Evie replied that it would take a little more time. Grayson was not pleased.

They were horrified to see Grayson winch the horse to the tractor with ropes and haul him up by brute force. The horse broke his leg and had to be destroyed. It turned out that the trailer had an unstable floor, which is why the poor animal had balked. None of this bothered Grayson. Nobody was allowed to question his orders.

Self-doubt filled her mind. Was she going about this in the right way? Should she just confront her father and tell him that she wanted to find her mother? But why risk making him madder? He hated the mere mention of Angela's name. He'd never even shown Evie pictures of her.

No. She would have to find out for herself. Fifteen hundred and eighty dollars would more than do it. Evie began to smile a little at the thought. And the sight of those three men in bright racing silks with their mouths wide open as mighty little Kazzam sped past! Evie found herself chuckling aloud at the memory.

"Why so happy, carrot-head?"

Evie spun to look directly into the face of her stepsister, Beatrice. The girl was standing in the shade of a lilac bush. Evie would've walked right by had she not spoken.

Beatrice was twelve, dark-haired, delicate, and graceful. Everything she did, she did perfectly. She'd won the gold medal in her first gymnastics competition. As soon as she'd begun dance classes, her instructor had asked her to be one of the background dancers in a television show. In the family, it was understood that she was perfect. It had been that way since the day she'd arrived.

Suddenly self-conscious, Evie slumped. She was five-foot-six and Beatrice was barely five feet tall. She felt too tall around her. And too clumsy. And too freckly and too red-haired. "Happy? I was just thinking about something."

"Must've been funny." Beatrice sat on the stone bench beside the path and held out a toasted whole-wheat bagel slathered with cream cheese. "I don't want this. Do you?"

Evie was suddenly ravenous. She'd been up since five that morning and hadn't eaten since the muffin and banana she'd grabbed on her way out the door. "Yes! Are you sure?"

"I'm sure." Beatrice sniffed. "It's my second. Sella's trying to fatten me up."

"Happy to help," said Evie as she took a big bite and sat down beside her. "Thanks. I'm really hungry."

"She keeps pushing food at me. I'm just naturally thin." Beatrice crossed her legs and bounced a foot as she flicked a piece of dust off her pink cotton sundress. "Where were you all morning, anyway?"

"Out riding. Why?"

"You missed my synchronized swimming recital. Mommy's mad."

Evie stopped chewing and wiped her mouth on her sweaty arm. "Was that today? I'm sorry, Beebee!"

Beatrice rose from the bench and stretched like a Siamese cat. "No big deal."

"Were you fabulous?"

"Everybody said so."

"I wish I'd seen you swim."

"I thought you missed it on purpose."

"Why would I do that?"

"Because you're afraid of water."

Evie swallowed. It was true. The mere smell of chlorine caused a tightness in her chest and the need to sit down. "No. I really would've loved to see it."

Beatrice twirled, pointed a toe, and skipped up the walk to the house. "Next time."

"Sorry!" Evie called to her departing back. Nobody had actually told Evie about Beatrice's swimming recital. She knew about it, but since she'd never been officially invited, she'd never promised to go. Which allowed her to sneak away to the Caledon Horse Race. Now it looked like she was in trouble again.

"Hey, Evie!"

Evie's thoughts were broken by another sibling.

Her seven-year-old half-brother, Jordan, appeared. He had light brown floppy hair and a sweet face.

"Hey Jordie. What's up?"

"Where've you been all day?"

"Fooling around with Kazzam."

"Who's Kazzam?"

Oops. "I mean No Justice."

"Why'd you call him Kazzam?"

"It's the name of the horse that won the Caledon Horse Race. I heard it on the radio today and I liked it."

"It's a cool name."

"Yeah, I think so, too." *That was close*, thought Evie.

Jordie looked down at his runners. "Um, Mom wants to talk to you. She's kinda mad about something."

"Beebee's recital?"

"Yeah."

"Did she send you to find me?"

"Yeah." Jordie dug the toe of his sneaker into the grass. "Um, I can say I can't find you, if you want."

"Nah. I'm going up to the house now anyway."

"I'll go with you."

Evie put her hand on her little brother's shoulder as they walked. She was touched by how he stood up for her. She stood up for him, too. And sometimes it backfired.

The previous summer, their father was chastising him in the back garden for bringing a tame rat home from day camp. Jordie had traded his lunch for it. Evie knew how much he loved it, and she approached them to offer to help look after it. Their father had glared at her, then grabbed the frightened rat by the tail and hurled it on the rocks below the garden. It broke its back. The gardener climbed down and smashed it with his shovel to put it out of its misery.

Through her stunned tears, she'd asked Grayson why he'd done that. He'd answered, "The fact that you have to ask makes it worse." Again, point made. Nobody should question his orders. Again, confusion and fear.

Evie and Jordie entered the house through the kitchen door. She took off her filthy riding boots and stood them neatly on the boot rack. "Can you talk to Paulina while I have a quick shower? She hates it when I'm dirty."

"Sure." Jordie took off running.

Evie climbed the back stairs two at a time. She passed the open door of Beatrice's pink-and-white, lace-and-satin bedroom. It had an ensuite bathroom and a big bay window with a cushioned window seat. Her childhood dollhouse was decorated exactly the same, and sat in the middle of the sitting-room area beside the television.

Jordie's room was just as big. It was all in shades of blue and very much a boy's room. Trains, boats, cars, trucks, and all sorts of other toys were tidied every day by Sella. Sella had lived with the family for longer than Evie could remember and had become a second mother to her when she was three, after her own mother had gone.

Up Evie climbed to her room, tucked under the roof. She loved it. There was barely space for a single bed and a dresser, but it was very private. The small window looked over toward the stables and she could see all the paddocks. Paulina let her decorate it any way she wanted. Paulina never went up there, so it really didn't matter if it suited her lavish tastes.

On Evie's walls were pictures of horses and nothing else. Posters of jumping horses, bucking horses, mares and foals. She loved them all, but her favourite was the poster of jockey Imogene Watson winning the Queen's Plate on Firestone Stable's Mike Fox. Evie could just imagine the thrill of that day.

Evie had chosen a green-and-red plaid bed cover and had collected cushions with horses embroidered on them over the years. Whenever she saw one, she bought it with her savings unless it was too expensive. Sometimes theme cushions were totally overpriced.

Evie pulled off her grimy clothes and jumped into the small shower in the hall. She soaped herself, washed her hair and rinsed it, grabbed a towel and was dressed in clean navy shorts and a white T-shirt within five minutes.

She raced down the stairs and walked into the huge living room, decorated in shades of pink and ivory by some famous guy Paulina had flown up from Miami. She was a few minutes late, but at least Paulina wouldn't spend ten minutes yelling at her about her lack of personal hygiene.

Her stepmother, back from her riding lesson, lounged on the overstuffed white couch with satin cushions, her stockinged feet propped up on an ottoman. Tick and Tock, her tiny brown chihuahuas, were tucked beside her with their bug-eyed heads comfortably resting on her stomach. She'd removed her boots but hadn't changed out of her riding clothes. She never got dirty. People made sure that the horses and tack were spotless.

True to his word, Jordie sat on an armchair right beside her. He caught Evie's eye and tried to wink. He'd been practising, but he still scrunched up his entire face.

Paulina casually stretched her arms and ran her fingers through her long dark hair, posed like the fashion model she'd been before marriage. A full glass of red wine sat on the pink-lacquered coffee table.

"I've got a bone to pick with you," she said, levelling her dark brown eyes at Evie until they became a squint.

Whenever Paulina said that, Evie imagined her taking a pickaxe to a dog bone. She tried not to smile. "I'm sorry."

Paulina snapped. "Don't say you're sorry before you know what to be sorry about."

Evie nodded and stopped herself before she could apologize again. "Is it about Beebee's recital? I really —"

"Wanted to come?" Paulina finished her sentence. "If you'd wanted to come, you would've been here when we left at eight." She stroked Tick and Tock's soft, hairless bellies. "But you weren't here, were you?"

Evie shook her head.

"Where were you? What was so important that you missed Beatrice's synchronized swimming recital?"

"Riding," Evie answered truthfully.

"Riding?" Paulina cocked an eyebrow knowingly. "And which horse were you riding, may I ask?"

Evie felt trapped. Paulina knew that her father had forbidden her to ride Kazzam. She didn't answer.

"It was No Justice, wasn't it?"

Evie nodded. She couldn't lie.

Paulina's mouth was smiling, but her eyes were not. "So now you've succeeded in making everybody in this family unhappy. I hope you're proud of yourself."

Evie was honestly puzzled. "How've I done that?"

"Well, I'm upset that you missed Beatrice's recital.

Your father will be upset that you rode No Justice. Jordie is upset when people are upset, and Beebee is upset that you stole her bagel."

Evie shook her head, astonished. "Her bagel? She *gave* me her bagel!"

"That's a lie!" Beatrice appeared in the doorway. "Evie stole it right out of my hands. She's so much bigger than me!" The girl's bottom lip trembled and she threw herself into her mother's arms.

"There, there, sweetie," Paulina comforted Beatrice. "Sella will make you another."

This was crazy. Evie knew it was useless, but she had to defend herself. "But I —"

"But nothing." Paulina checked her manicured fingernails. "Stealing food. Shame."

Jordie jumped up. "Mom, Evie doesn't steal food!" He ran to Evie, on the verge of tears.

Evie put an arm around him and whispered, "It's okay, Jordie."

Paulina sat up straight, knocking the small dogs to the floor. She spoke loudly over the yapping of her chihuahuas. "Leave my son out of this!"

Grayson Gibb stalked into the room, smiling coldly. "What's going on here?"

Paulina gave a melodic little laugh and shrugged apologetically. Her face changed in front of Evie's eyes. Gone was the shrew. In its place was the model with a heart of gold. Was it possible that Paulina was afraid of Grayson, too? It had never occurred to Evie until that moment.

"Nothing important, dear," purred Paulina. "Your daughter, Evangeline, rode No Justice today instead of coming to our Beebee's recital. And then she stole her lunch." She smoothed back her glossy dark hair from her face. "We're just sorting it out."

Grayson assessed Evie carefully. His eyes narrowed and his nose wrinkled like he'd sniffed something putrid. "Never go near that horse again, if you know what's good for you." His voice got quiet and he growled, "And you must not steal food. You'll end up like your mother."

4

Escape

Evie was banished to her room for the rest of the day without dinner. She sat down on her bed, completely worn out from her early morning and the adrenalin rush of the horse race, and demoralized by the scene that had unfolded downstairs. Her eyes closed and she flopped back. As soon as her head hit the pillow, she was asleep.

Her growling stomach woke her at six o'clock that evening. But she couldn't go downstairs to get food. She was being punished.

Beatrice had set out to get her in trouble. *Miserable brat.* She'd lied about what happened and then called *her* a liar. Over a bagel? In her sister's never-ending quest to be the favourite she never balked at making Evie look bad, but this was ridiculous. What was going on with her?

And what had her father meant about her mother stealing food? Was her mother a thief, as well as all the other rotten things he'd called her?

Evie thought of the long night ahead with nothing to do. She wished she had a television in her room like Jordie and Beebee. If she hadn't thrown out her cellphone, she could've called Aunt Mary to set up a time and place to meet.

She still couldn't believe she'd tossed her phone into the river. Why, why, *why* had she done that? She longed to share today's triumph with Cassie and laugh off her hurt about being sent to her room with Rebecca. Evie wondered again what her friends had been up to lately. Phoneless, she was simply not in that world. *Who am I kidding? I'm not in that world anyway.* It hurt every time she thought about how they'd all turned against her.

She did have a book that she loved, *Horse Play*, written by Elizabeth Elliot. She read it once a year, at Christmas, to treat herself and to imagine what a nice family might be like. It was about a girl and a horse, and all the adventures they went through together. *Like me and Kazzam,* she thought. But she didn't want to read it now and spoil her December ritual. Evie made a mental note to buy all the books that Elizabeth Elliot had written with her newly won money, if there was anything left after finding her mother.

There was a light tap at the door. Evie rolled off her bed and turned the handle. She peeked into the hall. Nobody was there. She saw something lumpy in a white napkin on the floor by the door and picked it up. An enormous sandwich and an apple!

Evie looked down the staircase. Jordie's head popped around the corner. He winked — an improvement on his earlier effort. He put his forefinger up to his mouth and disappeared.

The sandwich tasted better than anything she'd ever eaten in her life. Her sweet little brother had stuffed big hunks of tender chicken with mayonnaise and a huge wedge of crisp lettuce between thick slices of whole-wheat bread and peppered it liberally. She got a big glass of water from the bathroom to drink with it and ate every crumb. It was a complete meal. Even an apple for dessert.

Evie hesitated before biting into the apple. After winning the race, Kazzam deserved it, not her.

That gave her an idea. Her worry about a night of boredom disappeared. He *would* get the apple. Time for a practice escape.

Without another thought, Evie went to work. She packed a small knapsack with three spare shirts, socks, underwear, toothpaste and brush, deodorant, a hairbrush, and a light windbreaker. She dressed in jeans, socks and runners, a T-shirt, a sweatshirt, and a baseball cap. All dark colours.

She took the sheets off her bed, tied them together, and twisted them with knots. She looped one end and tied a lead shank she'd borrowed from the barn through it. She attached that to the sturdy hook she'd screwed tightly into the wooden baseboard a few days earlier, in preparation for her escape.

Evie opened the window as far as it could go and looked down to the veranda roof. She'd have to be careful not to slip off.

To make this a true dress rehearsal, she put Aunt Mary's phone number in the front pocket of her knapsack and slid the envelope full of prize money into the zippered pocket.

Now she was ready. She stood up and looked at the sky. It was seven-thirty and still bright outside. Time to go.

Quietly, she pushed the sheet-rope out the window and fed it down until it was all outside, hanging almost to the veranda roof. She tugged on it hard — the hook was secure. *All systems go.*

Evie wriggled through the window, feet first. Her legs blindly moved around until her feet found the first knot and held tight. Then the next knot, and her hands grabbed on. *This is easy,* Evie thought as she climbed down the rope, knot by knot. She felt the shingles with her sneakered feet and relaxed. Taking a deep breath, she let the sheet-rope swing next to the outside wall.

Getting to the ground from the roof was a bit trickier.

Evie crept to the far end of the veranda. When she'd cased it earlier, she'd marked this as the best place to climb down. The veranda roof met the wall here, so the eaves were sturdy and the bushes below were tall enough to hide her. There were no windows here, either, for someone to look out and spot her.

She sat on the roof, turned around, swung her legs over with her belly to the eaves, and inched down, down, down, then a little farther down.

Evie thought her toes should be touching the porch railing by now, but she felt nothing beneath her. Leaning her weight on her chest, she pointed her toes and stretched. Nothing. She let gravity pull her down a little farther. Then she slipped.

She grabbed at the eaves with all her strength and caught herself. Willing her heart to stop thumping, she held tight, but she still couldn't find the railing with her feet. It was farther than she'd estimated. She should've measured.

Soon her arms would give out and she'd have to let go. Could she trust that the porch railing was just below her feet? It might be only an inch away, or she might have seriously miscalculated and would tumble down.

She had two options. Go up or go down. Option one was out. She was hanging so precariously that she couldn't possibly get back up. She had no choice but option two. She'd have to rethink this part before the real escape. Impulsive again, she thought. *Stupid, stupid.*

Suddenly the eavestrough pulled away from the wood with a crack. Her feet hit the railing and she tumbled backwards into the bushes. She fell hard, accompanied by the loud crash of broken branches and crumpling metal eavestroughs.

Tick and Tock began yipping and yapping. She counted the seconds. *One. Two. Three. Four. Five.* Nobody came running out to see what had caused the noise. Evie began to breathe again. Luckily for her, Tick and Tock barked so much that they were always ignored.

Evie hoped she hadn't done any damage to herself.

She wiggled her various body parts. Her fingers and toes moved — that was good — and so did her arms and legs. Her neck turned both ways easily. *All good.*

When she was sure the coast was clear, she hightailed it to the barn, slinking from tree to tree, crouching all the way.

Once she reached the stable, she exhaled. *Home free.*

The entire barn was quiet. Not a soul in sight, except the barn cats hunting mice, and the horses, munching and crunching their hay and occasionally slurping water. Evie loved those sounds. And she loved the smell — leather and horse and manure and clover — a poignant medley of smells that always lifted her spirits.

Kazzam raised his head from his hay and softly nickered to her. "Hi there, Mister Racehorse. You were beyond brilliant this morning."

She took the apple out of her knapsack and offered it to her sleepy black horse. She held it for him as he took half of it in his teeth and chewed it up.

The other horses smelled the apple and began to snort.

"I know you all think it's not fair, but Kazzam raced his heart out today." She gave him the other half.

Nine other horses in that aisle refused to accept her logic and stamped their feet and whinnied.

"Okay! I give up!" Evie gathered up carrots in the feed room and fed each horse a delicious crunchy treat, one by one. Now the horses in the other aisles smelled carrots and began to demand their share. Horses deem it rude if you let them sniff something good but don't let them eat it, so Evie grabbed more carrots and handed them to the impatient animals as quickly as she could.

The setting sun bathed the walls of the barn in a rosy glow as she went back to Kazzam's stall. She brought some brushes to curry him, and he was very content with her total attention. When she groomed the dip in his back, he reached his neck around and groomed the dip in her back, too, with his front teeth.

She chuckled. "Nice, Kazzam. That feels good." Out in the field, if a horse is itchy in a place he can't reach, he scratches another horse in that place with his front teeth to show where to scratch him. "Horse etiquette," said Evie aloud. She loved watching how horses relate to each other. In that way, she'd learned how to relate to horses herself.

As Evie curried Kazzam she considered the various ways to get back into the house undetected. The original plan was to climb up the way she came. Now she knew that would not be possible. If she was extremely lucky she could get Jordie's attention and he could let her in the back way. If not, Sella might still be in the kitchen.

All of a sudden the barn lights came on. Evie froze. Footsteps approached. Two men were advancing along the aisle in her direction. Quickly she gathered the brushes. She sat down in the straw under the water bucket with her back to the stall wall next to the aisle. Kazzam stood with his head over her. She dared not peek out.

"We don't have an offer." That whispery voice could only belong to one person. Evie's blood went cold. "And we won't. But you know that, Jerry. People are laughing."

"He's the best we've ever had for the Queen's Plate, Grayson. Faster than Thymetofly by half a second at three-eighths of a mile. He can run." Jerry Johnston, their racing manager, spoke urgently.

"He can run but nobody can stay on him." Her father and Jerry stopped at Kazzam's stall, inches from her. "Put all your attention on Thymetofly. There's only one option for No Justice. You know what I mean."

"Try another jockey?"

"You think jockeys don't talk to each other?" Grayson Gibb snorted meanly. "Do you think at all?"

Evie cringed in sympathy with Jerry.

"Look, I hear you, Grayson, I do. But No Justice is good. We shouldn't give up on him. I feel it."

"You feel it?" Her father scoffed again. "Well, I pay for it." Grayson's voice was a growl. "I refuse to spend another penny for him to be trained and fed and worked and shipped to the races, just to have him dump another jock. Get rid of him."

Grayson Gibb's voice had become louder. He was standing right over her. Evie stayed as still as she possibly could. Was he looking down through the bars at her? Could he see her? She almost peed herself with fear.

"He's a mean one, too. Look — his ears are flat back."

Evie knew that Kazzam's ears were back because he was protecting her from a perceived enemy. Actually, a real enemy. *If my father finds me, I'm a goner.*

Grayson grunted angrily. "Look at him. He wants to bite me. Ha! Bite the hand that feeds him. I'm going to teach him a lesson." Evie heard the click of the stall latch.

She stiffened. She knew what came next. Kazzam was about to be beaten within an inch of his life. And she'd be discovered. There was nowhere to hide. Nothing to do but wait for it. *Dear Lord of creatures great ...*

"Stop, Grayson," said Jerry quickly. "Please. He's a valuable animal. Give me just a little more time."

"You're not listening. Every day he's here, he costs money." Grayson took his hand off the stall latch, stepped closer to Jerry, then hissed, "Get rid of him, Jerry. If not one way, then the other."

"I'll try."

"Do more than try. I want No Justice gone." Grayson paused, then spoke very quietly. "He's insured for a lot of money. Don't make me spell it out."

"Yessir. Tomorrow."

"Hear me. Clearly. If you don't make this happen by tomorrow, I know someone who will."

The conversation was over. Jerry Johnston scooted away down the aisle and Grayson Gibb strode back the way he'd come. The lights went off.

Evie gasped for air. She collapsed against the wall and stayed where she was, trembling wildly. She tried to think. Kazzam had escaped a beating this time, but what was this insurance her father was talking about?

She made her decision. No Justice *would* be gone by tomorrow, she vowed. She could not leave him to the whim of her father. She hadn't planned on having a horse with her when she went to find her mother, but things had radically changed.

Evie got Kazzam's saddle and bridle out of the tack room, along with her helmet. She quickly slipped the bit into his mouth and the bridle over his ears. The saddle pad was embroidered with "Maple Mills Stables" and their tree logo in blue, so she turned it over for anonymity. She popped the saddle over his back and buckled the girth nice and tight.

She led him out into the growing dimness. It was warm and the air was still, and smelled sweet to her nose.

Soon it would be dark, but there was a moon rising, and it would be bright enough to throw some light. And with a sky so clear, she knew it wouldn't be long before the stars peeked out.

She leaned toward the horse's warm muzzle and stroked his gleaming neck. "We're going on an adventure, Kazzam," she whispered. "I'm not sure exactly where, but you'll be glad to be away from here, and so will I."

Kazzam nickered. It was deep and soft, from way back in his throat, and the sound cheered Evie. The horse was communicating with her as best he could. He bumped her gently with his nose.

"You want to get going? Fine with me."

Evie led him to the mounting block beside the entrance and hopped onto the gelding's back. Silently, they trotted from the stables across the grass. She looked behind. There were no hoofprints to give them away. The Caledon racetrack had been overly dusty that morning, but now Evie was grateful that the weather had been so dry.

The Maple Mills Stables gates were electronically operated, so they couldn't get out the front. Farther south along the road was another, much smaller gate. Evie and Kazzam went directly there.

The second they were off the property, she dropped her head in relief. Her heart stopped racing.

"We made it, Kazzam. Prison break!" Parts one and two of her plan were accomplished.

They picked up a trot and went south on the gravel road.

5

Magpie

Kazzam's strides were rhythmic and strong as they trotted south for half a concession, then turned east.

Tomorrow, she'd figure out what to do about contacting Aunt Mary, but right now they needed a place for the night. Somewhere with food and water for Kazzam, and a dry spot where she could sleep. Somewhere safe, where Grayson Gibb would never look. There was only one location she could think of — the abandoned Henson property. It was about ten kilometres from Maple Mills with two highways to cross. If she remembered correctly, it had a paddock with grass and a walk-in shelter attached to the old barn.

The Hensons' children had sold the farm to developers and moved their elderly parents into Golden Years seniors residence. Apparently, the developers had gone bankrupt, and the farm had been vacant for many years. She wondered briefly how the Hensons had adjusted to city life. They'd spent their entire lives farming, and now they were without even a balcony to enjoy the fresh air. But then again, they were known for their miserable temperaments. Maybe their children didn't care. Certainly, Evie thought, she'd have no trouble putting *her* father into a home.

Whatever, the old farm was about to serve a new purpose. A halfway house. A refuge for her and Kazzam.

This was not how Evie had imagined part three of her plan. Heading off into the night with a horse and no definite destination was out of her comfort zone. What if Aunt Mary wasn't home when she called? Or on holiday? Would she and Kazzam have to stay hidden for weeks until she answered? What if her father called the police when he noticed his horse gone, and she was sent to jail? Evie's head was spinning.

Keep cool. It'll all work out. One thing for sure was that she could not turn back. Not on her life.

Traffic was light as they hacked along in the dark. Kazzam didn't seem to mind the occasional cars and trucks that drove by. He stepped out with energy and purpose, ears forward and alert. Evie patted his neck and said, "You seem to know where we're going, boy!"

They trotted along for twenty minutes, and Evie began to feel good inside. Free. The stars popped out of the dark blanket of sky, one by one, and the fresh night air was exhilarating. Evie thought of herself as brave and adventurous; a woman of the world, a person who would fulfill her destiny, stop at nothing, take matters into her own hands. She sang show tunes aloud. "The hi-ills are ali-ive with the sound of mu-usic...."

The first of the two highways came into view. The Henson property was right there in front of them, directly ahead. There were four lanes of traffic, and the road was busier than she'd expected on a Saturday night. The bright headlights and the loud engine whines were unfamiliar to Kazzam. He'd never seen this many cars and trucks moving so fast. She felt her first pang of concern and tightened her legs on her horse's sides.

Kazzam began to hesitate. His head went up. His steps got shorter and his body movement became a bit stilted. Too late, Evie realized that he'd picked up on her anxiety, so she tried to calm herself. She took a deep breath and made an effort to relax her body. She brought Kazzam back to a walk, and cooed, "Good boy, Kazzam. No problem."

The horse snorted. He shook his head. He pranced on the spot and twisted, trying to turn back. His every instinct was to run away from the scary sights and sounds. Evie stayed very still on his quivering back and tried to get things under control. She patted his neck and kept speaking quietly. "Easy boy. Good boy. Easy there, Kazzam."

Then he reared up on his hind legs and whinnied.

Evie worried that her plan was about to fail before it had really even started.

No, she thought, *I cannot fail. It's not just about me anymore. If I turn back now, what will happen to Kazzam?*

She took her feet out of the stirrups, hopped down to the ground, and stood with the nervous animal. He pulled away and pawed the ground. Thoroughbreds are high-strung, and once excited take a while to calm down. Evie was patient. She didn't fight him, but didn't let him race away, either. After five minutes of practising patience, Evie felt Kazzam's apprehension abate. He lowered his head and snorted.

She said, "Let's walk for a bit, okay, boy?" She calmly ran up his stirrups so they wouldn't bump his sides and proceeded to lead him down the side of the road toward the busy highway.

To soothe the horse and herself, as well, she began to sing an old gospel song she'd learned at camp. "Rocka ma soul in the bosom of Abraham, Rocka ma soul in the bosom of Abraham, Rocka ma soul in the bosom of Abraham, Oh-h, rocka ma so-oul...."

It seemed to work, and Kazzam kept walking forward. The lights changed, thankfully, as Evie and her horse got to the intersection. The north- and southbound traffic came to a halt. Evie kept her eyes forward and marched onto the highway, still singing loudly. Kazzam kept pace and together they managed to cross the road.

Relief flooded her body. She kept walking and singing until they were well past the highway. When she saw that the ditch along the road was steep enough to use as a mounting block, she said, "I'm getting back up, boy."

She pulled the left stirrup down along the leather and kept walking. She led Kazzam into the ditch. Still moving forward, she lightly jumped up into the saddle before he knew what was happening.

Kazzam remained settled and content, and they trotted on until the next highway. This one was half the size of the first, and the traffic was minimal. Evie tried not to show any concern and continued singing, "... the ci-ircle of li-ife...." By good fortune, there were no cars when they got to the intersection, and they rode right through to the other side.

Evie smiled broadly. The two highways had been safely crossed and they had only three more concessions to go — one straight ahead, then a left turn and two more. They trotted the first two and walked the entire third, to cool Kazzam down.

There, in front of them, the old Henson barn stood black against the night sky. It looked spooky with its missing boards and tilted silhouette. But at least it was still there. The farmhouse was not. In its place was a huge pile of caved-in bricks and lumber.

They walked along the road, past the old driveway and the falling fences, until they got to the barnyard gate. Evie slid down from Kazzam and gave his ears a rub.

She led him through the unhinged gate toward the dark, decrepit building. It leaned dangerously to one side and smelled of mouldy hay and wood rot. Kazzam shook his head and cleared his nose. His eyes rolled at her.

"I know. But it's better than nothing, don't you think?"

Evie wasn't sure herself. It looked like it might fall down.

Kazzam fidgeted and didn't seem too happy about this place. Evie couldn't blame him. The stables at Maple Mills were luxurious, especially by comparison.

Evie continued to investigate. By the light of the moon she could see a separate fenced area with a small building. That might be a possibility. The split-rail fence was rickety but still standing, and the ancient board gate was still on its hinges. She unlatched it and pushed it open. The ensuing creak was loud enough to startle Kazzam.

"Easy, boy. You've escaped a dire fate at the hands of my father and faced two highways tonight. A little rust shouldn't upset you."

He trembled with apprehension and snorted, but walked through with her. She closed the gate behind him slowly to minimize the noise, then looked around the small yard.

In the dark it was difficult to know exactly the condition, but the walk-in shelter seemed to be okay. In any case, it was much better than the derelict barn, and the roof leaked no moonlight. After assuring herself that the fences enclosed the paddock entirely, she took Kazzam's saddle off and removed his bridle. They would stay here for the night.

She watched him check out the small field and nibble

some grass. He then dropped to his knees and rolled over onto his back to give it a good scratch. He rolled over twice before he stood up and shook his body from head to toe. Evie was satisfied. Horses don't roll unless they feel safe.

Evie carried his tack into the shelter and looked for a place to put it. She squinted into the murky darkness and waited until her eyes adjusted. At the back in the corner was a pile of odds and ends. A broken pitchfork, ceramic bits and pieces, a rubber pail, and — what luck! — a dusty old wooden sawhorse. *Maybe it's a sign that things will turn out well,* she thought, as she placed the saddle on the sawhorse and hung the bridle on the end. *Who needs a fancy tack room?*

Out of the corner of her eye, she saw a large, irregular, light-brown lump on the ground. What was it? She kept perfectly still and stared at it. It didn't move. She could not identify it by sight. Cautiously, Evie crept closer to see what it was. She really didn't want to find a dead body, animal or human, and the hairs on her neck stood up straight.

Gathering all her courage, she kicked it hard. It was a pile of burlap feed bags.

Evie shuddered, then suddenly laughed. *What an idiot! Talk about an overactive imagination!* She lifted the top bag and shook it out. It didn't smell bad at all. Maybe a little like wet dog, but not rot or some disgusting dead thing. The burlap bags would really come in handy. She rubbed Kazzam down with the one she had in her hand.

Evie felt good that she'd thought of this place. They had shelter, there was grass in the paddock for Kazzam to eat, and the pile of burlap feed bags could serve as her bed for the night. The only thing missing was water.

She fumbled around, looking for a tap. She *had* seen a large aluminum basin upside down beside the gate. Interesting. She strode toward it and smacked right into something metal and large, stinging her thigh. An old-fashioned water pump. *We're getting closer,* she thought, rubbing away the pain.

She grabbed the handle and pumped. It squeaked noisily and the handle worked far too easily. Evie knew little about water pumps, but the phrase "priming the pump" came into her head. What did it mean? Knowing that might have been helpful.

She kept pumping. If nothing happened after a few minutes she'd have to go in search of water. She'd noticed lights up the road at the next intersection. If she remembered correctly, there were a few houses there, a gas station and a variety store.

But something was happening. The pump handle was becoming harder to lift up and push down. Promising. All at once, water gushed out. Evie thought it looked rusty in the moonlight, so she kept pumping madly until the water became clear. She grabbed the basin, turned it over under the spout, and resumed pumping. She washed out the basin as best she could and began to fill it up.

Water, beautiful, clear water came rushing out. Wonderful, plentiful water for Kazzam. The gelding wandered over and sniffed it. He splashed it with his upper lip and sniffed it again. The water kept coming as Kazzam put his mouth into the cool liquid and drank his fill.

When the basin was full to the brim, Evie rinsed her hands and arms and face. She let the water run down her back and front, and she combed it through her sweaty hair. Now she leaned over the trough and drank as much as she wanted. It tasted surprisingly good.

Evie felt content. A wave of fatigue came over her. She stretched her arms over her head and yawned. It had been a very long day, starting early that morning with the big Caledon race. She'd call Aunt Mary first thing in the morning and hope that her aunt was there to take the call.

Evie gratefully sank into the pile of burlap, using her sweatshirt as a pillow and her windbreaker as a blanket. It was a warm, breezeless night, and the sound of Kazzam quietly foraging grass comforted her. She was sound asleep within minutes.

She dreamed that a cold, wet nose was sniffing her face. She rolled over. The nose pushed at one of her hands. She moved her arm and adjusted the windbreaker.

Now something thumped on her back. Evie sat up quickly, wide awake, and looked around. She could see nothing. The moon had disappeared, and the sky was pitch-black. She could barely make out the silhouette of Kazzam, outside grazing.

What was in her shed? What had come so close? And why was Kazzam so tranquil when some large creature with a cold nose might have attacked and eaten her?

Evie decided that it must've been a dream. It had felt very real, but if any animal had been there, the gelding would've been tense and pacing and totally upset. She sighed and drifted off, telling herself to quit imagining things. Soon, she was back in a deep sleep.

The next morning Evie awoke and yawned happily. In daylight, she was pleased with what she saw. The shelter was old but sturdy, and the paddock wasn't overrun with burdocks and weeds, the way one might expect of an untended patch of grass. Kazzam was having another drink at the basin, and he looked rested.

She stretched. She'd get up and go to the variety store along the road to pick up a few things to eat. Her stomach rumbled at the thought. She'd find a phone there, too, to call Aunt Mary. They'd figure out where to meet in Toronto and how to find Evie's mother. The only question was whether Kazzam would be fine at the Hensons' for the day. Evie wasn't quite sure. She'd have to think about it a bit more.

Also, she had a huge amount of cash. Maybe she should bury some in case she was robbed? Evie would take just enough money and hide the rest.

As she lay considering how much money to bring to the store, she realized that the right side of her body was very warm. Much warmer than her left. She glanced to her right and there it was.

A dog. A large black dog. Nestled into the edge of the pile of burlap. That's why the bags had a dog smell. This was the dog's bed. The cold nose and the heavy thumping in the night. It'd been a tail! It all made sense. It *had* been real!

Evie studied the dog as it slept. It was curled up so she couldn't tell if it was male or female. It appeared young and healthy. Its black coat was short and shiny. The dog wasn't wearing a collar, although fur was missing where a collar might have been, and Evie could see some sore, red skin. She dared not pat the dog before she knew if it was friendly, but why would it sleep beside her if it didn't want company?

Evie couldn't help herself. She stroked one of the dog's long silky ears. It looked up, surprised, and in one quick motion darted away. Now she was able to take a good look. The dog was female. Her body was long and lean and much taller than it looked curled up. There was a little white crest on her chest and a splatter of white on each of her four paws. She stared at Evie with innocent, unsure, dark-brown eyes. They inspected each other, and after a minute both decided the other was okay. The dog wagged her long, skinny tail just a little.

Evie spoke softly to her. "Good girl. Nice girl."

The dog's tail wagged more. She crouched down to Evie, licked her nose, and then retreated. From the back of her throat came a gulping noise. Not a growl or a whimper, just an odd little noise.

Evie smiled. "What's your name, girl? Are you lost?" She stretched out her hand for the young dog to sniff. The dog came close again, still wagging her tail. Evie sat up. The dog approached, made her funny throat sound, and lay down exactly in the spot she'd spent the night, right beside Evie.

Evie stroked her soft black fur. She said, "You need a name. Everybody does. Hmm. You're black and shiny and you make the oddest noise I've ever heard from a dog. More like a dove. I'll name you ... Magpie. Yes, Magpie it is."

Evie took a good look at Magpie's neck. It was raw but not infected or bleeding. She'd get something to help it heal when she went to the store.

Evie already felt very attached to this long-legged animal that had appeared out of nowhere. Maybe because they were both looking for a better home. *It must be destiny.* Why else would they both have come to this exact place at exactly the same time? Something intangible had drawn them together.

Same with Kazzam. He was nervous around and suspicious of other people. She'd watched the grooms piling bales of hay behind his back feet so he couldn't kick them when they combed his tail. And he needed two grooms to pick the dirt out his hooves. One would hold his tail while the other would lift his feet. Even then, they watched their backs because he bit very quickly and accurately. It was worse when they tried to ride him. His buck was legendary. One by one, the exercise riders had refused to get on him.

For whatever reason, Evie and Kazzam were attached to each other. She would do everything she could to protect him from her father.

She stretched again and smiled, feeling optimistic about her plans. Things seemed to be falling into place.

6

Aunt Mary

It was already warm and the day ahead promised to be hot and sunny. Evie tidied herself up as best she could. She tucked some money and Aunt Mary's number in her pocket, and hid her knapsack with the rest of the money under the pile of burlap sacks. She patted Kazzam's neck. "I'll be back before you know it. Don't go anywhere. Stay and eat grass. I'll try to buy some oats."

Magpie followed Evie through the gate and down the road. *Maybe someone in the store will know who this nice dog belongs to.* But she hoped not.

She walked along the highway with Magpie, who had her ears pricked up and her tail wagging happily. Evie smiled and skipped a couple of steps. She felt positive about her adventure as she double-checked her pocket for Aunt Mary's phone number.

When they reached the store, Evie asked Magpie to sit on the porch to wait. "Bert's Variety" was written in faded letters over the entrance, and a bell tinkled as she opened the screen door. The old floors were wooden and the place smelled of ice cream. She followed her nose. There! A whole array of tubs of assorted flavours. Evie's mouth watered. Maybe breakfast could start with dessert!

An elderly man stood behind the counter, possibly Bert himself, reading a newspaper. Evie approached him. "Do you have a pay phone I could use?" she asked.

The man looked at her over his glasses and pointed to an old white telephone on the wall. "Local?"

"Yes. I live on the Third Line, west of Highway 10."

"I meant is it a ... *local* ... *call*." He over-enunciated the last two words as if Evie were hard of hearing.

Deafness seemed to be a theme, thought Evie. "It's to Toronto. Is that local from here?"

"Yes. Be brief." He resumed reading and muttered, "Nobody asks for the phone anymore, all those cells and text messages, twitters and tweets. I don't understand any of it, and I don't intend to learn."

With the phone in her hand, Evie found herself very nervous. Aunt Mary would not be expecting her call. What should she say? Evie scolded herself. She really hadn't prepared this part of the plan very well. She took the letter out of her pocket and pressed the numbers carefully.

Ring. What if she had to leave a message?

Ring. Should she hang up?

Ring. "Hello?"

"Oh!" she stammered. "It's Evie Gibb. I —"

"Evie! Hello dear! This is your aunt Mary."

Evie was tongue-tied.

"Are you still there?"

"Um, yes."

"Are you at home?"

"No, I, um —"

"Where are you calling from?"

"Um, the corner of the ... Fifth Line and Little Creek Road."

"Bert's Variety?"

"Yes! How do you —?"

"I'm just a few concessions from you right now."

Evie was confused. "Don't you ... live in Toronto?"

"My cell number has a Toronto exchange. I live on a farm very close by. Can I pick you up for a visit?"

Evie thought hard. This was too fast. But it was what she wanted, wasn't it? "Yes. Where, um, where should I wait? In the store?"

"Good idea. I'll be there shortly."

"How will I know you, Aunt Mary?"

There was a slight pause. "I'll know you. Sad we've never met. But we'll make up for it. I'm old and grey. And I don't expect there'll be too many people there on Sunday morning this early."

"Okay. I'll wait here."

"Goodbye, dear." Aunt Mary hung up and so did Evie. The man behind the counter continued his muttering.

"Well, I never. This girl and that racehorse, I don't understand. She came out of nowhere and disappeared into thin air. With the horse! Kids today."

Slowly, the man's words sank in. Evie turned to him and asked, "Excuse me? Who are you taking about?"

He peered at her. "Don't you listen to the radio or read the newspapers? Are you one of those people that only sees what's on Facebook?"

"I, well, I've been sick."

He nodded and poked the paper with a yellowed fingernail. "Ever hear of a horse called Kazzam and the deaf girl, Molly Peebles?"

Evie decided it was safer to nod yes than to say anything.

Besides, she was speechless.

"They won that Caledon Horse Race, you know?"

Evie nodded again.

"By eight lengths! But nobody knew 'em or where they come from. Folks're yacking about it. Seems they were going under assumed names!" He shook his head darkly. "I don't understand. If any a my kids did that...."

"So, who are they?" Evie rounded her eyes and tried to look fascinated, which wasn't hard. "This ... deaf girl and her horse? Where did they come from?"

"Turns out Kazzam is a big-time racehorse, a devil it seems, by the name of No Justice. He was a favourite for the Queen's Plate till he was banned for bucking. And get this! The girl is the rich brat of Grayson Gibb. *You* heard of him. Maple Mills Stables? How d'ya like them potatoes?"

"Wow." Evie was sweating. "Amazing. What's the, um, deaf girl's name?"

"Last name's Gibb, I'd guess. I didn't know he had a deaf kid. She hasn't confessed, but time will run out." He pointed knowingly at her. "Took off with her father's horse!"

Evie gasped, then recovered by pretending to cough. "May I borrow the paper after you've read it, please?" She really needed to know how much trouble she was in.

"Take it. I'm finished." He folded the newspaper in two and handed it over the counter.

"Thanks." She tucked it under her arm.

"Are you buying anything today or just taking things for free?"

"Oh! Yes! I've got to pick up some things for my mother. I was so shocked by your news I totally forgot!"

The man looked smug to have been the bearer of such good gossip. He nodded curtly and began to sort the lottery tickets.

Evie gathered her groceries as quickly as she could and put them on the counter. Peanut butter, bread, jam, orange juice, milk, a box of rolled oats for Kazzam, and a bag of dog kibble for Magpie, plus a tube of antibiotic ointment for the dog's scraped neck. She put everything on the counter, satisfied that it would do for now.

As the man added everything up, Evie snuck a peek at the article in the paper. *Oh, no!* Along with the article was her picture. She stared at Kazzam's filthy face and herself covered in dirt and smiling with her fist in the air. Not good. Anybody could see through the grime. And even though his white, heart-shaped star was hidden with the face mask, Kazzam had a distinctive jawline and wide brow, and his small ears were unusual — the tips pointed together, almost touching. If a person had seen him once, it would not be difficult to recognize him.

Evie couldn't stay here and wait for her aunt. Bert would put her face together with the face in the paper any minute and call the police. She was a wanted woman! Evie had to keep moving.

She pulled the money out of her pocket and waited for him to make change. Her chest tightened with fear. Time moved so slowly!

While he was counting out the change, the man stared at her over his glasses.

Evie froze. *Here it comes.* She prepared to run.

"You say you been sick, girl?"

Evie quickly remembered her lie and nodded.

"Well, you don't look so good now. Get yerself home and back to bed and stop spreading yer nasty germs."

She nodded again, grabbed the bags, and left the store. Magpie was still outside, thumping her long, skinny tail against the wooden porch.

"Gotta go, Magpie. Come."

"Hey! Girl!" Bert yelled from inside the store.

Evie almost fell over with fear.

"You forgot yer change."

Evie stepped back inside, grabbed the money, and then took off. She jogged quickly along the road toward the deserted barnyard, eager to distance herself from Bert and his prying eyes. She checked over her shoulder to see if he was following her. Only Magpie.

Just as she shut the rusted gate behind them, Evie saw a white, four-door truck and a two-horse, goose-neck horse trailer pull up at Bert's Variety store. She put down her groceries and watched. Even from that distance she could clearly see a tallish, slim, silver-haired woman get out of the driver's side and stride into the store. She was wearing riding breeches and boots.

This must be Aunt Mary, thought Evie. But could it be? This woman walked so briskly, and Aunt Mary was actually her great-aunt, her mother's aunt. Evie expected a cane and bad hips. Maybe even a walker.

Warm breath rustled her hair. Evie lifted her right hand and cuddled Kazzam's nose on her shoulder as she continued to watch.

The woman came back out. She stood on the porch and placed her hands on her hips. She looked up the road and down. Then she cupped her right hand over her eyes and seemed to stare right where Evie stood with Kazzam. Finally, she got in the truck.

Evie panicked. Should she wave or hide? She was sure the woman had seen them. She picked up the groceries, receded into the shadows, and hid in the shelter, thinking hard. When she'd called Aunt Mary from the store, Evie hadn't known about her picture being in the newspaper. Would her aunt feel honour-bound to take her back to Maple Mills and her angry father? Is that why she'd come with a horse trailer?

Evie didn't know what to do. Could she trust Aunt Mary or not? It came down to that. But how could she trust someone she'd never met?

She peeked around the corner of the shelter. The white truck and trailer were indeed coming south, in her direction.

Kazzam, his black coat shining blue in the sunlight, stood in full sight, grazing on the fresh grass in the paddock.

She could not get away in time if she tried. Evie waited for whatever it was that would happen next.

Nothing. The truck and trailer drove right by.

Evie stood up and watched them pass. Now what? Aunt Mary was the only one who could tell her about her mother. Evie had promised to meet her in the store, and she hadn't kept her promise. Would Aunt Mary want to help her now? Evie inhaled deeply to calm her troubled brain.

She'd think this out later. Right now, she was very hungry and knew the animals would be, as well. She poured some kibble out for Magpie and watched her gobble it up with great appetite.

The oats weren't horse oats, but they were better than nothing. Evie found a stick to stir them, as well as an old rubber pail. After cleaning out the cobwebs, she mixed the oats with water, stirred until they were all wet, then brought the pail to Kazzam. He stuck his nose in the pail and ate them all up.

"Good boy!"

Magpie stood quietly while Evie smeared ointment on her sore neck. It would heal quickly. It looked like the dog had caught her collar in a fence or on a nail and had struggled to get free, leaving the collar behind.

Now that her animals were looked after, Evie went back into the shelter, sat down on the burlap bed, and opened the grocery bags. She found another stick and spread peanut butter and jam on a piece of bread. She ate it quickly, guzzled down some orange juice out of the container, and made herself another sandwich.

"That looks delicious!"

Evie started. Girl, dog, and horse all stared at the lady in riding clothes, standing beside the maple tree in the paddock.

"May I have one, too?" she asked, walking toward them. "I'm your great-aunt Mary. I came as soon as you called and had to leave my breakfast in the toaster."

Evie nodded dumbly. She handed her the sandwich she'd just finished making. *Now what? Is she upset?* In a daze, she started spreading peanut butter on another slice of bread.

"May I sit down?"

Evie stammered, "Oh! Of course!"

"Did you want me to find you?"

Evie blushed deeply, filled with unease. "I didn't know it was you in the white truck and trailer. I mean, I thought it might be you, but you're a lot, um, a lot less old than I thought you'd be and you got here really fast."

Mary sat and bit into the bread. "So why didn't you wait for me in the store like we agreed?"

Evie took another bite and decided to answer truthfully. She pointed to the newspaper. "I saw that article and the picture after I called you. It says who I am and that I disappeared with a horse."

"I wondered. I understand. I saw the article first thing this morning, too. Not bad. Chet Reynolds writes well, and he was kind to you."

Evie stopped chewing. *Chet Reynolds must be the reporter who followed me home after the race.*

Aunt Mary continued, "That's why I drove past the

front lane and came in the back way. I wasn't sure if old Bert was watching. He likes to know everyone's business." She chuckled.

Evie studied her. Aunt Mary was cool, and she thought quickly. "Thanks."

"Great sandwich," said Mary. "Nothing like PB and J."

"I'm glad. It's all that's on the menu today."

Mary laughed. Evie noticed the multitude of little lines around her eyes, and the grey streaks in the faded blond hair. Her skin was freckled all over, like Evie's, but wrinkled and loose at her neck and elbows.

"How old are you?" Evie asked.

"Just over sixty. I know how old you are."

Evie nodded, remembering the birthday card she'd received. "Yeah. Sixteen."

They finished their breakfast sitting on the burlap bags. Magpie had gotten over her shyness and rested her head in Mary's lap, looking up at her with beseeching brown eyes.

"You do look like your mother, Evie," said Mary thoughtfully. "That's a compliment. She's lovely. Always was." A brief cloud seemed to pass over her face and then disappear. "Nice dog. Is she yours?"

"No. She turned up last night and slept with me on this bed." Evie looked at Magpie fondly. "I guess I really can't keep her if she belongs to somebody else."

Mary nodded her approval. "Good girl. I'll call the Humane Society and some local vets, and if nobody's missing her, she's yours. She might have an implanted chip. A vet can check that out."

"Okay. Sounds good."

"And what about the horse, Evie?"

Evie felt suddenly chilled. "What about the horse?"

71

"He doesn't belong to you, either."

Evie jumped to her feet. "My father told Jerry to get rid of him by today! I couldn't leave without him! They all think he's horrible, but he's a wonderful horse. He hurts people sometimes, but that's because they don't understand him. He's just afraid!"

"There, there," soothed Mary as she stood and put her hand on the girl's shoulder. "I see the problem. But you must understand. He's a valuable horse and people might think you stole him."

Evie admitted to herself that it didn't look good.

"Let's get Kazzam on the trailer, and you and Magpie and I will drive to my farm. You'll be far safer there than out here. Somebody else is bound to recognize him if I did."

While they were talking about him, Kazzam had strolled up to the two women. Evie patted his nose and thought about what to do. Aunt Mary made sense. "Are you going to call Dad?" she asked quietly.

"Not yet." Mary scowled a little. "He's not my favourite person, and I'm not his."

Evie considered Aunt Mary carefully. There just might be a chance of this turning out okay.

7

Parson's Bridge

Kazzam had loaded easily onto Aunt Mary's trailer, and Magpie sat happily at Evie's feet in the front seat. Still, Evie couldn't help but feel apprehensive as they drove along the road.

"We're almost home," said Aunt Mary as she checked the side-view mirrors to make a turn.

"It's pretty over here. Less rocky and more rolly."

Mary laughed. "Ho ho, hey, hey! Rock and roll is here to stay!" she sang.

Evie laughed, too, even though she had no idea what her aunt was talking about.

"Did you bring your prize money with you?" asked Mary.

"Yes. I thought I'd need it to visit you in Toronto."

Mary glanced at her and smiled. "I have a safe at home, or I'll help you put it in the bank, if you like."

After driving a few minutes more, she said, "My farm is just up this road, but let's drop in here first. Magpie might be chipped. I see my vet's in her office today, even though it's Sunday."

Mary parked the rig along the driveway of a small vet clinic attached to a red-brick farmhouse. Magpie looked wary, so Evie got out, too. The black dog leaped down and followed them into the reception room, tail wagging.

The woman behind the counter smiled. "Hi, Mary!"

"Hi, Diane. I saw your door open. Do you have time to scan this dog for a chip? My niece just found her."

"Ann's cat was hit by a car and will be here soon, but I'll give your pup a quick scan first." She came out from behind the counter with a small hand-held device. Within seconds she said, "I've got it." She patted Magpie's head and said to Evie, "I'll call your aunt later when I track down the address. Let's hope this sweet dog finds her rightful home, whether it's with you or the person who got the chip put in."

Evie knew the vet was right. If she'd been the one to lose Magpie, she'd be heartbroken and would want her returned. But still....

Mary, Magpie, and Evie got back in the truck and continued on to Mary's farm.

"When we get home," said Mary, "we'll get No Justice settled and make a quick call to the Humane Society to see if someone's reported a missing dog. Then I need a coffee or two before I talk to your father."

Evie's stomach did a flip. "I thought you weren't going to call him."

"I said not yet. I didn't say I *wouldn't* call him. You're his daughter and Kazzam is No Justice — his racehorse. He needs to know you're both safe."

"He doesn't care about either of us!" exclaimed Evie. Her face flushed as anger tightened her throat. "He wants Kazzam gone, and he wants me gone, too. I mess up his perfect family."

Mary glanced at her sympathetically, then turned up a lane that was marked with a small sign that read Parson's

Bridge. "That may or may not be how your father sees things, Evie. It's your truth, though, and I can see that you're hurt."

The farm was simple and appealing. The small yellow farmhouse sat to the left of the curving lane, on the far side of a large field. The lane forked, and a little barn was straight ahead. It looked like a four-stall. The boards were unstained, weathered wood. The fences surrounding the fields were split-rail made of old cedar, and there were three very contented-looking horses in the front field. One was a lanky bay, one a sway-backed chestnut, and one a small palomino. Evie much preferred this farm to the ostentatious Maple Mills Stables with the electronic gates and twenty-four hour surveillance.

Aunt Mary parked the truck beside the barn and turned off the engine. She smiled warmly at Evie. "We have a lot of talking to do, don't we?"

Evie liked Aunt Mary so far, but experience had taught her that when in doubt, keep quiet. She wasn't sure how much talking she wanted to do.

Mary seemed to sense what she was thinking and added, "In time. We have lots of time to talk after we get settled in."

Remarkably soon, all the settling in was done. Kazzam backed off the trailer, looked around, snorted a couple of times, then relaxed as he was led to a grassy paddock beside the other horses. At first, they squealed and pranced and pawed over the fence, but after a while things became calm.

Magpie and Aunt Mary's dogs got along right away. She had two labs, a black one named Simon and a yellow one named Garfunkel. The three dogs discovered interesting things to smell and ran around getting to know each other.

Aunt Mary showed Evie into the little yellow house. Evie quickly decided it was just the right size. The kitchen, living area, and dining area were all one room, and Aunt Mary's messy pine desk stood over in a corner.

"Now, I desperately need a coffee. Let's see what I can put together for a snack," said Mary. "But let me get my messages first. The bathroom's right over there if you want to wash up." She pressed the message button and scribbled down a couple of things on a pad while Evie went to use the little washroom.

It was pretty, with ivy-patterned wallpaper in green and white. She refreshed herself as best she could. When she came out, face and hands clean, the table was set for two. Evie was surprised at how quickly Aunt Mary had assembled a tall glass of milk, a plate of cookies, sliced apples, and grapes, along with her steaming coffee.

"This looks delicious." Evie was suddenly very hungry.

Mary's eyes sparkled. "I'm glad you like it. Turns out it's all that's on the menu."

Evie chuckled as she sat down and helped herself.

"So, I called the Humane Society and Animal Control. No dog of Magpie's description is reported missing at the moment, glad to say."

"Thanks, Aunt Mary. I sure hope I can keep her. I've never had my own dog and I love her already." Evie wiped her mouth on the paper napkin and paused. "Can I ask you something?"

Aunt Mary nodded. "Of course you can. Ask me anything."

"Why haven't we met before, ever, when we live so close to each other?"

Mary smiled at Evie a little sadly. "That's a long story. I'm happy to share it with you, but the short answer is because I'm on your mother's side of the family. The Parson side."

"I haven't met any Parsons before. So, you're my mother's aunt?"

"Yes. My brother, Ted Parson, was your mother's father, and her mother was Alicia."

"I have grandparents?"

"Well, they died, so you don't actually have them anymore."

"And the Gibb side doesn't speak to the Parson side?"

Mary's eyes saddened. "When your mother and father got married, your father decided that the Parsons didn't exist. That decision didn't sit well with us, and we continued to try to connect. When Angela had to leave Maple Mills, he decided that *she* didn't exist, either."

Evie felt tears pop into her eyes. "My mother *had to leave* Maple Mills? Why?"

Aunt Mary sat deeper in her chair. "She could no longer be cared for properly. She needed professional help."

Professional help? Was her aunt saying her mother had a serious disability? Or a mental illness? Evie wasn't sure how much she could take in all at once. She wanted to find her mother, to move in with her to get away from Grayson Gibb. She didn't want to hear that she was really ill.

"All my life, since I was little, I was told she was dead."

"No, Evie. She's not dead."

"She's alive?" It came out as a whisper. "For real?"

"Yes, dear. For real. She's alive."

Evie took a shallow breath. Alive, not dead. But in what shape? She felt the pieces of her history shift into a different formation and grabbed the seat of her chair. "Where is she?" Evie's voice was hoarse with emotion.

Mary put down her coffee mug and stared out the kitchen window. Evie followed her gaze and saw nothing but blue sky and the green leaves of the tree outside.

"I know you want to find her. You made a big effort to get in touch with me." Mary looked directly into Evie's eyes. "But still, it'll be tough to hear. She's in Toronto."

"Toronto?" Evie knew by her tone that there was more.

"Yes, dear." Mary smiled with kindness. "She's doing her best. She's worked in stores and cleaned houses. For a while she sewed clothes, but right now she doesn't have a job. Sometimes she has an apartment. Right now she doesn't."

"So where does she live?"

"I'm not exactly sure."

"What are you saying? She's living on the street?"

"Possibly."

Evie blinked. Was she a street person? Were all the nasty things her father said true? That her mother stole food and was a flighty, irresponsible, despicable person? Evie tried not to let her imagination run rampant. She tried not to picture Angela with a swollen belly and missing teeth, begging for money and wearing filthy rags. Evie listened intently as Mary continued.

"Angela became addicted to pain medication after she fell off a horse and shattered her leg. You were just a small child. Not even three years old." Mary sat forward and ran her fingers through her silvered hair. "I blame the doctor. He gave her too many prescriptions for OxyContin and she became dependent on them. That's how it started."

Evie sat motionless, slumped in her chair. "Holy."

Mary sighed. "She should've gone into a rehabilitation facility. Instead, your father sent her away."

"But kept me with him?" This didn't make sense to Evie. Her father wouldn't have wanted a child to look after. Especially her.

"He persuaded Angela to sign away all claims to you, and with you went her estate."

This was a lot to take in. "Her estate? I don't understand."

"Grayson was not a wealthy man when he married your mother. The money belonged to Angela."

"And so?" Evie spread out her hands.

"And so, when Angela was convinced that she was a horrible mother, she made a deal with Grayson. As long as you were raised well and loved and cared for, she was happy to leave him with her money."

"He *never* loved me or cared for me!" Evie's heart was thumping. She worried that she couldn't get enough oxygen into her lungs.

Mary reached out and rested a hand on Evie's shoulder. "She never knew that, dear. She always thought that you were better off with Grayson."

This is crazy! Evie's head felt like it could burst. "But why? Why would she ever think that? She knew him! She must've known better!"

"She didn't."

"She would've loved me!" Evie tried not to cry. She couldn't imagine a mother leaving a child at all, let alone to such a man as Grayson Gibb. "Something must have happened."

Aunt Mary looked pensive. "Let me just say, she was in a very bad way. She thought you'd be better off."

"She was wrong!"

"She made her choice with the information she had. That's all she could do. We all do that, Evie. We're not always right, but we only know that later."

"Why didn't anybody help her?" she heard herself yelling. "Like her parents? Her friends? Or you?"

Mary answered very quietly, her head down. "I should have done more. I feel guilty every day. I wasn't aware of her addiction until later." She looked up. "May I speak honestly?"

Evie nodded. She wiped the sweat and tears from her face. "Yes. Why stop now? I need to know everything."

"Grayson was very possessive about her. He kept us away. He wanted her all to himself. I thought at the time it was newlywed stuff and that he'd get over it. But he became more and more controlling as time went on, not less. Nobody knew that Angela needed help until she was gone."

"But what about her parents — your brother and his wife? My grandparents. Didn't they know what was happening in their own daughter's life?"

Mary tilted her head. "I guess you don't know anything about the Parsons, do you?"

"No. I told you. Not a thing."

"Let's sit over by the window to watch how the horses are getting to know each other. I'll fill you in."

When Evie stood up she felt dizzy and grabbed the back of her chair. It quickly passed, but she was careful as she walked over to the couch where Aunt Mary sat.

Mary had noticed. "I'm sorry. I've told you more than you can absorb at one time. Let me ask you some questions about yourself instead."

Evie sank into the soft cushions. She let her body go limp. *Nice.*

"What do you like to do? Besides riding, of course."

"Nothing, really." Evie tried to think of something interesting, but she really had nothing more to say. Lately, riding Kazzam was all she liked to do.

"So," Mary tried again, "tell me about school."

Wrong topic. "It's ... okay." Mary was a very nice woman, but Evie was not about to confide her problems.

"Tell me about your friends."

What friends? Evie blushed. She hated blushing and was embarrassed about how red her face could get, which made her blush more. She tried to hide her face with her hair.

Mary lifted a strand of red hair from Evie's face and said very sweetly, "It's healthy to blush, Evie. It means you're a sensitive, honest person. Be proud of it."

"Proud?" Although she felt irritated, Evie couldn't help but appreciate Aunt Mary's kind sentiments.

"So, tell me about school."

"I'm in grade ten. It's okay."

"Hmm. Just okay. Friends?"

"Didn't you already ask? Can we talk about something else? It's been a tough year."

"How so?" Aunt Mary waited for an answer.

"What are you, a psychiatrist?"

"Oops. I guess I hit the No Go button."

"Are you making fun of me?"

"Not at all. I won't ask any more questions. We're done."

"Are you mad? I can't tell."

"No. I'm not mad." Aunt Mary looked thoughtful. "But ... you asked me a lot of questions. And I'm happy to answer them." She sat back into the cushions. "I'd just like to know you a bit better. I'm not trying to be nosy."

Really? Why did Aunt Mary keep asking these crappy questions if she wasn't nosy? Evie felt miserable. She wasn't used to talking about herself. Who cared, anyway? People asked questions, then never listened to the answers. Besides, she admitted to herself, her brain was still trying to absorb what Aunt Mary had told her about her mother.

However, now that she'd found Aunt Mary, she had to comply with what she wanted. At least a little. "I'll answer all horse-related questions."

Aunt Mary chuckled. "Agreed. Who helped you train No Justice to win the Caledon Horse Race?"

This, she could handle. "Well, he was already fit. He won a race ten days ago."

"I don't think it counts as a win if the rider isn't on his back when he crosses the finish line."

Evie hadn't realized that Aunt Mary followed the races. "He thought he won. He beat all the other horses."

"Good point. So how did you do it? It's not easy to train a horse to win. I know that. It takes a lot of hard work, knowledge, patience, and diligence."

"Thank you." Evie felt herself blush again. "We ran every night at eleven o'clock. Nobody knew. I copied what the trainers did, but at night."

Mary's eyebrows rose. "And nobody helped you?"

"No. I tacked him up and off we went."

"Weren't you a little afraid? Word has it that nobody can stay on that horse."

Evie looked out to where the sleek black horse was grazing. His coat shone midnight blue in the sunlight. "He and I have a way of understanding each other, I guess. I don't do anything special. I just ride him. We just run together."

Mary lifted an eyebrow. "Well, well. You're a real horsewoman."

Evie shook her head. "No, I'm not. My stepsister Beatrice is a good rider, and my stepmother, too. They win ribbons all the time. I'm not good enough to compete."

"Says who?"

"Says everybody. I don't care anyway." She found herself fidgeting with her hair. She stopped herself.

"I'm sure you're a very good rider. If you ever want to try showing in the hunter ring, Paragon is a lovely horse. You'd do very well with him."

"Thanks, Aunt Mary, but my form is all wrong. I never get anything right. Anyway, I only like riding Kazzam."

Mary smiled and nodded. "Maybe we can go for a hack on the trails later."

"That'd be great," Evie said, happily surprised. "He likes to see new things."

"But first I have to call your father." At Evie's gasp Mary put up her hand. "You know I do."

"But … there's something else." Evie had no choice. Aunt Mary had to know. "I'm not totally sure what I heard." She paused and then blurted it out. "My father might have Kazzam killed if he goes back."

"Killed?" Mary's eyebrows shot up.

Evie continued, even though when it was spoken aloud, it sounded lame. "He said that Jerry had to get rid of him by today or … that he's insured for a lot of money."

"Wow." Mary sat quietly as she thought it over. "Grayson isn't my favourite person, I've told you that. But I can't believe he'd have a horse killed for insurance money. It's the lowest of the low and too great a risk."

Evie hoped that Aunt Mary didn't think she'd made it up. "I heard him say it, that's all. I thought I should tell you before you call him."

"You were right to tell me. And I understand your concern. But the facts remain the same, Evie. You are his child and the horse belongs to him. I cannot harbour you both without contacting him."

"It's not like Dad cares about me or Kazzam. But if you call him, can you tell him that Kazzam can stay here?"

Mary nodded.

"I won't give him back," Evie said, "unless I know he's not in danger."

"Agreed. I want you both to stay here as long as you want. Magpie, too." Mary crossed to the telephone and held it up. "Number?" she asked. As Evie told her, she pressed the buttons.

It seemed a long time before someone answered.

"Hello," said Aunt Mary. "This is Evie's great-aunt, Mary Parson. Could I speak with Grayson, please?" A worried look passed over her face. "Oh, dear … I see. Thank you, Sella.… No, please don't bother him.… Thank you. I'll call back later."

Mary hung up the phone and turned to Evie. "Your father is talking to the police right now, but not about you." She put her hand on Evie's arm. "It seems that your little brother went missing last night."

Evie jumped to her feet. "Oh, no!" She clasped her hands together. "Last night? Poor Jordie!" Evie felt terrible. She had no doubt that he ran away because of her. "I should've told him what I was doing so he wouldn't worry. But I didn't know I was leaving so soon myself, and anyway, he might have let it slip by mistake, and I couldn't take that chance!"

"What do you want to do, Evie?"

Evie's mind raced. Jordie was only seven years old! She said, "Please drive me back. I think I know where he might be hiding. Nobody else knows."

Aunt Mary nodded and grabbed her handbag and keys. "Don't worry, Evie," said Mary. "We'll find him."

They unhitched the trailer from the truck and closed the tailgate. As soon as Evie climbed in, Magpie jumped up and sat at her feet with bright and expectant eyes. "Can Magpie come?" Evie asked.

"Sure." Mary got behind the wheel and started the engine. She turned the truck around and drove down the lane.

Evie glanced at the beautiful ebony gelding as they passed his field. Kazzam lifted his head with curiosity, but looked peaceful. Evie was glad she needn't worry about him while they were gone.

All the way to Maple Mills, Evie kept an eye out for signs of her little brother — along the roads and in hedges and fields — in case he'd tried to follow her in the dark.

They turned up the Maple Mills drive and stopped at the security pad. Evie told Aunt Mary the correct numbers and they waited while the gates opened.

Only now did it occur to Evie what she might face when her father saw her. She felt immobilized. He knew what she'd done. "He's going to be mad."

"Yes. The best way to handle this is head on."

"Head on?"

"Yes. Deal with it directly. It's a fact that you left without telling anyone and a fact that you took Kazzam. Or rather, No Justice." Mary glanced at her. "Admit it, say you're sorry, and then get down to business."

"Which is finding Jordie."

"Exactly."

"Okay. Right. I can do it." Evie inhaled deeply and gathered her courage. "If you'll protect me."

Without hesitation, Aunt Mary said, "To the end."

Police cars were parked at the house. Evie counted four of them. What had she started?

They stopped the truck. Evie walked ahead with Magpie, and Aunt Mary followed right behind. The front door of the house was wide open.

Evie saw Jordie's running shoes on the mat. She held them up to Magpie's nose, then set them down. "Here, girl. This is what Jordie smells like. Take a sniff."

Beatrice came running from the kitchen. "Evie! Mom saw you with my bagel and I didn't want her to get mad at me and she was already mad at you anyway!" Tears popped into her eyes. "I didn't mean for you to run away!"

"It's okay, Beebee!" Evie was stunned. Beatrice had never been this nice to her before. Maybe she didn't hate her, after all. "I didn't leave because of the bagel. Really. It's not your fault."

"Then it's all *your* fault!" The smaller girl stepped back and hit Evie, hard, on her shoulder. "I hate you!"

"Ouch!" That answered *that* question.

"Now Jordie's gone, too! All because of you! He thought you hanged yourself, but there was no dead body hanging from your sheet, so he went to find you!"

Evie looked at Aunt Mary over Beatrice's angry head.

Aunt Mary stepped closer. "Beatrice? I'm Aunt Mary. I came to help."

Beatrice turned and stared at her with suspicion. She wiped her face with her arm and sniffed.

Evie noticed a movement through the kitchen door. It was Sella. Under her glossy black pageboy, her small, dark face was tense and her deep-brown eyes were hollow. *Something's wrong*. Evie nodded a greeting. Sella tried to smile, flicked her eyes quickly to her right, then disappeared from sight.

"What are *you* doing here?" a voice hissed.

8

Jordie

Grayson Gibb swept tiny Sella aside, then strode out of the kitchen and into the hall. He towered over them, glaring past Evie and right at Mary. His eyes glinted like steel. He began to smile, which made Evie think of a rabid dog baring its teeth. Her blood ran cold. She wanted nothing more than to run back to the safety of Aunt Mary's truck.

"Hello, Grayson." Mary sounded calm to Evie, and she looked very composed, although her own knees were trembling. "Evie came to visit me. Both of us are here to help find Jordie."

"Get back in your truck and leave." The tall man stood ramrod straight, inches from Mary, looking down at her with hostility, even though his mouth was still smiling. "You're not welcome. You should know that by now."

Evie stared at him, uncomprehending. "Jordie's missing! You can't turn away help!"

"You call it help?" said Grayson, still focused on Mary. He laughed rudely. "I call it interference. I've never needed your help, Mary. Not with Angela, not with Evie, and not with Jordie. Stay out of my business."

Mary blinked, but stood firm. "When it's family business, it becomes my business."

"You never stop pushing yourself where you don't belong. I'm in charge of this house, and I demand that you leave. Immediately." His face darkened.

Evie slowly put the picture together. How many birthday cards had been delivered that she'd never seen? "Dad? What are you saying? Has Aunt Mary tried to help us before?"

He turned his cold gaze on Evie. "Your aunt is an interfering busybody who has no place here," he rasped. "She thinks she can solve everyone's problems. What Angela became is no fault of mine." For the first time in her life, Evie saw confusion on her father's face. Fear, even. But then the insecurity vanished, replaced by the familiar aggression.

"And you, young lady." He pointed a finger two inches from Evie's nose. "You caused this whole situation. My wife has taken to her bed and won't come out. I'll deal with you later. You get to your room, you ... horse thief!"

"I won't do a thing until Jordie's found!" Evie ran out the door. She looked back and yelled to her father, "And I didn't steal Kazzam! I saved him! I heard what you said to Jerry Johnston!"

Evie ran toward the stables with Magpie right behind her. She felt wronged. She'd come back to help, in spite of her father's certain wrath, but her father could never accept that there was an ounce of good in her. He was horrible to her. And to Aunt Mary, too. It'd been awful to listen to him hissing at her!

But right now she had to find Jordie. "Please let him be in our secret hiding place," she prayed. Whenever their father was mad at them, really mad, Jordie and Evie went to a special place. Beatrice didn't need it. She did no wrong in his eyes, or Paulina's.

Evie ran as fast as she could. Just as she was passing the stables, Jerry Johnston stepped out.

"Whoa there, girl," he called good-naturedly. "Just the girl I've been looking —"

"Jordie's missing!" panted Evie. "I have to find him."

Jerry's brow furrowed. "Oh, no. You go, but take this. Call me." He reached into his pocket. "It's about No Justice." He handed Evie a business card. "It's important."

"I'll come back as soon as I find Jordie."

"Evie, I won't be here. I've been fired."

"Fired?"

"I knew it was coming." He looked resigned.

Evie had trouble keeping up with everything that was happening. "I'm so sorry." She put the card in her pocket. "I'll call you!" she said, and sped away.

Why had Jerry been fired? And why had Grayson never told her about Aunt Mary? Evie had never known that Aunt Mary had been trying to connect until now. What else was Grayson hiding?

She jogged through the back hayfield. Once past the treed fenceline, she scrambled down the brambly embankment and stepped from rock to rock across the stream. It was low for this time of year, she noticed. *All this dry weather.*

Magpie shot past her, all excited. Her nose was to the ground and her tail wagged madly. She had a scent!

Just past the oldest and biggest maple on the farm was a rocky ridge. Evie and Jordie had dug a small cave in the far side and had furnished it with old stools and sacks. She'd taken a green curtain from the Goodwill box and tacked it up over the entrance to keep out the wind.

Magpie's nose brought her to the mouth of that cave. The big black dog stood there panting, wagging her tail and looking proudly at Evie.

"Good girl, Magpie!"

Evie knelt down in front of the cave and pulled back the curtain just a little. "Jordie?" she whispered, hoping against hope.

"Evie? Is that really you?"

Evie's body went limp with relief. "Yes. It's me." She was suddenly exhausted. "I'm so glad you came here. I'm so glad you're safe."

Jordie's head popped out from behind the curtain. His face was stained with tears. "I thought you were gone for good." The little boy crawled out and hugged his big sister. "I thought you were dead! I saw the sheet and I thought.... I don't want to go home if you're not there!"

Magpie pushed into the embrace and licked the boy's face.

"Who's the dog?" he asked. He reached out and gingerly touched her head. Magpie lay down on her back and allowed him to rub her tummy, which made Jordie smile. He wiped his teary face on his sleeve.

"Her name is Magpie and I found her last night. Or she found me. I hope I can keep her."

"She's super cool!"

"She likes you. She found you with her nose!" Evie watched her little brother pat the dog. "I'm so sorry, Jordie. I'd never hang myself, I promise. But I should've told you I was going."

"Was it because Dad's so mean? Or Mom?"

Evie snorted. "Try both. I'm not exactly their favourite."

"I know. Beebee is. But you're *my* favourite. Don't ever go away again!"

Evie had to be honest. "Jordie, I need to go away again. Just for a while. I need to find my mother."

"But your mother is dead, Evie. Dad says so." He stopped playing with Magpie and looked at her earnestly.

"He told me that, too, but Aunt Mary says she's alive and living in Toronto. I want to meet her."

"Who's Aunt Mary?"

"My mother's aunt."

Jordie looked skeptical. He wiped his nose on the curtain. "If she's alive, why isn't she your mother instead of Paulina?"

Evie wasn't sure how much to tell Jordie. "She's been very sick. Maybe I can help her get better."

Jordie stood up and brushed himself off. "Then I'm going with you. I can help her get better, too."

Evie saw how eager he was to come, but she shook her head. "It's not a good idea." There was no telling what her mother might be like, or in what shape. Her imagination conjured up an emaciated, horrible, wrinkly lady with a shaking, outstretched hand.

Evie wondered if *she* could handle it, let alone a seven-year-old.

Jordie persisted. "I won't be a problem, Evie. I'll help! I'll stay quiet and I won't eat anything if there's only enough for you." A single tear fell down his cheek.

"Oh, Jordie!" cried Evie. She hugged him tightly and said, "We have to go back to the house. Paulina won't come out of her room, she's so sad that you're gone."

"She's drinking her red wine. That's why she's in her room!" Jordie was indignant.

Evie knew he was probably right, but the police were looking for him. "She's drinking because she's unhappy. Come on, let's go."

Magpie sat up and sniffed the air.

Jordie stared at something behind Evie. His eyes grew round. Evie spun around to see Beatrice climbing down the embankment.

"Did you tell her?" whispered Jordie.

"No. Did you?"

"Never! This is *our* hiding place!"

"Jordie!" yelled Beatrice, stumbling awkwardly toward them. "Jordie, you're safe!"

"What's with her?" asked Jordie. "She's looking for me? She never cared about me before!"

"Funny, I thought the same thing. Until she hit me." Evie rubbed her shoulder.

"What're you two ... whispering about?" demanded Beatrice, red in the face and catching her breath. "You always keep ... secrets from me."

Evie answered, "We were saying how nice you are to be looking for Jordie."

"Why ... wouldn't I? He's my ... brother!" She put her hands on her knees and gasped for air. "Idiot!"

"How'd you find me?" Jordie wanted to know.

"I followed ... Evie. She runs ... fast. Mom's gonna be so mad."

The three kids trudged back toward the big white house, followed by the only happy one in their little group — Magpie. Every flower, every stump, every rock was a delight to her. Somehow, her mood became contagious. How could they be sad when there was so much to enjoy? Soon Evie found that her spirits had lifted. She noticed that Jordie was smiling, too, and the dark cloud that usually followed Beatrice had gone. All because of Magpie.

Once they got to the house, Sella met them at the door. The housekeeper threw her arms in the air and clapped, overjoyed to see Jordie. She hugged him until he begged for mercy. Then she wiped her eyes and said, "Missus is asleep. Don't wake her. And Mister is in his office with Aunt Mary." She made a quick sign of the cross. "He's going agaga."

That was Sella's way of describing the rage that some-times possessed their father. *Not a good sign*, thought Evie.

"Come, come! I have so much to eat!" When Sella was upset, she made food. Evie smiled. They followed her into the kitchen and she promptly shut the door. This was another habit. Sella always tried to protect them from Grayson's temper.

Before Evie could take a bite out of a deep-fried chicken leg, the kitchen door opened. Aunt Mary came in and closed it softly behind her.

"Evie, your father wants you to come home with me. Can you get some clothes together for a little visit?" Aunt Mary was flushed but composed.

Jordie's eyes bulged. "Who are you?" he said through a mouthful of warm bread.

"I'm Evie's Aunt Mary." She smiled at the small boy.

"I wanna come, too." Jordie looked like he might cry again. "I need to be with Evie."

Mary sat on the stool beside him. "I'll invite you and Beatrice soon." She included Beatrice in her smile. "But your father would like Evie to visit me for a while first. Alone. Then we'll talk about both of you coming, okay?"

Beatrice stared at Mary, picking at her bread. "I'm not going. You're not my aunt. I have dance practice and it's horse-show season."

Mary's eyes took in her slight frame and defensive manner. "Wonderful! Evie tells me you're a lovely rider and such a good swimmer."

Her compliment made Beatrice relax slightly. "I am."

Evie stood up. "Jordie, I won't be gone long. I'll write down Aunt Mary's number. You can call me anytime."

"I'll give it to them, Evie," said Mary. "You go get packed." She looked more than a little stressed.

Sella put her hand on Evie's shoulder. "You go now, quickly, my dear. Beebee and Jordie will be fine with me. You know I'll look after them good."

Evie hugged the housekeeper. "I know that, Sella. You always do."

She gave Jordie a warm embrace. "I'll see you before you know it." The little boy nodded bravely as tears filled his eyes.

Evie went to give Beatrice a hug, but the smaller girl shoved her hard. "Just go already!"

Somehow that made things easier. More normal. Evie ran up the stairs two at a time. She wanted to go back to Parson's Bridge, but Grayson was so weird and she hated leaving her siblings with him. *They'll be fine,* she told herself. *Just fine.* Paulina was their mother, after all. They should stay with her. And Sella would look after them.

Once they were in the truck and through the security gates, Aunt Mary let out a huge breath. "I forgot the effect he has on me!" she exclaimed.

"My father?" asked Evie.

"Yes. Grayson is a formidable man."

"So, what did he say about Kazzam? Is he mad that I took him?" Evie needed to know.

"Yes, he's mad. But he knows where the horse is." Mary blew air through her teeth. "He told me to feed him for now, and that at least he's not paying for him."

"So I can keep him?"

"I wouldn't go that far. Let's just say that he doesn't want us to drive him back today."

Evie sighed. "That's a start. And did he say anything about us winning the Caledon Race?"

"Not a thing."

It would've been too much to ask for a little praise, thought Evie bitterly. *Not one of his high-priced jockeys could even stay on!*

"I'm sure he's very proud of you," said Mary.

"I'm sure he doesn't give a crap."

"Don't be so sure. It's hard to know what people think."

Evie snorted. "How did you convince him to let me go with you?"

"It was actually his idea. Jordie and Beatrice will be better behaved without your extremely bad influence."

Evie felt defensive until she saw the sparkle in her aunt's eyes. "Not funny. Do I have to live with your awful sense of humour?"

"Family trait. Get used to it."

Evie groaned, but briefly wondered if her mother shared that trait. "So really. Why did he let me go?"

"I was surprised, I admit. He's so controlling. But it *was* his idea. Paulina needs her own children with her for a while. He thought it would be better this way. For a while."

"And now the translation." Evie felt hollowed out, and tried to keep the hurt out of her voice. "Paulina kicked me out and he agreed. And Kazzam was thrown in to sweeten the deal."

"But, Evie, dear, you left home yourself first."

"It's not the same at all." Or maybe it was. She didn't want to live there, anyway. "I'm so confused."

"I'm sure you are, dear. It'll work out. It always does, one way or another."

"I don't even know what you just said!"

Aunt Mary chortled. "Just words, Evie. Meant to comfort you."

"Thanks." She watched miserably as the fields went by.

"Did you like how he told me I wasn't welcome and to stay out of his business?" asked Mary.

"That's my father for you." Evie chuckled begrudgingly. "You and he talked for a long time. What did he say?"

"It was mostly a rehash of what he said to me in the hall. That I wasn't welcome in his world. That he had done everything possible for Angela before she left."

"You mean, before he kicked her out." *Like me.*

"He can't think differently, Evie. It's his defence. It would kill him to think otherwise, to imagine that he'd been wrong. Or negligent."

Evie remembered another thing she wanted to clear up. "It sounds like you've been a pest since my mother left."

"You mean to Grayson?"

"Yes. He called you an 'interfering busybody.'"

Mary nodded. "I am indeed and will remain so." She gave Evie a serious look. "I keep trying to right the wrongs, and I'm not ashamed of that. He kept me away from you, though, until you found me."

Evie twisted her hair and slumped, full of undiagnosed emotions. Lots to think about. Her throat tightened, but she managed to say, "I'm glad I found you."

"I'm glad you did, too, my dear," said Aunt Mary softly. "I'm glad you did, too."

Magpie plunked her head onto Evie's lap and stared at her with love. She rubbed the dog's soft ears between her fingers. "Maybe we'll hear about Magpie's chip when we get back. I hope nobody's going to claim her."

"She is a lovely dog," said Mary. "Somebody must be missing her. Don't get your hopes up too high."

Evie had only known Magpie for a day, but the thought of losing her was quite distressing.

Her mind turned to the reason she'd sought out Aunt Mary in the first place. "When do you think we can go see my mother?"

"How about tomorrow?"

Evie's breath caught in her throat. "Tomorrow?"

"Oh, what was I thinking? Tomorrow is Monday. You've got school."

Evie shook her head. There was no way she was going back to school. Not now, maybe not ever. A little white lie would solve this. "No, I don't. It's a PA day."

"Professional Activity? Great. Then why not? The sooner the better."

The thought of meeting the woman who was her mother was intimidating, but somehow easier to face than her classmates. "Yes, why not?" she echoed.

When they drove up the lane at Parson's Bridge, the sun was just beginning to set. The entire sky was striped with variations of reds and blues, and the little yellow house had turned pink. *It's beautiful,* Evie thought. Kazzam, grazing in the field, had a pink halo, and the three horses in the next field were rosy, too.

"What are your horses' names?" Evie asked.

"The tall bay is Paragon. He's a show jumper. The retired old chestnut with the blaze is Bendigo, and he was a racehorse. The palomino quarter horse mare is Christieloo."

"They're beautiful."

Mary nodded, pleased at the compliment. "Thank you. I think so, too. I just got Christieloo. She's a rescue."

"Really? Rescued from what? She looks great."

"She wasn't malnourished, but she was neglected and smacked around. I'm going to start from the beginning and retrain her. She doesn't accept people telling her what to do yet. She's very suspicious."

"Maybe I can help."

"That'd be wonderful. You'll be an enormous help."

Evie felt a thrill in her chest. She looked forward to working with the little mare. She felt sure she could make a difference. Kazzam had been suspicious, too. Very.

Just then, she remembered the card in her pocket. "I have to call Jerry Johnston."

"Jerry?"

"Yes. I almost forgot. I don't know why he wants me to call."

Mary looked at Evie knowingly. "Let me guess."

"What?"

"Jerry thinks about racing and racing only."

"But he doesn't know...."

"Trust me, he knows. Everybody knows you're Molly Peebles. Jerry believes in Kazzam. And Jerry wants to talk to you about racing. I have absolutely no doubt."

"Wow." Evie felt her entire mood lighten, but she couldn't let herself get too excited. "If you're right."

"Oh, I'm right. I've known Jerry for thirty-odd years. I know how he thinks." She parked the truck beside the house and looked toward the barn. "Speak of the devil."

Evie followed her aunt's gaze and saw Jerry Johnston getting out of his car.

"He couldn't even wait for your call," said Mary.

9

The Breeze

Aunt Mary was right. All Jerry Johnston wanted to do was talk about racing. And Evie was very happy to listen.

They sat together in the living area beside the kitchen as the sun set through the big windows. Evie enjoyed a mug of hot chocolate, Aunt Mary sipped a glass of white wine, and Jerry talked while nursing a beer.

"I saw the tapes. Evie, you were sensational. You let No Justice run his own race. He had a really rough start. Most jocks would have freaked and started whipping, but not you. You made sure he knew he wasn't in trouble with you, and then you helped him get back in the game. You tried to manage him on the stretch, but as soon as you saw he wasn't buying, you changed your tune. You left him alone and he won like a champ. A real champ." Jerry wiped a tear from his eye. "See what you did? You made a grown man cry."

Evie sat very still with her eyes wide open. She wasn't used to being complimented. She liked it, but was a little uncomfortable.

"Well," said Mary, "high praise, indeed. So what are we going to do about it?"

"We're going to run No Justice in the Queen's Plate. He's already entered, and renewed. Purse is one million dollars. He's the best Canadian-bred three-year old I've ever seen." Jerry Johnston was almost bouncing on his chair. His face was so animated that Evie looked to Aunt Mary for reassurance.

"It's okay, Evie," she said with a grin. "Jerry gets like this when he's got a plan cooking."

Evie raised her eyebrows and looked back at Jerry. "I like your plan, I do, but is my father really going to allow him to race? And do you have a jockey?"

Jerry picked up his beer and swallowed the last of it in one gulp. "Good questions. Both of them. The jockey problem is real. Nobody wants to ride him. But we can get around that, with luck. It's all in the details."

"And Grayson?" asked Mary.

"Grayson isn't going to like it. That needs more thought. Another detail. But Grayson ordered me to get him off his payroll, which has happened, thanks to you taking him in. We can make this happen. We have to. No Justice will win it. I think he's got —"

"Can I ask you something else?" Evie interrupted.

"Of course."

"Why were you fired?"

Jerry wiped a bit of beer foam from his lips. "Look, it was coming. Your father and I had serious disagreements. The surprise is that I lasted so long."

"Disagreements about *all* the horses? Or only Kazzam?" asked Evie.

"In truth, only about that black racehorse of yours. I didn't want to give up."

"You wanted to overturn the ban?" asked Mary.

"Yes. But before that, I wanted the vet to take a few x-rays to see if he was bucking out of pain. I wanted to change his feed in case the oats were making him too hot. Try blinkers. A different bit. A new jockey."

"But Grayson didn't want to spend any more money," guessed Mary.

"Right on," Jerry nodded. "It's like this. Grayson can't stand anybody challenging him and I challenged him anyway. I'm not the first person he fired for that reason."

Evie decided to ask the question that had been on her mind since the night she ran away. "Would my father ever have a horse killed for insurance reasons?"

Jerry looked stricken. "I would never do that!"

Aunt Mary intervened. "That's quite a loaded question, Evie." She looked at Jerry. "Evie thought she overheard Grayson saying something about that in the barn."

"She heard right. But he wouldn't actually do that. It was just a way of emphasizing his point."

"His point being for you to get rid of No Justice by the morning," clarified Mary.

"Exactly. And Evie solved my problem, and his, by running away and coming here. End of story."

"Thanks, Jerry," said Evie. "I'm glad about that." And she was. It was a great relief to know that Kazzam was not in danger of being killed for the insurance money.

"Stay for dinner, Jerry?" asked Mary.

"No, thanks. Gotta run."

"Another beer?"

"Love one, but no. I'll take a rain check."

"But as you've pointed out," Evie said, "there are a lot of details to work out. When are we going to do that?"

"Lots of time."

Evie had yet another question. "How old do you have to be, to be a jockey?"

Jerry scratched his nose. "Eighteen. And apprentices must be at least sixteen. Why?"

"Just curious," answered Evie, reddening as she hoped that her question hadn't appeared precocious.

Jerry didn't notice and went back to his train of thought. "We need to keep No Justice in training. He needs to be racing fit by June 24." Jerry stood and straightened his tie. "I'll come back tomorrow to train. What's a good time for you, Mary?"

"We're going to Toronto. Can we make it 6 a.m.?"

"Good. See you then. We'll breeze him." Jerry left the house as quickly as he'd arrived.

"Breeze him?" Evie asked as the kitchen door slammed.

"Let him run," answered Mary. "Not push him, just let him run. You're the rider, it seems, at least for tomorrow." She winked as she took the wineglass and mugs to the sink.

Evie sat in a daze. She was going to help train Kazzam to win the most prestigious race in Canada. *Amazing!* "I'm sixteen. Can I be an apprentice jockey?"

Mary turned quickly, eyebrows raised. "Not a simple thing. But it's something to work toward."

Evie smiled. She vowed to try.

"Come on, girl! It's late. Gotta look after the horses."

Evie and Aunt Mary walked across the grassy slope to the little barn, followed by the dogs. Tails were wagging and Evie was happy to observe that Magpie had been accepted as one of the pack. In a very short time, Simon and Garfunkel had completely welcomed her.

Aunt Mary prepared the horse feed, mixing crunch with oats and a scoop of flax seed that had cooked in the slow cooker all day, to keep their coats glossy. Evie threw down some hay from the loft above and put a flake in each stall. She filled the buckets right up to the top with fresh water. Now they were ready to lead the horses in from the field to their freshly bedded stalls.

Aunt Mary gave Evie a halter and lead shank, and they walked out to the gate. The horses all came running, three in one field and Kazzam in the next.

"Whoa, there, buddies," said Mary, smiling. "Everybody's getting fed. You'd think I starved them."

She opened the gate and slipped a halter on Bendigo.

"You take Paragon, Evie. He's next."

They walked in with the first two and returned for the others. On the way back to the fields, they noticed that Kazzam and Christieloo were sniffing noses and checking each other out over the fence.

"See how they're standing together?" said Mary. "They've chosen to be friends. With the others gone, they can introduce themselves without fear of a jealous kick or bite."

Magpie had her dog friends and now it looked like Kazzam had a friend, too. At Maple Mills, nobody took the time to notice if horses liked each other or not, because two horses were never allowed to be in the same field. Separate turnout was the way race-horses lived their entire working lives to avoid the risk of a debilitating kick. This was way better, Evie thought. These horses were allowed to be horses, and

Aunt Mary treated them like individuals, not merely revenue-generating units. Evie felt a wave of contentment. She smiled. Aunt Mary was pretty cool, she thought. Being here might just work out.

Aunt Mary led Christieloo, while Evie put the halter on Kazzam. She stroked his neck as they walked in the cooling evening air. "Do you want to run in the Queen's Plate, boy?" she whispered. Kazzam lifted his upper lip and tossed his head. His loud neigh rang through the hills. Evie threw back her head and laughed aloud. Even though she'd just been kicked out of home, she had not felt this happy for a long time.

Once the horses were looked after, they returned to the house and washed up in the bright kitchen. Aunt Mary told Evie where her room was, and Evie headed upstairs with her knapsack.

When she opened the door, she was stunned. "Oh … my … gosh!" she whispered. Her room was perfect. She spun around and fell spread-eagled on the bed. Then, she lifted her head to be sure she wasn't dreaming and giggled. She *must* be dreaming. A multipaned bay window overlooked the little stable, and a tiny gas fireplace was under a mantel. The wallpaper was a riot of colourful flowers, and the bedspread, bedskirt, and curtains were ivory eyelet. Antique embroidered cushions were thrown on the bed — horse-themed cushions, just like what Evie loved to collect. *How amazing!* she thought. She had so much in common with her aunt Mary. A lovely, comfortable, deep-pink armchair with matching ottoman finished the bedroom, sitting in the bay window ready for Evie to cuddle up with a book.

She put away her few clothes in drawers that had been built into the closet, took another unbelieving look around the room, then descended the stairs to the kitchen.

"It's the most beautiful bedroom in the entire world!"

Aunt Mary's head was in the refrigerator. "I'm so glad you like it," she said as she took out food and set it on the counter. "I'll make us some eggs while you feed Magpie, Simon, and Garfunkel. The kibble is in the mud room and the bowls are on the floor. They'll need water, too."

Evie jumped into action, feeling like part of the family, included and helpful. Her entire life until now had been on the outside looking in. The concept of family had been a strange and unrecognizable one. How could it be that she'd feel like this in a strange house, with a person she'd never met until today?

She filled water bowls and poured out the kibble, then called Simon and Garfunkel. Because Magpie was new here, she fed her outside. She didn't want a food fight on the first day. Once the dogs had gobbled their dinners, she let Magpie in. "You feel like family, too, don't you, girl?" she whispered, and patted her head.

"Welcome to Parson's Bridge, dear Evie," Aunt Mary said. She put dinner on the table. Sliced tomatoes, fresh bread, and a cheese omelette. "I want you to feel right at home."

Evie suddenly choked up. She couldn't speak, so she just nodded.

That night, Evie slept better in her eyelet bed than she had for a long, long time. When the sun began to creep through her curtains, lighting the flowery wallpaper with streaks of lemon, she stretched and yawned and smiled from ear to ear.

Her alarm hadn't yet rung. She luxuriated in the down bed, thinking. This morning, she was going to exercise Kazzam with Jerry Johnston, the famous Thoroughbred trainer. Was this really happening to her, the misfit? The loser? The girl with no talents and no discernible future, and no friends since the embarrassing incident? Things were changing for the better. She stretched her arms and grinned.

And after the breeze, they were going to Toronto to find her mother. Angela. The woman who'd given birth to her.

Evie stopped smiling. Because Angela had disappeared when Evie was only three, she had very few memories of her, and even these were hazy. She wasn't sure if they were even real.

Uneasiness settled in. What kind of person would she find? Was her mother crazy? Doped up? Did Angela want Evie to find her? Her stomach dropped. Evie became increasingly unsure about the Toronto expedition.

Maybe the truck wouldn't start. Or she might fall off Kazzam and break her leg. Evie scolded herself for her negative thinking. Finding Angela was the whole goal! They were going to Toronto today and that was that. End of story.

Evie got out of bed and pulled on her riding pants and a T-shirt. The alarm rang and she quickly shut it down.

When she crept down the narrow stairs to the kitchen, Aunt Mary was already up. A bacon sandwich and orange juice sat ready at her place at the round kitchen table. The house smelled delicious.

"Sleep well?" asked Aunt Mary with a smile. She was dressed for the barn in jeans and a polo shirt.

"Best sleep of my life."

"Good! Sit. Eat. I've already fed the dogs. Jerry is down at the barn already. He's excited about this."

"So am I!" Evie ate every crumb on her plate and downed the juice.

Mary took a steaming mug of coffee, and they walked down to the stable with the three happy dogs.

The air was clear and cool. Evie inhaled deeply and filled her lungs with fresh morning scents. She loved the smell of country air — pine, earth, wild flowers, and the unmistakable, glorious scent of horse. She took in the way the morning sun lit up the fields in striations of pink and green through the evaporating mists rising from behind the trees. Gorgeous. She felt overwhelmed.

"Better late than never!" chided Jerry as they walked into the barn.

"We're exactly on time!" retorted Mary. "You're always early. That's your problem, not ours."

Kazzam stood in cross-ties in the aisle. The horse bobbed his head at Evie and nickered. She let him nuzzle her as she scratched his ears.

Jerry brushed Kazzam's silky black coat with vigour. He glanced at Mary briefly. "I asked Murray to come. He's on his way."

"Murray Planno?" questioned Mary.

"Yep. Gotta get this thing happening and we need his help to do it."

"You don't waste any time!"

"Turns out he was at the Caledon Horse Race. Said the girl knows her stuff."

Evie was puzzled. "What are you talking about? Who's Murray?"

"Murray is the racing steward," answered Mary. "He's the man who can get things organized for No Justice to be allowed to race."

"But how?"

"Later. Lots of time to fill you in. Right now, just ride this horse and show us what he can do." Jerry leaned down to pick the dirt and pebbles out of Kazzam's hooves. "This is a fine animal. His muscle tone is excellent and his spirit is keen. I'm glad to see it."

Kazzam *did* look fine. Evie was very proud of him. He wasn't a big horse, but his conformation was perfect for speed, with broad chest, strong neck, sloping shoulders, muscular hind end, straight legs, and springy pasterns. His coat shone with health and his tail was full. He stood still and picked up each hoof in turn, and his eyes sparkled with mischief and intelligence.

"Good feet, too," added Jerry, from his bent position.

"Very important in a racehorse."

Kazzam suddenly arched his neck down to Jerry's buttocks and gave him a nip. Jerry stood up quickly.

"Kazzam!" scolded Evie.

"Leave him alone," said Jerry. He rubbed his sore rear.

"As I said, he's got spirit. I like that."

10

Murray Planno

Evie put on her helmet and gloves and opened the door to the tiny tack room to get Kazzam's saddle and bridle for the breeze. It was neat and well organized, and smelled of linseed saddle soap and leather. Evie loved everything at Parson's Bridge.

"Put that saddle back, Evie," said Jerry. "We're using *this* one." He pointed to the saddle rack in the aisle.

"A racing saddle?" asked Evie. There was not much to it. It weighed hardly anything. "I've never used one."

"Get used to it."

"If you say so." Evie returned her saddle to the tack room. When she came back Jerry was already leading Kazzam out the door. She followed them outside and along the fence where the other horses had assembled with great curiosity. She took a minute to give the noses of Paragon, Bendigo, and little Christieloo a kiss along the way.

Jerry gestured impatiently. "Murray's late. Come, Evie. I'll give you a leg up."

"Where should I take him?" she asked as she zipped up her crash vest and snapped on her helmet.

Jerry pointed to a huge open field behind the barn. "There. It's a mile and a quarter."

Evie nodded, noting the wide, mowed track all along the inside of the fence. She took Kazzam's reins in her left hand and grabbed his mane in her right. She bent her left leg and Jerry cupped his hands under her shin. "On three. One, two, and three."

She jumped on three, and sprang into the saddle. Her heart pounded with excitement. This was her first day of training with a real trainer! Kazzam felt the excitement, too. His body was tense and his ears alert. She patted his neck and cooed gently to calm him.

Jerry and Mary stood together talking. They nodded and gestured. It looked to Evie like they were discussing something serious.

"Good boy, Kazzam," she whispered. She organized her short stirrups and got familiar with the small racing saddle. It felt like she was crouching over Kazzam's neck, with only her feet holding on to his body, not her calves as she was accustomed. She tried different degrees of hip flexion and finally got somewhat comfortable.

Kazzam's skin was twitching. He wanted to run. "We're going for a breeze," Evie said to the horse. "I'm going to train you to run in the Queen's Plate. You have to be good for your jockey, too, whoever agrees to ride you." She kept talking, hoping to soothe his nerves. "You've made it hard on yourself. You have to stop dumping people."

Kazzam tossed his head up and down impatiently. "Hang on, boy." He began to dance. She looked at the adults, still deep in talk. She would not be able to hold him much longer. "Hello?" Evie called. "Jerry? Aunt Mary?"

"Keep him walking until Murray gets here," Jerry yelled. He didn't look at her, and Aunt Mary held up one finger to signal to wait one minute more.

Suddenly Kazzam reared up on his hind legs and took off at a gallop.

"Sorry!" Evie yelled. She steered Kazzam into the big field Jerry had pointed to. She prayed there were no groundhog holes.

Once in the field Evie let up a little on the reins. Immediately, Kazzam surged forward, surprising Evie with the force of his impulsion. They flew. She crouched as low as she could over his back, like in the poster of Imogene Watson on her bedroom wall. The stirrups still felt way too short.

When they rounded the first bend Kazzam stretched out, easily covering the ground and reaching a speed that Evie remembered from the Caledon Horse Race. She let him go. Evie wondered if they were going too fast at the first turn, so she pulled him in a little. He resisted and ran faster. Evie felt icy needles of fear in her chest. This was a little scary. She had no brakes whatsoever, and with the stirrups so short, no legs to hold on with.

Decision time. Bail and break her neck, or go with the flow. She forced herself to inhale and realized that she hadn't breathed for a while. Odd, she thought, why people do that. Why do we stop breathing when we need air the most?

While she was wondering about breathing, Kazzam's strides had become steadier and more rhythmical. He'd found his perfect racing speed. This was not scary at all. In fact it was thrilling and totally awesome. They pounded along the grass track and around the corner, heading back toward where they'd begun.

The home stretch. Like the big time.

Evie started to smile. This was really cool. Really, really cool! She could ride like this for years. The shortness of the stirrups made sense, now that she was perched up on top like a little bird, letting Kazzam have complete use of his back, haunches, and shoulder muscles.

Tears of speed and joy mingled on Evie's face. Nothing in the world could stop them now!

They tore up the ground as they pounded toward the gate where they'd begun. Jerry was waving a big, white feed bag to get her attention. Evie noticed a person standing with them, looking down at something in his hand.

Aunt Mary started waving at her, too. Evie wasn't sure she could stop Kazzam, but try she must. "Whoa, boy," she said. "Steady, Kazzam." He slowed just a little, so she patted his neck and relaxed the reins. "Good boy."

By the time they sailed past the gate, Kazzam's strides had eased. Then, he simply transitioned down into a trot and then a walk.

"Nice work, Kazzam!" Evie said as she walked him away to let him cool down. He was breathing hard but not puffing, and his coat was hardly damp with sweat. Regardless, she knew how important it was to keep a horse walking until his breath was perfectly normal. She looked over at the adults huddled together. They were talking with great animation.

After ten minutes of walking, Evie slid to the ground. She rubbed Kazzam's forehead and kissed him right on the nose.

"Well, golly be!" exclaimed a hearty voice. "We got something here for sure!"

Evie turned to see who was talking. She gulped.

There, in a plaid vest barely covering his big belly and a crumpled old fedora hat, was the same man who'd been the judge of the Caledon Horse Race. The same man who had handed her the prize money.

Evie stood fixed to the ground beside Kazzam and watched him chat with Jerry, dread growing in her stomach.

"He's a stunner, Jerry. The real deal."

"I wouldn't steer you wrong, Murray."

"You never have. I never doubted you. But, Jerry! His time is crazy fast!" Murray lifted the stopwatch up and showed the face to Jerry. "For a mile and a quarter? Crazy fast!"

Mary saw Evie's discomfort and came over to her. "Great ride, Evie."

Evie ignored her praise and turned away. "That man?"

"Murray Planno?"

"He gave me the prize money. He thinks I'm Molly Peebles."

Mary put her hand on Evie's shoulder. "He knows the whole story. I told you, everybody knows." She smiled warmly.

Evie relaxed a little.

Mary continued, "Because No Justice was banned from racing the last time he dumped a rider, we need a steward to overthrow the ban. We need Murray to help us." She turned Evie around to face her. "In fact, it's only because Murray was at the Caledon race that day that he agreed to even think about it. He's a fan of the horse."

Evie checked Aunt Mary's face to see if she was just trying to make her feel better. "Really?"

"Really. Let me introduce you." Mary took Evie by the arm, with Kazzam by her side, and approached the men. "Murray, I'd like you to meet my great-niece, Evangeline Gibb. Evie, I'd like you to meet the racing steward, Mr. Murray Planno."

Evie mumbled, "Pleased to meet you."

Murray slapped her on the back. "Wow, girl! You can ride! And what a horse!" He reached out to slap Kazzam's neck.

Kazzam reared back, startled by Murray's enthusiasm, and Magpie came out of the barn growling softly.

"Steady boy," said Evie to Kazzam. She grabbed Magpie's neck fur to keep her away from Murray. He seemed nice enough, she thought, but he didn't know the effect he had on animals.

Jerry got down to business. "You see why I want him to run, Murray. We need the ban lifted."

"Agreed. Done. He's not a loony, and man, can he run!"

"So you'll help?"

"Yes, I will. And I have a perfect jockey for him."

Jerry and Mary glanced at each other anxiously.

Murray waved away their concerns. "I know all about his jockey problems. But he's got speed and my jock wants to win. It'll be a great show for the folks. I can see the press!" Murray spread his hands in the air as if the headlines were hovering over his head. "'Devil Horse to Run in the Plate,' followed by 'Devil Horse Bedevils Field!' and then, 'Devil Horse Leaves Them in the Dust!'"

Jerry grinned. "Thanks, Murray! Appreciate your help. We don't have a lot of time. Queen's Plate's coming right up. What's the next step?"

Murray pursed his lips and rubbed his hands together in thought. "Grayson doesn't want him, right? Wants him sold ASAP?"

Jerry nodded. "Right. My thought was that once we —"

"I'll buy him. I brought my trailer, just in case."

"We don't want to sell him, Murray," Mary said quickly.

"We called you to help us lift the ban."

"But he's for sale and I'll buy him. Today. Right now." Murray pulled his cellphone out of his shirt pocket and pressed some numbers. "I'll get the ban lifted."

Evie stood quietly, stunned. She wasn't sure what was going on. Kazzam nuzzled her pocket and found the mint she'd forgotten to give him. Absentmindedly she stroked the black horse's nose and felt his soft ears. Things were happening way too fast.

"Grayson! Glad you answered. Planno here with J.J. What'll it take for me to own No Justice?"

Aunt Mary put her hand on Evie's shoulder. Jerry looked dumbfounded.

Murray grinned hugely. "Done deal, Grayson. I'll bring a certified cheque to you this morning when my bank opens at nine." He pressed *end* and did a jig on the spot.

Jerry had pulled himself together. "Murray, hold on. We fully intend to run this horse ourselves...."

"I'm sorry. He's mine. And *thank you* for calling me! I'm loading him up and taking him home." Murray unfastened Kazzam's girth and handed Evie the saddle. "Oh, Jerry? Special bonus. Grayson's real happy with you for selling the horse this fast. Maybe he'll give you back your job." He winked broadly at them. "Win win, and all that."

Mary was speechless. She went into the barn and returned with a lead shank and Kazzam's halter. It was black leather with his registered name, No Justice, stamped into a brass plate on the side.

Evie unbuckled the bridle with a hollow stomach. This horse was her friend. This horse was the reason she had any happiness in her life at all. He'd been her secret project. He loved her, and she loved him!

Kazzam seemed to understand that Evie was upset. He nestled his face into her torso and held still.

Murray stepped between them. "I know how you feel, girl. But think of the horse, not yourself. I'm his best chance. He'll be famous. Be proud of his future."

"I've got lots of money," Evie blurted. "I'll buy him back from you."

Murray laughed good-naturedly. "And how much money is that?"

"One thousand, five hundred and fifty dollars, minus twenty dollars' worth of groceries."

"Ho, ho, ho. Understand, this is the horse of my dreams." Murray grabbed Kazzam's bridle behind his ears and slipped it off over his head. "You shoulda thought about buying him before I did." Expertly he replaced it with the halter and snapped on the lead shank. He turned to go.

Kazzam reared up and twisted away. He ran off, dragging the lead shank from his halter.

Evie felt her Aunt Mary step beside her. "You have to help. You're the only person who can get that horse on the trailer."

Anger boiled up in Evie's chest. "No way! Kazzam doesn't care who has money and who owns him on paper. He trusts me! He doesn't trust anybody else!"

Mary's voice became more formal. The cool edge made Evie pay attention. "He's not your horse, Evie. He belonged to your father. Your father has sold him to Murray. Now get out there and catch him before he breaks a leg."

Evie didn't like it, but she understood. If Kazzam stepped on the rope, he could go tumbling and injure himself badly. She would buy him back one day when she had lots and lots of money. Murray wouldn't laugh at her then.

She walked out into the field and picked up two blades

of grass. She whistled through them the same way she'd called him every night to train.

Kazzam stopped running. He turned and looked at her, startled. Then he began to trot back to her, ears forward, an expectant, happy look in his eyes.

Tears ran down Evie's face. She was betraying him. Why was life so complicated and wrong? If Kazzam could choose his owner, it sure wouldn't be Murray.

Silently, Evie led her beautiful black horse up the ramp and tied him in the horse trailer. "I'm so sorry, Mister Racehorse. This doesn't make sense to me, either. But I'll be there if you need me," she promised. "I'll come and get you if you're in trouble, no matter what."

Evie rubbed the heart-shaped star on his forehead for the last time and walked down the ramp to the ground. She couldn't look back. She kept walking, right up to the house and into her room, where she fell on the bed face-first. She couldn't even cry.

Magpie followed her. She jumped on the bed and curled up beside her. Evie reached out and rubbed the dog's fur. At least she had Magpie.

Aunt Mary entered Evie's room so silently that when she touched Evie on the shoulder, Evie startled and shot up from the bed.

"More bad news, Evie."

"What could be considered bad after that?"

"Diane, my vet, just called." Mary paused. Her tone was gentle. "I'll just say it. Magpie's chip was inserted by the Humane Society when she was adopted. The chip located her owners, Mel and Rod Usher. They want her back."

This couldn't be true. Evie searched her great-aunt's face for any sign of teasing. There was none. She slumped back onto the bed and moaned.

"I'm sorry, my darling girl," said Aunt Mary. "I wish these things weren't happening, too."

Evie looked into Magpie's earnest face. The dog tilted her head one way and then the other, trying to understand what was making Evie so miserable. "It's okay, girl. It'll be okay. Someone is missing you terribly. *I* would."

To Aunt Mary she said, "Let's get this over with. Can we take Magpie home now?"

"Yes. You're a brave and wonderful girl. I know how hard this must be."

Aunt Mary was wrong. Evie knew she was neither brave nor wonderful. She wanted to get under the covers and die.

11

The Ushers

After showers and breakfast, Mary and Evie got in the truck and were on their way to Toronto. Magpie sat at Evie's sandalled feet, looking up at her questioningly with her head in the girl's lap. The dog knew something was about to happen, but she didn't know what. Only that her new friend was sad. The dog was right, Evie thought. *I am sad.*

There was a lot on her mind. After all the thinking and planning and imagining, today Evie would actually meet her mother. But did her mother want to meet *her*? If she'd wanted to reconnect, wouldn't she already have done that?

To make a good first impression, Evie had put some effort into her appearance. After the breeze, she'd washed her long red hair and brushed it into a ponytail. She was wearing her embroidered, white sleeveless blouse with her jeans. She hadn't packed anything else, anyway, but when she'd checked her appearance in the mirror, she thought it would do just fine.

She sat quietly, with one hand on Magpie's head, unable to speak. On top of her nervousness about meeting her mother, her heart was so heavy she thought it might drop to her feet. The loss of Kazzam plus the agony of returning Magpie was too much to bear in one day. The black dog tilted her head and made her funny throat noise.

"You know it's the only thing to do, Evie," said Mary kindly. "You can't keep a dog that doesn't belong to you."

"Or a horse!" Evie spat out. She surprised herself with how loud and bitter her voice sounded. "Why didn't Jerry or you or I buy Kazzam first? What was the big plan, anyway? To race him against my father's wishes? With no jockey? It wouldn't have worked. It was all stupid."

Mary drove in silence for a few minutes. "You're right, of course. In retrospect, Jerry and I wanted to take one step at a time. But we had no idea that Murray would want to buy him. If we'd bought No Justice and the ban wasn't lifted, we'd own a racehorse that wasn't allowed to race. He'd be worthless."

"At least he'd be mine!" Evie retorted. But she softened a little as she thought about her aunt's logic. It made sense that a racehorse that couldn't race wasn't worth much. "I should've offered Dad all the money I won in the Caledon race right when I heard him tell Jerry he wanted Kazzam gone. He might've taken it."

Mary chuckled. "As you were hiding in the stall? I would've loved to have been there for that discussion."

Evie imagined her father's shocked face when she jumped up from Kazzam's stall with her hands full of money. "Surprise! I'll buy him!" She began to chortle.

Mary joined her. "Boo!"

"Where did you get that money, young lady?" demanded Evie in her father's raspy voice.

"Good imitation!" praised Mary.

Magpie wagged her tail, relieved that her people were happy again. She burrowed her face into Evie's lap and thumped her skinny black tail on the floor of the truck, staring at her with intense, shining eyes.

"Oh, Magpie," said Evie. "I do love you so." She wiped away the tear that had dropped onto her cheek.

"Here we are," said Mary, checking numbers on the road. "One Six One Seven. Rod and Mel Usher, right on the mailbox."

Evie looked down the rutted lane to the rundown cottage. It might have been a lovely place, once, she thought, but bedsprings and old tires were strewn around the yard, and a battered tin doghouse sat in a grassless patch with a long rope tethered to an iron stake. A dog collar was still attached to the end.

"Are you *sure* this is the place?" Evie asked.

"Yes. This is it."

Magpie began to whine soulfully. Her ears went flat on her head.

"That collar?" whispered Evie. "I bet that's hers. I bet she escaped and we're bringing her back to her prison."

"We can't jump to conclusions and make this worse. Magpie belongs to these people, Evie. We have to do the right thing."

"Even if they tie her up like that? It's not fair at all! Let's go before anybody sees us." Evie had never felt more certain of anything in her life. "Now!"

Just then, the peeling door of the house creaked and opened. A skinny woman came out and waved timidly. She had limp, light-brown hair pulled back with bobby pins, and was dressed in an ill-fitting, faded, calico dress. But she looked friendly and eager to please. Evie wondered if she'd been hasty — this woman didn't appear to have a mean bone in her body.

"Well, if that's Mel, she looks very nice," said Mary, echoing Evie's thoughts.

Magpie whimpered and began to shake. Evie patted her soothingly. "Magpie seems to think otherwise."

The woman was followed by a large man wearing a sleeveless undershirt and baggy, green work pants. His bare arms were covered in tattoos, and he apparently hadn't shaved in days. He blinked in the sunlight, then looked at the truck and marched up.

"Here might be the problem," whispered Mary. "Keep Magpie on the floor for a minute." She rolled down her window halfway and didn't get out. "Hello!"

"You brought my dog?" asked the man pleasantly.

"Are you Rod Usher?"

"Yeah, and this is Mel." He pointed to the woman, who smiled. "Vet said a lady driving a white Ford F-150 with a fifth wheel has my dog." He peered into the truck through Mary's window. "Vixen!"

Magpie whimpered loudly. Warm urine trickled onto Evie's foot. *Poor thing!* Evie thought. The dog was so frightened she couldn't control her bladder.

"Vixen! I hear yer whining, sucky baby." Rod Usher grinned down at Magpie with nicotine-stained teeth, making the dog tremble even harder. "She's a silly one. Look at her shake!" He gave a forced-sounding laugh.

Evie wasn't sure what to do. Magpie was certainly frightened of this man. Was he cruel or just rough? She looked at Aunt Mary for guidance.

"Good thing she was chipped," said Mary, buying time.

"Yeah. The Humane Society do it to all the animals."

Mel spoke for the first time. "They spay 'em, too. We got her to hunt with Rod, but she's scared of the gun, and she can't even make pups to sell."

"Enough, Mel!" Rod barked. Mel retreated. "We don't have all day to listen to yer gab."

Mary's brow furrowed. "Too bad your dog got lost," she said. "How did it happen?"

Rod narrowed his eyes and grimaced. "She got *herself* lost." He glanced sharply at Mel, who smiled weakly again. "Stupid bitch don't have sense enough t'come home."

Without warning, Rod reached into the truck over Mary's half-open window and opened Mary's door.

Evie was terrified, but Aunt Mary was furious. "How dare you break into my truck! Step back right now."

Rod put up his hands and backed up a step, laughing in what Evie thought a derisive way. Mary shut the door, threw on the locks and put the truck into reverse. She hastily began to back up. Then there was a loud, metallic *clunk*. Mary slammed on the brakes.

Mel Usher stood right behind the truck with a shovel, raised with menace. "Gotcha. Move again, I'll bust your tires," she hissed through broken teeth.

"Good girl," praised Rod. "Smacked 'em good."

What had they gotten into? wondered Evie. A horror movie? This was getting nasty.

Rod leaned on the driver's side door of the truck and leered at Mary. His teeth badly needed cleaning, Evie thought.

Aunt Mary reopened her window just a crack. He spoke quietly. "Now, you let that dumb dog out, or you're not going anywhere."

Mary's voice shook with fury. "This dog ran away from you and now I know why. I'm not leaving her here." Mary clutched the steering wheel with white knuckles. "Sue me."

Evie was horrified. Aunt Mary was provoking a really scary-looking man. She waited for what might come next.

"Sue you? Now, that's a mighty fine idea," drawled Rod, a crooked smile lighting up his face as he eyed the truck. "You have plenty of money, seems." He hoisted his green pants up higher. "Mel! Get over here!"

Mel scuttled over beside Rod and waited for her orders, like a private in some underground mercenary militia.

"We're gonna sue her. What d'ya think of that?"

Mel nodded and nodded. "Yeah!"

Evie thought that one word sounded oddly hollow, and she suddenly felt badly for Mel. She was just like Magpie in this situation — bullied, likely mistreated, and almost a prisoner. No, Evie thought, *actually* a prisoner. Mel probably had nowhere else to go. Evie shuddered.

Rod scratched his chest under his shirt. "But lawyers are expensive."

Mel began nodding again.

Mary glanced at Evie knowingly. Evie had no idea why.

"Will you sell her to me?" asked Mary. "I've got one hundred dollars right here."

Rod's eyes glinted greedily. For the first time since Murray Planno bought Kazzam, Evie felt a ray of hope.

Rod spat on the ground, thinking. "Make it two and you got yerself a deal."

Evie smiled. Aunt Mary would pay it and they could go. Thank goodness. But she'd underestimated her aunt's steel.

"I said one hundred. She's worth nothing to you. She won't hunt and she can't have puppies."

Rod jerked his head around and sneered at Mel for letting that out. "Two or no deal."

"A lawyer's going to cost you a whole lot more than that, and I'll guess you won't walk out of court with the dog at any rate, after the jurors see her living conditions." She indicated the battered doghouse and rusting chains.

"Two hundred or you don't leave at all." Rod's face had turned red. Mel held up the shovel again.

Evie couldn't take any more. "I've got two hundred dollars!" she yelped.

"Evie," Mary said sharply. "What are you doing?"

"Buying a dog! Nobody can take her from me if I own her!" Evie reached into her knapsack and pulled out two crisp one-hundred-dollar bills. She bunched them up, opened her window, and threw the money out.

As Mel and Rod ran around the front of the truck to collect it, Aunt Mary wasted no time backing up the rutted lane. She hastily checked to see if any cars were coming before she spun her wheels on the gravel shoulder and raced away.

A kilometre down the road, they both exhaled.

Evie realized that her hands were clutching Magpie's loose skin at her shoulders. "Oh, Magpie, I'm sorry!" she exclaimed while she rubbed the dog's fur.

"Well, you own a dog, my dear," said Mary happily. "And you sure have a story to tell!"

Evie shuddered. "I can't believe what just happened. They were so awful! And you were so calm!"

"I'm glad you thought so, Evie, but my heart almost jumped out of my chest."

Mel's timid, scared face flashed in Evie's mind and she said, "Poor Mel."

Mary nodded. "She likely has no idea that she can get out of this situation. If she even wants to, that is."

"Why wouldn't she?" asked Evie. "Rod's a creepy guy."

"It's not always so easy. People don't always realize what's wrong in their lives. She'll have to be ready before she makes such a big decision."

Evie couldn't imagine why leaving Rod would be such a big decision.

Mary continued, "Mel probably thinks she deserves to be treated badly. Rod's bullying tactics are working."

Evie thought about this. "That's so sad. Horrible, even."

"Yes, it is."

"Can you stop the truck for a minute?" asked Evie. "I need to clean up the pee on the floor."

"Poor dog!"

"I almost did it myself, too!"

Mary started laughing, and Evie joined in. Mary pulled over to the side of the road and let Magpie out. The dog seemed ashamed of herself for making a mess, but found good smells to sniff in the tall grass and soon began to wag her tail. Evie and Mary mopped up the puddle with an old towel, then scrubbed the floor with the sanitizing hand wipes that Mary kept in the glove compartment. Once done, they climbed back into the truck and were on their way.

Magpie lay happily on the now-clean floor at Evie's feet. *Imagine,* thought Evie. Just two days ago, she hadn't even met her aunt Mary, and now she felt closer to her than anyone else on earth — at least anyone with two legs. Mary was proving herself quite a lot more than just a little old lady.

"We'll take Magpie back to Diane for shots and worming and a good checkup." Mary turned and smiled. "Now. Let's go meet your mother."

12

Angela

Aunt Mary drove south on Highway 410, then east off the ramp to Highway 427, which they followed south until turning east on the Gardiner Expressway, overlooking Lake Ontario. The day was sunny and the sky was clear blue. Evie watched the cars and huge trucks as they passed them and were passed by them in the four busy lanes. To add to the difficulty of driving safely, motorcycles sped in and out of traffic. She wondered why there wasn't an accident a minute.

Evie gazed out her window. Lake Ontario was enormous. She couldn't see land on the other side. It was calm and beautiful on this day in June, and there were all kinds of sailboats taking advantage of the perfect weather.

Every November her family travelled this route to see the prize livestock and exciting international horse shows at the Royal Agricultural Winter Fair. In November, the sky was grey and often there was snow, but today felt like summer.

"Lately, I've been finding Angela on the corner of Queen and Spadina. Or rather, I go there and she finds me. Let's look there first." Aunt Mary turned onto

Lakeshore Boulevard. "If she's not there, she might be at the little park nearby. Or the cafeteria where they serve hot lunches."

"Okay," answered Evie as she twisted her hair. Her mouth was dry. It was a bit crazy. She was going to meet a homeless woman. "Does she actually live on the street? I mean, no bed, no roof?"

"She's had an apartment, on and off. At the moment I believe she's sharing a place with other people. She won't tell me the address."

"But she doesn't know we're coming. What if she's not around?" Evie found herself hoping that would happen.

Mary shrugged. "We can only try."

Evie watched her great-aunt's profile. She needed someone like Aunt Mary in her life. And maybe, just maybe, her mother would turn out to be good, too, regardless of all the things her father had said about her. She crossed her fingers.

They got into the correct lane to turn north on Spadina. As they waited for the light, two young men approached. One came up to the truck shaking a can.

Aunt Mary rolled down her window. She asked him, "Are you hungry?"

"Yeah." The man wore a black sweatshirt with the hood pulled up on his head, and low-slung baggy jeans.

Aunt Mary reached back and lifted a paper bag from the floor of the back seat. She handed it to him. "Two cheese sandwiches, two apples, and a few cookies. Enjoy."

The man stepped back in surprise. The other man joined his friend. "No!" he barked. "We need money!"

Mary calmly took back the bag, rolled up her window, and drove on when the light changed.

Once again, Evie was surprised by her aunt's actions. "You brought a packed lunch to give away? Why?"

"There are always people who need help, and I'm pleased to assist them. Look at the floor behind you."

Evie saw four brown paper bags, just like the one the men rejected. "Why didn't they take it?"

"If they're hungry, they're very happy for food, so I offer it. If they want money, they want it for drugs or alcohol. I'm happy to feed them, but not to help them get high."

This made perfect sense to Evie.

"Besides, your mother will be hungry, and if there are others with her, I want her to be able to share."

This is insane, thought Evie, her head reeling. She felt an enormous pang of dread. She really did not want to meet her mother if she was anything like the men who'd just come looking for money. She wanted to get out of the city and back to Parson's Bridge.

"Don't worry, Evie," said Mary, reading the expression on her face. "People are way less strange once you meet them face to face. We're all just humans, no matter what our differences. And no matter where our paths changed direction."

Aunt Mary parked the truck in a public lot on the south side of Queen Street. It was crowded and a close fit, but it was in the shade and outside, not in some huge parking garage. Evie wondered how people ever found their cars again, with all the levels and ramps.

"We'll leave Magpie in the truck," said Mary as she lowered the windows for ventilation. "She's in the shade and we won't be long. She's better off here than being frightened by all the hustle and bustle. She's not used to it."

Evie nodded. To Magpie she said, "You stay, girl. I'll be back."

A cooing noise came from Magpie's throat, but she cocked her head and stared at Evie, as if trying to say something.

"Don't worry, Magpie. Good girl." Evie rubbed her silky head and closed the truck door.

Mary put the lunches in her large handbag and clicked the locks. "Ready?"

No. Evie was definitely not ready, but she couldn't see a way out of this. This *was* what she'd wanted. Her stomach was in turmoil. "What are we waiting for?"

"That's my girl," said Mary with a smile. She put an arm around her niece and together they started off down the street. They walked together for a few blocks, jostling though the lunchtime crowds and looking in all the store windows.

As they walked, Evie tried to find a way to say it. Finally, she steeled herself and began hesitantly "I've always wanted to know about my mother. That's why I called you." She paused, almost changed her mind, but continued, "I hoped I could go live with her and get out of Maple Mills. Away from my father." Her words came out faster now. "But I really thought she was dead, even if I hoped she was alive. I didn't factor in that she might be so ... you know ... damaged. Do you understand?" She stopped walking. "Okay, I admit it. I'm scared to find her."

Mary rested her hands on Evie's shoulders. "Humans are animals, Evie. And like animals, they become stray when they can't cope. It's easier for you to reach out to a stray dog like Magpie than a stray person, but we humans aren't that different. Your mother is just a stray person. There's nothing to fear."

"I hear what you're saying, but I'm still afraid. Can we do this some other time? I'm not ready. I thought I was."

"We can go home right now."

"I don't want to see some awful, dirty drug addict and have to call her Mom!" Tears rolled down Evie's cheeks. "My father said she was crazy. *Is* she crazy? How am I supposed to deal with that?"

Aunt Mary nodded. "I understand." She looked around. "Let's pop into this café and sit for a bit. Hungry?"

"No. Not at all." In spite of that, Evie let herself be led into a small coffee shop. Mary sat her in a booth beside the window and went up to the counter. In a few minutes she was back with a coffee for herself, chocolate milk for Evie, a roast-beef sandwich, and two big cookies.

"One's chocolate chunk and one's ginger," she said with a smile. "They're freshly baked. They both looked good and I couldn't decide. Let's split them, okay?"

Evie nodded. She took a sip of the chocolate milk and a bite of the ginger cookie. "I'm sorry I'm such a coward."

"Nonsense! There's a right time for everything."

"But I made you come all this way! I'm really sorry for wimping out."

"Please! I love adventures, and we've already had one today with Magpie."

"And with Kazzam, don't forget," added Evie. She was starting to feel better. "I don't like that Murray Planno bought him, but Kazzam will win the Queen's Plate either way, and I'll be so proud. And I totally loved riding him today. He felt so great. So fast!"

Mary nodded. "You ride beautifully, my dear. You have good instincts. You asked me about becoming an apprentice. Would you like to train to be a jockey?"

"Yes." Evie blushed with sudden shyness. All her life she'd secretly harboured this wish, but had never admitted it out loud. She'd never believed it even possible. Evie thought of the poster on her bedroom wall back at Maple Mills. "Imogene Watson is my hero."

Aunt Mary nodded. "She's fabulous. It's a lot of work to become a jockey. A lot of training and discipline."

Evie agreed. "Do you think I'm too big?"

"Not at all."

"I'm five-six and 115 pounds."

"Perfect. Height isn't the issue, it's weight, and that's a good weight. But as I said, it'll take time and training."

"And a horse to ride," Evie added glumly.

"There will always be horses for a good jockey."

"Not like Kazzam."

They ate in silence for a few minutes.

"I have an idea," said Mary. "Let's go to Woodbine Racetrack on the way home. Just to look around."

Evie's heart skipped a beat. "I'd love to! Then this trip won't be a total waste!"

"Nothing is ever a waste, Evie. Remember that. Everything leads to something, we just don't know what at the time."

Evie nodded, not quite sure what to make of her great-aunt's words. She finished her drink and devoured her share of the cookies and half the sandwich. She'd been hungry, after all, she thought, as she wiped her hands on a paper napkin. She glanced out the window.

She stared. "Look! It's Magpie!"

It was unmistakably Magpie. The long, lean black dog cut a distinctive profile. She trotted between pedestrians along the busy sidewalk, with her long, pointed nose to the ground.

"Well, I'll be a monkey's uncle!" Mary declared.

They watched in disbelief as Magpie sniffed past the café, then returned and sat at the door. Her eyes searched the window and door for familiar faces, and her tail thumped against the sidewalk.

"I guess we're finished lunch!" said Mary, standing up and grabbing her bag.

Evie dashed for the door and ran outside. "Magpie! How did you get out? And how did you find us, clever girl?"

Mary unclipped the shoulder strap from her handbag. Evie watched her double it to form a loop, which she put around the dog's neck. She threaded the loose ends through the loop, then clipped the ends together.

"There!" She handed the strap to Evie. "A collar and leash in one."

"Cool, Aunt Mary. Now, let's go to Woodbine."

"Yes, our city trip is over!"

But Magpie wouldn't move. She stared intently into the narrow alley between the café and the shoe shop next door, and her hackles rose. She held up one white paw, and her long skinny tail stuck straight out. A low growl emanated from her throat.

"Come on, Magpie," said Evie. "Let's go. It's only a squirrel or a mouse or a...."

A woman stepped out from the dark alley into the light of day. She was a bit shorter than Evie and dressed oddly in layers of faded clothing. She was underweight and ashen. She stared at Mary with half-lidded eyes.

"Angela!" Mary stepped toward the woman with open arms and hugged her tightly. The woman's arms hung limply at her sides, then returned the hug. Her eyes closed and her face crumpled. Tiny tears glistened on her cheeks.

Evie studied her carefully, keeping her distance, frozen to the spot. The woman's skin was blotchy, with traces of freckles. She looked frail, but stood erect. Aside from her clothes, the really off-putting things were her feet. Dirty, discoloured, ragged toenails stuck out of worn-out sandals. And her fingernails, too, thought Evie. Nicotine-stained and bitten. Not attractive.

This was a street woman. Not the television type, but a real one. She'd never seen a real street person before. The reality of the situation began to sink in.

Mary held Angela away to take another look at her, then embraced her again. "I'm so glad to see you, dear."

"Me, too," said Angela in a surprisingly clear voice. "I recognized your truck."

She'd followed them! Evie blushed at the memory of her hurtful words. She'd called her an awful, dirty, drug addict. She hoped this woman — her mother — hadn't heard them.

Over Mary's shoulder, Angela looked into Evie's eyes briefly. Her mother had green eyes flecked with gold, like her own. Angela smiled. Her smile was sweet and loving, in spite of the greyish colour of her teeth.

Confusion swirled in Evie's brain. She had no idea what to do or what to say. She stood and stared. Finally, Magpie solved the problem by dragging her over to get a good sniff of this new person, who'd been watching from the alley.

"Evangeline," whispered Angela. "You're beautiful."

"Thank you." Evie looked at Mary, desperate for assistance.

Angela coughed. Evie recognized it as a smoker's hack. Then she continued speaking, as if unaware of Evie's great discomfort. "I named you Evangeline after a poem I love by Henry Wadsworth Longfellow. I read it when I was pregnant. And part of my name is in your name. Angel."

"But you left me. With my *father*." Evie quickly covered her mouth with her hand. She hadn't meant to say that.

"You're right to be angry. I'm angry at myself, too." Angela reached out her hand, looking down. "I'll explain everything one day and hope you understand."

Evie nodded, afraid to open her mouth again. She found she couldn't accept the proffered hand.

That hand fell to Angela's side, but she didn't seem offended. "I hear you love horses."

"Yes! I ... I do," stammered Evie. "I want to be a jockey." She surprised herself again. Why did she keep saying things that were true, but that she'd never said to anyone before?

"Good. It's important to have a goal. Believe in yourself."

Aunt Mary opened her large purse and handed the paper-bag lunches to Angela. "Here, dear. Sandwiches for you and some for your friends."

"Thanks, Aunt Mary." The lunches fit nicely into Angela's knapsack. "Did you bring smokes?"

"Yes. They're in one of the bags. And here's my number again, just in case. You call me. Anything at all, anytime at all." She handed her a card.

Angela put it in her pocket and nodded.

Evie couldn't stop herself. She blurted out, "I don't understand why you're here, living like this. Why do you choose this life? I have so many questions and no answers."

Angela coughed and cleared her throat. "I want to answer them all. And I will." She began to retreat.

"Mom?" It felt strange calling her that. She didn't remember ever calling anybody that in her life.

Angela stopped. "Yes?"

"Can you answer some questions now?" Evie's voice croaked with raw emotion. "Like, why you let me think you were dead all my life? Why you never came to visit me or ever called or anything?" She was so upset her stomach ached and she felt the need to sit down.

Angela paused. Her face saddened. She chewed on a fingernail. "There are reasons." She squinted her eyes like her head was hurting. "But not today. I'm not ready. I'm seeing my daughter for the first time in thirteen years." Angela coughed again. She reached into a pocket and pulled out a cigarette. Her hands shook. "It's a shock."

It was like Evie wasn't even there! "It's a shock for me, too! Are you even thinking of how I feel?"

"Come on, Evie. It's time to go." Mary put her hand on Evie's shoulder. Evie recoiled and backed away.

To Angela, Mary cheerfully said, "Stay healthy, my dear, and call me. Please."

Angela lit her cigarette and silently drifted back into the alley. And then Evie couldn't move away fast enough.

13

Surprises

Evie and Magpie raced back to the parking lot. The girl leaned against the truck, panting for air.

She shook her head and sniffed back tears. Her mother had been in a hurry to get away, to score more drugs, or to do whatever she had to do. That was more important than it was to see her only daughter after thirteen years.

Aunt Mary arrived a moment later and clicked open the locks. "I left the windows too far down. Look at Magpie's paw marks!" Evie noted the long skid marks in the country dust that covered the truck door, and saw how she'd gotten out. The dog had squeezed herself out the window and slid down.

Mary chuckled and opened the door. "She's an acrobat!"

Magpie jumped in first and lay on the floor, and Evie sullenly got in herself. Mary started the engine. They were well north on Highway 27, almost at Derry Road, before they began to talk.

Mary spoke first. "Well?"

"Well, what?"

"What do you think?"

"I met my mother, who freaked me out, and I will never see her again. I won't be looking for her, anyway. She said she'd answer my questions but she couldn't take the time. What else is she doing today? She doesn't care at all about me."

Mary considered this. "She really does care, Evie. She wanted me to bring you to her. That's why I wrote to you about her in the birthday card." She sighed. "It'll take a little time for all this to sink in."

"And what am I supposed to make of it in the meantime? I'd love to know that!" Evie shook her head. She was flushed and sweaty and slightly nauseated. She wondered if she had a fever.

"I don't know how to answer you."

Evie stared out the window, taking in nothing. "All my life I've wondered what she'd be like. Well, she's a messed-up addict who wants nothing to do with me." Evie swatted away a tear, angry with herself for caring enough to cry. She snorted suddenly. "I spent years dreaming about her. She was beautiful. She was a princess with a sparkling tiara. Right!"

Mary sighed again. "Don't give up on her so easily, Evie. She'll answer your questions. All of them. I know that. Nothing happens in a day."

"Except this day. Too many things have happened," Evie muttered. She was slouched so low in her seat that she almost missed it.

The sign. Woodbine Racetrack. She sat up. "Are we here?"

"Yes, we are. This is it, the home of your mother's racing career."

Evie was startled out of her miserable mood. "My mother's *what*? She was a jockey?"

138

"Jockey and trainer. Mostly trainer because there were no female jockeys except in the Powder Puff Race and the Pink Ladies League. It was an old boys' club. Still is in lots of ways. She was good, Evie. Very good."

"Why didn't you tell me?"

"You never asked." She smiled and lifted her eyebrows. "There's a whole lot you don't know yet."

"Like what? Tell me!"

"All in good time."

"So when she smashed her leg, was it a fall from a racehorse?"

"Yes. Her horse was clipped from behind. Her horse tumbled, the horse that clipped him fell, and several others, too. Nobody was killed and the horses all got up, but it was a really bad accident. Your mother never raced again."

Evie knew that being "clipped" is when a horse crowds the one ahead and steps on that horse's heel. The results could be bad, like a ripped heel, or horses falling. "That's terrible. Did the jockey get in trouble for riding too close?"

"No. It's hard to prove wrongdoing sometimes."

"Or maybe the old boys' club turned a blind eye?"

Mary shook her head. "No sense in being cynical. Especially at sixteen." She chuckled.

They'd driven in through the main entrance and followed the interior road past the big stadium. Now they stopped in the small gravel parking lot beside the stable gate.

"I'll be back in a minute. Stay put."

Evie watched her aunt walk into a small building beside the automatic gate. Magpie snuck up onto the seat beside her, and Evie put her arm around the dog. "I'm sure glad you're mine, Magpie. Now and forever. Nobody will ever be able to take you from me."

Trucks and horse trailers and cars came and went through the gate, and Evie became more and more excited about going in. She put all thoughts of meeting her mother out of her mind as she watched the activity. She yearned to learn how this whole business worked. She wanted to visit the stables filled with Thoroughbreds and watch the trainers work. Vets and farrier trucks drove through the gate, and Evie tried to pick out the grooms, exercise riders, and jockeys. She wanted to learn about it all.

Aunt Mary came out all smiles, accompanied by a man in a navy-blue uniform. But as they approached, the man stopped. He pointed at the truck and shook his head. Mary looked somewhat crestfallen, but she nodded and shook his hand. He walked back to the office.

"What happened?" asked Evie as Mary opened the door.

"No dogs are allowed anywhere at Woodbine. It's a rule. I forgot all about it."

"Even if Magpie stays in the truck in the parking lot and we walk in?"

"She shouldn't be on the property at all. Tom said we can come back another time, no problem." Aunt Mary started the truck and drove toward Derry Road. "It's Monday, and not a race day, so we're not missing much."

"If you say so, but it looks pretty busy."

"It's always busy here. It's an entirely separate world."

"As long as we do come back, because I really, really want to look around." Evie was disappointed.

"We'll be back many times, don't worry."

Evie felt she owed Aunt Mary an apology. "I've been thinking. I was upset, meeting my mother, and I took it out on you and I shouldn't have. I'm sorry."

"Thank you, Evie. It takes a big person to admit that."

"I probably need to think about things for a while."

"Of course you do. You have a whole lot of new information to process."

Evie was glad her great-aunt understood. "I feel like I've known you forever."

Her aunt smiled. "I feel the same."

"You know, I called you because you used the word 'is' instead of 'was' in your birthday card." She chortled.

Aunt Mary raised an eyebrow. "'Is' instead of 'was'?"

"That's when I hoped my mother *is* alive, not *was*. It was weird finding her, totally weird, but you promised you'd take me to meet her and you did. I'm not sure if I'm glad I met her, but thank you."

❧

It was just after three in the afternoon when they turned in the lane to Parson's Bridge. They both saw the black horse at the same moment.

Evie blinked and looked again. "Aunt Mary? Do you see what I see?"

"I do. What the heck?"

Standing outside in the field, head bent contentedly over the grass, was Kazzam.

"Stop the truck!" yelled Evie.

Mary did just that. Evie and Magpie leaped out and ran toward him. Simon and Garfunkel started barking from the house and came running, too.

Kazzam lifted his head and nickered. He trotted over and met them at the fence.

Evie ducked through the fence and hugged his neck. "Kazzam, boy! I thought I'd never see you again."

She felt something warm and sticky on her hands. She looked and saw blood.

"Holy." Evie began to check him all over. "Aunt Mary! Come here!" she called.

Mary came running.

"Look at the blood! His chest and his legs. What happened to him?" Evie was shrieking now. "What did Murray Planno do to Kazzam?"

Mary grabbed her and held her firmly by the shoulders. "The horse needs you to be calm. Now, lead him so I can see him walk."

Evie took a deep breath, took hold of his halter and led him along the fence. She tried to control her anger and frustration.

"Now, trot him," called Mary.

Evie did what she was told.

"Okay, good. Slow him to a walk and bring him back." Evie led Kazzam back toward Mary.

"Is he okay?"

"Yes. He's perfectly sound. Let's get him inside and hose him down so we can see what's what."

As Evie led Kazzam toward the barn, Mary drove the truck and parked it. Just as Evie was about to enter the barn, her great-aunt rushed over to her, holding a ripped scrap of paper.

"Murray pinned this note to the door," she said. "Look."

She handed Evie the scrawled message.

Evie read it aloud. "'Deal's off. Blasted Gibb accepted my offer then doubled his price. Can't get a jockey anyway. Good luck to you. P.S.: His horse kicked my trailer to hell and back. Gibb owes me.'"

Evie and Mary looked at each other in astonishment and said in unison, "Let's call Jerry!"

Mary pulled out her cell and texted the trainer that No Justice had returned. "I give him two minutes to text me back," she said, smiling. "He'll be curious."

Her cell dinged. "Two seconds!" she exclaimed. "I'll

tell him to drop over," she said to Evie as she typed a return message. "He's not far."

They led Kazzam into the barn and over to the wash stall. Once the water was warm enough, Evie hosed him down, starting with his feet and moving up gently. Blood mixed with water and pooled at the drain.

"Everything is superficial," observed Mary. "A few scrapes and cuts. Not many and nothing deep."

"Do you think he got them all from kicking the trailer?" asked Evie. She couldn't imagine how he got the chest scrapes.

"Depends. Murray doesn't beat horses. Kazzam might've fallen down in there."

"Ouch!"

"We'll wash him with antiseptic soap, then spread Furacin on his cuts. I'm going to give him some Bute, too, to reduce any swelling and make him feel better. He's better off outside grazing and moving around so he doesn't stiffen up."

Jerry's truck stopped at the barn door and the man appeared, completely out of breath. "Oh, forgot to turn off the engine!" He raced out again and was back in moments. "Tell me what happened!" he panted.

Once he was filled in, Jerry stood silently scratching his head under his hat.

"So now what?" asked Evie.

Jerry shook his head. "Murray Planno is still the guy we need to let No Justice run. He's the steward with the most seniority. I'm going to have a chat with him. This incident might actually help."

"How could it help?" Evie wondered aloud.

"Might, might not. If it makes Murray inclined to show Grayson up, it'll help. If he hates No Justice for kicking his trailer, it won't."

"Should we buy Kazzam now?" asked Evie. "So this doesn't happen again?"

"I know what you're thinking," answered Jerry. "Thing is, Grayson will screw us around like he tried with Murray, and I don't think there's anybody else out there willing to buy him, anyway."

Mary nodded agreement.

"So we take our chances?" Evie was uneasy. "But Dad can do what he likes if he owns him! I have a bad feeling about this after what just happened."

Jerry sniffed. "Best to face the beast." He pulled out his cellphone and pressed a button. "Grayson? Jerry here."

Evie was startled. To Mary she whispered, "He's calling my father?"

Mary nodded. "It takes courage to be in this business."

Jerry turned and walked away while he talked to Grayson Gibb in private.

Mary and Evie waited expectantly and were all ears when Jerry returned with a big smile. "All clear! He's calling our bluff!"

"What did he say?" asked Mary.

"To knock ourselves out. That if we think we can do something with that no-good blankety-blank — sorry, Evie — to go right ahead."

"Really? This is great!" Evie jumped up and down, unable to contain her excitement. Then all at once she stopped. "But the Queen's Plate isn't even two weeks away. Will Kazzam be okay to run?"

Jerry grinned. "A girl who thinks like me!" He went outside with his cellphone to call Murray.

Mary and Evie cleaned up the horse, and Evie led him back outside. He bumped her lightly with his nose as they walked along together. "I don't know what's going to happen next, boy, but I'm sure glad to have you back."

She rubbed his ears and forehead as she removed his halter and released him into the field. Evie watched him trot over to the fence where Christieloo stood waiting for him. Kazzam nickered to her and she returned his call. "A girlfriend, Kazzam?"

Mary and Jerry were deep in conversation as Evie walked back to the barn. "What's up?" she asked.

"No answer yet, but I've got a plan," said Jerry. "No Justice was nominated and his dues are all paid up until the final entry, so the paperwork is up to date. We'll work him as though we're racing while I figure out who'll be the jockey. Every morning at six, before it's hot, with one day off, and that's tomorrow so he can heal up a bit."

Evie nodded. "And I'm the rider?"

"I'm the trainer, you're the exercise girl. You understand the problem. You're not a professional jockey, not even an apprentice. You can get him ready, but somebody else will ride on the day. Are you okay with that?"

Evie nodded. "I know the rules. One day I'll be a jockey, but I have a lot of work to do."

"You've got the right idea," Mary said approvingly.

"Working hard is the only way to succeed at anything."

"That's how your aunt Mary succeeded, Evie," noted Jerry. "People think writing is easy, but that's a lot of bunk."

"Writing?" Evie asked her aunt. "Are you a writer?"

Aunt Mary smiled. "I've written a few books."

"A few!" said Jerry. "She's published a dozen of them. All best-sellers."

"Aunt Mary! I didn't know that. What kind of books? I love reading."

"They're mysteries. I'll give you one to read when we get to the house."

Jerry grinned. "They're really good, too. You can't put them down."

Evie studied her great-aunt. How many more surprises did she have in store?

"Gotta go," said Jerry as he headed for his truck. "Have No Justice tacked up and ready at six on Wednesday morning. Rain or shine. He's gonna have to run in dust or mud on the day, no matter what."

"Okay, Jerry. Let me know when you hear from Murray." Mary waved goodbye to Jerry, then headed to the feed room. "It's well after three. Let's get these horses grained and leave them all outside tonight."

Evie helped carry the buckets to the fields. She gave Kazzam his mixture of carrots and grain while Mary dumped oats in three feed tubs separated by a good distance to prevent kicking. Horses love their food and get jealous if they think one has more than another, even if they've been grazing on grass together all day long.

On the way back up to the house, Evie thought back on everything that had happened since she'd opened her eyes that morning. "What a day! I lost a horse and a dog, then I got them both back."

"And you finally met your mother, after thirteen years." Aunt Mary put her hand on Evie's shoulder as they walked.

"The dog and the horse are less complicated."

Mary smiled. "Give it time, sweetheart. Give it time." After a simple dinner of barbecued chicken and salad, Evie cuddled up on the couch with one of Aunt Mary's mystery novels. Jerry was right about it being a good read. From the very first page it was packed with excitement, and Aunt Mary really knew how to draw in her readers. It reminded Evie of her favourite book, the one she read every Christmas. She glanced at the cover.

"Aunt Mary!"

Mary's head came up from her computer as she sat at her desk. "You startled me!"

"I just realized. Your pen name is Elizabeth Elliot. My favourite book is *Horse Play*. I can't believe it!"

"That's a very nice compliment. I'm glad you like my writing." Aunt Mary settled back into her work.

"How could I not know?"

"Very few people know what I do, and I like it like that. Now, I've got another book half-done and it won't write itself."

"I get the hint. I still can't believe it's you!"

14

Honest Talk

Darkness fell. It had been a very eventful day, and now it was time for peace and quiet. Evie was intently wrapped up in her book. Aunt Mary sat quietly typing at her desk.

Both of them were startled by a tentative knock on the front door.

"The dogs aren't barking," was the first thing Mary said. "And it's ten o'clock."

They heard the knock again, a little louder. "I'm not expecting anyone," she said.

"Do you think it's a burglar?" asked Evie anxiously.

"Burglars don't knock," said Mary, rising from her chair. "I have no idea who it might be."

Evie got up, walked into the hall, and flicked on all the lights. Aunt Mary was right behind her.

"Why *aren't* the dogs barking?" whispered Evie.

Mary shrugged and opened the door. On the steps, arms locked with each other's, stood Beatrice and Jordie. They looked small and frightened. The three dogs were right behind them, wagging their tails.

Jordie spoke up. "Can we come in?"

"Of course! Come in, kids!" Mary's surprise showed

in her widened eyes as she ushered them in, dogs and all, and locked the door behind them.

"What are you doing here? Does Dad know? Paulina?" Evie hugged them both tightly until Beatrice shoved her away.

"Let's let them get comfortable before we interrogate them," Mary said as she led the way back into the cozy kitchen area. "Come on, I'm making hot chocolate, and Evie's popping some cookies into the oven."

Evie sliced the packaged cookie dough with the happy feeling of being part of a family. Belonging. That feeling again. It might be the most important thing of all, she thought.

Jordie was shivering in his shorts and T-shirt, so Aunt Mary wrapped him in a soft blanket on the couch. Beatrice nestled in beside him, happy with hot chocolate and fresh-baked cookies. Magpie sniffed their faces and snuck a lick on their cheeks.

"What a funny dog!" said Jordie, laughing. He patted her head. "She remembers me from when she found me."

After letting them settle in for a few minutes, Mary said, "You know I have to call Grayson and Paulina. They'll be worried about you." She spoke gently, but Evie remembered the morning she'd met Aunt Mary, and knew that the firm tone meant there was no point in arguing.

Beatrice nodded solemnly. "I suppose so."

"Before I call, maybe you could tell us what's been happening at home?"

Jordie answered. "Mom stays in her room. She won't talk to anyone."

"And Dad's never home, but when he is, he won't talk to anyone, either. Even me." Beatrice's small face crumpled. "And I'm his favourite."

"Is Sella still there?" asked Evie.

"Mom keeps firing her, but she won't leave." Jordie chewed on a nail, then continued, "But I heard Dad say he won't pay her anymore."

"Why did you leave tonight?" asked Evie. "Did something happen?"

Beatrice and Jordie glanced at each other. Neither spoke.

"You don't have to say anything," said Mary kindly. "It's late, and I'm sure you're both very tired. You walked a very long way."

Evie knew that they couldn't have walked from Maple Mills. "How did you get here?"

Beatrice sniffed. "Sella drove us. She's going to live with her sister in Brampton."

Jordie added, "Dad wasn't home and Mom wouldn't let us into her room. Sella was crying and said we couldn't stay alone and she knew you would help."

Beatrice said, "Sella told us Dad went agaga and ordered her out and she had to leave or the police would take her."

"But why?" None of this made sense to Evie. "Sella does everything in the house!"

Jordie started to say something, but Beatrice silenced him. "We don't know for sure, Jordie!" she whispered fiercely. "It's gossip." She held up her fist to keep him quiet.

"But it's true! I know it is! I saw them kissing!" The little boy cowered and shifted away to avoid a punch on his arm.

Beatrice dropped her fist and slumped deeper into the couch. "I know it's true, too. Mom and Kerry. And now Dad knows."

"Kerry Goodham?" asked Evie.

"Who's he?" asked Mary.

"Kerry's her coach. Her jumping instructor. But why fire Sella?" asked Evie. "She has nothing to do with it."

"Dad said that Sella knew they were kissing and she should've told him. It's not Sella's fault!" Jordie was clearly distressed.

"Of course it's not her fault," soothed Aunt Mary. "She did the right thing bringing you here. Does your father know where you are?"

Jordie shook his head. "He wasn't home."

Mary stood and picked up the phone. As she pressed the numbers, she told the kids, "Your father loves you, and your mother, too. They need to know you're not in any danger."

They all listened while Mary left her message. "Hello Grayson and Paulina. It's Mary Parson. Sella drove Jordie and Beatrice to my farm tonight and she's going to her sister's. Please call me when you get this message and we can discuss the situation further."

She hung up and yawned. "Now, it's way past my bedtime. Come with me."

The children were only too happy to follow her up the stairs and climb into the twin beds in the room next to Evie's. Within minutes, all the lights were out.

❧

Aunt Mary woke everyone up at seven the next morning. Evie was not happy about that, since she hadn't been able to put her book down the night before. She'd nodded off around two in the morning.

"It's a school day!" said Aunt Mary gaily, and rushed down the stairs. "Rise and shine!"

The three kids appeared downstairs shortly thereafter to find orange juice, muffins, and cereal with bananas and berries laid out on the counter.

"I can't go to school dressed like this!" whined Beatrice.

"I left my homework in my room and it's not done!" Jordie complained.

Evie had a more serious concern. "I haven't been to school for ... a ... couple of days," she confessed. "I'm a little worried about going back."

Mary creased her brow and put her hands on her hips. "What time does school start?" she asked. "Eight-thirty?"

"Nine o'clock," answered Jordie. The girls nodded.

"We don't have much time if we have to go to your house first. Grab some fruit and a muffin, and drink some juice."

She clapped her hands. "Now, everybody in the truck. Dogs stay home. I've already fed them, Evie, and Kazzam looks really good this morning." Mary put some fruit and muffins in three separate bags, along with a sandwich and a couple of cookies.

They were out the door in five minutes and on the road to Maple Mills. "I assume somebody has a house key?" asked Mary.

Evie yawned and said, "There's a hidden key." She looked glum. "I don't see why you're making us go to school. We're in the middle of a family crisis."

"Life goes on. A job is a job, and your job is school. The longer you procrastinate, the harder it'll be."

The kids groaned.

Mary ignored them. She drove quickly, and soon they were at the imposing gates of Maple Mills. Evie told her the gate code and they drove through.

Evie was pleased to see horses out in the fields. It looked like business as usual, until she caught sight of Yolanda, leading Thymetofly to his pasture. Instead of her usual sunny smile, she had a despondent look on her face.

Evie rolled down her window. "Yoyo!"

Yolanda looked up, startled, then smiled broadly. "Evie. Are you okay?"

"Yes! And Kazzam, too."

"You had me worried, I can't lie."

"I'm sorry, Yoyo. I'll explain everything...."

Yolanda put up a hand. "I figured it out, Evie. And I understand why you ran away and took No Justice. I'm just glad you're okay."

Mary stopped the truck and hopped out. She spoke to Yolanda. "I'm Mary Parson, Evie's great-aunt. How are things around here?"

"Truthfully? Nobody knows. Les still has his job and so do I, but Jerry's gone, we're down to two grooms, and ten horses have been sold."

She looked into the back seat. "Hi, kids!" They waved back. To Mary she said, "It's nice to meet you. I heard a bit about you from Angela. She really liked you."

"Thank you. That makes me happy."

"I can't be caught talking, you know what I mean, so sorry, gotta go. Bye, everyone." Yolanda and the big horse continued on their way to the field.

"Bye, Yoyo!" called Evie, thinking that she should've left a note for Yolanda before she left. And Jordie, too. More people had missed her than she would've thought.

When Mary drove up to the house, Evie shivered with unhappy memories. "Is Paulina here?" she asked.

Beatrice answered. "She'll be sound asleep. But you're not in any trouble. She doesn't care about you. No offence."

Evie shrugged. They got out of the truck and approached the side door. Evie went into the bushes and turned over a rock. She came out with the key and opened the door.

"Hurry, kids," said Mary. "Get dressed, pack a few things, get your homework, and hurry outside. There's no time to lose."

They all rushed upstairs. While Beatrice and Jordie dressed and got organized, Evie changed into clean clothes and packed. She had absolutely no intention of ever returning to Maple Mills. Quickly, she threw her beloved cushions into a pillowcase, removed her favourite posters from the wall, and put her only book into her suitcase with her clothes. She lugged it all downstairs.

She stopped, stunned. There, in the front hall, stood Paulina. She wore a fluffy pink bathrobe and matching slippers. A white silk negligee hung unevenly to her ankles, and she had sleepy eyes and uncombed hair.

"So the rats are leaving the sinking ship?" Paulina said unhappily.

"Hard to say whether this rat is leaving or was already tossed out," responded Evie. She was pleased at her quick wit, and found herself smiling.

"What's wrong with you?" asked Paulina with a furrowed brow. "What could you possibly be happy about?"

Aunt Mary ushered Beatrice and Jordie into the hall.

"Hello. You must be Paulina. I'm Mary Parson."

"Mary Poppins? Did Grayson hire you to take Sella's place?" Evie noticed the confusion on Paulina's face.

"Something like that," said Mary cheerfully. Then she looked at Paulina and asked seriously. "Do you know where your kids slept last night?"

"Here, of course!" Paulina took offence. "Why?"

Evie felt embarrassed for her. Paulina's answer confirmed that she really had no idea what her children were doing. Sella was needed more than ever.

Mary checked her watch. "Got to run, Paulina, we're late for school. Since Sella's fired, the kids will be visiting me for a few days. I've left my contact numbers on your kitchen counter. Call me, please. I'd love to talk."

Paulina's face crumpled and her shoulders slumped. "I don't know why I can't look after my kids. Grayson's so … angry … I can't seem to get it together."

Beatrice ran up and hugged her mother, and Paulina began to cry. Jordie said, "It's better this way, Mom. Just for a while." He started to cry, too, and joined his sister in the hug.

Evie was ready to cry, too, even though she was not included. She knew how bad it was to have Grayson angry at you. "Aunt Mary will look after them until you and Dad sort out … everything," she said. "Really."

Mary agreed. "I promise, Paulina. Please call me."

Paulina nodded and wiped the tears from her cheeks.

Mary spoke gently. "All you need is a bit of time right now. Everything will work out fine."

"Thank you. Really." Paulina tried to smile.

Evie could see how tough this was for her. She saw a different side of her stepmother, a more sympathetic one, and felt badly leaving her alone in the big empty house.

"Call me?" Aunt Mary said. She picked up as much of Evie's stuff as she could and swept it out the door and into the truck. They managed it all in two trips.

"Let's get you to school," Mary said to the kids. She started the engine and drove out, chattering to fill the silence. "Your mother will be just fine. She'll come visit soon. She's always welcome. She'll sort this out and come to get you when she's ready."

Jordie and Beatrice sat mutely in the back seat, clutching their duffle bags. Jordie's eyes were round and red, and his bottom lip quivered. Beatrice appeared hostile and ready to bite someone. Evie thought they both looked lost.

"Okay!" Mary made an effort to sound jolly. "Where's Jordie's and Beatrice's school? Are you at the same one?"

"Yes," answered Jordie stoically. "It's the Abergrath School, and it's close to the new shopping centre."

They arrived in the parking lot of the school. An older building, it was covered in ivy, and the windows were leaded. The big front door was closed and all was quiet. It was very apparent that they were late.

Mary marched right into the school and, with directions from the receptionist, went straight to the principal. Evie followed along for moral support, with Jordie and Beatrice clinging to her. They overheard most of the discussion. Evie thought it was very smart of Aunt Mary to explain the situation without giving too many details or painting Grayson and Paulina in a bad light.

They left the younger kids there and headed for Evie's school. Evie said, "You made things a lot better for Jordie and Beebee. Now the teachers will understand and will give them a break." She stared out the window and mumbled, "It's not going to be so easy to help *me*."

Mary pulled over to the side of the road and stopped. "Maybe it's time for an honest talk."

Evie didn't answer. An honest talk was not what she wanted.

"We can sit here all day."

Evie wasn't sure how to begin. She turned to face Aunt Mary. "You notice I don't have a cellphone?" she asked.

Mary nodded. "I assume it's because you didn't want your father tracking you when you left home."

"That crossed my mind. But no. It's because I don't want to read what the kids at school are saying about me."

"What are they saying?"

"I don't know! That's the whole point!"

"Well, what do you think they're saying?"

156

"Look, I'm not popular, okay? I don't have any friends right now." She kept her eyes on the scene outside the truck. Across the road an elderly man was mowing his lawn.

"That's hard for me to imagine."

"I'm sixteen and I've never been on a real date."

"And so?"

"So I...."

"Go on."

"So my friend Amelia, past tense, said this guy had a crush on me. He's very hot and I liked him. I asked him to a party she was having. He turned me down. He talked to Amelia and she told me what he said. But she told me on Facebook. She put it on her wall. About me asking him out and him thinking I'm a loser. And worse. That I was a skid. Then everybody jumped on, even my best friends. I was shot down big time by one of the most popular guys, if not *the* most popular, in school." She cringed unhappily, reliving her humiliation. "I thought he was nice, too. I haven't been to school since."

"When was that?"

"About a week ago. Maybe longer."

Mary inhaled. "You haven't been to school for over a week and nobody's called?"

"Maybe they called. Paulina wouldn't do anything about it, and Dad never picks up messages." She slumped down in her seat and wished she could disappear. "There. You're the first person I've told. Now you know."

"Thanks for telling me, Evie. What's his name?"

"Not that it matters."

"I like to know the enemy."

"Mark Sellers."

"Mark. Well, he's probably forgotten all about it. And Amelia certainly played her part. Don't leave her off the hook."

"She was just reporting facts."

"On Facebook? A little public, don't you think?"

Evie rankled. "What do *you* know?"

"I don't, but I was your age once, and I did things way more embarrassing than asking a guy out and getting turned down. This problem is quite fixable and not a big deal."

Evie sat up straight, outraged. "This is a big deal for *me!* The whole school is laughing at me! What do you know, anyway! You're old and you've never even had children!"

Mary sat staring at the steering wheel.

Immediately, Evie felt awful. Aunt Mary was only trying to help. "Look, I'm sorry. I —"

"No offence taken. I was too blunt."

"I only meant that you've probably never done anything stupid in your entire life, so you couldn't know —"

Mary cut her off. "So I couldn't know how you feel? I think I do." She sounded strange and upset. "I had my own pain when I wasn't much older than you."

Evie didn't interrupt. She listened.

"I don't talk about it, but I had a child when I was very young. You can imagine." Mary swallowed with emotion.

A child. Evie dropped her head. She tried to assimilate this new information.

"Everybody at school talked about me. Made fun of me. Nobody wanted to be my friend. So I think I *do* know how it feels to be the one that people talk about. The difference is that nobody 'Facebooked' in those days." Aunt Mary hesitated, and then said so quietly that Evie could barely hear, "It was hurtful, nonetheless."

Evie blushed, horrified at herself for being so insensitive. "I didn't know. I really am sorry, Aunt Mary."

"I know. Apology accepted. I'm only telling you because you must understand something very important."

Mary looked into Evie's eyes. "Everybody has a story. Everybody has pain. Look outside yourself. Those kids who you think are laughing at you? They're all afraid that somebody else will laugh at them. Remember that."

What Aunt Mary said made sense. "What happened to your child?"

"She was adopted into a good home."

"Do you know if she's okay?"

Mary looked at Evie sadly. "I know that she's not okay."

"Oh." Evie didn't think she should ask any more questions, although she was very curious. "You're right. My problem looks small next to that. Very small." She straightened her back. "Now I'm ready to go."

Mary pulled back onto the road and drove to Evie's school. They didn't say a word until they were parked.

"Thanks for the ride. And for the honest talk." Evie opened the door of the truck to get out.

"I'm coming in with you. The school has to know why you've been away."

"This is *my* problem, Aunt Mary. I can handle it."

"It's best that I speak to the principal."

"You're not my guardian. They don't even know you."

"They will." Her aunt got out and marched to the front door.

Evie was exasperated. She sat in the truck for a few seconds, then reluctantly grabbed her bookbag and followed Mary in. When she got to the principal's office, the door was closed. She peeked through the glass and saw Aunt Mary sitting across the desk from Mr. Chumar. They were engaged in animated conversation. Evie plopped herself down on the bench in the hall.

How had she let Aunt Mary take charge? she wondered. She'd called Aunt Mary to help find her mother.

Full stop. Not to live with her or to let her take control of her entire life. Now, Aunt Mary was talking to the principal, and who knew what she was saying? Regardless of how helpful she was trying to be.

Evie was so preoccupied that she didn't notice the person standing in front of her.

"Evie?"

She looked up and stared into the face of the boy who'd ruined her life. "Mark!" She felt her cheeks redden.

"You haven't been to school for a while."

Evie remained silent. She hoped he'd squirm.

"I've been looking for you. All week. I wanted to talk to you. About … you know."

Evie swallowed hard. She was afraid of what words might come out of her mouth, so she kept it shut.

"I called but you never answered. And you didn't return my emails." Mark shifted his weight from one foot to the other. "I guess you're mad."

Evie met his eyes levelly. "Well, I'm here now, so talk."

"Look, I didn't see the crap Amelia wrote until the next day. By then a whole lot of people had written stuff, but I didn't know it would keep getting worse, you know? It was just crap. I thought it would go away."

Evie didn't answer, even though Mark looked genuinely upset. *Let him boil in his own juice,* she thought.

"I would've gone to Amelia's party with you, but … my mother needed help painting the garage. She turned it into a rehab spa to make some money. It wouldn't be cool that I couldn't go because my mother wouldn't let me, but that's the truth." Mark looked very uncomfortable. "Amelia twisted what I said. I told her off. I should've done that on Facebook, but I didn't. I mean, it didn't mean anything."

Evie shrugged and snorted. "It didn't mean anything to *you*, that's clear. It *did* mean something to me. You let people think that you called me a loser and a skid."

"I'm really sorry." Mark's ears blushed.

Evie found that she believed him. At least, she believed the blush. "Did you really say those things?"

"No! That's the whole point. She made them up!"

Evie tilted her head and examined him. Mark, with his earnest brown eyes and thick, wavy brown hair, was very good-looking. "No big deal. I don't care anymore."

"You don't?" Mark gave her a wary look.

"No."

"You don't care what all the others —"

"I don't *know* what all the others think and I don't want to. They're all trying to be cool, like you. They'd rather laugh at me than be laughed at themselves." She was happy to have Aunt Mary's words to repeat.

Mark's face broke out into an enormous grin. "Wow! I felt bad and all along you were okay with it!" He shifted his bookbag and prepared to walk away. "Cool! See you around!"

This wasn't quite what Evie had been going for. "You can still feel bad, okay? It was really embarrassing. And if you think you're a badass, you're not."

Mark stopped retreating. One eyebrow lifted. "What?"

"You hurt me. But you felt bad." Evie stood and looked directly at her tormentor. "A badass wouldn't care."

"If you say so." Mark eyed her carefully.

"So if what you say is true, you can get on Facebook and tell the truth. It's not too late."

He reacted like he'd never noticed her before. "What?"

"You heard me."

"I'll … do it." He spoke with uncertainty.

"Now."

Mark nodded slowly and smiled. "Now." He cocked his head quizzically. "Hey, why haven't you been at school? What have you been doing all week?"

"Training a racehorse."

"A racehorse? You mean, like a real racehorse that races on a track?"

"That's what I mean."

"Cool! Can I watch?"

"Maybe someday. If you don't put it on Facebook."

Mark was about to object when he saw the slight smile on Evie's lips. "Cool." He walked away, then turned back and laughed. "A racehorse! Wow." He walked a couple more steps, then turned again. "Gotta get to class. Catch you later!"

As she watched him make his way down the hall, Evie's heart rate steadied. She was proud of the way she'd handled that conversation and realized that an enormous weight had been lifted from her. She literally felt lighter. Mark had been trying to reach her and he'd been worried about her feelings. Aunt Mary had been right. This was a very fixable problem.

Her aunt and the principal emerged a minute later. She stood up from the bench.

"Hello, Evie," said Mr. Chumar. "Your aunt Mary filled me in. We'll not deduct marks for the tests you've missed, but it's important that you catch up quickly. Final exams are next week."

"Thanks, Mr. Chumar. I'll go to classes now and ask each teacher —"

"It's better that I do that. At the end of today, come back here to see me."

"I will. I'll work hard to catch up. Thank you."

Mr. Chumar shook her hand. "You're a fine young woman. Well done." He blinked and returned to his office.

Evie was puzzled. She turned to her aunt. "What did you say to him?"

Mary put a hand on her shoulder. "That this week you rescued a dog, a horse, and your little brother. That you located me to help you find your sick and presumed-dead mother. That you are a remarkable young lady who deserves a second chance."

Evie was not sure that she could live up to this new image. "I'm glad you're in my corner. Thanks."

"My pleasure. Have a good day at school. See you later."

15

Angela's Revelation

Within a few days, the Gibb children had developed a rhythm in their new home at Parson's Bridge.

Jordie and Beatrice took the school bus daily to Abergrath and back, and then Mary drove them to their various activities after school. Jordie had kung-fu and piano. Beatrice had dance and swimming, which Evie couldn't imagine. The thought of being submerged in water terrified her. It always had.

At six every morning, Evie and Mary worked Kazzam before Evie showered and hopped on her school bus. From eight every morning until the children returned, Mary worked in the barn and wrote her new book.

Things were much better for Evie at school. Aunt Mary had helped her out big time by telling the principal about Evie's heroic deeds. It had travelled all around the school and made her a bit of a celebrity! She was the gutsy jockey who'd rescued her brother and saved animals. She was the girl whose mother had a tragic story.

Eve found that she was actually glad to be back. Mark had done what he promised and righted the wrong on Facebook. In fact, he'd confessed to liking her! It'd made a huge difference. Rebecca, Hilary, and most of the other kids in her classes included her now. Amelia still avoided her, and Cassie, too, in solidarity, but Evie was okay with that. It was their problem, not hers.

She was ready for her exams the following week. There were four: history, English, math, and science.

At seven o'clock Friday evening, Mary was working at her desk after a supper of burgers and salad, with ice-cream cones for dessert. The three dogs were fast asleep on the carpet, and the kids were doing homework on the dining-room table.

The telephone rang.

Mary answered on the second ring. She spoke quietly, and nobody paid any attention until she hung up and stood. "Evie. Your mother will be okay, but she's in the hospital. She was hit by a car on Queen Street."

"How bad?"

"She's unconscious. They found my card in her pocket." Mary looked at her watch. "I'm going to see her. Does anybody want to come?"

Evie closed her books. "I'm coming."

Beatrice wrinkled up her nose and frowned. "Can I stay here? My favourite show is on at eight."

"Certainly. The dogs will babysit."

"I'm almost thirteen! I can stay on my own."

"I know, Beebee." Mary tousled her hair. "I just always feel better with the dogs around. Jordie? Your choice. Stay with Beebee or come. We'll be back around nine-thirty or ten."

He squirmed in his seat. "No thanks. I'd rather stay here. I hate hospitals. Is that okay?"

"Of course it's okay. I'll have my cell if you need me. Bedtime at nine. Evie, let's go."

As they were leaving, Mary told the kids, "Don't open the door to anybody. Call me if there's anything wrong at all, and call Mr. Gregg next door if you need help. If it's an emergency, call 911." She hugged both and locked the door behind her.

One hour later, Evie and Mary were riding up the elevator at St. Michael's Hospital in downtown Toronto. Evie felt scared, even queasy. She could not imagine what they were going to see.

The elevator door opened. Evie hesitated. "If she's unconscious, why are we even here?"

Mary took her by the arm. "They need us to identify her, and the doctors need permission to treat her. We're very lucky. St. Michael's is considered the best in North America for their work with people like Angela. Still, it never hurts for family to show up. For motivation."

Evie was puzzled. "What do you mean, motivation?"

"She's a homeless person. We don't want anyone to think Angela has a lesser value." Mary's voice was steely.

Of course. Some people would say good riddance to an addict off the street. Evie herself had wondered how much value her mother added to the world.

Mary spoke to the nurse at the desk and they waited a couple of minutes until a middle-aged woman appeared to show them where Angela lay.

"Thanks for coming so quickly," the doctor said. "I'm Dr. Janette Graham," she said. "Follow me."

At room 718, the doctor stopped. "Please take a good look and tell me if you recognize this person."

They both looked through the door window. Together they said, "Yes." Mary added, "That's Angela Parson."

"Will you sign this, please?" asked Dr. Graham as she handed Mary a clipboard with a pen. "It's to confirm your identification of the patient."

"Angela," corrected Mary firmly as she signed.

Dr. Graham chuckled. "I'm from Jamaica. I know better

than to judge a person from the outside." She looked at her watch and tapped it twice. "You have ten minutes to sit with her. I'll be back." Dr. Graham strode off.

Evie liked the doctor, especially her no-nonsense attitude. She and Mary entered the room. There were three beds curtained off from one another for privacy. Angela occupied the one closest to the door.

She lay very still. Her face was pale, and her freckles had all but disappeared. A monitor was hooked up to her arm, with a drip going into her vein. Evie couldn't tell how badly she was hurt, but a cut on her forehead had recently been stitched up. The skin around it was bruised.

Mary pulled a chair closer to Angela's bed. She motioned Evie to do the same. "We're here, dear Angela. It's Aunt Mary and Evangeline."

For five minutes, Evie held one hand and Mary the other. They didn't speak. There were occasional sounds coming from the other patients — little grunts and groans and rustling of bedclothes. The minutes ticked slowly by.

Then Angela's fingers wiggled in Evie's hand. "She moved!" Evie whispered.

"That's great!" Mary smiled. "Oh, this hand, too!"

Angela's head swivelled a tiny bit. Then she opened her eyes, one at a time.

"Angela?" asked Mary quietly. "Can you see us?"

Angela's mouth curled up into a tiny smile. "Hello." Her eyes squinted, then relaxed, then widened. "Where am I? Ooh, I hurt. What happened?"

"You were hit by a car this evening," replied Mary. "We came as soon as we heard."

"A car?" Angela's eyebrows pulled together. "I hurt. I need something. I … I don't … remember a car."

"That's okay. You'll remember in time. Right now it's important that you rest and get better."

Angela moaned. "I hurt all over. Can you get something for the pain? And a smoke?"

"The doctors will look after you," said Mary. Her tone was stiff and Evie looked at her quickly. "They'll give you what you need and nothing more."

Evie realized that Angela was asking for drugs, but not just for the pain. She was an addict. Evie must remember that and try to understand that getting drugs was foremost to her.

She tried to think of a topic of conversation. "Aunt Mary told me that you were a jockey. I never knew that. Is it true?"

Angela nodded, then winced. "Ouch. I shouldn't do that. Yes, I was a jockey. They called me 'Jockey Girl.' They meant it as an insult. But I loved the name."

"I want to be a jockey, too. Like you."

Angela's eyes cleared. "Have you got my horses?"

Evie was surprised. "What horses?"

"At Maple Mills. They're my horses. All of them."

"No Justice? Is he yours?"

"He's three now, isn't he? Sire is Nobleman, dam is Judge Joody. He should be small but very fast."

"He is! How do you know his breeding?"

Aunt Mary answered Evie's question. "I keep in touch with your mother." To Angela, she said, "But until this minute I never knew they belonged to you."

"It was never important. But now it is. I want Evie to ride them." She tried to lift her head. "I hurt all over. I need something."

Evie squeezed her hand. "I call No Justice 'Kazzam.' I don't know why. Well, I guess I do. He's kind of magic to me. And he surprises people with his speed. A la Kazzam!

He comes from behind and wins. Plus I had to race him under a different name so I could win money to find you."

"You did? And you won?"

"Over a thousand dollars."

"Good girl." Angela was fading. "I'm glad you found me. I think about you. All the time." Her eyelids began to droop. "I'm going to get better. For you."

"For me?" Evie wiped her tear-wet cheeks.

Angela nodded. "Get me something for the pain. And a cigarette. Can you get me something?"

Mary said, "I'll tell the doctor." She signalled to Evie that they should go.

"Aunt Mary and I will bring you pictures." Evie stood up and moved her chair back. "I'll take some nice ones of Kazzam. No Justice, I mean. He's gorgeous."

Angela nodded and her eyes closed. Within seconds she was fast asleep.

Evie studied her face. She'd been so dismissive of this woman. Now, she was beginning to see her mother as a real person. She'd had real ambitions and a real past. But for many reasons, she'd become something she'd never wanted to be. Never expected to be. Maybe she could get back to the person she was before. *Maybe*. Evie crossed her fingers.

As they left the room, Dr. Graham appeared. "Good timing," she said. "Your ten minutes are up."

"My mother's awake and talking," said Evie. "That's good, isn't it?"

"Is she making sense?"

"Yes. I think so."

"Then it's good." Dr. Graham made a note on her board and looked through the window at the sleeping Angela. "Excellent, in fact."

"How long will she be here?" asked Mary.

169

"Well, aside from minor cuts and bruising, her only injury was a slight concussion. I'll check later, after she sleeps for a while. She needs sleep more than anything. We'll watch her overnight, then make a decision about when she can go home."

Evie felt a pang. Where was home for her mother? Behind an alley somewhere near Queen and Spadina?

"I don't have to tell you about the drugs in her system," Dr. Graham continued. "We'll want to keep her here as long as possible and manage her withdrawal. I'd love to see her in a treatment facility." She looked at Mary directly. "There's a long wait for the fully covered ones."

"Private would be fantastic. I'll gladly pay the bills."

"Good. I'll make some calls."

"Thank you so much. Call me." Mary handed the doctor a card. "Please don't let her leave before contacting me."

"I promise. We'll watch her. I'll write it in the notes, too, so there's no misunderstanding."

"As soon as she wakes up again, please tell Angela that she'll come live with me. Okay?"

"Yes, I will." Dr. Graham's voice softened. "How many times have you been through this?"

Mary answered slowly. "Many times. And my heart has been broken many times. But I'll try again. And again and again. I have to."

The doctor took her hand. "That's the right thing, no matter how it turns out this time. Never give up on her."

Aunt Mary opened her mouth, but only a croak came out. Her whole face seemed to crumple.

Evie put her hand on her aunt's arm. "We won't," she said. She knew that was what Aunt Mary was trying to say.

On the way home from the hospital, Evie asked, "Was the doctor saying that my mother might not want to go to rehab after all? That she'd go back to drugs again?"

"Exactly." Mary drove along the Gardiner Expressway for a few minutes before saying, "It's tough. Nobody says, 'I want to be a drug addict when I grow up.' But once addiction has its claws in a person, it's very tough."

Evie didn't understand. It seemed so easy. Just stop taking drugs. "Why do people get addicted, anyway?"

"I don't pretend to be an expert. I'll give you some stuff to read."

"But you've learned a lot from experience." Evie really wanted to know. "Why is it so hard to stop taking drugs? Especially when a person knows they'll end up like my mother?"

"But they don't know that. Everybody thinks it won't happen to them." Aunt Mary inhaled slowly and released the air completely before she explained, "You know how when you hold your breath too long, your lungs start aching, and it gets unbearable until you have to breathe?"

Evie nodded. "Yeah."

"It's a little like that."

"But you need air to live," quizzed Evie. "You don't need drugs."

"No, you don't, but your body screams for them once you're addicted. It's a physical reaction. Addicts are in great pain when they go without. Serious suffering. Shaking, sweating, spasms, nausea, vomiting, diarrhea —"

"Enough!" interrupted Evie. "I get the picture. So why not stop taking them before you get addicted?"

"Because you don't know you're addicted until you try to stop."

"So my mother took OxyContin for pain after her injury, then when her leg was better, she was addicted?"

"Bingo. Then she couldn't stop. That's when she needed to go into a rehabilitation facility and get the drug out of her system."

"But my father thought he could fix her himself with no help from anybody else."

"And he couldn't, Evie. She needed professional help. The brain becomes hard-wired to want those drugs, and the body craves them, feels it *needs* them to survive."

"Like needing air."

Aunt Mary nodded. "Same thing with people addicted to cigarettes. There are a lot of addictions, Evie, and they all start out the same. Whatever the substance, it makes the person feel better at the beginning."

"And then it turns bad."

"It turns really bad. People choose the drug over everything else in their life."

Evie nodded. "Even over me, her own kid."

"Please understand. She was convinced that you'd be better cared for by your father."

Aunt Mary had told her that before, but Evie still didn't believe it. "Has Angela ever gone to rehab?"

"She's tried. Maybe four or five times over the years, she's signed herself up without telling me or anyone else. But there's a waiting list. By the time she gets in, she's back into the Oxy. And whatever else she can find, I guess."

"That's awful! But Dr. Graham said there's somewhere she can go if we pay for it."

"Yes, there is. And Dr. Graham will work on it."

"It's worth it! I'll give her all my winnings."

Aunt Mary reached over and patted Evie's arm. "I will, too, Evie. Trust me. I'd spend every last cent on that girl."

Evie agreed. "I hope she can do it this time."

"She's got a good reason this time. You."

That reminded Evie about something her mother had said. "What about the horses, Aunt Mary? How is it possible for my mother to own them?"

"I don't know. I always assumed they belonged to Grayson, along with everything else Angela signed away."

"I hate to even ask, but could she be confused about it?" Evie felt she needed to explain, "Because of the drugs and her concussion?"

"Possibly, but I think she really believes it."

"Okay. I have no right to say it, since I'm a guest, too. I'm a little nervous about her coming to live with us. If she might, you know, start using drugs again."

Mary laughed. "Me, too. But it's family. You're family! Beatrice and Jordie are family. That's what we do for each other. And my little house is happy to be filled with wonderful people."

"That's really nice." Evie thought she'd never be as good a person as her great-aunt. "You never finished telling me about Angela's parents — your brother and his wife. My grandparents. Why didn't they help her?"

Mary sighed deeply. "They were both killed in a car crash. On the night of Angela's marriage to Grayson. They were broadsided by a drunk driver."

"Wow." Evie hadn't expected that. "I never knew."

"Grayson decided not to tell you anything about your mother's side of your family," said Mary.

"But why?" Evie still didn't understand. "I mean, unless your side of the family were all criminals or something."

Mary glanced at her and smiled drolly. "A far as I know, none of us has been in jail."

"So why, then? Do you know?"

"Evie, you ask all the right questions. Maybe it had something to do with his need to control Angela. He didn't want anybody else influencing her in any way." She paused. "And maybe it was about the family money."

Evie remembered her aunt mentioning money the day they met. "Tell me about that."

"My brother was a very wealthy man, and they worried that Grayson was marrying Angela for money. They forced a prenuptial agreement on them so that if there was a divorce, he wouldn't get half the family money."

"I bet that didn't go over too well."

Mary snorted. "With Grayson's control issues?"

Evie had an awful thought. "But ... there was no divorce. Is that why he told people that Angela was dead?"

"Angela signed everything over to him anyway, so it didn't matter."

"But my father knew she was alive and he got married again. To Paulina. How is that possible when he wasn't divorced?"

Mary looked at her kindly. "It's not a legal marriage, dear."

"I feel like I'm in a movie about amnesia. I don't know anything about who I am!" She wanted to scream. None of this was Aunt Mary's fault, but knowing that didn't make it any easier.

"Please, Evie. Be patient. I'll tell you everything soon."

By the time they pulled into the driveway of Parson's Bridge it was quite dark, but the outlines of the horses grazing in the fields were still visible against the sky. Just the sight of them gave Evie comfort.

They parked the truck and tiptoed into the house. The three dogs greeted them at the door, wagging their tails.

"All's quiet," whispered Mary. "The kids went to bed like I told them, wonder of wonders. Take the dogs out for a few minutes, Evie, will you? I'll check my messages."

"Okay, sure." Evie let out the dogs and followed them.

Simon and Garfunkel raced away, while Magpie stayed with her. She rubbed her ears and patted her sides. The dog's body under her sleek black coat felt full of life and energy.

The last of Evie's stress disappeared, replaced with an inner calm. Animals did that to her, she realized. Maybe they were *her* addiction. She giggled at the thought.

"Go catch up with the others, Magpie! Have some fun." Magpie just tilted her head and stared at her. "Go on, it's okay." Then the dog was gone, her black coat rending her invisible in the dark.

Evie filled her lungs with the delightful aromas of June.

She was very happy to be outside in the balmy night air.

As her eyes adjusted to the darkness, she gazed over to the horse fields. Christieloo, Bendigo, and Paragon were grazing contentedly, and Kazzam stood napping at the fence.

Evie wandered down the hill and climbed into his field. The horse heard her footsteps and became alert. His neck straightened and his head turned. Then he trotted over, giving a little nicker of recognition.

"You're a good boy, Kazzam," cooed Evie. He put his head down and gently pushed into her chest. She scratched behind his ears and rubbed between his strong jaw bones, then patted his neck. "You're fast. Mom says you were bred that way. Kazzam? Can you win another race next week? This time, I want you to win for my mother."

16

The Woodbine Test

The next day was Saturday, and the morning was wet and rainy. It had rained all night. Since she didn't have to rush off to school, Evie and Kazzam went for a quiet hack on the trails after the daily training. Followed by Magpie, of course. The dog loved nothing better. So much to smell, so many small animals to flush from the bushes! The fields and woods had turned emerald green. Birds sang loudly, outdoing each other with their talent, and frogs and insects chirped and hummed. It gladdened Evie's heart, and her horse's, too. Kazzam was playful and full of energy, hopping and spooking at nothing at all. His antics made her grin.

Daily, Kazzam was getting fitter, exactly on schedule. A full second had dropped off his time on the mile-and-a-quarter track, without even trying, it seemed. Evie had sat on his back, perched high and holding on to the horse with the insides of her feet. She'd basically just let him run, but they'd devised signals. When she leaned further forward with her hands up his neck, he ran faster. When she rested her weight into the saddle a little and sat up, he slowed. When she wanted him to stop, she relaxed and said, "Whoa, boy," then waited until he came to a halt.

Riding Kazzam was the most joyful part of her day. The horse was smart and sensitive. As long as he felt respected, he was happy, and when he was happy, he could learn. He was a quick learner, too, Evie thought, provided he understood what she wanted. That was Evie's job. She was careful never to rush him or to force an issue, but when she needed him to know something, like yielding to the pressure of her leg or changing leads, she quietly persisted until he got it. She and Kazzam were quickly developing a mutually respectful relationship. Evie felt that she was doing her part, and gladly left the administration details to Jerry and Aunt Mary.

Saturday afternoon, Evie settled down to the business of preparing for exams. While Evie was busy doing that, Aunt Mary drove back to the Toronto hospital to see Angela. When she returned several hours later, she reported that Angela was much improved and had agreed to come live with them until a space at the right program opened up.

Altogether, it had been a very productive day.

By Sunday morning, the sun was out again and Evie trained Kazzam before the day got really hot and humid. Their workout was really fast. Kazzam's speed was the best ever. Evie knew from his ever-improving performance and energy that the program was working. She was getting more and more excited about the Queen's Plate. Kazzam was a contender, she could feel it. Evie slapped his neck and said, "I'm so proud of you, Kazzam! Good boy!"

She knew that Jerry was working hard at getting a jockey. Evie wondered who would get to ride him at the Queen's Plate. She felt jealous. Quite jealous. The only jockey she wouldn't resent was Imogene, only because she was her hero.

Evie's mind was busy as they trotted along the trails. Her mother was moving in. Soon. Maybe even in the next week. Evie knew she should try to be as good a person as Aunt Mary and welcome Angela just as generously. But how was it going to work out? What was the plan for helping her mother get clean? Evie admitted to being afraid of the unknown.

She turned her mind to Mark. They'd been flirting at school. Evie smiled and felt the blush creep into her cheeks. School was fun now. Turns out that her old friends had never deserted her. Well, except Amelia. Cassie had let slip that Amelia'd had a crush on Mark herself. That was the gossip, and it made sense to Evie. Cassie was slowly softening, and Hilary and Rebecca thought that *Evie* had deserted *them*! And really, she had. She'd thrown away her phone and left school, assuming the worst. She hadn't been fair to them. She hadn't given them a chance.

As Evie and Kazzam emerged from the woods, Magpie stopped suddenly, pointed her nose and one paw, and then tore across the field with lightning speed.

"Be glad Magpie's not entered!" she said to Kazzam, laughing. Evie saw that Jerry Johnston's truck was parked at the barn.

When Evie slid down from her horse, she patted his nose and gave his head a hug. "You're the best horse in the world. You're my secret weapon."

Jerry and Mary approached with thoughtful faces.

Evie looked from one to the other, not sure what was going on. Mary took Kazzam's saddle off.

Jerry Johnston looked serious. "Evie, we need to talk."

Evie's throat constricted. *What've I done now?*

"Tomorrow is the day. Half a mile."

"Okay." Evie still wasn't sure where he was going with this.

"Mary will drive you and Kazzam to Woodbine for a run at six in the morning. With three other horses. Out of the gate. I've set it up. Three stewards will be there, including Murray Planno. Three jockeys, three trainers, and the official starter."

Evie was having a hard time understanding. She searched his face for clues. She looked at Mary. "What's this all about?"

"Are you in?" asked Jerry. "Yes or no."

"Of course I'm in! But tell me what I'm in for!"

"No need to shout," said Jerry.

"We have a problem," Mary explained. "Not one available jockey will take a chance with No Justice. I fully appreciate their concerns. It's dangerous enough out there. They're worried about being bucked off."

"So?" prompted Evie. "That's not a surprise, is it?" Again, she looked from one adult to the other.

"And," Jerry answered, "if we're going to run No Justice in the Queen's Plate, we need two things: to get his racing ban lifted, and for you to become an apprentice jockey. And we'll do both at one time. Tomorrow morning. For a short test run."

Evie was astonished. Her eyes widened and a tentative grin slowly crept across her face. "Apprentice jockey. So I could...."

"Ride him, yes." Mary completed Evie's sentence.

"In the Queen's Plate?" Evie thought her heart might stop. "You're not kidding? Because that would be so cruel...."

"No joke." Mary smiled at her great-niece. "If Kazzam behaves himself tomorrow, he'll be allowed to race. He's already been entered, so that's all good. And since you're only sixteen, you need parental consent."

"My father will never give his consent!"

"Your mother signed her consent on a legal document yesterday when I visited her."

Evie shook her head disbelievingly. Things were happening so fast. "She did? What does she think?"

"She's thrilled. Totally thrilled. She told me she'll be at the Queen's Plate in person to cheer you on."

Evie let that pass. No way would her mother make the race. "You knew about this yesterday and didn't tell me?"

"We weren't sure we could pull it off. Now we're sure, thanks to Jerry for doing all the organizing."

Jerry smiled proudly. "As long as you want to do this."

"I want to do this *so* much," said Evie. She felt like doing cartwheels across the field. "I really hope he runs well tomorrow." She crossed all her fingers.

Jerry patted her on the shoulder. "He will. I have no doubt. If there's any justice in the world."

Evie did not say what she was thinking, that the horse's name was No Justice. "Oh!" she exclaimed. "My exams. I have two exams tomorrow. I write history at nine!"

"I know," said Aunt Mary. "Don't worry, I'll have you back in lots of time. You ride at six. We cool him out. We load him up and bring him home. I drop you off at school by eight-fifteen at the latest. Lots of time. If you agree."

"I do!" Evie inhaled and relaxed her shoulders. "Okay. And Beebee and Jordie?"

"They'll get ready for school by themselves tomorrow and catch the bus at the end of the lane. They'll be fine."

"You thought of everything. Thank you. Both." Evie surprised Aunt Mary by hugging her tightly and totally startled Jerry by turning to hug him, too. Then she ran to the house to study. She couldn't stand still for one minute more. Magpie raced along with her.

The next morning Evie and Mary were up at four, quietly getting ready to go. They whispered and tiptoed around the house so as not to awaken Beatrice or Jordie.

By four-thirty the dogs were fed, and breakfast cereal, bananas, orange juice, and muffins were on the counter. The kids' lunches were made and their clothes laid out. Lastly, Mary wrote a note of instructions and taped it to the fridge.

They walked down to the barn with the dogs at their heels. Dawn was creeping up the horizon with a pinkish glow, and the morning air was fresh. Mary got the truck and trailer set up with hay and a large container of water. She packed the racing saddle, leg wraps, cooling blanket, and brushes.

While Mary organized the equipment, Evie went out to bring Kazzam in from the field and to polish him up.

To her surprise, Christieloo was in the same field, grazing right alongside him! She must have jumped over the fence sometime in the night. The minute she led Kazzam into the barn, Evie said, "Aunt Mary, you'll never guess! Kazzam and Christieloo were out together and totally happy!"

Mary smiled. "I wondered if that might happen. They're very fond of each other and have been since the first day."

"Should we keep them together?"

"Yes. Otherwise, she'll jump back anyway, or worse, he'll jump in with all three and that might be quite … eventful."

Evie knew exactly what she meant. Horses are very territorial and the other geldings might gang up on the new guy. "Not good before the big race."

Evie turned her attention to Kazzam. The black horse could sense Evie's excitement. He was extra alert, with his nostrils a little more flared than normal and his ears a bit more forward. "You're quite right, boy," she told him as she picked out his feet, "Today is a very important day. But you know what to do. Just run. That's what you like to do, so just do it."

Evie led Kazzam onto the trailer and they were ready to go. She shivered with nerves. Mary hugged her and said, "You'll be fine. It's in your blood. Let's get going!"

By five-fifteen the Parson's Bridge trailer stopped at the stable gate. This time, Magpie was not in the truck and they were allowed through. Jerry Johnston was waiting, his truck idling on the other side.

He waved through his open window. "Just in time. Follow me."

Evie's eyes took in everything. It seemed early to her, but the place was bustling with activity. They drove past the staff barracks and the backstretch, and along the dirt road between long, low horse barns. Horses were being led or ridden, cars were moving around, and people of all ages, heights, and weights seemed to be everywhere. She saw a truck delivering feed. There were veterinarians, one examining a horse's leg, another checking eyes. Over at one of the long, lean-to buildings housing rows of stalls, referred to as shed-rows, was a farrier, hammering on a shoe.

Mary had been right. This place was a world unto itself.

Evie was mesmerized. So close to the biggest, most modern city in Canada, and yet these scenes could've taken place a hundred years ago. Well, except for the vehicles, she thought. But nonetheless, it felt romantic to Evie, and she wanted to drink it in. Her neck swivelled left and right in her effort to miss nothing.

"Jerry's pulling in here," said Aunt Mary. "This is the plan. It's quite simple. He'll look after the people, we'll look after the horse." She parked her rig beside Jerry's truck.

Evie nodded. "Suits me." Jerry's job sounded too complicated to her, anyway, with three of this and three of that plus the official starter.

Jerry glanced briefly at Mary and Evie, then pointed to a building. Mary waved and called, "We'll meet you at the starting gate." Jerry nodded and walked in.

Evie climbed into the trailer through the little side door beside Kazzam's head. She gently patted his nose and scratched him under his chin. "Remember what I told you? Just run, nothing else. No nonsense, No Justice. Let's have some fun on the big-boy track."

Mary handed her the bridle. Evie slipped off his halter and replaced it with the bridle. She appreciated how he opened his mouth to take the bit. "Saddle?" she called through the side door. Mary passed her the saddle, and Evie dropped the chest bar so she could step beside him and safely place it on his back. She slowly tightened the girth until it was secure.

Evie needed a moment to collect herself. She stood beside her beautiful gelding and took a long look at him. Kazzam's ebony coat gleamed with health. He held his head proudly and his ears were alert. His eyes were calm but had the sparkle of spirit. Evie gazed at his graceful, long neck, his perfect legs, and his wide chest. "You are a great horse. Today, we'll show them you belong here. It's in your blood."

Aunt Mary poked her head over the rear ramp. "Time to go. Are you ready?"

"Ready."

Mary dropped the ramp and unhooked the tail guard. Evie backed Kazzam off the trailer and onto the dirt. He raised his head as he smelled the air. He sniffed in all four directions and snorted loudly, then he opened his mouth and whinnied. Loudly. Other horses returned his greeting, and suddenly the air was vibrant with the primitive calls of wild horses.

Funny, Evie thought. *We people think it's all about us, but horses have their own society with their own language and their own objectives.* This was a perspective that Evie hoped always to remember.

Mary interrupted her thoughts. "Jerry gave me the signal. Let's get you mounted." She gave her a leg up on the count of three. "Okay. Come this way."

Evie, riding Kazzam, followed her great-aunt along the dirt road past all the shed-rows. Kazzam was excited and danced a little, but Evie knew he was not fearful. She felt quite elegant on this stunning black beauty and thought that people must be admiring her horse as they passed.

They turned right and headed for the tunnel under the turf course. Horses and riders passed them, going in the opposite direction, having already completed their daily exercise.

When they emerged from the shady tunnel, the track appeared in front of them, huge and panoramic. Evie took it all in, looking around at the endless Polytrack surrounded by the wide turf track, with the enormous grass infield in the middle of the oval. *Wow,* thought Evie. *It's gigantic.* Her heart raced. She inhaled slowly, trying to contain her excitement.

So this is how it looks from the back of a horse. She'd watched countless races, a few times in person, but mostly on television, and the track had looked so much smaller. Less scary. *But this is good scary.*

Kazzam, too, was feeling thrilled. He pranced sideways and arched his neck until his nose touched his chest. "Easy, boy," soothed Evie. "No monkey business. It's me up here, remember?" She rested her hands on his taut neck and scratched his neck through his silky mane with her fingers. "Just you and me. We'll be fine."

"Evie?" called Jerry. His voice seemed faraway.

Evie looked around and spotted the trainer in a small crowd of people. These were the people who would deem Kazzam fit to race or not, and accept or reject her as an apprentice jockey. She counted ten people, plus Mary.

Three stewards, three jockeys, three trainers, including Jerry, and an official starter. Aunt Mary stood out. She was wearing her bright red shirt and was easy to spot.

Jerry pointed several times to somewhere behind her, and hollered again. "Evie!"

"Yes?" She yelled to be heard.

"Follow those horses and get ... in ... the ... gate!"

Three horses cantered past her.

"These horses?"

"Yes! Those horses!"

Evie turned Kazzam and began to trot in the same direction. Up ahead was a tall, roofed, white starting gate on wheels, which had been towed onto the track. There were places for up to eight horses, all lined up in a row.

Kazzam got jumpier and jumpier as they neared. "Please, Kazzam. Please. This is our last chance." She let him canter and prayed he would behave himself.

Kazzam lowered his neck and shook his head in agitation. He hopped, but didn't buck. He allowed Evie to slow him as they arrived at the gate. The other horses were already locked in.

There were two men waiting for her: the assistant starters. They indicated that she ride into the empty spot at the end. Her throat held an enormous lump and she couldn't speak, so Evie nodded. She hoped Kazzam couldn't tell how nervous she was.

Who am I fooling? she asked herself. He knows me better than I know myself. With that thought, she chuckled and relaxed. "You're doing better than I am, Kazzam," she said aloud.

"Pardon?" asked the older man.

Evie opened her mouth to answer, but he didn't give her a chance.

"Did you call him 'Kazzam'?" he questioned.

The young man asked the older man, "Like, as in the horse that Molly Peebles rode?"

The older man nodded. "The deaf girl."

Evie breathed deeply and smiled brightly. She had no idea how to correct their misunderstanding. Anyway, she needed all her concentration for the task ahead.

"My daughter wants to be just like Molly here," the older man said. He took hold of Kazzam's bridle to lead him in.

Kazzam did not like people doing that, and he swerved away from the man's grasp. Evie waved her apology and pointed to herself to indicate that she'd get him in place herself.

Both men stepped back. The younger one said, "Go ahead," with exaggerated facial movements.

"Okay, boy," she whispered. "Easy does it." One hesitant step at a time, the horse entered the box.

"Go, Molly!" and "Good luck!" said the men as they clanked the gate shut behind the trembling horse.

Evie looked down the endless stretch of track ahead and waited for the bell to ring.

17

Win, Win, Lose, Lose

"Dear Lord of creatures great and small, please prove to these judges that Kazzam is fit to race in the Queen's —"

The starting bell rang. Just like in the Caledon Horse Race, Kazzam stalled. Again, Evie watched as her competitors raced away, this time kicking up stinging pellets of Polytrack instead of dust.

"— Plate. Amen."

Perched high on her little jockey saddle, Evie couldn't squeeze her legs to hang on, so she pressed her feet into him. She knew to be patient, to let him decide when to go. Was he waiting to see what strategy was needed? Did he want to avoid the crush of horses at the start? Whatever his reason, Evie remembered how far he'd leaped the last time. She grabbed as much mane as she could and leaned way forward.

"Please go, Kazzam," she whispered.

A second passed. And another. Each second was interminable.

"Soon, Kazzam?"

Kazzam sprang out of the gate like a giant kangaroo. Evie held on with every fibre of her body. He accelerated from zero to thirty miles an hour in seconds.

This is fast, she thought. Very fast. Yet even as she thought he'd neared his top speed, he stretched out and ran faster, closing the gap with every stride.

Evie had read that the fastest recorded speed of a Thoroughbred racehorse was Petro Jay in 1982, at Turf Paradise in Arizona. He was clocked at 40.18 miles an hour. Faster than Spectacular Bid at 38.2 and Secretariat at 37.5. Why she was thinking statistics at this moment baffled her.

Kazzam's pace was still surging. Evie was on top of a galloping machine. Tears streamed down her face as they rushed onward into the wind.

Kazzam was running so fast the three horses ahead of him appeared to be standing still. The small black horse ran wide to the right and passed them all on the outside — one, two, three — effortlessly! He was hurtling now, nose straight ahead and legs flying.

Evie loved his great spirit, his desire to win, and she knew he would use every ounce of his courage until the job was done. He powered past and left the others completely and utterly defeated.

The assistant starters appeared with flags waving, ending the race. Evie couldn't see clearly through her blurry eyes, but she swore they were both grinning.

She lifted her weight off Kazzam's back and rode him around the bend, asking him to slow. His speed diminished incrementally until his gallop became a canter, then a lope, then a trot, and finally a walk. Evie patted his neck, first with her right hand and then with her left. "Thank you. Kazzam, you are truly a champion."

Aunt Mary, with her bright red shirt, came running out from the group of people, waving her arms. Evie could see she was very excited. "Evie! Beautifully done!"

Evie rode over to her aunt and hopped to the ground.

Mary hugged her tightly. "Do you have any idea how fast you were running?"

"You mean Kazzam," corrected Evie as she caught her breath. "I just sat on him."

"Yes, of course. Kazzam, actually No Justice, was clocked at 37.6 miles an hour!"

Evie beamed. "Faster than Secretariat and slower than Petro Jay."

"You've certainly been studying up on racing," said Mary with undisguised admiration.

Evie nodded and hugged Kazzam's neck. "I've got a racehorse. Why wouldn't I?"

Jerry Johnston appeared at their sides. He could hardly contain himself. "Slam dunk. Well ridden. Thought you'd lost it out of the gate, but —" he paused and shook his head in disbelief "— but, wow, child, you can ride."

Evie was touched by the man's sincerity. "Thank you," she said. "Do you think Kazzam can run this Sunday?"

Jerry swallowed, fidgeted, and sniffed. "These people need to conference and make a final decision before we know for sure." He looked over his shoulder. "But if they decide against him, there's no justice in this world."

There it was again. Did Jerry know what he'd said? "No justice as in No Justice or as in no justice?" she asked.

Jerry looked startled. "My, my," he said with a sheepish smile. "I won't say that again!"

Mary looked at her watch. "It's six-fifteen," she said. "Let's cool out No Justice and get on our way. Your history exam is beckoning."

"And then my English," added Evie.

Jerry put his hands on his hips and studied Evie with approval. "Write your exams with a light heart. No Justice was a gent and you rode magnificently." He waved goodbye to Evie and Mary as they walked back to the shed-rows and their trailer with Kazzam. "I'll be in touch!"

Mary patted Evie's back. "You really impressed those people, dear. They were a bit negative starting out, about both No Justice and you. Him because they were certain he was dangerous, and you because they don't like jockeys under eighteen years old. Especially girls, most of them."

"What did they say after the race?"

"They were amazed at No Justice's speed, for one. And how gutsy he is, even in a hopeless situation, so far behind. But the real test is that they have to be satisfied that he isn't a danger to himself, his jockey, or to other horses in a race. In my opinion he passed with flying colours."

"And my age?"

Mary grinned. "At first you seemed quite young and confused, really, when you didn't know where the starting gate was and all that. As soon as they saw how you waited for No Justice to decide to run, then let him run a perfect race, they changed their minds, one by one."

"Who was the first?"

"Imogene Watson."

Evie stopped walking. "Imogene Watson? She was there, watching? She was one of the three jockeys?"

Mary's eyes glowed. "Yes. She was the first to say you deserve a chance to become an apprentice."

Evie's entire body was covered in goose bumps. "Oh my gawd! Imogene won the Queen's Plate in 2007!" She looked back, hoping to see her hero.

"You'll meet her one day, Evie. Just not today. We've got to get you to school on time."

⚶

Both of Evie's exams went well. She loved both subjects. If two exams had to be on the same day, it was lucky that it was these two.

History was even fun to write, since it was mostly true and false with three essay questions that she chose out of nine possibilities. She thought she might have aced it.

Between exams, she'd gone outside to eat her lunch while brushing up for English. She'd enjoyed reading the books they were taking — though not as much as Elizabeth Elliot novels — and felt ready for that section. Evie felt good about how she did in the grammar section, too.

At three o'clock, she sat on the wide stone steps in front of the school and waited for Aunt Mary to pick her up. The sun felt warm on her face. Evie put her bookbag behind her head and leaned back with her eyes closed. Now that her work was done, her whole body relaxed. What a perfect day, she thought, smiling to herself. The test race had been utterly thrilling, and two exams were over.

"Sleeping Beauty, I presume?"

Evie sat up and looked into the grinning face of Mark Sellers. His eyes shone bright chestnut in the sunlight, and his dark-brown hair gleamed.

"So who are you, the handsome prince or the bad fairy?"

He plunked his bag on the steps and sat beside her. "Just call me Handsome."

"Great nickname."

"Thanks." Mark nudged her with his arm. "People are talking about you."

Evie cringed. *Oh, no. Not again.*

"They're saying you're cool. You know, riding Thoroughbreds and everything."

"One Thoroughbred. Only Kazzam. But that's great. Better than talking about what a loser I am."

Mark shook his head. "Look, I'm sorry. I was a real jerk. I should've blasted Amelia on Facebook that same day. Will you ever forgive me?"

"I already have. But I'll never forget. You let me hang."

"How can I make it up to you?" Mark pleaded. He looked genuinely stricken, then brightened. "Hey, are you going to the prom next weekend?"

"It's the Queen's Plate. I'm riding." Suddenly she worried about jinxing herself. "Touch wood." She knocked on her head, then held up her two hands and crossed all her fingers.

Mark stared. "You're kidding."

"No. If everything works out, and it might not, I'm riding No Justice in the Plate." She kept all her fingers crossed.

"Then I'm coming. I've got to see it!"

A small fire began to burn inside her body. "Cool. That's how you can make it up to me."

"Isn't the race in the afternoon? I'm coming, but can't you come to the prom with me that night?"

She smiled from ear to ear. "Yeah. I'd like that."

"Cool." Mark took her hand in his. At his touch, Evie felt a pulsing sensation travel through her body. Her mouth went dry and she couldn't move.

"Cool because I'll have the coolest girl ever with me. The winner of the Queen's Plate!"

Evie wished that this minute could last forever. Mark Sellers and her, sitting on the steps in the sun, holding hands. She felt like a popular girl, a novel experience.

"Evie! Hello! Over here!"

Aunt Mary's truck pulled up at the curb. Evie looked at Mark dreamily. "Science tomorrow?"

"Science tomorrow. See you then." He released her hand reluctantly and slowly stood.

Evie grabbed her bookbag and ran to the truck, face flushed. She looked back to see him waving goodbye. She raised her hand in a quick motion, then got in and closed the door.

"Handsome boy," said Aunt Mary.

"That's his nickname."

Mary chuckled. "What's his real name?"

"Mark Sellers. And yes, *the* Mark Sellers."

"Well, well!" Mary said with raised eyebrows. "Young love. It's a wonderful thing."

Evie agreed, but "wonderful" was such an inadequate word. "Full of wonder."

"Indeed. So, let's pick up Beebee and Jordie and get home. Lots to do." Aunt Mary checked her mirrors and pulled onto the road. "Murray called. He thinks you and No Justice will really pump up attendance and betting and get the Queen's Plate in the news."

Evie stopped daydreaming about Mark and sat up straight. "What did you say? So we passed the test? I'm an apprentice?"

"Yes. Didn't I tell you?"

"No! That's huge!" Evie bounced in her seat and shrieked with joy. She stuck her head out the window and hollered, "I'm riding in the Queen's Plate!"

Mary laughed gaily.

Evie felt on top of the world. It was truly hard to believe this news! She was just sixteen. The only race she'd ever ridden was the amateur Caledon Horse Race. Should she pinch herself? Could this be real?

They drove to the Abergrath School and waited for Beatrice and Jordie. Children seemed to pour out of the doors and down the stairs, dispersing in various directions. School buses pulled out.

"Do they know you're picking them up?" asked Evie.

"Yes. I told them last night and put notes in their lunches, too."

As the minutes ticked by, fewer and fewer kids emerged. "It's too quiet," said Evie as she got out to stretch her legs. They'd stiffened from her earlier ride, and sitting all day in exams hadn't helped. "Should I go see what's holding them up?"

"Good idea. I'll wait here in case they show up." Mary turned on her phone and checked her emails and messages.

Evie walked into the school. It was empty except for the occasional teacher and cleaner. She walked to the office, where an assistant was putting on her blazer.

"Hi. I'm looking for my little sister and brother. Beatrice and Jordie Gibb. Have you seen them?"

"No, sorry. All the kids are gone. Do you want me to call anyone to help?" The woman's face creased with concern as she checked her watch.

"No thanks. My aunt is outside. If they show up, can you ask them to call Aunt Mary?"

"I would, but I'm just leaving. Sorry."

Aunt Mary appeared from down the hall. "Evie? Beebee left a message."

Relief washed over Evie. "I'm so glad!"

The assistant was relieved, as well. "Thank goodness. Well, we have to lock up now."

"Thanks for everything," said Mary, walking with Evie toward the door. She seemed kind of tense.

"Where are they?" whispered Evie.

"Apparently Paulina came to get them at school."

"Paulina?"

"Yes. She's their mother, after all. It's as it should be."

"Then why are you gripping my arm so tightly?"

"Oh! I'm sorry," said Mary as she released her hold.

"It's just that Beebee sounded ... uncertain."

"Can I listen to the message?"

"Yes. In the truck."

They walked together across the parking lot. Evie was concerned. Paulina's moods were unreliable. She was likely to return her children as quickly as she took them. And without Sella the housekeeper, Paulina couldn't cope. Sella was the person who'd raised them, not their mother.

When they got in the truck, Aunt Mary retrieved the message for Evie to hear. Beatrice's plaintive voice could be heard clearly:

"Aunt Mary? Evie? It's Beebee? And Jordie, too? Um ... Mom is here. At the school? Um ... she's here to take us to where she lives now? She said it's okay. Is it okay?"

Evie and Mary sat in silence, both considering what to think about the call.

Evie said, "You're right. Paulina is their mother."

"And remember, they were to live at my house just until she got organized."

"Yeah, but why didn't Paulina tell you she was picking them up so you'd know where they were?"

Mary pursed her lips. "I guess that's the troubling thing. And Beebee sounds confused."

"Poor Jordie. I'm sure he's confused, too."

"Do you know Beebee's cell number?"

Evie shook her head. "She's not allowed to have a cell."

"Well," said Mary briskly as she started the truck. "Let's get home. Nothing to do but wait. Beebee didn't leave a number, but Paulina will call later, I'm sure."

Evie wasn't so sure. Beatrice's voice had been quite tentative. Was Paulina even sober when she picked them up? Adults were sometimes so unfathomable.

As always, Evie's spirits lifted as they turned into the lane at Parson's Gate. The horses were out in their

195

fields, grazing in pairs. Bendigo and Paragon in one field, Christieloo and Kazzam in the next. They looked sleek and healthy, and the little farm with its yellow house, wooden fences, and charming barn seemed to welcome them home.

The three dogs raced up to the truck when they parked at the house. Tails wagged and tongues flapped. Magpie leaped into the truck as Evie opened her door. "Down girl!" she commanded with a laugh. "You must have really missed me today."

"Time is simple for dogs," mused Mary. "They miss us while we're away, but when we get home it's like we were never gone. After the welcome, that is."

"But really, if a dog's year is seven of ours, each minute must feel like seven."

"Who knows? They're not talking," Mary winked.

When they got to the house, the message light was blinking. Mary said, "Might be Paulina. Get some milk and a snack, Evie. Help yourself." She pressed the button.

"Hello, Ms. Parson. This is Dale Green at St. Michael's Hospital. You're listed as the sole contact for Ms. Angela Gibb. Please call immediately at extension 4357."

Mary wasted no time. She pressed the numbers. Evie waited with apprehension.

"Yes, this is Mary Parson. You left a message about Angela Gibb.... Yes, I'll wait."

Mary spoke to Evie. "I'm on hold."

Evie asked, "Why do you think they called?"

Mary shook her head. "We'll know soon."

Evie clamped her mouth shut. She sat on a stool at the counter and tried not to imagine disaster.

"Yes, hello, this is Mary Parson. I'm returning your—. Yes, I'm her.... No, I didn't know.... When did she leave?... How did it happen?... Yes, I understand.... Okay.... Yes,

I will.... Of course.... And you call if you hear anything at all?... Thank you very much."

"What happened?" asked Evie. "What's wrong, Aunt Mary? You look so worried. Tell me, please!"

Mary leaned against the counter and rubbed her face with her hands. She spoke very quietly. "Angela left the hospital."

"She's gone?"

"Yes. This afternoon. Nobody knows where she went."

"Is she well enough to leave?"

"Not really. They hadn't discharged her, anyway."

"How did she get out? Dr. Graham said they'd watch her."

"Angela wanted to go outside for a smoke. She wasn't allowed to go alone, so she convinced an intern to join her."

"And she escaped?"

"Yes. She slipped away. The oldest trick in the book."

"So she's not ready to be helped."

Mary turned to Evie slowly and put a hand on her shoulder. "That's my guess."

18

Christieloo

It was after five on Monday afternoon. It had already been a big day, with the test race at Woodbine and two exams, plus the stress of Angela leaving the hospital and Jordie and Beatrice being picked up by Paulina.

Evie's science exam was the next day and there was a lot of information Evie needed to review. She flipped through her textbook, trying to concentrate. She reread passages and tried to memorize graphs and pertinent points.

But studying was a lost cause. No matter how she tried to focus, Evie continued to worry about her sister and brother, and she was very concerned about where her mother had gone.

At least Beatrice and Jordie were together, she figured. And fine, if you didn't count how bleary and moody Paulina got once she opened her bottles of wine. Which would've started around noon.

But Angela had been hit by a car and wasn't well enough to leave the hospital. On top of that, she didn't have a clean place to go. How would she find food to eat and a warm bed when she was so weak? *She could've called Aunt Mary. She could've called me.* Evie was worried and frustrated. *She said she wanted to get better for me. Yeah, right.*

Evie slammed the books shut and gazed out the window of her room. How had Aunt Mary been so patient with Angela? All those years of almost getting help, then disappearing back into her addiction.

The sight of Kazzam distracted her. *My Queen's Plate horse*. Evie still couldn't quite imagine it. His black coat glistened in the late-day sunlight, and Christieloo, with her bright golden colour, made an attractive contrast.

She thought about riding him on a hack. Just to clear her brain. But no. He'd had his test at Woodbine that morning, so she should let him rest. Evie's eyes fell on the little palomino quarterhorse. What about Christieloo? Aunt Mary had asked her to help. She'd said that the mare was a rescue and had some trust issues. Right up Evie's alley.

Evie felt her sluggishness wash away, replaced with purposeful energy. She jumped up and ran downstairs. "Aunt Mary?" There was no answer.

"Aunt Mary?" The house was empty. Evie saw a note on the wooden counter and picked it up.

Hi Evie. Didn't want to disturb you. Gone for groceries. Back soon. Study hard! Love, M

Evie looked outside and saw that her aunt's truck was gone. She was disappointed. Christieloo was a pretty little mare and in the few minutes since she'd hatched the idea, Evie had developed a huge desire to ride her.

No harm in taking a walk to get some fresh air before getting back to the books, she thought. *And it's never a bad idea to check the horses' water supply.*

Evie opened the back door. Three dogs popped up their heads and stood and stretched. Tails began to wag and six earnest eyes begged her to do something fun.

"Okay! Can't refuse this kind of pressure." She strolled down the slight slope feeling better and better with every breath. Magpie stayed at her side while Simon and Garfunkel raced into the woods.

As she neared the pastures, four horses raised their heads at the same time. They watched her approach calmly.

"Good day!" she called gaily. "How's the grass? Up to your liking?" Evie grinned and hopped a step, then two, then broke into a happy dance. She was so glad to be outside, away from her science books.

Now all the horses looked wary, which made her laugh.

"Never seen a happy dance before?" she asked aloud, gyrating with her arms waving and her feet prancing.

The horses snorted and shied away. Kazzam began to buck and off he ran. Evie got the message. Her enthusiasm seemed like aggression to them, so she reluctantly reined in her jubilance and settled down.

Evie climbed on the fence and watched for five minutes, until finally the horses were peaceful again. She'd disturbed their tranquility. Now their curiosity was taking over.

Horses are innately curious, Evie reflected. It was a trait she'd learned to use in training. Instead of going to them, if you were patient enough they would come to you.

Bendigo and Paragon ambled to the fence and sniffed her. By then, Kazzam had stopped caring. He was off by himself, busy grazing.

Christieloo hung back with Kazzam, curious but cautious. Evie patted Bendigo and Paragon, and scratched their ears. Five more minutes passed before they tired of the attention and returned to the grass. Magpie wearied of the inaction and wandered off to join the other dogs.

Now Christieloo approached. Her nostrils gently sniffed Evie's hand and breathed out warm, fragrant air. Evie admired the mare's thick white tail and glossy blond coat. She quietly touched the delicate skin on her nose and made soft cooing noises. Then she began to stroke her, first around her head and neck, then further back along her sides. Evie gradually climbed over the fence and stood beside her.

"How much do you know about people riding you?" Evie asked. "Aunt Mary knows but she's not here, so I'll have to find out for myself. With your help, Christieloo."

Evie kept the low, quiet chatter going while she took the halter from the fence and slipped it over the mare's ears. "Aunt Mary will be home soon, so she'll help, and soon we'll be hacking through the woods as happy as can be." She rubbed Christieloo's chest and stroked her legs all the way down to her feet.

"Do you know how to pick up your feet for a person?"

Evie held both front feet in turn and set them down. "Very good, sweet mare. Very good! We'll try the hind feet later, when someone else is here." Evie knew how easily horses are startled and that sometimes their first instinct is to kick out.

A lead line was looped over the fence beside the halters, and Evie took it. She snapped the clip on the left side of the halter, then tied the other end to the right side. "See, now we have reins," she whispered.

With one hand holding the halter, Evie leaned on Christieloo's back. The mare stepped away, but didn't seem bothered, so Evie tried again. She stepped up on a log and pushed down a little where the saddle would sit. The mare was interested in what was happening. Evie began to massage her back and could tell that it felt good, because

Christieloo lifted her upper lip and flipped it back, exposing her teeth, then began to make chewing motions. Evie persisted, and within minutes, the little palomino accepted Evie's entire weight. There she was, stomach down, feet dangling off the ground on one side and head and arms on the other, her body bent right over the mare's back.

Evie slid off, dropped to her feet, and praised Christieloo. "What a clever girl!"

She looked around. Aunt Mary still wasn't home. Should she continue? Why not?

Evie stood beside Christieloo's shoulders and faced forward. She held the right rein in her right hand and the left rein in her left, then began to walk with her. She steered her in circles until she was quite sure the mare knew what Evie meant when she pulled one way or the other. And then they worked on steering plus "whoa." Evie would stop her randomly with the voice command and a gentle tug.

"You know all this, don't you?" Evie said aloud. "I'm wasting your time, but how was I to know?"

Evie walked the mare over to the fence. She leaned over her back again and grabbed her mane with both fists. Careful to avoid startling her in any way, Evie slowly slid herself astride onto Christieloo's bare back. She sat there quietly, feeling the mare's uncertainty beneath her. The other horses were grazing on the far side of the next field, totally bored with her presence, and Kazzam didn't seem to care. If that changed, and if any of them came charging over, Evie would hop off. Quickly. All bets are off when a horse joins the herd. She'd keep an eye out for that.

She squeezed her legs together, just a little, and Christieloo moved forward. "Nice, girl! Well done." They walked in a big loop to the left, halted, and then walked in a big loop to the right. Evie asked her to do a large figure eight, and switched directions after stopping in the middle. "So you know walk, whoa, turn left and right. You know how to move away from my leg. What else do you know, Christieloo?"

Evie now urged the mare into a slow trot and then halted. "Very good!" Soon they were doing figure eights at a trot and halting whenever Evie asked.

"Have you ever cantered with a rider?" Evie asked the mare. "Is this the time to try?"

As soon as Christieloo was in a forward trot, making a large circle to the left, Evie put more leg on and sat down squarely. She tapped the mare's side with her right leg. Immediately Christieloo began to canter on her left lead. *More of a lope*, Evie thought. Quite easy to ride and very manageable, even bareback. They cantered in loops to the left, loops to the right, and when Evie decided to canter the figure eight, Christieloo swapped her leads perfectly.

"You're amazing!" called Evie. "Utterly amazing!"

"No kidding!" a voice answered from the fenceline.

"Aunt Mary!" Evie brought Christieloo to a halt and walked her over to the fence, all the while wondering how to explain. With a tough exam tomorrow, she really should not have been outside her room, let alone on a horse that she'd been told had problems. How much trouble was she in?

Aunt Mary's mouth was not smiling. Not a good sign.

"I know I should've waited. I'm sorry. I couldn't study because I'm too worried about Beebee and Jordie and mostly my mother, so I came outside just to breathe fresh air, then I sort of found myself thinking about riding Christieloo."

"I'm not mad, Evie. I'm quite pleased that you've made such progress. I had no idea how much Christieloo knew. I haven't been on her back yet."

"Really?" Evie slid to the ground and praised the mare. "Good girl, Christieloo. Good girl."

"The minute I put the bit in her mouth she started misbehaving. Her teeth have been checked and they're fine, so there's no problem there."

"I didn't use a bridle. Maybe the bit is her problem."

She removed the halter and rubbed her soft nose. As soon as Christieloo realized she was free, she spun and bucked, then trotted off to graze beside Kazzam, who welcomed her with a quiet nicker.

Evie turned back to her aunt. "But really? You haven't been on her back? She was so eager to be good. I love her!"

Aunt Mary smiled. "You have a wonderful way with horses, Evie. You're gentle with them. And patient. They trust you, and you teach them how to learn."

Evie felt herself blush. "Thanks, Aunt Mary. I thought you looked mad."

"You had me worried, I have to admit. You shouldn't have done this alone. You know that, don't you?"

Evie nodded. "I do. It might've gone wrong."

"And when it goes wrong, it goes wrong quickly. You might've gotten yourself, and this nice little mare, into serious trouble."

Evie dropped her head. She knew it was true. "I know. I'm sorry."

"Well, everything turned out fine. Just don't do it again. Or I *will* be mad. Very mad. Come help me unload the groceries. Do you know everything you need to know for your science exam?"

Evie whistled through her teeth unhappily. She'd felt so lighthearted while she was riding Christieloo, and now all that good feeling drained from her body.

Mary put her arm around her shoulders as they walked to the truck. "Can I help?"

Evie shook her head. "No. Unless you can tell me that Beebee and Jordie are okay and that my mother isn't lying doped up in a ditch." She shrugged theatrically, trying to lighten up the serious things she'd just listed. "That's all. And that my science exam is cancelled."

Aunt Mary picked up the theme. "Tall order. I'm not sure I can make those three wishes come true. How about some peanut butter with chocolate-chunk ice cream instead?"

Evie made an effort to put her worries aside and smiled. "It's worth a try."

They carried in the bags of groceries and put the food away. The dogs were underfoot, hoping for a spill or good will. Aunt Mary ordered them out. "Scat, ungrateful brutes," she said as she opened the door, then shut it behind them. "Give them an inch."

The phone rang. "I'll get it," said Mary. "You get your ice cream." She picked up the receiver. "Hello?"

Evie was scooping a generous amount of delicious-looking ice cream into a bowl when she glanced at her aunt and stopped in mid-scoop. Aunt Mary looked dumbstruck.

"Who is it?" whispered Evie.

Mary ignored her. "Why do you think she'd be here?" asked Mary. "Uh-huh. Well, she's not in."

Evie stepped closer and tried to hear. Mary pulled away and said into the phone, "I'd rather you didn't, actually. Thanks, and goodbye."

Evie waited expectantly.

"The press. It's that reporter, Chet Reynolds, who broke the story about Molly Peebles."

"What does he want?"

"What do they all want? A story."

"Didn't you tell me that one of the reasons people

are glad I'm racing is the publicity for the Queen's Plate? Molly Peebles, Kazzam, outlaw horse, all that?"

Mary nodded. "Yes, I did say that, didn't I?" She opened the fridge and placed the lettuce in the crisper. Then she straightened. "It was a reflex. I hate people nosing around, but you're right. This time, we *want* publicity. Even so, we can't appear too eager."

The phone rang again. Evie looked at her aunt. Mary nodded. Evie took a deep breath and picked up, expecting the reporter. "Hello?"

"Evie?" It was Beatrice.

"Beebee! Are you and Jordie okay? Where are you?"

"We're fine. Mom took us to Newmarket."

Beatrice sounded strong and impatient, to Evie's relief. Gone was the hesitant tone of her message.

"Is Sella there with you?"

"No, she's fired, but Mom has a, well, friend here and that's who we're living with."

"I was worried! Is everything okay?"

"If you're asking if I miss you, I don't."

Evie grinned. The old Beebee was back in full glory. "Can I talk to Jordie?"

Long seconds passed before Evie heard the little boy's voice. "Evie? I miss you. I made Beebee call the number Aunt Mary gave me."

"I'll see you soon, Jordie. I'll come visit, okay?"

"Come soon. Mom came to school and took us here. It's okay here. I thought you'd worry, but we're okay."

"You're a good boy, Jordie," said Evie, her eyes full of tears. "I *was* worried. Really worried, but now I'm not. Thanks for calling. Can I call you, too? Can I have your number?"

Beatrice came back on the line. She read out the number and then said, "Bye." The line went dead.

Evie hung up and turned to Aunt Mary. "I'm so glad they're okay. They're somewhere in Newmarket at a friend of Paulina's. At least they're safe."

The phone rang again. Mary and Evie were startled.

"Three in a row?" said Mary. "We're suddenly very popular. This time, I'll get it. Next time it's your turn." She answered the phone. "Hello? ... Yes, Chet. Evie just got in. She's right here." Mary held it out for Evie to take.

Evie put the carton of ice cream back in the fridge and took a big spoonful of chocolatey, peanuty deliciousness from her bowl. Mmm, it tasted good!

"Evie?" asked Mary, pointing at the receiver.

"Like you said," Evie said softly. "We can't appear too eager." She swallowed her mouthful and took the phone from her aunt.

"Hello Mr. Reynolds, this is Evie Gibb. Just a minute, please." Evie covered the receiver with her hand, stared at her aunt, and flicked her head. She couldn't pay attention with Mary's face right up to the phone.

"Sorry," whispered Aunt Mary. She walked over to the kitchen area and noisily began to prepare dinner.

"You're where? Here?" Evie looked out the kitchen door and there, through the door window, stood the reporter. "Persistent or something?" she asked, and hung up.

"Why'd you hang up on him?" asked Mary, bewildered.

Evie didn't answer. She walked to the door and opened it. "Chet Reynolds, meet Mary Parson. Mary Parson, meet Chet Reynolds."

Chet was average height and dark-haired. He'd shaved since Evie had talked to him at the Maple Mills gates and had either brushed his hair or got it cut. Whichever, he looked a lot more presentable than the last time she'd seen him, and he stood at the doorway, uncertain of his welcome.

Mary dried her hands and said, "Please come in, young man. Have a seat over there and I'll get you something. Tea? Coffee? Beer?"

"Thanks, Ms. Parson. I'd love some of that ice cream."

He smiled at Evie, who filled another bowl and took both bowls over to the sofa, where Mary had indicated. Chet sat down and said, "I won't take up much of your time."

Evie had to get a confession out of the way. "I was acting like a spoiled snob when I told you to go away before, you know? After the Caledon Race, at my father's farm?"

Chet nodded slowly. "You made a very believable rich brat. So, who are you really?"

Evie blushed. She always did it at the wrong time. "I'm just me. Evie Gibb. I would've been in deep trouble if my father found out I took Kazzam, so I had to lose you."

Chet laughed. "You didn't lose me, in spite of your act."

That remark made Evie angry. "Your story caused me a lot of trouble! I had to run away with Kazzam."

Chet nodded. "And you came here, to your Aunt Mary's? Have you always been close?"

"I'd never met her before. She's my mother's aunt, and she sent me a birthday card with a message —"

Mary interrupted as she set down a tray with coffee, a creamer, and sugar bowl. A few chocolate-chip cookies were on a plate beside the coffee. "Evie has a big exam tomorrow, Chet. We'll have to get to the point."

"Five minutes, ten max. As soon as I've finished this delicious ice cream. And a cookie. And a cup of coffee. It all smells great."

Mary sat down beside Evie. She took her hand and squeezed it. Evie glanced at her. Mary shook her head slightly and said, "Evie's sixteen years old, Chet. I'd like you to remember that when you write this piece. Can we keep family matters out of it?"

Chet took a spoonful of ice cream. "Very good," he said.

"You didn't answer my question."

"Family is the really interesting thing about this story."

"In that case, I hate to be rude, but this interview is over."

Evie sat up straight. "What about the story of the Queen's Plate and Canadian horse racing? Isn't that interesting? Established in 1860 by Queen Victoria. Great horses like Northern Dancer, Alydeed, and Izvestia cleaned up. Izvestia still has the fastest time ever at a mile and a quarter — two minutes, one and four-fifths seconds — in 1990."

She took a breath and went on, with some urgency. "Let me tell you what to write, Chet. This is the story of No Justice, a little black horse with a great heart, who never got a fair shake. He's ready to prove himself in Canada's most prestigious race, the first jewel in the Canadian Triple Crown, followed by the Prince of Wales and the Breeders' Stakes. No Justice is about to have justice served! Isn't that a great story?"

Chet and Mary stared at Evie. Chet began to smile. "A horse story." He set down his coffee cup. "Make you a deal. I'll write the horse story. If you win the Plate, you tell me the people story."

Evie didn't want Aunt Mary to tell her not to do this.

She stood up quickly. "Yes. That's a deal. But you have to tell the *right* horse story. I'll give you all the details. Kazzam's breeding, his training, his problems. And if you sneak in any personal stuff I don't like, the deal is off when we win."

"*If* you win."

"Right. If we win." Evie touched the wooden arm of her chair so she wouldn't jinx herself.

Chet considered this. "I'm not used to people writing my stories for me."

"I'm not used to talking to reporters *or* riding in the Queen's Plate."

"Point taken. We'll find our way as we go. What am I allowed to say about you in the first article?"

"Say whatever you like, just don't bring my family into it. Just yet."

Chet smiled at her again. "I'll do my part. For this to work for me, you can't talk to any other reporters about this. I want the story exclusively."

Evie shook his hand. "You have my word."

"I'm a witness," said Aunt Mary. She put her arm around Evie's shoulders. "Now scoot, Mr. Reporter. This girl has a big exam tomorrow."

"I'm gone," he said to Evie, and smiled knowingly. "I actually believe you might win. See you at the finish line."

19

Temptation

Evie woke up on Tuesday with the knowledge that she was about to fail her science final. Absolutely nothing had seeped into her brain, and she'd studied well into the night. She turned her head and looked at the clock on the bedside table. Six o'clock. The alarm was set for six-thirty.

Magpie lifted her head from her doggy bed beside Evie's and flapped her ears loudly. Her eyes were bright and intense, ready and eager to begin her day. Evie put her pillow over her head and tried to ignore her. The dog stood up and stretched herself from sleek head to long toes, then poked her nose under the pillow and nudged Evie in the cheek with her cool black nose.

"Go back to sleep."

Magpie wagged her slender tail and shook her ears again.

Evie gave in. "You need to go out. Aargh."

She and her dog tiptoed downstairs, only to find Aunt Mary already up, dressed, and sipping coffee.

"When do you sleep?"

Mary laughed. "I'm trying to finish a chapter. Can I get you some breakfast?"

Evie rubbed her eyes and worked her fingers through her tangled hair. "No. Thanks. I'll have a shower first." She let Magpie outside and climbed wearily back up the stairs.

Later, as Aunt Mary drove Evie to school, Evie was glum and uncommunicative, totally unready to face her exam.

Mary chatted as she drove. "I just spoke to Jerry. He's so nervous he makes me laugh. We can't exercise No Justice today since he raced yesterday, but tomorrow morning good and early we train. Okay?"

Evie nodded.

"This week is critical. No sprints, just easy gallops Wednesday, Thursday, and Friday. Saturday he gets off, and then Sunday is the big race. It's the eighth race of the day and it'll be run around five. Then we'll ship out."

Evie nodded again. She tried to stay miserable about her exam, but a little buzz of adrenaline was growing in her body. "Have you heard anything more about my mother?"

Mary frowned. "Not a thing. I'm driving to Toronto to look for her after I drop you off."

"What'll you do if you find her?"

"The usual. Give her some food and try to bring her home." Mary sighed. "I'll try. But she won't come unless she's ready. Same old story."

Thinking of Angela always succeeded in twisting Evie's gut. She changed the subject quickly. "Did Chet Reynolds write the story?"

Mary kept her eyes on the road. "After your exam this morning, we'll pick up a paper."

"You didn't go online?"

"Is that an accusation? I'm old, I get it. I'll learn how to do that another day."

Evie chuckled. "A little sensitive?"

"Get out there and ace your exam, will you?" Mary stopped the truck in front of the school and unlocked the doors. "Youth is a condition that only time can heal."

"Very funny." Evie hopped down. "See you in a few hours?"

"If I don't die of old age first."

Evie groaned but felt a tiny bit better. "Good luck with Angela." She waved to her aunt and entered the school. She couldn't lose her feeling of despair about the exam. Every time she tried to recall any facts, she drew a blank. This was going to be a massacre. A dismal zero.

Mark Sellers came around the corner as Evie opened her locker.

"Hey, Evie! Great story about your horse today!"

What? "You're kidding! What's it say?"

"Read it yourself." He produced a section of the *Brampton Expositor.* "It was in the *Globe and Mail,* too. I saw it online."

Evie couldn't help but wonder if Aunt Mary knew about the story all along but didn't want to distract her. Or maybe it was bad? Evie grabbed the newspaper from Mark.

It was just below the fold on the front page of the sports section, with a close-up of Kazzam. In bold print it read: "Will Justice be Served to No Justice?" She'd even written the headline!

"Great pic of the horse," said Mark. "He's a real black beauty."

"Let me read it," said Evie. Chet Reynolds had basically written the story just as Evie had wanted, with the focus on the history of the Queen's Plate and No Justice's life and racing career. It mentioned that he'd won the Caledon Horse Race under the assumed name of Kazzam with Molly Peebles aboard, and that Molly Peebles was actually

Evangeline Gibb, who would ride him this Sunday. It was all written according to the deal. And Mark was right about the picture of Kazzam. He looked impressive and regal, posing in Aunt Mary's field with the farmhouse in the background. Evie speculated that it had been taken by Chet before he came to the house.

"You read fast," said Mark when Evie looked up.

"But do I retain anything? That's the question, and I dread the answer I'll get in today's exam."

Mark took her hands in his. "You'll do great. Biology is all about animals and vegetation — zoology and botany — and you love that stuff."

"There's a difference between loving animals and being able to name their dissected body parts."

Mark laughed. "You're funny."

"I'm serious!"

"Come on, let's get going. It can't be as bad as you think."

Two hours later, Evie was finished the exam and looking around the huge, open room. Roughly eighty kids sweated over their papers on desks lined up in long rows in the gymnasium.

Mark was two rows over, writing away. He appeared workmanlike and confident. *He really is a cute guy,* she thought, *hunched over his desk in his white T-shirt and torn jeans. More hot than cute. His lips look so kissable....*

He glanced up and caught her eye. He smiled slowly.

Wow. Evie felt her face turn bright pink. She looked at Mark's strong arms with their smooth, rounded muscles, and wondered how it would feel to have them wrapped around her, tightly. Evie's entire body was drawn to him as if they were human-size magnets, and a film of sweat broke out on her skin. The longing in his eyes told her that the same was true for him.

Lordy. She looked away. With great difficulty Evie pulled herself back to the task at hand. There were still about ten minutes before the time was up, and she read over as much as she could. Unbelievably, her mind was less blank than she'd feared. Instead of a zero, she thought she'd passed, and on the high side might get a sixty or sixty-five. A miracle. She put down her pen when the bell rang.

The students shuffled and stretched as they handed their papers to the supervisor at the front of the room and filed into the hall.

Mark fell in behind her and hooked his arm through hers. Evie clutched his arm to her side with her elbow. She tried to walk steadily but thought her knees might give out. She noticed the wistful looks of other girls around her. Rebecca and Hilary slid by, and each of them gave her a thumbs-up with an unsubtle wink.

Evie tried not to giggle but couldn't restrain herself.

"What if we study for French together this afternoon?" Mark asked in her ear.

Evie's entire body tingled. "Great idea." She very much wanted to spend time with him. "Aunt Mary's outside waiting. Come to my house."

Mark looked around. He whispered, "I was thinking you could come with me. Nobody's home." His eyes pleaded.

Evie felt a thrill in her stomach. Mark's face was so close to hers. Her temperature rose dramatically. She couldn't think clearly. She wanted to go with him. She wanted to slip her arms around him and pull his face close to hers and feel his lips on hers. She'd never kissed a boy before, except in grade two, but that was on a dare and it didn't count.

Evie felt light on her feet. Mark's heat was melting her, and she very, very much wanted to go home with him. But what would she say to Aunt Mary, who'd be outside waiting? That thought brought her back to some form of sanity.

Summoning all her willpower, she forced herself to step back. "I don't think so. Do you mind? Another time?"

"Are you chicken?" His eyes sparkled.

"Chicken? What do you mean?"

"Do you think I'll do bad things?" He smiled so sweetly that Evie had a hard time resisting. Oh, it was so tempting.

"Define 'bad.'"

"You're flirting! Naughty girl."

Evie blushed and her underarms began to feel damp. She was out of her depth and starting to feel confused. "Look, I'd love to but I can't. Aunt Mary won't understand."

Mark grinned and raised his eyebrows. "Tell her that a bunch of kids are going. That we have a last-minute tutorial or an exam-prep session. Please?" He got close again.

Evie felt his warmth. "I … I don't know." She was torn. Aunt Mary might buy it. But she felt uneasy. Mark was the most popular guy in school. He could have any girl he wanted. Did he think she was just another one? Maybe she didn't know him well enough. "Sorry, Mark. I really am. I'll see you tomorrow, okay?" She pulled away awkwardly and felt like a total dork.

Evie walked out to the front steps, hoping Aunt Mary would be there waiting. She wasn't.

Mark Sellers came up beside her. "Evie?" His face looked defensive. "Are we still on for Saturday?"

Evie was startled. The prom. With everything else that was happening, she'd actually forgotten about it. "Yes!" She needed a dress. "But wait. You said *Saturday?*"

Mark nodded. "Yeah."

"The Queen's Plate is Sunday. I thought the prom was *after* the race, not the night before."

"And I thought the race was Saturday. Does it make a difference?"

"Yeah. It does. A lot. I can't go out the night before the race. It's actually a really big deal. I didn't realize, Mark." Evie felt her entire social life collapse. "I screwed up. I'm sorry."

"So you're not coming to the prom with me?"

Now she was miserable. "I can't. I'd love to, but I really can't. There's so much to do before the race and I need a good sleep."

"You're ditching me?" Mark looked genuinely shocked.

"No! I'm trying to tell you. I need to focus on the race. I have to give it all my attention. It's the highlight of my life! Can we go out Sunday night? There's no school on Monday."

Mark became insistent. He grabbed her hands with his and drew her close. "Then come with me now. We'll study French, and ... I just want to, you know, get to know you better."

Evie tried to regain her composure, but it was no good. Her brain was whirling. She felt the patches of sweat grow on her shirt, and she didn't want him to notice. She just wanted to go home. "I'd like that, too. But I'm sorry, Mark. It's too soon. Not today."

"You're really not coming?" asked Mark. He looked so surprised that it confirmed to Evie that most other girls would've gone home with him. Which made her dig in her heels even more. She refused to be just another girl!

"I can't." It was easy now.

His lips got tight. "You're mad."

"I'm not mad. I'm just not coming."

"No prom and you're not coming today? Your choice." Mark looked annoyed.

"My choice."

The familiar truck stopped at the steps and Aunt Mary waved. *Thank heaven!* Evie raced down the steps and jumped in, leaving Mark standing alone.

"Anything wrong?" asked Aunt Mary.

"No. If you don't count wrecking my entire social life."

"How did you manage that?"

"Mark Sellers asked me to the prom and I said yes. For some reason I thought it was after the race, but it's before. I can't go to a dance the night before the Queen's Plate!" She slumped. "He doesn't understand what a big deal this race is for me. I told him I can't go."

"Ouch."

"That's not all. He wants me to study French with him this afternoon and I said no to that, too."

"If you want, I can drive back and pick him up."

Evie wondered how much to tell her, but confessed, "He doesn't want to come to our house. He wants me to go to his house. And nobody's home."

"Oh."

They drove along in silence.

"Great article in the paper today," said Mary. "Exactly as you laid it out." She tried to coax a smile from Evie.

"It was super. I read it, too." She looked out the window. "Anything new about my mother? Did you find her?"

"No luck. She's not where she usually is and nobody's seen her. Or that's what they say."

"That's not good. I sure hope she's okay."

"Mmm. Me, too."

Nothing else was said all the way home. When they drove up the Parson's Bridge driveway, Jerry Johnston's truck was in full view.

"I'm glad he's here," said Mary. "We have a lot of details to work out before the race."

Jerry stood in front of his truck, glowering.

Evie said, "What's up with him?"

Mary shook her head. "We're about to find out." She stopped her truck and got out, immediately swarmed by dogs.

Evie jumped out and the dogs turned to her with their outpouring of affection. "Hello pups," she said. Magpie leaped up and licked her right on the mouth. "Thanks, Mags. At least I got kissed by someone who loves me."

She was startled by an outburst from Aunt Mary. "I don't believe it! What a cad!"

That got Evie's full attention.

Mary turned to face her. "Evie, your father has vetoed No Justice running. He called Jerry right after he saw the article. He's furious."

Vetoed No Justice?

"What does that mean?"

To judge from the look on her aunt's face, it was certainly not a good thing.

"He refuses to let us enter him, Evie. No Justice cannot be entered in the Queen's Plate."

"I thought he already was!" Evie was confused.

Jerry took off his cap and combed his hair back with his fingers. "No Justice was nominated and renewed, but he must be officially entered before the draw on Thursday."

"The draw?"

"For the post order. There's a draw to see which horse goes in which slot. And a ten-thousand-dollar fee, to be paid that day."

Evie's head was reeling. "But my father said we could go ahead and knock ourselves out!"

"He changed his mind."

"But what about yesterday? Racing three other horses with judges and all that? Getting approved as an apprentice jockey? Lifting the ban on Kazzam?"

Jerry looked sad, and also frustrated and angry. "Waste of time."

Evie sat right down in the dirt. *Impossible*. How many things could go wrong in one day? A day that was still far from over.

"What do we do now?" she asked. She looked up at Mary and then at Jerry.

Jerry pursed his lips. "Nothing we can do. Grayson's call. It's over. The son of a bitch."

"Aunt Mary?"

Mary bit her lip. She looked down at Evie as she sat on the ground and shrugged dismally. "No Justice is technically his horse. He makes the decisions. We save our ten thousand dollars, I guess."

Jerry nodded gloomily. "Silver lining."

"But we don't win the million!" Evie couldn't believe it. She got to her feet and brushed herself off. "Are you both giving up?"

Mary reached out to comfort her. "At least you can go to the prom now with Mark."

Evie was taken aback. "Are you joking? He's probably already asked somebody else. I can't believe it! We've been working so hard and Kazzam is totally fit and ready to run!"

Jerry and Mary looked at each other sadly. It was apparent that Evie was on her own.

"It's your fault, anyway!" she howled. "You wouldn't buy him after Murray Planno brought him back!"

She stomped off to the house with Magpie right behind her. She climbed the stairs and flopped angrily onto her bed. *What would Imogene do?* she wondered. *She'd fight to the end. But how? Plead with Grayson Gibb?* Evie imagined his surly face and could hear his high-pitched, growly voice tell her she was full of it.

Just a minute! In the hospital her mother had said that she owned all the horses. She sat up. *What if that was true?* Dare she believe it?

Evie raced down the stairs at full tilt, knocking into Aunt Mary at the bottom. Her aunt fell to her knees, then struggled to her feet.

"What's going on, dear?" Mary asked, aghast, brushing herself off.

"I'm sorry! I'm so sorry!" Evie helped her stand. "My mother said she owned all the Maple Mills racehorses. Is that true?"

Mary thought for a second, then walked over to her computer and turned it on. "Angela did say that, didn't she. Let me check."

Evie sat at her side, trembling with anticipation.

"Okay, here we are. No Justice, owned by Maple Mills Stables, sole proprietor — sorry, Evie — Grayson Gibb."

20

703556 Ltd.

Bright and early Wednesday morning, Evie saddled up and walked Kazzam to the training field. Aunt Mary was still in bed. Jerry was nowhere to be seen. They'd think she was crazy to continue training, but what if she found a way to race, against all odds, and Kazzam wasn't fit?

She asked him to canter and then let him breeze. It felt so good to be riding him, so wonderful to be out in the June morning air with nothing around her except fields and horses and dear Magpie, sitting on the edge of the field, head tilted, watching them work. No humans in sight. No Mary and Jerry, who'd given up without a fight. No confusing Mark Sellers. Nothing but animals and bliss.

Kazzam lengthened his stride and began to run. Evie lifted herself out of the saddle and leaned on his neck. The fresh, cool breeze whipped past her, billowing her T-shirt and pulling tight the skin on her face. This was heaven.

Once the training run was over, they walked the mile path through Aunt Mary's woods. This is what Magpie waited for each day. Her sleek, black dog darted and dashed through underbrush, chasing down every scent, returning to check on Kazzam and Evie every minute or so, wriggling with delight.

When they returned to the barn for Kazzam's hosing down and breakfast oats, nobody disturbed them. It was a very peaceful time of day. As she soaped the bridle, Evie saw her contented smile reflected in the small mirror that hung on the tack-room door. She was always happy in the barn.

She led Kazzam back out to his field and released him.

Immediately the horse sought out a patch of dirt. He circled, buckled his knees, and dropped to the ground to roll. "Have a good scratch," she told him. "Bet that feels good." She watched while he rubbed his back in the dirt and groaned with pleasure. He flopped on his right side, then rolled over again onto his left. When he was good and ready, he stood and shook himself all over, spraying wet dirt and dust in a wide halo. Then he casually walked away without a backward glance.

Evie and Magpie headed up the gentle slope to the farmhouse. It was nearing nine o'clock. This afternoon was French, her second-last exam, and math tomorrow. Then she'd be free! She'd studied thoroughly for French and planned to review her verbs and vocabulary all morning.

Aunt Mary stood at the kitchen door with the telephone receiver in her hand. "Evie?" she called. "What's the number of Paulina's friend?"

Evie ran to the house. "Is something wrong?"

"The school wants to contact Beatrice and Jordie."

Evie found the piece of paper on which she'd jotted down the number and gave it to her aunt, who read it aloud.

"Please let me know if there's anything else you need," Mary said. "I'd like to help if I can." She hung up the phone. "So?"

223

"I'm going to Abergrath to talk to the principal myself. I can't interfere too much since I'm not family, but neither Grayson nor Paulina can be reached." She looked perturbed. "The kids haven't shown up for school since Paulina picked them up last week."

Evie reassured her. "You do know, Aunt Mary, that Paulina isn't exactly the responsible kind. She's probably forgotten all about school."

"School's almost over, anyway," Mary conceded.

Evie nodded. "And they don't have exams in those grades."

Mary sighed. "Let's hope you're right. Better not buy trouble."

"Especially when it's free."

Mary laughed. "Okay, then. You go study and I'll zip over to visit the principal. Have some breakfast. See you later."

Mary was gone, leaving Evie alone with the dogs in the house. It was a lovely, sunny day, and she hummed as she sliced a banana into her cereal and poured on the milk.

She'd gallop Kazzam tomorrow and the next day. Saturday he was to have off and Sunday was the big day. The question was how to get him back in the race. She needed to think.

Aunt Mary's computer sat on her desk. It wouldn't hurt to check a few things herself. She ate her cereal as she surfed and searched.

Evie had googled her mother in her quest to find her, but never thought to try "Angela Parson," only "Gibb."

When she googled "Angela Parson," she got the whole history of her schooling, racing, and training career, including her horrible accident and hospitalization. It was noted that she was an heiress of considerable wealth.

Evie then tried "Angela Gibb," but now she was

looking for something different. On a very boring page of numbers and business references that Evie didn't understand, Angela was listed as sole owner of a privately held company called 703556 Ltd. The president was Grayson Gibb. Evie printed out this page, then sat back to think.

It was not impossible that within this company were the horses. Grayson Gibb was the sole proprietor of Maple Mills Stables, but Angela was the owner of the numbered company. Evie went back to work, but try as she might she couldn't get any details of the contents of this company. It was private and therefore all the assets were private, too.

But here at least was hope! If the company owned the horses and Angela was the owner, not Grayson Gibb, could Angela overrule his wishes?

Then Evie slumped, discouraged. Even *if* she was the owner of the horses and even *if* she wanted to overrule her ex-husband, how could Evie find Angela when Aunt Mary had failed?

Evie went back to her French studies. She was ready to go when Mary returned to drive her to school.

Once in the truck, Evie asked, "So what happened at Abergrath?"

"Nothing. They tried the number you gave me and left a message. Apparently they're staying with somebody named Kerry Goodham."

Evie groaned. "I should've known."

"Why? Who is he?"

"You know, the hot young hunter-trainer who teaches Paulina. Remember? The one Jordie and Beebee told us about when Sella was fired for not tattling?"

"Oh, yes." Mary rolled her eyes. "I forgot his name. People make such dumb choices sometimes."

"He *is* nice, though. Far nicer than my father."

"Hmm." After a couple of minutes, Mary asked, "Are you ready for this exam?"

"Yup. *Je pense que oui.*"

"*Bon.*"

"Oh, I used your computer this morning. I hope you don't mind."

"Not at all."

"I'll show you later, but maybe Angela owns the horses, after all. There's a company called 703556 Ltd., and she's the sole owner. My father is the president."

Mary raised her eyebrows and glanced at Evie. "Oh? I'll check it out. But please, Evie, don't hold your breath. The race is in three days. Grayson Gibb always dots his *i*'s and crosses his *t*'s. I can't believe there's anything we can do about it."

Evie decided not to argue. "Thanks for the lift."

"I've got some errands to run and I'll pick you up at three-thirty, okay?"

"*Merci beaucoup. A bientôt.*" Evie jumped out and went up the steps with her French books under her arm. She kept her eyes down and successfully avoided bumping into Mark. He was likely doing the same thing, which was okay with her.

The exam went well, which was one good thing. Evie checked it over before handing it in and waited on the front steps in the sun for her aunt.

She felt tense, nervous that Mark might show up. What could they say to each other? It was over before it began. She felt stupid. He was only toying with her, anyway. After yesterday, she had good reason to believe he thought she was easy. He thought he could take her home, do what he wanted, and throw her out, and that made her feel sick. Heartsick.

School was almost out for the summer. She should be feeling joyful. Instead, she was close to tears.

Mary's white truck appeared and Evie ran for it. "Home free," she said, her laugh one of relief.

"You can run but you can't hide," said Aunt Mary. She indicated the person who'd emerged from a small blue compact car in the parking lot and was striding quickly toward the truck.

"Do you think he saw me?" asked Evie, ducking.

"Yes, I do. He was watching out for you. Time to face the music, sweetie."

Evie sat up. She steeled herself and looked out her window.

Mark stood there with a very serious expression on his face. "Uh, I've been thinking, Evie. I was an idiot yesterday. I want to start again."

He actually looked nervous, Evie thought. *Good*.

"There's no school tomorrow. Thursday. Can we go out? See a movie, maybe? Grab a burger?"

Mary nudged her.

Evie wasn't ready yet to jump at the offer. "And then go to your house?" she tested.

"No!" Mark's eyes looked startled. He blushed, and Evie's heart leaped at his honest reaction. "I'm sorry about yesterday. I was disappointed, that's all." He actually blushed more deeply, to Evie's growing delight. "You're not like other girls."

"I guess you're not like other boys, too, which I worried about after yesterday." Evie smiled to lessen the sting of her words. Then she conceded, "I was wrong about the day of the prom and I'm sorry, too."

"I feel a whole lot better now." Mark's lovely, slow smile grew on his face. He bobbed his head a little.

"Me, too. And it might turn out that I'm not riding in

the Queen's Plate, anyway. Maybe I'll be free on Saturday night, after all."

"What happened?"

"Long story."

"Tell me tomorrow. I'll call you later to make a plan."

"Deal." Evie gave him a quick wave goodbye as Mary drove out of the lot.

"Well, that's a turnaround," Mary said.

Evie bounced on the seat. "Whoo-hoo!"

"And I'm glad to see you're accepting the inevitable."

"About what?"

"About the Queen's Plate. It's Grayson's decision and there's nothing to be done."

"Did you check out that company — 703556 Ltd.?"

"I did. It's nothing but a holding company for tax purposes. Grayson is the president and sole beneficiary."

"But Angela is the owner?"

"It's in her name, but Grayson has power of attorney."

Evie was glum. "You found out all that?"

Mary nodded. "I'm sorry."

Evie looked out the window and blindly watched the countryside go by. Was this the end of her Queen's Plate dreams?

"Why don't you ride Christieloo again this afternoon? I'll ride Paragon. We'll go for a hack."

Evie tried to smile. "Sure. Sounds like fun."

"No Justice needs some time off, and then we can start to retrain him as a jumper or a trail horse."

"That's if my wonderful father doesn't give him away."

Mary inhaled sharply. "He wouldn't do that."

Evie snorted. "Right."

"Evie, listen to me. I understand your disappointment, but you must let this go. No Justice is not running on Sunday. Make the best of it. Go to the prom with Mark. He seems like a good guy."

That gave Evie a great idea.

Mary and Evie went for their hack that afternoon. Evie was thrilled with Christieloo. The little mare was safe and reliable and a great riding horse. Whatever her problems, they were in the past, Evie thought. Possibly it was as simple as the mare not liking her former owners. And it was clear Christieloo and Kazzam were very good friends, and just like people, horses are happy when they like their companions.

Like her and Mark, Evie thought, and smiled. She didn't know him well yet, but she liked what she knew so far. *A lot.*

That evening, Evie thought it was time to put her great idea into effect. All the chores were done. Mary was typing away at her computer, engrossed in her next book.

Unnoticed, Evie snuck upstairs with the phone. "Mark? It's Evie. Can you get your mother's car tomorrow? Early?"

21

Secret Mission

Mark Sellers arrived at Parson's Bridge at exactly seven-thirty Thursday morning. Evie watched him stop the little blue car in front of the farmhouse.

She threw open the kitchen door and called, "You're just in time!" She ran down the path toward him, and was so excited that she skipped a step.

"Are you skipping?" Mark asked.

"I always skip when I'm happy." Evie laughed. She hadn't realized it until that moment.

He grinned. "I'm happy to see you, too, and very curious about your secret plan. Where are we going?"

"I'd like to bring along my dog, Magpie, if it's okay."

Mark gave her a sidelong look. "Sure. Any other little surprises?"

"You never know." Evie smiled brightly.

"So? When are you going to fill me in?"

"As soon as we're out of here."

Mark raised his eyebrows. "Then we better get going."

Within minutes they were on the road, with Magpie happily lying on a blanket on the back seat.

"Okay? Are you going to tell me what we're doing

and where we're going? Might be a good idea, since I'm the driver," Mark said.

"Keep going southeast," answered Evie. "First, let me give you the background. My father nominated No Justice, you know, the horse I call Kazzam, for this year's Queen's Plate. I won't bore you with all the details, but when he read Chet Reynolds's article in the paper on Monday, he decided not to let him run."

"So, no race for your horse?"

"No race. Aunt Mary and Jerry Johnston, the trainer, have given up. They don't want to hear any more about it. But when I met my mother — and that's another long story — she told me that she owned all my father's racehorses, including No Justice."

Mark glanced at her. "And so? Go on."

"So, I want to find my mother again and get her to help."

"So you called her?"

"No. I have to talk to her in person."

"And that's why I have my mother's car? To drive you where?"

"Toronto."

Mark pulled over to the side of the road. "Evie, do you know how much gas that'll take? My mother'll kill me."

"I'll pay for the gas. I have a whole lot of money. Kazzam and I won it in the Caledon Horse Race." She pulled several fifty-dollar bills from her pocket. "See?"

Mark whistled at the sight. "Do you have an address?"

"The corner of Spadina and Queen."

"Hmm." Then he nodded. "Okay. Off we go!" Mark drove south on Highway 410 toward the 401. "Tell me all about this mother of yours, Evie. I'm a little curious, and we've got an entire hour to kill."

Evie wasn't at all sure she wanted to tell him, but once she got started, the whole story came out. Paulina and her flirtations, Grayson the control freak, Angela slipping away from the hospital and living on the street, Beatrice and Jordie, finding Aunt Mary. Listening to her story, Evie realized how odd it must sound. "I'm not making this up, Mark."

He snorted. "No chance! Truth is stranger than fiction and this is really strange." He glanced at her. "I'm not judging, Evie. I didn't mean that. It's just...."

"I know. Your family's normal."

"Normal? What does that mean? We're normal on the outside, I guess, but my dad lost his job and my mom is a retired nurse and she's trying to get a spa set up in the garage as a business. There's a lot of stress. They argue all the time, and my sister thinks they're getting a divorce."

Evie felt sympathy for him. Stress at home was very familiar to her. "I'm sorry."

"Thanks. I'll need to know which exit to take. What's her address?"

"She lives on the street, remember?"

"Oh. Actually, the street."

"Well, that's not clear. Aunt Mary said she shares a place with some people, but she always finds her on the street. More accurately, Angela shows up if she wants to be found."

"Am I ready for this?"

Evie shook her head. "Probably not. I know I'm not, but it's my last chance."

"Why did you bring Magpie? Am I allowed to know?"

"You'll see. Easier than explaining."

They parked Mark's mother's car in the same lot Aunt Mary had parked before. Evie put Magpie on the leash and bought a ticket at the machine.

"Okay. Last time we were here, Aunt Mary and I walked that way." Evie pointed west along Queen Street. "Then we had lunch in that little restaurant. When we came out my mother appeared from that alley beside it."

Mark shuddered. "Spooky. Do you want to try it again?"

"Might as well. It worked last time."

They walked along the street. Mark seemed intrigued with the noise and pace of life in Toronto. "I'm glad we came," he said. "Whether we find her or not, it's great to hang out."

"I'm glad you feel that way. Okay, this is the restaurant and that's the alley. Keep walking. She might be watching."

"What? That's kind of creepy."

"Just keep walking."

Mark and Evie strolled past the restaurant. There were small tables set outside, full of people eating breakfast and enjoying their coffee. They stopped at the lights at Spadina.

"Why don't we check out a few stores and go another block?" suggested Evie. "If my mother is following, that'll give her time to think about talking to us."

"This is really odd."

Evie laughed. "You think?"

"I've never known anyone with a street mother before." His words were meant to be jovial, but Evie heard his unease.

"Just wait'll you meet her," warned Evie. "This'll be a whole new experience for you."

"Look, I'm fine with it, really, but just say the word and we're out of here."

"I know exactly what you're saying. Trust me, I felt the same when Aunt Mary and I were here. But she's really quite nice. I mean, she has some odd mannerisms, but I don't want you to worry. She doesn't bite. Except her nails."

"Good to know."

One block west of Spadina, Magpie began to wag her tail. She started to whine.

"What is it, girl?" Evie knelt and rubbed the dog's ears.

Magpie pulled the leash out of Evie's hands and dashed between two stores.

"Magpie!" Evie called. The dog was gone.

Mark started to follow, but Evie held him back. "Give it a minute, Mark."

They waited on the street. Sure enough, Magpie reappeared with company. Angela.

She had her hand on Magpie's back as they walked toward them. The cut on her head was oozing a little through the stitches, but her hair was brushed and it looked to Evie that she'd made a quick effort to look respectable. She was unsteady on her feet, however, and Evie wondered if she might be in need of food.

"Hi, Mom," she said, as if this was a daily occurrence, and picked up Magpie's leash. "I'd like you meet a friend of mine. Angela Parson Gibb, this is Mark Sellers."

"Very nice to meet you, Mark." Angela spoke softly. She scratched at her arm. Evie noticed a strong smell of stale tobacco.

Mark was very tense. Evie nudged him.

"Hello!" he shouted. "Nice to meet you, too!"

Angela smiled. Evie saw the glint in her eye. Angela missed nothing. She knew how shocking this was for Mark.

"I really need to talk to you, Mom. Do you want to have breakfast with us?"

Mark glanced at Evie in horror. Evie grabbed his arm and pinched it hard.

Angela tilted her head. "I'd love to."

They made their way back to the little café. Luckily, a couple was leaving and there was an empty table outside. Evie procured it before the table was cleared and tied Magpie to a chair.

"Perfect," she said. She gestured at Mark and Angela. "Sit down, please!"

The waiter brought out a menu, gaped at Angela, and then quickly disappeared. Evie saw him speaking with animation to an older, stout man behind the counter. It was clear that they were about to tell them to leave.

Evie considered how Aunt Mary might handle this. She would be friendly and respectful, but assertive. Most of all, she would not want Angela to be embarrassed. With her back straight, Evie stood up. "Excuse me for a minute?"

Mark stared at her, asking for help with his eyes.

"I'll be right back. Promise."

She went into the restaurant and approached the two men. "That's my mother out there. The faster we're served, the quicker we'll be gone."

The man behind the counter twisted his mouth. His eyes repeatedly glanced to their table and back. "We don't serve street people. Bad for business. It's policy."

Evie pulled out a one-hundred-dollar bill, then scanned the menu on the wall. "One cheese omelette, three assorted sandwiches — chicken, ham, tuna — and three chocolate milks. Plus one coffee with milk to go and three orange juices." She placed the hundred on the counter. "Keep the change." Then she added politely, "And get those dirty dishes off the table now, please?"

Evie sat down again with Mark and Angela, and stroked Magpie's silky ears. "Breakfast is on the way."

The waiter quickly followed her out. He hurriedly removed the dishes and wiped the table clean.

"Nice work," said Mark with admiration.

Evie nodded her thanks and inwardly thanked Aunt Mary for her inspiration.

"Mark was just telling me that Grayson refuses to enter No Justice," said Angela. She coughed her smoker's cough.

Mark nodded. "She got right down to business and asked me why we came today." He looked at Angela with respect.

"He's a smart young man, Evangeline." Angela returned his approving gaze for a second, then looked away.

Evie raised an eyebrow. "You two hit it off rather quickly!"

"Seems so," Angela agreed.

Evie leaned forward. "And yes, that's exactly the reason I needed to find you."

The omelette came, soon followed by a platter of sandwiches. Angela began eating the omelette. "Go ahead, Evangeline. Tell me all about it. I'll listen while I eat. I'm very hungry. Mark? Please join me."

Angela finished her eggs and began working on the sandwiches with Mark. Evie was pleased that her mother's appetite was so good and told her the entire story.

"So that's it, Mom."

Angela sat back, cradling the hot coffee in both hands. Her colour was much improved, and she seemed to grow stronger by the minute. "This is simple."

Evie sat up straight. "Really? I'm all ears." She waited until Angela had lit a cigarette and taken a deep pull.

"There's a brown leather box containing my legal papers, my will, and other important things. It's in the stables at

Maple Mills. It's plastered in behind the wall of the feed room, under the table along the eastern wall."

"The table where we clean the tack?"

"Yes. Knock low on the wall. You'll hear the empty spot. But do it privately and don't get caught. Don't stay to fill the hole. It's under the table and nobody will notice right away." She chewed on a nail and then took another puff.

"Okay." Evie wasn't sure that she could sneak in and out with the box, without detection. But she would try.

"In the box are the ownership papers for 703556 Ltd. Listed are all the assets, including the horses."

"Is No Justice listed?" asked Evie hopefully.

"No. The company was formed long before he was born, but Grayson still keeps all the racehorses in this company." She scratched her head and ground out her cigarette. "Take the box and all the contents to Aunt Mary's house for safekeeping."

"I will."

"Now find some paper for me to write on. Please."

Evie jumped up and ran into the restaurant. The owner and waiter were still peering at them through the window. She came out with paper and a pen, and placed them on the table.

"Give me a minute, kids."

Evie and Mark watched while Angela fidgeted and squirmed. Then she carefully wrote out her intention to enter No Justice in this year's Queen's Plate. Her jaw worked constantly and her foot tapped relentlessly. Finally, she signed it. "This should do. Get J.J. on this right away. I've named him trainer. You'll likely get a fight from Grayson, but disregard him. I've overridden his authority."

"Thank you so much," said Evie. She was astonished at how capable her mother was. And how knowledge-able. "Do we take this to the stewards?"

"Give it to the stewards at Woodbine the Thursday before the race. In the morning, before the draw."

"Today is Thursday!" said Evie, aghast. "Is it too late?"

"What time is it?"

Mark checked his watch. "Quarter to ten."

"Go now. Right to Woodbine. Remember, this is a legal document. It will allow Jerry to enter No Justice." She pointed to the last paragraph. "And this serves as a voucher for the $10,000 entry fee from my company, 703556 Ltd. Do it now."

"What about the box from your hiding place?"

Angela stared at Evie purposefully. "Listen to me carefully. Go to the indoor Walking Ring at Woodbine. Right away, call J.J. to meet you. Call Aunt Mary, because No Justice needs to come, too. He'll need to be there from the time of entry, today, under guard, until after the race."

"And the leather box?"

"It's not essential today, but bring it on Sunday. They might need documentation, but more importantly my company cheques are in it."

Mark and Evie looked at each other. Evie was begin-ning to feel overwhelmed about getting this done within an hour. She stood. "Are you sure that's everything we need to know?"

"Yes. Now, you must be going. Lovely meal. Thanks." Angela winced as she stood.

"Are you okay, Mom?"

"Yes, dear. I got up too fast."

"Come home with us, please? To Aunt Mary's?"

Mark agreed. "Yes. Right now. I've got a car."

"I'm not ready yet. Soon. Scoot, now. Goodbye."

"One thing first, Mom." Evie held her arm. "We need to look after that cut on your head. I think it's infected."

"I'll go to a walk-in clinic."

"No, you won't, and you know it. Mark, please take her to that bus shelter with Magpie?" She pointed.

Angela resisted. "You don't have time."

"Sit there with Mark. I'll be right back."

Before Angela could say another thing, Evie dashed to the Shoppers Drug Mart on the corner. She returned in a couple of minutes with a small bag. Mark and Magpie and Angela were seated in the empty bus shelter. Angela was smoking. Several people stood impatiently outside, waiting for the streetcar, obviously avoiding them.

Mark grinned. "Best way I know to clear a seat."

Angela smiled wryly. "Happens all the time."

"Works for me." Evie took the disinfectant and gauze out of the bag and went to work. Angela tightened her lips together and grabbed the bench so firmly that her knuckles went white. When the job was done to Evie's satisfaction, she smeared antiseptic cream over the wound and covered it securely with a new bandage. "Done." She handed the ointment and spare bandages to Angela. "Keep it clean and put this on it three times a day."

"Thank you. Now go. Quickly. But drive safely." Angela gracefully rose and then leaned down to pat Magpie. For a second Evie glimpsed the shadow of a beautiful woman.

Magpie stretched her neck as high as she could and made her little throat noise. "You're a dear dog," said Angela. "And so well behaved. But next time, wait until I'm ready for company before you find me."

Evie and Mark laughed at her unexpected sense of humour.

"And thanks for not mentioning my escape from the hospital. Now scoot!" she said. Then, as quickly as she'd appeared, she was gone.

Mark and Evie, with Magpie on the leash, returned to the car with haste. They didn't have much time. Mark backed out of his spot and waited impatiently for an opening in the heavy traffic before driving onto Queen Street.

"I like the big city, but this is why we live in the country," he said. "So many cars! It's frustrating."

"Can I borrow your cell?" asked Evie. "Since you're the reason I threw mine out?"

"Will you never forgive me?" Mark grinned and handed her the phone. Evie made the required calls.

The first was to Jerry. It rang four times, then went to message. Evie spoke quickly. "Hi, Jerry. It's Evie. I just met with my mother. She wrote something and signed it. We're racing! I need you to get to the Woodbine walking ring ASAP and get Kazzam to Woodbine. Call me back right away on this cell."

She pressed the numbers for Aunt Mary. Again, no answer. She left a similar message. "I hate it when this happens!" she growled.

"Don't worry. They'll call back. We'll get to Woodbine and hope for the best."

Evie threw herself back into the seat and tried to relax. The traffic cleared a bit when they reached the Gardiner Expressway, and moved very well as they headed north on Highway 427.

"We're almost there and they haven't called back!" Evie wailed. She felt like screaming.

"Cool down," said Mark. "They'll call." He glanced at her. "Your mother surprised me, Evie."

"Are you trying to distract me?"

"Yes." He smiled. "She's quite smart. She really knows her stuff. And she's a good person."

Evie was on edge and a little defensive. "Why are you surprised? Just because she became an addict doesn't make her more stupid or less nice."

"I didn't mean to insult her. I just meant...." He seemed to struggle for words.

Evie softened. She had such mixed emotions herself. "You're trying to say that you didn't expect a street person to be so with it and lucid?"

"I guess. I expected a drug-addled, crazy person who smells bad and yells a lot."

Evie thought about it. "She does that, too, I guess, at times. She ran out on the street last week, asking people in cars for money to buy drugs."

"Is that when she got hit?"

"Yeah. And she doesn't smell too bad, but soap would help."

"Soap always helps." Mark turned right on Rexdale Blvd. "Now I know why we brought Magpie along."

"Great sniffer on her." Evie chuckled. "Okay, it's quarter to eleven and we're here. And speaking of Magpie, she can't be seen or we'll be kicked out."

22

The Draw

Mark looked for some trees to park the car under, but the entire Woodbine parking lot was bathed in sunlight and full of cars. The draw was obviously a big deal.

"Where's best for Magpie?" he asked.

Evie reached into the back seat and stroked her silky ears. The dog gazed back with adoration shining in her eyes. "Over there." She pointed to the only patch of shade, cast by a tall television truck. "We'll leave the windows down to let in the breeze. It's not too hot, and we won't be long." She poured a bottle of water into a dish and put it on the floor of the back seat.

Mark parked in a remote corner. "Let's hope she doesn't bark."

"My biggest problem is how to get Kazzam entered if Jerry doesn't show up." Evie got out of the car, holding the letter her mother had written. She put it in her pocket.

"Can't you do it yourself, with that letter?"

"No. The owner or the trainer has to enter him, and Jerry's the trainer. Obviously, my mother can't."

Mark nodded as he clicked the locks shut. "Where's the Walking Ring?"

"Right over there." Evie pointed to the left of the

covered walkway that led to the big building.

Mark and Evie ran across the cinder path where the horses walk out to race. They entered the indoor Walking Ring. It was packed with people who'd been there since nine that morning, and the party was well under way. There was a definite tingle of excite-ment in the atmosphere. Everybody but the two of them was dressed up, and they were the youngest in the room.

Evie checked her pocket again to make sure she had Angela's letter. She clutched Mark's hand. "Jerry and Aunt Mary still haven't called. I'm going over to Murray Planno and ask him to help."

"Who's Murray Planno?"

Evie pointed across the crowd. "A steward. In the plaid jacket and crazy vest."

"I'm coming with you."

A buffet table loaded with a great variety of delicious-smelling food stood along the far wall, and Murray was there loading his plate and chatting with a group of men who were all laughing at something he'd said. He was the King of Woodbine, holding court.

As they approached, one of the men turned around. It was Jerry. She hadn't recognized him without his hat.

"Mark! There! It's Jerry!" Evie exclaimed.

Jerry caught her eye and elbowed his way right to her. "Evie. Got your message."

Evie told him about their trip to Toronto and what her mother had said.

Jerry nodded excitedly. "That's what we hoped!"

"But I need Kazzam to be here, too, and Aunt Mary hasn't called me back!"

Jerry patted her shoulder and grinned. "Under control. Now give me that letter your mother wrote. I hope it'll do."

Evie handed it over and watched while he read it.

Jerry's grin expanded into his entire face. Evie wondered if his head would split open. "Exactly right," he said. "Good work! Fireworks to come!" He danced a few steps on the balls of his feet. "Mary will love this!" Then he leaned closer and whispered in Evie's ear, "You can stop worrying about that insurance issue. If Angela legally owns the horse and he was killed, the money would go to her, not Grayson!"

Evie gasped. Jerry had obviously taken her concern seriously. "You don't trust my father, do you?"

"Not as far as I can throw him. But now, I must get copies made and get this done. Get some food, girl," ordered Jerry. "And take your friend." For the first time, Jerry took a good look at Mark. "Who are you?"

"Mark Sellers, sir," Mark answered. They shook hands firmly.

"Nice young man," Jerry said to Evie with a nod. "Now eat, both of you. The proceedings are about to start." Jerry disappeared from sight, intent on his mission.

Evie was too excited to eat, but Mark dug in. While he filled his plate, she looked around to see who was here. Famous jockeys, well-known trainers, and elegantly dressed owners mixed with one another with confidence. People spoke animatedly, telling stories and connecting, doing business and selling horses.

Evie picked out a few familiar faces, including the people she'd met getting her apprentice-jockey status. She waved at Imogene Watson, who smiled broadly and waved back. Amazing that she remembered her from the test run! Evie's heart swelled with pride.

Then she saw her father. Right over by the far wall, smiling as usual and chatting jovially with a group of men. He was in his element.

Then he saw her, too, and glowered. Evie's chest constricted. Suspicion pursed his mouth, and he jutted his jaw in apparent consideration of why his daughter would be there. Evie watched his eyes squint as he put two and two together.

"Who's that?" asked Mark. "That guy over there who looks like he'd enjoy murdering you?"

"My father."

"No, couldn't be. That guy, tall, with the yellow suit and purple tie."

"My father."

Mark stopped chewing. "What's his problem?"

"You'll see," she muttered. Suddenly she wasn't sure she wanted to do this. In fact, she was sure she didn't. She had to put a stop to this whole thing. Where was Jerry?

Before she could change the plan, Murray Planno called everyone to order. "Time for the draw!" he bellowed. He held out a big white hat with slips of paper in it.

Evie balled her hands into fists and bit her lip. Mark put his hand on her shoulder. "It'll be okay."

Murray tested the microphone, then resumed his speech. "Come up when I call your name. There were thirteen entries until one minute ago. Now there are fourteen."

Everybody inhaled at the same time.

"As you know, each person reaches in and picks a number. Then, from one to fourteen, he selects his starting position. Here goes."

Evie noticed how quickly the mood in the room had changed. This was serious business, not just a party.

Murray called out the first entry. "Passenger Pigeon. Owner: Blue Ridge Stables. Trainer: Elliot Stone. Jockey: Irv Walla. Elliot? Come on up."

A man nervously walked up, flexing his fingers. He cracked his knuckles and deep-breathed.

"A rattler in that hat, Stone?" called a man. Everybody laughed, easing the tension. Elliot Stone's lip quivered in an attempt to smile. Suddenly, his hand shot into the white hat and he pulled out a slip.

Murray took it. He paused for dramatic effect, then read it out. "Three."

Elliot bobbed his head and stepped away.

Next, Murray Planno called out, "Thymetofly. Owner: Maple Mills. Trainer: Les Merton. Jockey: Abe Moxy."

Her father's horse. Evie knew he was fast and fit. He'd been trained by Jerry, too, but since Jerry had been fired, Evie guessed that Les Merton had taken over. The tall man walked up and drew the number six.

"Pirate's Dream. Owner: Fox Ridge. Trainer: Christopher Higgins. Jockey: Luke Henry."

Murray called out name after name. The big horses, the ones most favoured to win, were Thymetofly, Paradise Found, LaLaLady, Gasparilla, and Roustabout, and attention was paid when their names were called. As people chose their number, they became more comfortable and the undercurrent of chatter became louder.

There was only one left.

Murray cleared his throat. Suddenly there was dead silence. Curiosity reigned. Who was the new entry? people wondered. The fourteenth horse?

Murray held the final name, and read aloud, "No Justice. Owner: Angela Parson Gibb. Trainer: Jerry Johnston. Jockey: Evangeline Gibb."

Immediately the room was buzzing like a giant hive of bees.

"Preposterous!" hissed an uncomfortably familiar voice. Evie froze.

"This is ridiculous." Grayson Gibb stepped up to the front. He smiled broadly, including the entire room with his large presence and charm. "The horse is mine. I didn't enter him for obvious reasons. How is this possible, Murray?" He held his palms up in a gesture of dismay and amazement.

Murray looked uncomfortable and answered, "It's all in order, Grayson. Let's talk about this later in my office." He wiped beads of sweat off his brow.

"We're among friends. There's been a mistake. We can talk about it right now." Grayson was still smiling, but his skin was bright red and beginning to mottle. Evie had seen him mad, but never this mad. She was unable to breathe.

Jerry Johnston spoke up. "Pardon me, Mr. Planno. May I speak?"

Murray nodded.

"Mr. Planno, Mr. Gibb. This is a valid entry. I have here in my hands a document that cancels your power of attorney over the horses in 703556 Ltd. and gives me that power. I am the trainer of No Justice and have the right to enter this horse and to choose his jockey."

Murray spoke up. "Agreed, subject to legal verification of that document before the declaration of winner."

Jerry nodded curtly in acknowledgement. He stood at ease and seemed sure of himself, so Evie began to breathe again. She still couldn't look at her father.

Grayson sputtered, "Really?" He spun and grabbed the document from Jerry's hand. "This is worth nothing!" He bunched it up, then glared at Evie, apparently trying hard to retain a semblance of good humour. "With all respect, this child is incapable of riding any racehorse, let alone one that bucks. It'll end in disaster. This entire thing is a charade and an insult to racing. I insist, Murray. Scratch No Justice!"

No one dared speak. All eyes were on Murray now. The tension was overwhelming.

To his credit, Jerry didn't cower. "If you've had your say, Mr. Gibb, the paper you took is one of several copies. Mr. Planno has the original in his possession."

A murmur rose in the crowd as everyone quietly commented to others.

"And Evangeline Gibb has been deemed worthy of the title of apprentice jockey by the Ontario Jockey Club. She's a very capable rider and on behalf of the Jockey Club, I'm offended by your remark." Jerry Johnston stood tall and expanded his chest as he continued, "Perhaps I didn't make the owner's wishes clear. I have the power of attorney over *all* the horses in 703556 Ltd." He cleared his throat and looked directly at Grayson. "Your entry, Thymetofly, is included in that company." He paused dramatically. "I therefore have the right to decide not only about No Justice, but about Thymetofly as well."

Like a tennis match at Wimbledon, all heads pivoted to witness how Grayson would respond.

Grayson dropped his charm. His eyes narrowed and all but disappeared. His face contorted. Evie thought that if looks could kill, Jerry would be dead. "Ridiculous!" Grayson barked. He then turned to Murray Planno. "Stop this nonsense, man!" he demanded. "I will take my complaint to the top and delay the running of the Queen's Plate!"

Murray's head tilted to the side. He licked his lips nervously and tucked in his chin. "Under these circumstances, I feel it's best for the management and the stewards to have a private conference." He mopped his dripping brow again.

Jerry saw a bargaining opportunity and took it. He stepped closer to the stage beside Grayson. "If I may, Mr. Planno? If Grayson Gibb agrees to drop his complaint against No Justice, I will allow him to run Thymetofly."

All eyes turned back to Grayson. Seconds passed with no sound in the room. To Evie, it felt like hours. She started to worry about Magpie in the car outside.

"Deal," he pronounced in a harsh whisper.

The tension was punctured and the crowd exploded into applause. Grayson held up his hand for silence. He smiled broadly and laughed. "And just for the record, No Justice is no threat." He gestured with his hands expansively. "I could not care less if he runs. You'll see. And as for the jockey?"

Evie withered as Grayson pinned her to the wall with his beady blue gaze. His voice was overly solicitous. "I only hope that she doesn't cause an accident with her rank inexperience and rank horse."

The entire crowd gasped as one. The culture of the racehorse industry is very superstitious, and what Grayson had said was akin to a curse. The noise level became deafening as Jerry strode up and took the last slip of paper from Murray Planno's hat. It was number fourteen.

Aunt Mary appeared beside Evie. "Well, well," she whispered in her ear. "Lots of fun."

Evie spun around to face her. "Aunt Mary! You're here! Where's Kazzam?"

"Safely in his stall with a guard. The CEO of Woodbine assigned him stable five and ordered security."

"How did he get here?"

"I drove him here as soon as I got your message."

"Why didn't you or Jerry call me back?" Her tone was impatient.

"I tried a few times, but had no reception. Plus, we were a little busy, getting all this together in less than an hour, including a stop at the bank."

Evie stared at her. "Oh, Aunt Mary! Thanks so much!" Tears fell from her eyes. "I'm sorry."

Mary hugged her tightly. "It's okay, dear girl. It's okay." She pulled a tissue from her purse and wiped Evie's tears away. "I have to say, I'm really impressed with you. You found your mother and got what we need. You're going to race on Sunday, after all!"

"Angela knew exactly what to do." Then something her aunt had said registered. "The bank? Why did you have to stop there?"

"To get $10,000. I knew Angela wouldn't have it."

"But she wrote a voucher."

Mary shook her head. "They wouldn't have accepted it. Jerry and I were going to have to find the money anyway, to enter you. Luckily, I just received my latest royalty cheque for my books."

"Thank you, Aunt Mary! I'll pay you back!"

Mary hugged her niece. "Let's worry about that another day."

Mark stepped between them. "No prom for you, girl."

"Do you mind about that?" Evie had forgotten all about the prom again.

"Are you kidding? This is much more exciting than a prom! I'm dying to know what comes next."

As Evie looked across the room to where her father stood with Les Merton, she wondered the same thing.

Mary smiled as Jerry approached. "Jerry 'J.J.' Johnston, you are the man of the hour."

"True. Man of *this* hour. Who's the man of the next hour?" He joked in an effort to appear modest, but he looked mighty proud. "Mary, is No Justice looked after?"

"Yes. Twenty-four-hour guard."

"Good. But after Grayson's reaction, just to be extra sure I'll get someone to sleep in his stall."

Evie was shocked. "Kazzam will hate that, except if it's me. I'll stay with him."

250

"No, you will not," countered Mary. "You have your last exam tomorrow. You'll study for it tonight and then get a good night's rest."

"But who, then? You know Kazzam. He can be...."

"Yes, I know," said Jerry. "I have someone in mind who the horse knows and likes, but I can't tell you who that is at the moment. Trust me."

"Don't I have a say in this?" grumbled Evie.

Jerry was direct. "No."

Mary said, "Hush. The start-position selection is about to begin."

Jerry nodded. "We choose last. We get what's left. My guess is you'll be running next to the rail."

"Let's get out of here before your father kills you," said Mark hastily. "Look. He's coming this way."

23

The Leather Box

At exactly eleven-fifty-five on Friday morning, after an early half-mile training session with Kazzam at Woodbine and immediately after their math exam, Mark Sellers drove Evie through the imposing gates of Maple Mills Stables in his mother's blue compact car.

"Holy," he said. "Quite some digs."

Evie was too tense to answer. She would not relax until she had Angela's leather box in her possession and kept her fingers crossed that her father wouldn't show up. Evie had called Yolanda right after the draw, and she'd been very helpful. Together they'd devised a plan.

Just as Yolanda had predicted, nobody was around.

The horses were finished working, the stalls were all cleaned, and the grooms were on lunch break.

Yolanda met them at the tack-room door and ushered them in. "We have to hurry. I'm shipping Thymetofly in half an hour," she said to Evie. "I never know about helping you. Am I helping you get *out* of trouble or into more?"

Mark laughed. "Fun, though, eh?"

Evie didn't laugh. She was all business. "Yoyo, guard the door? Mark, let's do this fast and get out of here."

"Remember our signal?" asked Yolanda. Evie nodded. Three short knocks meant that something was amiss. She closed the tack-room door behind them, and the two teenagers ducked under the long, wooden table that was used to soap and oil the saddles and bridles.

Evie tapped along the wall where her mother had instructed and quickly found the hollow area. Mark broke the plaster with the hammer and reached around until he found the box. "Got it!"

"Beauty," whispered Evie. "Let's go!"

Mark crawled out and placed the dusty box carefully on the table. He brushed himself off while Evie tried to conceal the plaster chunks and dust under a mat.

They heard three quick knocks on the tack-room door and froze. "Oh, no," gasped Evie.

They listened intently. Yolanda began talking loudly in the hall. "Good afternoon, Mr. Gibb. Lovely day again today!"

"Thymetofly should be ready to ship to Woodbine."

"Yes, sir. He's ready now."

"Mistakes will not be tolerated. No sloppy errors."

"Understood, sir."

"Who's here with you, Yolanda? In the stable?"

"Just me, sir. Getting Thymetofly ready to ship, sir."

"There's a blue car at the door. Is it yours?"

"No, sir," Yolanda said a little hesitantly.

Grayson Gibb's tone intensified. "Whose is it, then, if nobody's here? It's a security issue."

"I'll make sure it's taken care of, sir."

"It's be gone immediately."

"Yes, sir."

"Yolanda," he snarled, "you know better."

"Uh, yes, sir."

"You know what I'm talking about."

"Uh ... no, sir."

"You know better than to let your boyfriends visit you at work. Ever. But today? With the Queen's Plate on Sunday? Shame. Mistakes will not be tolerated." With no warning, he threw open the tack-room door.

Mark stood with his back to the table, hiding the box and the hammer as best he could. His mouth hung open in astonishment. Under the table, Evie stayed as still as a mouse.

Grayson eyed him from head to toe. He growled, "What have we here?"

All Evie could see were Mark's feet, glued to the floor.

Yolanda tried to make things seem normal. "Uh, Mr. Gibb, this is, uh...."

"Mark Sellers, sir."

"And who are you exactly?"

Evie prayed that Mark would play along. If he said he was Evie's friend, her father would go crazy. And if he knew of its existence, he'd surely confiscate Angela's leather box.

"I dropped over to say hello to, uh, Yoyo, on her lunch break. I didn't realize it'd be a problem, sir. I apologize."

"Yolanda neglected to tell you the rules?"

"I didn't tell her I'd be coming. Sir. I just got here and she told me I couldn't stay. I'm leaving now. My error, not hers."

"Do I know you from somewhere?" Grayson asked, sounding very suspicious.

Evie clenched her jaw and hoped that Mark would not reveal that they were in the same room as Grayson just the day before, and a witness to Grayson's humiliation at the draw.

"I don't believe we've ever been introduced," answered Mark truthfully.

Evie relaxed. By now she should know to trust Mark. Grayson Gibb harrumphed, then spoke to Yolanda.

"Drive Thymetofly to Woodbine. Leave the trailer there. Leave the truck, too. Disobey at your peril. You're fired. Empty out your apartment and be gone by the weekend."

He stalked out of the stable. Seconds later, an engine started with a rumble. Evie, Mark, and Yolanda listened until the long, black limousine had fully departed.

"Oh, Yoyo," said Evie, crawling out from under the table. "I'm so sorry, I can't even begin to tell you how much."

"You're not as sorry as I am, believe me." Yolanda looked wretched. "It's surprising I've lasted this long. I've been here fifteen years. He's firing people left and right."

Evie felt terrible. Mark looked embarrassed. Evie said, "We'll help you load Thymetofly. Then we'll get out of here. I'll think of a way to help you, Yoyo. I promise."

"Better you just leave. No hard feelings. I know you didn't mean for this to happen."

"Oh, Yoyo. I'm really sorry."

"Please go quickly. I'll be in even more trouble if he comes back and finds you here."

"Thanks, Yoyo. I'll call you later. And again, I'm sorry."

Yolanda nodded sadly and continued preparing for her trip to Woodbine Race Track. "Bye, Evie. Good luck Sunday."

"You heard about me riding Kazzam?"

Yolanda nodded. "I babysat him all last night for Jerry."

Of course, Evie thought. Only Yolanda could sleep in a stall with Kazzam and not get bitten or kicked. "Thanks, Yoyo. Thanks so much."

Tears streamed down Evie's face as they got into the car.

"Get in the back seat on the floor, Evie," said Mark. "With that box, better safe than sorry."

Evie did as she was told. She was crushed at what she'd done to her old friend. Yolanda had always helped her, including today, and that had cost her her job.

Mark drove silently for a few minutes, then said, "I'll bet Jerry will have a job for her."

Evie got off the floor and sat up on the back seat. "Jerry doesn't have a job himself."

"Well, maybe your aunt Mary?"

"She doesn't need any help. Maybe she'll let Yoyo stay for a while, though. There's an apartment over the garage."

Evie watched out her window and noticed that they were almost at Parson's Bridge. "I have to do some chores this afternoon. You're welcome to hang around and help."

"Uh, love to, but I have some errands. I promised my mother she could have her car back this afternoon. Groceries and all that." He chuckled. "Can't monopolize this baby forever."

"Sure. Anyway, thanks for, well, everything. Going to Toronto with me to find my mother, the Woodbine coup, the Maple Mills caper. Everything."

"So I'll swing by later? After dinner, around eight?"

"That'd be great, because I won't see you tomorrow. And don't forget to try to get a ticket to the Queen's Plate. It's on me. I really want you to be there. For good luck."

Mark nodded and waited. "Aren't you getting out?"

"The child-lock is on."

"Oops. Now try."

Evie got out of the car carrying the leather box, then she leaned in Mark's window. She kissed his startled lips.

She started to pull her head away, but Mark's hand held her head. He kissed her again, a longer, slow kiss.

He released her and she straightened up. "Holy. I think I'm dizzy."

Mark smiled. "Me, too. Gotta go now or I never will. See you later."

Evie watched Mark drive down the lane. She was still very upset that she'd caused Yoyo to get fired, but she was elated at the same time. Her lips felt hot from Mark's kiss.

"Evie!" called Aunt Mary from the house. "Come in!"

Evie was greeted by Magpie as she rushed to the house.

"What is it, Aunt Mary?"

"I just got a call from Jerry. Two things. First, Yolanda was fired."

Evie took a quick breath. "I know. It's my fault. She was helping me get this from the tack room," she explained, holding the leather box for Aunt Mary to see, "and my father came in. She covered up for me, and he fired her."

Mary stared at the box. "That's Angela's."

"Yes. It's got all her documents in case we need them."

"How did you find it? It's been missing for years!"

"My mother told me where it was and said to give it to you for safekeeping."

"Let's open it and see what's there," said Mary.

"What's the second thing?" asked Evie.

"Oh, yes. No Justice is acting up. The grooms say that he's making a fuss and upsetting their horses."

"Is Yoyo at the track yet with Thymetofly?"

"I think so. She called Jerry for a lift home and he's on the way."

"Can you ask her to stay with Kazzam until I get there? I can pay her from my race money."

Mary nodded. "Good thinking. We should hire her for the duration of the race." She called Yolanda and then Jerry. "Done. We'll drive over to see what's up with your horse, but first, let's get this box open."

The lock was rusty and bent, and the hinges were welded together with disuse. Mary got out her toolbox and pried it open as carefully as she could with a flat screwdriver.

Evie stared in wonder as the lid opened. Covering the contents of the box was a piece of multicoloured silk. She reached in and pulled it out. As it unfurled, Evie could see it was some sort of garment. Bright pink polka dots on a white background with periwinkle-blue stripes on the sleeves. She gasped as she held it up. It was a silk shirt.

"Her racing silks!"

Aunt Mary's eyes misted. "I remember like it was yesterday, Angela winning her first race in those very silks."

Evie held it up to her chest. "They'll fit, too. Can I wear them?" She had a lump in her throat.

Mary nodded. "Yes. Your mother would want you to. It's her horse you're riding. You're her jockey."

"Perfect." Evie sniffed back her emotions as she looked for whatever else she might find. She picked out a much smaller piece of silk, half pink polka dots and half periwinkle-blue stripes.

"That's a helmet-cover for your hard hat. It fits right on."

Evie nodded and reached in again. Manilla envelopes and legal papers were mixed in with a birth certificate, social insurance card, and other personal papers.

"We can look at all that later, Evie. I'll sort out what we need. But now, we must get to the track and make sure No Justice settles down."

Evie had an idea. "Is there another stall available?"

"What are you thinking?"

"Christieloo. He loves her. I think she'd calm him down if we could take her there."

Mary nodded with enthusiasm. "Great idea. I'll call Jerry and see if it's at all possible."

While Mary tried to organize a stall, Evie looked through the papers in her mother's box. They were yellowed from age but quite legible. At the very bottom was an envelope with Evie's name on it.

Very carefully, she unsealed it. Inside were photos. Evie as a baby. Evie in her mother's arms. Taking her first steps. Laughing at the beach. Eating ice cream. In a smaller envelope was a lock of silky, red, curling hair. Evie got a tissue to be sure none of her tears stained these precious things.

As she looked at herself as a baby and at her mother's face, a great realization dawned. She'd been loved by her mother. Adored. Not discarded and despised as she'd always believed. This was a big moment, one that she couldn't take in all at once.

"Jerry arranged for a stall right beside No Justice," Mary said, "and Yolanda is there now, waiting for us. Let's go."

Evie placed everything back in the box except the silks and helmet cover. Aunt Mary promised to wash them and get them pressed for the race on Sunday, just two days away.

As quickly as possible, they got Christieloo loaded onto the trailer. The dogs understood by now that they should stay to guard the place, and Bendigo and Paragon were happy to keep munching on the early-summer grass.

Forty minutes later, Mary's rig passed through the east gate of Woodbine and headed for stable five. Christieloo hadn't stirred the whole way.

Evie looked at all the racetrack sights and activities. They were beginning to look familiar. She was starting to feel like she belonged. Even so, her heart beat faster and she could feel her excitement grow. She wondered if the pros still got excited.

Horses being led, farriers tapping on shoes, grooms hosing horses down, trucks delivering hay and feed. It was such a wonderful world, Evie thought. She was part of it now.

At stable five, Mary parked the truck and trailer. Jerry and Yolanda emerged from the doorway together.

Evie jumped out and found herself apologizing yet again. "Yoyo? I'm so sorry about what happened. You were only helping me and —"

"It's okay, Evie," said Yolanda. "It's for the best. I haven't been happy there for a long time."

Jerry added, "There's always a job for a person as good with horses as Yolanda is. It'll work out."

"Thanks, Yoyo." Evie gave her old friend a hug. "And thanks for helping us out here."

Christieloo whinnied, followed by a loud thumping in the shed-row.

"Let's get her off!" ordered Jerry. "No Justice is causing a lot of trouble in there! That's why they moved the horses around and made room for Christieloo. They weren't just being nice."

They went into action. Mary and Evie dropped the ramp. Yolanda backed the mare out. Then they walked into the barn together with the mare pulling hard.

"Christieloo knows where she's going," enthused Yolanda. "Right to No Justice's stall!"

It made them all laugh to see how excited the horses were to be reunited. Once again, Evie was reminded how their connection to others of their species was the same as people's. Kazzam had been upset in a new place with no friends. Like she would be, herself.

"Aunt Mary? Can we lead them around together for a while? Let them see what the place looks like?"

Mary nodded. "Good idea."

Jerry agreed. "Hand-walk them. Let them graze a little, sniff around. It'll do No Justice good. Might settle him a bit."

"I have nothing better to do," joked Yolanda. "And nowhere else to go!"

Mary spoke firmly. "You'll stay with us, Yolanda. Move in today. Until you find something suitable, consider yourself part of the family."

Yolanda's face crumpled as she tried unsuccessfully to hold back a deluge of tears. "That'd be so, so great!"

That evening, Yolanda packed all her belongings into boxes and drove them over to Parson's Bridge in her compact car. Mark dropped over as promised, and he and Evie helped carry her things up to the apartment over the garage.

Just as they were unloading Yolanda's last box, the heavens opened up. The rain came down in sheets, drenching them all in seconds. It pounded so hard that they couldn't hear each other speak.

Yolanda organized her things into a livable situation and popped into the house before driving back to Woodbine for her guard duties. She joined Mary, Evie, and Mark, who were chatting in the kitchen.

"I feel like a great weight has been lifted from my shoulders!" she exclaimed, pouring a second cup of coffee. "Thank you for letting me stay, Mary."

"My pleasure entirely."

"Even though it's raining cats and dogs out there, I feel happy! I had no idea how awful things had become for me at Maple Mills."

"Thanks to *me*," Evie teased. "I got you fired."

"Let's not go there," warned Yolanda. "You owe me, big time!" She tossed a napkin at her playfully.

Mark shook his head. "That was one scary moment when you got fired, Yoyo. Grayson Gibb is not someone I want to meet in an alley."

"Or anywhere else, if he's mad," seconded Evie.

"So totally true." Yolanda stood up. "Now, I'm off to my night job. Sleep well in your warm bed, Evie, knowing I'm on guard, suffering for you."

Evie's eyes twinkled. "As it should be!"

Mark went home soon after Yolanda left, and Mary went back to her writing.

Evie picked up the phone and made a call. "Jordie? It's Evie. Are you guys okay?"

"Yeah," answered her little brother. "But I like it better when you're around. I miss you lots and lots!"

"I miss you lots and lots, too, Jordie." Evie pictured his earnest face and felt a pang of love for the little boy.

"When can I come see you?"

Evie chuckled. "Are you and Beebee doing anything on Sunday afternoon?"

24

The Ladies' Room

The next morning, Mary bustled about the little yellow farmhouse as they prepared to leave. She took a sip of hot coffee and asked Evie, "Ready in half an hour?"

"I'm ready now," said Evie. "I get to tour the jockeys' room today. I can't wait. Are my mother's silks ready?"

"For the tenth time, yes."

"And what about all the other stuff I'll need?"

"We'll sort it out today. Don't worry."

"I can't help but worry!" Evie retorted as she opened the door. "I'm racing in the Queen's Plate tomorrow!" A howling gust of air rushed in with a spray of cold water. "Unless it's called off because of rain."

"It's never called off except when there's lightning. And then it's only delayed, not cancelled."

Evie saw it first. An envelope had been wedged between the door and the frame. "What's this?"

"There's only way to find out," said Mary. "It's addressed to you. And it's soggy."

Evie paused as she studied the handwriting. Her throat constricted. "It's from my father. I don't want to read it."

Mary's voice was soft. "Take your time, Evie dear. But you might want to know what's in it."

Evie knew she was right. If she didn't read it now, she'd worry until she did. She closed the door, shutting off the roar of wind and rain. It seemed to Evie that the whole world became silent as she tore open the letter.

Evie read aloud. "'Dear Evangeline. I fought hard against you racing. The reason is I don't want you hurt. No Justice is dangerous and has injured many people. Now that it's final, I accept it with good grace. You've proven you're committed to this sport. I wish you every success in the Queen's Plate. I'm proud of you. Be careful and stay safe, your loving Father.'"

Evie's knees buckled and she slid to the floor.

※

They drove through the downpour, windshield wipers working hard. Evie was confused. She'd been so excited about seeing the jockeys' room. Now, her mind kept trying to sort out her father's letter. He'd signed it "your loving father." He'd said he was proud of her. She wanted so much to believe that! She played back the conversation she'd overheard between him and Jerry in the barn. Was he getting rid of Kazzam so the horse wouldn't hurt her? His meltdown at the Draw, too. Was he worried about her safety? And his anger that she'd gotten Kazzam qualified to race? It all made sense. Her heart expanded with hope.

Mary glanced at her. "A penny for your thoughts."

"My father's letter. I feel so much better. We don't have to worry about Kazzam anymore." Saying it out loud made it seem true.

Mary glanced at her. "Hmm."

"You don't believe his letter?"

"Do you?"

"I want to. It makes sense if he's been trying every way he can to stop me from riding Kazzam. I didn't know until right now that he ever cared!" Evie found herself sobbing.

Mary kept her eyes on the road. As Evie's sobs subsided, Mary very quietly reached out and held her shoulder. "I have a little story to tell you. About a turtle and a scorpion."

"You're kidding."

"One day, a scorpion needed to cross the river. He couldn't swim, so he asked a turtle to carry him to the other side. 'But you'll bite me and I'll die,' said the turtle. 'I won't bite you, I promise!' said the scorpion. 'Because if you die, I'll drown.' The turtle saw his logic. He agreed to help him, so the scorpion crawled on his back and they began their journey. When they were halfway across, the scorpion bit the turtle in the neck. Poisoned, the turtle asked, 'Why did you bite me? Now we'll both die.' The scorpion answered, 'Because that's what scorpions do.'"

Evie's jaw clenched as she stared at the raindrops racing sideways on her window. "You're saying my father can't change. That he's a scorpion."

"I'm telling you a story."

"Right. Just out of the blue."

"It has meaning only if it applies."

Evie argued, "I know you hate him. But maybe, just maybe, he's not what you think. Or what I used to think. Maybe he *has* changed! What if he's a good person now? I want to think he cares...."

"Evie, I understand. I do. And I'm sorry I've upset you. I'm on your side. I'm just ... not sure about that letter, and I'm trying to help in my own inadequate way. It was a bit of a surprise, you have to admit."

Evie's anger abated a little.

"Take it day by day. If your father truly feels the way he says in his letter, it will soon become very clear."

Evie sniffed and wiped her eyes. What Aunt Mary had said seemed intelligent. She'd wait and see. And pray that her father's letter was true.

"You'll see, Aunt Mary. My father is not a scorpion."

*

Soon, they arrived at stable five.

Yolanda came out to greet them, huddling under a broken green umbrella. "They had a peaceful night and all's well."

"Did you get some sleep?" asked Mary.

"Enough to last me through today."

They rushed out of the downpour and into the stable. Kazzam contentedly munched on hay and sipped from his water bucket. Christieloo's presence had certainly worked miracles, and the staff was glad that the banging and neighing had stopped.

"Well, I'll see you both later," said Evie. "I'm going to check out where I go tomorrow."

Yolanda and Mary wished her luck. In slickers and rain boots, they led No Justice and Christieloo over to the wet grass to stretch their legs and graze. Horses love the rain, Evie observed as she strode in a different direction. They don't mind getting wet at all.

She headed for the jockeys' room, on the other side of the indoor Walking Ring. Even though she was expected, she felt quite nervous. Sweat dripped from her underarms and mixed with the raindrops as she looked through the glass door of the jockeys' private sanctuary.

In front of her was a hall with a room on the right and an open booth farther along. At the end of the hall was a door to the left, and people were walking in and out. It looked like the hall turned and continued right. She steeled herself and walked through the glass door.

The man in the booth lifted his head from some papers he was working on. "Evie Gibb. You're the new girl. Breathe in here," he ordered, and handed her a small tubular machine. She took it, too startled to object.

"I said breathe."

She did as she was told.

"You're okay," the man said after reading the meter.

"What is that thing?" Evie asked.

"A breathalizer. Everyone who has anything to do with horses has to be checked. Sign in there." He pointed to a ledger. He smiled at her very briefly. "And welcome."

"Thanks," said Evie. She tried to smile back.

"Now you know what to do tomorrow." The man resumed his work. "The ladies' room is down the hall here on the right."

"Thanks," she said again. She wandered further along the hall and looked into the door on the left.

She heard what sounded like people being sick to their stomachs. Then a very short man appeared at the door.

"What are you doing here? The ladies' is down that hall." He pointed.

"Thanks, but I don't need it."

He looked at her like she was an alien and then laughed. "I get it! Hey, guys!" He called into the room. "Newbie Gibb here doesn't need to use the ladies' room!"

Within a few seconds, Evie was surrounded by curious jockeys. She was being studied and examined like a science project. She felt too tall and too young and most of all, too inexperienced. Certainly out of place. Questions came at her from all around.

"Where've you ridden?"

"Any stakes races?"

"Where'd you come from, anyway?"

"No Justice is tough. Are you ready to be dumped?"

"Don't get dumped in front of me!"

"You stay away from me with that horse!"

"Bump me and I'll smack you."

"Do ya know how to steer?"

"Do you know how to ride? Your father says not!"

Evie didn't know what to do or say. She stood with her mouth open, understanding how unwelcome she was. She wanted to sink into the floor.

Then from behind her came a woman's voice. "Leave her alone, you bullies. You all know better."

Evie turned around to see Imogene Watson's angry face. "Cool it! She's new, get over it. We were all new once."

Evie was grateful for the intervention. "It's okay, really," she said, still shaking. "I know everyone's worried about No Justice and me. For good reason, too." She'd found her voice and looked at the men. "I promise not to bump into anyone. My horse has a bad reputation, but he's never dumped me. We'll run a fair race and stay out of your way. That's all I know how to do, anyway. I'm not a fancy rider."

Imogene took her by the arm and stood with her. "Apologies, men?"

One by one, Evie saw the faces of the jockeys soften, and one by one, they mumbled monosyllabic grunts and returned to the men's room.

The last to go was the man who'd appeared first. "You're okay, girl jockey," he said as he turned away. "You'll do fine. Just mind your p's and q's."

"You, too, Irv," retorted Imogene.

The vomiting noise began again. Evie looked at Imogene questioningly.

"They're just flipping," she answered. "Making weight. It's a struggle for some of the guys to stay so light." She walked down the hall. "Come with me. I'll show you around."

Imogene led Evie past some hooks on the wall.

"That's where the valets hang our silks." Evie noted that she pronounced it *va*-let and not the French va-*lay*. "Every race, you wear the silks of that stable, and they're hung in reverse order of your races so you always have the right ones on top. Your hook is already marked, see?"

Evie smiled when she saw her name on the wall. "Wow. I get a valet?" she asked. "With only one horse to ride?"

"You certainly do," said a man from farther down the hall. "I'm Bart Myers and I'm your valet." He carefully hung Angela's pink-and-white and periwinkle-blue silks on the hook. "Mary drove these over just now. It's been a long time since I've seen the Parson silks."

Evie was intrigued. "Where did you see them before?"

"I was your mother's valet."

Evie's eyes widened. "Really?" She stared at this man.

He was middle-aged, a little taller than she was, and slight. He had a kind, practical look.

Bart lifted his chin proudly. "Angela Parson was my favourite, long before Imogene came along. She looked a lot like you, Evie. And she was a good jockey."

Imogene said, "It was way worse than now. Females had a bad time of it. Your mother had the odds stacked against her to get rides."

"You're the one who broke the mould," Bart responded. "Just so you know, Imogene's working hard to level the playing field for the generations to come."

"I'm trying my best."

Evie agreed. "I've had your poster on my wall since you won the Plate on Mike Fox."

Imogene's face broke into a wide smile. "Then I've got the perfect thing for you. The saddle I rode on that day. You can use it tomorrow."

"No," said Evie, awed. "I couldn't."

"Yes you can! And you will. It's good luck."

"And I have something special, too," said Bart. "Just a minute." He hurried back down the hall.

"Where's he going?" asked Evie.

"To the laundry room where silks are washed and boots and jodhpurs are cleaned."

Bart reappeared with a short pair of shiny boots. "I've saved these for many years. They were your mother's."

Evie reached out and held the lightweight, patent-leather boots to her chest. There was a slight hint of mildew. She was overcome.

"The only things you need now are some britches and a helmet. Come with me!" exclaimed Imogene. She dashed into a room on the right.

Evie couldn't move. Her feet were planted on the floor with her mother's boots clutched tightly in her arms.

Imogene popped her head around the corner. "Come on!"

Evie, with Bart's kindly help, dislodged herself from her stupor and followed Imogene. If ever she thought she was dreaming, it was now.

Bart deposited her at the doorway of the female jockeys' room. Before he left her, he asked, "How much do you weigh?"

"About 116, maybe 118 pounds."

"Great. You're allowed 126. We'll pop you on the scales and add the lead."

Evie nodded. "Whatever. Just tell me. I don't know anything. At all."

"I'm here to help. We all are. You'll do great." Bart stepped back and stuck out his hand.

Evie shook it. "Thank you, Bart. Really. So much."

"Are you coming or not? I don't have all day," came a voice from the ladies' room.

"Go," said Bart. "She's got a race in two hours."

Evie followed Imogene. The room was spacious with separated sections in the walls around the room. There were about ten of these cubbyholes. Each cubby was like a little window seat with shelves and drawers on the side for storing clothes and other personal items. Imogene had one, and because there were more cubbies than female jockeys, she spread her stuff over into the next.

To Evie's delight, Imogene showed her the one she could use herself.

"I get a cubby?" she asked. "In the ladies' room at Woodbine? Fantastic."

"Of course you do. You're riding in the big race."

"I really am."

"Pinch yourself, girl. Here." Imogene pulled a pair of white riding pants out of a drawer. "These'll fit you. I've got some new ones, so keep them."

"Wow. Thanks."

"And a helmet. This is one you can use, but I'll need it back." She took a spare off the highest shelf. "The silk cover hides the scratches. And here's a pair of goggles for tomorrow. You'll only need one. The track is polyfibre, so not much kick-up, and it's going to be sunny. Leave everything in your cubby. It's safe."

"You're so ... I don't know what to say ... amazing! I can't thank you enough."

Imogene tilted her head and looked at Evie. "We all help each other. That's what we do. Someone helped me when I first started out. You'll pass it on, I know it."

Evie nodded solemnly. "I will. I promise."

"Want some advice?"

"Yes, anything." Evie waited for criticism.

"Keep doing what you're doing. The guys don't mean any harm. They all know about No Justice. You let them vent out there, then you treated them with respect. I like that."

"Well, I know what they're worried about. I'd worry about me, too."

Imogene laughed merrily. "Glad to hear it. So, just ride your race and stay out of trouble. It'll go the way it goes, like it always does."

"Mike Fox was tough to ride, people say."

"It's true. He's a lady's horse — no man can ride him."

It took a few seconds for Evie to get the joke. A lady's horse generally means an old, quiet plug. She burst out laughing.

Imogene pointed to the door. "Now get out of here. I've got to study the sheets and get into the zone. See you tomorrow. Be here three hours before the race."

"Thanks so much, Imogene. I'll never forget this."

"Stop thanking me and get out!" Imogene gave her a quick hug and cheerfully pushed her into the hall.

Bart was waiting. "We should get you weighed before you go. Great gal, Imogene."

"For sure. I can't believe all the stuff she gave me."

"She's a generous person. Come. Let me show you what she invented."

"She invented something?"

"Follow me." Bart led Evie down the hall and into an enormous room with huge washing machines and dryers. A rotating conveyer belt packed with hangers of freshly pressed racing silks reminded Evie of the dry cleaner's, but many times bigger.

A man sat at a desk sorting name tickets and laundry stickers. They walked past people sewing and cleaning boots and pants.

"Here it is, Evie. The Equiciser. The equestrian exerciser." Bart pointed to an elaborate sawhorse.

"How does it work?"

"Get on. You'll see."

Evie sat in the saddle. She bent her knees tightly and put her feet into the stirrups.

"Now ride it," said Bart. "Like you're in a race."

"Sweet!" exclaimed Evie. "It moves like a galloping horse!"

"That's the whole idea. It simulates the movement of a racehorse so jockeys can practise their technique as long as they like, without wearing out horses."

Evie kept on riding the Equiciser. Faster and faster.

Within minutes she felt her balance improve. The machine moved better when her body was right over the neck and when she stretched her arms forward with each stride.

"This is great, Bart!" Evie enthused. "It's teaching me things." She slowed the machine and hopped off.

Bart smiled. "Now, be sure to get a good rest tonight and pray for sunshine. Tomorrow is the big day for us all."

25

Midnight

After leaving the jockeys' room at Woodbine on Saturday afternoon, Evie went to check on Christieloo and Kazzam. They looked good. They'd eaten all their food and were drinking water, and were peeing and pooping as usual. Nothing at all to worry about. But as she stroked Kazzam's forehead with its distinctive heart-shaped star, Evie couldn't quite shake the feeling that something would go wrong.

People said that it was normal to have nerves before a big race, and Evie knew that with the dark skies and dismal rain, her imagination must be working overtime. She should get a grip. Besides, she told herself, as well as the stable security guards, Yolanda would be right there watching over Kazzam.

Since the Thursday draw, she'd been waiting for some kind of retaliation from her father, but none had come, not even a threat. His letter was sincere. It had to be. He was not a scorpion.

Evie climbed into bed Saturday night after organizing everything she could think of for the race the next day. She was showered and ready to go, with her clothes laid out and necessities packed. It was still early in the evening, only nine-thirty, but Evie needed a good night's sleep, like Bart had advised.

She drifted off to sleep, comforted by thoughts of Yolanda and the security at Woodbine. She slept deeply and dreamlessly.

Suddenly, at midnight, thunder crashed right over the farmhouse. Evie sat straight up in bed, her heart pounding. A tongue of lightning split the sky into sections, accompanied by another ear-splitting roar.

Anxiety flooded her body. Her pulse raced. Something was wrong. Kazzam, she felt sure of it. He needed her. She had to make certain he was all right.

Yolanda had a cellphone with her and the number was beside the phone in the kitchen. Evie got out of bed. Magpie leaped to her feet and shook her floppy ears. She stayed by Evie's side as she crept down the stairs in the dark.

The message light was blinking. Evie pressed it. Nothing but an electonic squeak. She played it again. Just a squeak. Evie's mind ran overtime as she considered all the horrible reasons someone had called but was unable to leave a message.

Evie quickly dialled Yolanda's number and waited. Her phone rang until voice mail came on. Evie left a message. "Yoyo? It's Evie. Did you call? Is everything okay? Call me."

She hung up and stood thinking. She called again with the same result. Why wasn't Yolanda picking up? Evie tried one last time, but as the seconds passed, she found herself bubbling into a panic. Something must be very wrong.

Evie needed to find a way to get to Woodbine. Magpie shadowed her upstairs to Aunt Mary's room. The bedroom door was closed. Evie knocked and listened. She knocked again, harder, and then opened the door. "Aunt Mary?"

The covers moved. Aunt Mary's sleepy head rose from her pillow. "What is it, Evie? Is everything okay?"

"Can you drive me to Woodbine? Please?"

"What time is it?"

"Twelve o'clock."

"Midnight? Evie, please, get back to —"

"I can't! Kazzam's in trouble, I know it. I can't sleep until I see him."

Mary sat up and turned on the light. At the sight of the older woman's tired face, Evie felt badly. But still, she strongly felt the need to see Kazzam. "Please?"

"Call Yoyo. She's right there and if there was —"

"I already tried but there's no answer. And she might have tried to call us because the light was blinking and there's no message."

"Evie, it's your imagination. Nothing's wrong. You've worked yourself into a —"

"Please, Aunt Mary? I need to see with my own eyes."

"I know, dear, but it's the middle of the —"

"I'll call Mark. He'll drive me. It'll take longer, but I won't be able to sleep until I get there."

"Did you have a bad dream?"

"Can I take the truck and drive myself?"

"You don't have a licence!" Mary sighed in resignation. "Okay. I'll drive you. You'll see he's perfectly fine, and then we'll get you back to bed. You need rest before tomorrow. And so do I."

"Thank you, thank you! Meet me downstairs?"

"In five."

"Make it three?"

Mary glared at Evie and began to get dressed. "Four."

Evie raced to her room, threw on her clothes, and

grabbed her flashlight. She was downstairs quickly and let out the dogs. They didn't like the rain and whined to come back in.

True to her word, Aunt Mary appeared and lifted the keys off the hook. "Leave the dogs inside," she said tersely. "Let's go."

They ran through the rain to the truck and were off.

The downpour showed no signs of subsiding. As they drove south, brilliant electric forks lit up the black sky, followed instantly by an unearthly crash.

"That was too close," said Mary, shuddering.

"It's a spooky night." Evie was on edge. She wanted Mary to drive faster. She saw how her aunt was hunched forward in order to see the road through the flapping windshield wipers and pounding rain, and resolved to keep her mouth shut. She didn't want to push her luck, but it was an effort.

"Relax. We'll be there soon," said Mary. "Get my racing licence out of my purse so we can go right through."

Evie heard the irritation in her aunt's voice and felt a little foolish. She wondered about the craziness of her impulse. She had no idea why she was so convinced that something was wrong. But the blinking message light was real. Maybe Aunt Mary was right, that it was just her imagination. Maybe a bad dream. She hoped so.

"We're here." Aunt Mary rolled down her window and presented her licence to the guard, who glanced at it and motioned them through.

Mary silently drove directly to stable five. Everything looked calm.

"I'll run in," said Evie.

"If you're not out in two minutes, I'm coming in."

Evie raced through the rain to the stable door. She walked in and then stopped still to listen. The barn was dark and very quiet. Too quiet. The normal sounds of horses eating and snoring and shuffling around in the straw were missing. The only noise she heard was a barn cat yowling from somewhere down the hall.

Evie's eyes adjusted to the gloom of the barn. She thought it better not to switch on the overhead lights and disturb all the horses. Or alert an intruder. She checked her pocket for the flashlight, just in case.

She passed the security room. The door was closed, but she could hear that the television set was on. She kept walking, peeking into the stalls as she passed. Horses stood quietly, not eating, just watching, eyes wide open.

Strange. *Something is going on and the horses know it.* The hairs on Evie's entire body raised.

Why isn't a guard out here? Where's Yoyo?

Evie crept along the hall, unsure if she should make herself known or remain silent. Each horse observed her as she made her way toward Kazzam's stall, beside Christieloo's.

Definitely not normal. They're all worried.

Odd that nobody was guarding the horses. Were they all watching TV?

Evie stopped. There it was again. A mewing sound, like a distressed cat. Then it hit her. *That's not a cat. It's a person.*

She followed the noise right to Christieloo's stall.

The palomino mare's eyes bulged with uncertainty. Evie reached over the stall door to pat her nose and comfort her, then heard the noise again, but louder.

Evie looked down. A dark shape lay in a large lump on the inside of the stall door. She took her flashlight from her pocket and turned it on.

"Yoyo!" she whispered. "Holy."

There, on the stall floor, gagged and tied up, lay

278

Yolanda. Her eyes flashed with fear. She struggled to get up, but was bound tightly and couldn't move.

Evie opened the door, knelt down, and began to work. First, she ripped the duct tape off the woman's mouth and nose. Yolanda gasped for air and inhaled deeply. Then Evie loosened the rope around her wrists, held together behind her back.

"No Justice!" Yolanda implored urgently, as soon as she got enough breath. "Go! I'll untie my legs."

Evie jumped to her feet and dashed to the adjoining stall. What she saw almost caused her to sink to the floor. "Kazzam!" she croaked. "Kazzam."

The horse's head sagged to his knees. His legs were apart, supporting his quaking body. His eyes were dull and his ears were flat back on his head. Blood was splashed across his head, scarlet against the white heart on his forehead.

His head rose when he saw her, and his eyes brightened. He drew a huge, shaky breath of air and snorted.

Evie stumbled into his stall. "Kazzam, what did they do to you?" She threw her arms around his neck, soiling her shirt with the sticky blood.

Kazzam nickered and rubbed his chin into her back, returning the hug unreservedly.

"Who did this, boy? What happened to you?" An image of her father popped into her head, but she rejected it immediately. She refused to believe he would do this, especially after his letter.

The little black horse snorted and pawed the ground. He seemed very much on edge. He shook his head and looked behind him. She'd never seen him so agitated. Evie wondered how much pain he was in.

Her heart ached to see the fight in him. Even bloodied and battered, he never gave up. He lived like he ran — all out. He chose the people he'd accept. Or not. He figured out the play of each race and insisted on doing it his way. Or buck off the rider. His spirit was what made him a champion, thought Evie. And that would never change until the day he died. She choked back that thought. *No! I didn't mean that! Please, please, let him not die today!*

But if it *was* today, if this was the end, she vowed to stay with him until he breathed his last breath. He deserved nothing less. She owed it to him, because Kazzam had trusted her, believed in her. Evie's stomach dropped. How had she let this happen? She should've been there herself to protect him! He was a sitting duck, locked in a stall, defenceless.

She became overcome with rage. She would see Kazzam avenged. This noble son of the racetrack would not be forgotten, even though someone, tonight, on the eve of his big race, had tried to cut him down before he could prove his worth to the world.

"Don't give up, Kazzam. Ever. I'll never give up on you," Evie promised as she tried to soothe him. She wiped her eyes and stood tall, filled with determination. She would rehabilitate her injured horse. Like Sella always said, where life be, there hope be.

Yolanda came up behind her, rubbing her sore wrists. "Let me take a look at him." She walked into the stall and began to give him a once-over, using Evie's flashlight.

Suddenly, the fluorescent overhead lights came on. Mary came running down the hall. "Evie? Yoyo?"

"Here, Aunt Mary!" Evie called. She stepped out to show her aunt which stall they were in.

At the same instant, Yolanda shrieked.

Evie spun around.

"The man!" screamed Yolanda.

Evie looked where Yolanda was pointing.

In the far corner of the stall, illuminated by the overhead lights, a man lay motionless and hunched up in the fetal position. He wore a filthy and torn security guard's uniform.

Mary stood with them, staring. "Is he dead or alive?"

"He sure lost a lot of blood," whispered Evie, looking at his clothes and the dark stain in the straw.

"That's the man who tied me up," said Yolanda, tightly clutching both women's arms.

"What happened, Yoyo?" asked Mary gently.

"This guard came up and started chatting. Things got strange and I started to call you. Then I must've blacked out, because I don't remember anything until a few minutes before Evie found me. When I woke up I realized I was gagged and tied up on the floor of Christieloo's stall. I found my phone in the straw."

"Well, this guy's not going anywhere. I'm getting help," said Mary firmly. "Anyone coming?"

Yolanda joined Mary and they marched purposefully to the guards' room.

Evie stayed in the stall. She cared only about Kazzam and how badly he was injured. He stood patiently as she slowly and carefully felt every inch of his legs. Nothing wrong there. She examined his chest, flanks, torso, withers, and neck. No punctures or stab wounds. His head was free of injury, too. Except for the sticky and drying blood, the horse seemed to be perfectly unharmed. But where did all the blood come from?

"My sweet horse," she murmured softly. "Are you okay?"

"No-o!" came a moan.

Evie almost jumped out of her skin. The man was conscious!

Kazzam stiffened. He backed up and lifted a hind hoof threateningly, aiming for the man's chest.

"Help me! That horse is vicious!"

Evie grabbed Kazzam's halter. "Easy, boy." To the man, she said, "You better stay exactly where you are, mister. Make one false move and this horse knocks your head off."

"He kicked me and bit my arm! Let me out!"

"You shouldn't have been here in the first place!" Evie took a look at him. His features were hard to distinguish in the dim light, and he held his right arm to his chest. She shot a glance down the hall, hoping that the guards were on their way. She didn't know how long she could keep up the tough-guy act.

The man moved his legs and whistled in pain. Evie prayed that he wasn't able to get up.

Kazzam quivered. His bottom lip tensed and the muscles in his jaw chenched. His ears flattened. Evie saw how much he hated this man and wished him harm. It was this man's presence that had made Kazzam so edgy, not pain, as Evie had first assumed.

"Look, kid," the man said. He sounded friendly now. "Let me go and I'll pay you five hundred dollars."

"Good try," Evie said.

"A thousand."

She was astonished. He thought she was bargaining!

"Fifteen hundred. That's it. Take it or leave it."

"Where did you get all that money?" Evie asked.

"That's none of your business."

The man clumsily tried to get up. He yelled with pain.

Again, Kazzam's ears flattened against his head and he threatened to kick.

"Okay, okay! Call off the horse!"

"Move and you're a dead man." Why were Mary and Yolanda taking so long?

Just then, Evie heard footsteps coming quickly toward them. *Finally!*

The man heard them, too. He lurched forward and tried to crawl out the stall door.

Kazzam reared. Then his front hooves came crashing down on either side of the man's torso. The man screamed. Kazzam stayed over him, not allowing him to move another inch.

"Good boy, Kazzam!" Evie said. She patted his neck and stood beside him, hoping that he didn't finish the job before the man was arrested. "Nice work."

At that moment Mary arrived, followed by a security guard, two police officers, and Yolanda.

"They were watching a porn flick," sniffed Yolanda.

The security guard took offence and pointed to the injured man. "He brought it! What were we to do?"

Efficiently, the two officers lifted the injured man from the floor. The officer in charge touched the brim of his cap. "Evening, Ms. Parson, Ms. Schmits. Thanks for your statements. We'll be in touch." He nodded briskly, and they disappeared down the hall together, assisting the hobbling perpetrator.

"I'm sure glad he's gone," said Evie, shuddering.

"Me, too. Now, let's see if No Justice is able to run tomorrow." Mary took a lead shank from the stall door and led the horse out.

He stepped out easily and with confidence. He had not sustained even one injury. Clearly, the blood on his body belonged to the intruder. He arched his neck, shook his mane, and let out a triumphant neigh.

Christieloo whinnied back. Every horse in the barn returned the call, and Evie felt a collective sigh in the stable. Within a minute, regular noises resumed. Munching hay, slurping water, passing gas. Several horses let out their urine. Tension had been felt by every single horse.

While Yolanda and Mary replaced his straw and filled

his hay net and water bucket, Evie hosed Kazzam down in the wash stall. "Interesting, Kazzam," she told him. "The thing that everybody hates about you, your distrust of people and the kicking and biting? Turns out it saved your life."

Christieloo and Kazzam were settled in their clean stalls and nodding peacefully when Mary yawned and said, "Time to go and get some sleep, Evie. Big day tomorrow."

Evie knew what she had to do. "I'm staying here."

"Nonsense," said Yolanda. "It's my job. Get out of here."

"Please. You two go. I'm totally okay. Please? I want to stay with Kazzam. I need to. For me. Now go home. I'll see you tomorrow."

Mary smiled proudly and placed her hand on Evie's shoulder. "You certainly will."

"Can you bring my riding stuff, Aunt Mary? It's all on the chair in my room."

"Absolutely." Then she asked, "How did you know, Evie? You were so sure No Justice needed you."

Evie shook her head. "I really don't know. But I'm sure glad we came here tonight."

Yolanda agreed. "Amen to that."

26

Race Day

The big day arrived. It was Sunday, the day of the running of the Queen's Plate.

The downpour had ended sometime after midnight, leaving the air fresh and clean. This very special morning dawned as bright and clear as any since 1860.

Evie had awoken several times in the night, wondering about the man Kazzam had beaten up, puzzling about what he'd been up to and why. Each time, she reassured herself that her horse was safe with her in the stall and then fell back to sleep in the deep straw.

Finally, she gave in to wakefulness as sunshine poured through the stable windows and the horses began to stir.

She climbed out of Yolanda's sleeping bag, stretched her arms and legs as she stood, and brushed the straw from her clothes. "It's today, Kazzam. It's finally today," she whispered to her horse. "Nobody can stop us."

The black horse nickered his agreement and pawed the ground before nosing around for discarded oats in the straw.

"One, two, and up!" Jerry said as he boosted Evie into the saddle. Imogene's saddle. Wearing Angela's riding boots.

They were in the outdoor Walking Ring at their appointed place. So far, the day had been a blur of excitement, and now she sat, numb, lost in her thoughts.

She had no right to be there. No right to be sitting in this saddle and wearing these boots. She hadn't earned it. She patted Kazzam's shiny black neck. Evie knew that she was here for one reason — because Kazzam allowed her, and no other jockey, to ride him. The horse had the speed. He was the star. If another jockey had wanted the ride, she wouldn't be sitting there, waiting for the race to begin.

It was noisy. The crowd was supposed to stay in the centre of the parade track, but the owners and their friends and grooms and trainers crawled around the place like ants.

Kazzam tossed his head and nickered. She stroked his withers absently, considering that just last night she thought he might die.

"Okay up there?" asked Jerry. A crease of concern crossed his brow when she didn't answer. "Evie?"

"Yeah. Right as rain."

He pinched Evie's calf to get her attention. "Rain? No rain today. It's a great day for a lope around the track."

Jerry hadn't heard her right, Evie thought. It didn't matter. They would run a good race. They'd make him happy.

Kazzam reared slightly, his front hooves leaving the ground, then coming down hard. Next, he hopped up impatiently with his hind end, then snorted loudly.

Her head cleared. "I get it, boy!" Evie laughed. Kazzam knew how to bring her back to the present. Kazzam knew how to give her head a shake. "We're going to do this," she promised him, "for your name in the history books. But mostly for my mother."

"She's talking to herself," said Jerry to her aunt. Evie heard him and saw his concerned look. He continued, "Last night was a big shock. And she's only sixteen. Do you think she's okay?"

"She's all right," answered Aunt Mary. She polished the toes of Evie's boots with a rag. "Aren't you, Evie?"

Am I all right? Evie asked herself. *Yes, I am.* "Let's do this!" she said loudly.

They smiled up at her at the same moment, with identical expressions of huge relief and great expectation.

At the sight, Evie began to laugh and she couldn't stop.

Their faces turned to worry again, simultaneously.

"Stop worrying!" she commanded them. "Seriously!" Evie forced herself to settle down.

Aunt Mary's eyes welled with tears. "I'm proud of you, dear girl. I love you. I'll see you at the finish line."

She patted Kazzam's neck and whispered, "You'll do us proud, No Justice, I know it." And then her slight frame disappeared into the crowd.

Jerry and Evie had a moment alone.

"You never needed my help with this horse, girl. The first time I saw you breeze him — it seems so long ago but it was only weeks — I saw how you let him run the way he needs to run. Follow that inner voice. It's a good one." Jerry patted her booted calf. "Remember, you're in slot one, on the inside track. No Justice likes to go wide, so don't let them squeeze you. And have fun, Evie. Enjoy the moment. Jockeys wait their whole careers for this race."

Evie nodded her thanks. Her throat was too full of emotion to allow her to speak. The trainer gave her a nudge and a hearty grin. "You know where I'm going? To put the last of my money on you. To win. Right now. Every penny."

Yolanda appeared at Evie's side riding Christieloo, who had temporarily become a track pony. They would accompany Kazzam to the gate. The two horses nickered and stayed side by side as if they were harnessed together. Immediately, Evie could sense the difference in Kazzam. Christieloo's presence made this whole experience less scary for him.

Yolanda had chosen to wear a bright, pink-and-white-checked blouse with a periwinkle-blue scarf. Angela's racing colours. She'd put effort into Christieloo's decorations as well, braiding pink and blue ribbons into the palomino's blond mane and tail. Her saddle pad was bright pink.

"Nice look, Yoyo," said Evie.

"For you, babe," answered Yolanda. She reached out and patted Kazzam's soft black nose. "He looks a heck of a lot better than he did last night. How are you doing, Evie?"

"Great. You?"

"Couldn't be better. Thanks for coming to the rescue."

"You would've done the same for me."

"True. That's what we do." The two smiled, sharing a moment of unspoken friendship.

"Come on, Evie. Time for the Post Parade."

Together they rode around the track in the outdoor Walking Ring, surrounded by the other Thoroughbreds and their ponies. The puddles were drying up rapidly.

Here, dignitaries mingled with common folk, and all took a good look at the horses that were about to run. Before they put good money down on bets, people sized up the competition and compared one horse to the next.

Disposition, fitness, soundness, and keenness were all on display.

Evie had no idea how Kazzam looked next to the others and cared not one bit. He was behaving perfectly, even with this big crowd and all the stress and excitement. Underneath her was a horse with a heart the size of the world. He'd proven it the night before by fighting off his attacker.

As an apprentice, she wasn't allowed a whip for her first five races, but she never carried a whip, anyway. Not with Kazzam. If he could win, he would win, that was all there was to it. He'd try to get in front. He'd try his best. That was all she could ask. That was all she *would* ask.

At her side, Yolanda broke into her thoughts. "There's Thymetofly. Looks good."

He was the odds-on favourite and every inch a champion. The eyes of the crowd were on him. He was a really nice horse, Evie thought, a good-looking bay, and she wished him well. Life would be better for him in her father's stables if he won. She recognized his pony, Jules. She was a stunning paint mare, and Beatrice had ridden her in hunter classes, winning many.

She looked around and checked out some others. Roustabout was a handsome chestnut with a powerful chest and haunches, but he was sweating a little too heavily, Evie noticed. Using up his energy before the race.

Despite the skill of jockey Luke Henry, Pirate's Dream had his nose tucked right into his pony's neck as if he wanted to go home and couldn't look at what was happening. Evie chuckled. She sympathized.

Passenger Pigeon strutted stiffly, showing how much he longed to get out and run. He might be a real contender, thought Evie. His jockey was Irv Walla. Now Evie put the jockey's face together with his name. He'd been the first jockey to come out of the men's locker room the day before.

Gasparilla and his pony were calm and collected, but to Evie's eye, not as fit as the others. His jockey, Juan Alou, spun his whip and switched hands. *Irritating nervous habit,* Evie thought.

Imogene's mount was LaLaLady, known for her sudden bursts of speed. Evie admired her sleek lines and gleaming light-bay coat. A nice filly, and the only female horse in the race. She was bucking. Not big bucks, just crow hops, but enough that her pony kept a good distance from the mare's back feet. Imogene handled the situation well. If Kazzam did that, Evie mused, because of his history everybody would be worried.

"Who's that, Yoyo?" asked Evie, looking at a horse she didn't recognize.

"The gelding with the long back?"

"Yes. Who is it?"

"Phil's Pholly. His jockey is Angel Barrera. Good guy."

Evie made a mental note. Something in the horse's eye got her attention. He looked smart, and more than a little sneaky.

"Holy! The governor general and his wife are here!" whispered Yolanda. Evie looked to the centre of the grass enclosure. A trim man dressed in morning coat and top hat grinned boyishly at the people in the ring. His wife seemed far more interested in the horses than the people. She studied them with a knowledgeable eye, and when Evie and Kazzam passed by, the horse gave her a little nicker. The woman smiled up at Evie. "Good luck," she mouthed.

Evie smiled back and mouthed, "Thank you." It meant a lot to her. Her back straightened and her resolve hardened. She wanted to show the world what she and her horse were made of.

"It's time," said Yolanda. "I'll get you to the gate."

"Number one all the way," asserted Evie.

Out on the big polyfibre track, Evie felt tiny. The stands were far in the distance. The green grass in the middle and on the sides was so bright that it hurt her eyes. She was glad that she'd been here once before, when she was given her apprentice status. Now, she saw that as her dress rehearsal.

Kazzam began to dance sideways. He was keen to run. "That's what we're here for, Kazzam, but not just yet." The horse tossed his head and began to prance.

Yolanda leaned in to grab his bridle. Before she could, though, Christieloo butted him with her head, hard, right on his neck. He jerked away, startled, and took a good look at the mare with his left eye.

Together, Evie and Yolanda laughed.

"That surprised him," said Evie.

"Smartened him up a bit," agreed Yolanda.

On both sides of them, and in front and behind, the contenders jogged and trotted on the long stretch toward the post. The colours of all the luminous silks were vibrant, and brilliant sunshine sparkled madly off the pond in the centre.

Evie could feel herself drifting into a fog again. Her muscles were going limp. This was exactly how she'd felt before the Caledon Horse Race. Strangely disconnected. But now she recognized it for what it was. Her body was storing up energy for when she needed it.

"Earth to Evie, earth to Evie," said Yolanda loudly.

"I'm all right," she mumbled.

"Here we are. Number one. I've got to leave you here. Will you be okay?" Yolanda sounded uncertain.

"I'm all right. Seriously."

"Do I have to head-butt you to wake you up? Like Christieloo?"

Evie snapped to. "We're ready to fly."

"That's my girl." Yolanda walked with Christieloo beside the gate and waited while the assistant starters got Kazzam into hole one, the closest position to the inside of the track. The gate clicked behind him.

Yolanda joined the other pony riders behind the post until the race began.

Evie positioned her goggles over her eyes and adjusted her helmet. She was alone with her horse. Ahead stretched the testing place, where horses vied for glory. Power, speed, endurance. That was what it was all about. "What are you thinking, Kazzam? Do horses care about glory?"

Eerily, Evie was sure she felt his answer. *No. We care about running the fastest … in any group.*

She was positive that was the correct answer.

As the other horses loaded, she bent her head and whispered, "Dear Lord of creatures great and small, please bring everybody home safely. Let the fastest horse win, not the best, cuz I know Kazzam is the best, no matter what happens today."

She thought back to the Caledon Horse Race, when she'd prayed to the animal gods to win. This was different, somehow. This was the big time. Winning would be the cherry on the chocolate sundae. A sundae still tastes delicious without it.

"They're at the post!" called the announcer.

Evie jerked into position. Very briefly, she glanced to her right. Thirteen riders sat forward over the necks of thirteen of the best three-year-old racehorses in Canada. Goggles over their eyes, hands forward, silks covering

292

their helmets, determined mouths, one-hundred-percent focus. In that split second, that little glimpse was etched into her brain. She would never forget it.

She also knew that they were tough and fast. Super fast.

Evie cleared her head and grabbed Kazzam's mane, ready for his enormous leap.

The bell went off. The gates shot open. "And they're off!"

A tremendous surge of animal bodies and radiant silks spilled out and away down the track like a tidal wave.

Once again Kazzam stood still while thirteen horses raced away. Evie waited and counted, holding on to his mane for dear life. *One, two, three, four—*

He leaped. They were off.

She landed in the saddle with her feet still in the stirrups and the reins still in her hands. She was getting better at this.

Within seconds she found Kazzam's rhythm. She reached her arms forward with every galloping rotation. His strides lengthened, then quickened, and the little black horse narrowed the distance between them and the second-last horse, Gasparilla.

Evie let Kazzam go wide around Gasparilla, and on they ran, still on the outside, easily passing Roustabout and three others running in a small herd. Now, Evie thought, they were in the race. This was a thrill.

Kazzam stretched out and continued to pick up speed.

Evie was having the time of her life. Her definition of winning as the cherry, not the whole sundae, had freed her. She raced for the sheer joy of it.

Evie felt light on her horse's back, barely touching him as he thundered, *thundered!* across the ground. She kept her eyes forward, looking through the frame of his perfectly pointed ears, and let the wind pull her cheeks back. She listened to Kazzam's hooves pounding, pounding, pounding, while his rhythmic breathing kept time. He was a one-horse band.

They sped by two more horses in a blink. *Zoom, zoom.* Evie was filled with elation.

Phil's Pholly was just ahead. Kazzam came up on his right with a steady gallop. As his nose levelled with Phil's Pholly's hip, the horse swerved wildly and cut him off. Kazzam got out of the way just in time, jumping with all four feet to the right and just managing to keep his balance. Evie almost came off in the unexpected movement. It scared her.

Now, things were serious.

Now, she wanted to win.

"Get past this guy," she urged. But Kazzam stayed where he was, right behind Phil's Pholly, waiting until he understood his options. He kept pace with the other horse and seemed to be using him as a shield.

In that fashion — Phil's Pholly with Kazzam right behind — they passed Thymetofly and then Paradise Found on the outside. Kazzam seemed uncertain about making another move on Phil's Pholly, so Evie waited.

There were four more horses ahead of them on the backstretch. She estimated that the race was half over.

Kazzam suddenly sped up and veered left, making his move to pass Phil's Pholly. He gave him lots of room, but Phil's Pholly swerved again and bumped him. The result could have been disastrous, but this time, Evie was ready and so was Kazzam. He jumped to the left and slipped behind Passenger Pigeon, coming up his inside. Now it was Passenger Pigeon who had to contend with the swerving horse. He didn't take kindly to it. In response to a shove, Passenger Pigeon hip-checked Phil's Pholly, forcing him aside. Kazzam sailed past them both on the inside rail.

The track was clear for seven or eight lengths. Evie let Kazzam get his bearings while she got hers. Those had been some close calls. Evie rose up in the stirrups and let him breeze. When his body lengthened out again, she hunkered down.

Three horses were running neck and neck, just ahead. They led the entire field. She recognized LaLaLady on the outside, next to Thymetofly in the middle, who must've come up from the back. She hadn't seen that happening and began to wonder what else she was missing. The third horse, on the inside rail, was Pirate's Dream.

Kazzam closed the gap handily. Evie knew he hadn't yet reached his top speed. She planned to let him sit in that position, right behind the leaders, in the catbird seat. When he wanted to move, he'd figure it out. In a horse race, he had the advantage of thinking like a horse.

He switched to his right lead. Until now, Evie hadn't heard any cheering from the crowd. As they turned onto the home stretch in front of the stands, she couldn't imagine she'd been able to ignore it. The noise was thunderous. It was deafening!

The race was closing in. Horses began to crowd them from behind in their final desperate effort to be first past the wire, and Evie got swept up in the mood. She really wanted to win. The chocolate sundae *with* the cherry. All of it!

Suddenly, right in front of them, LaLaLady moved away from the geldings, opening a slim gap. Perfect timing!

Evie pressed her toes into Kazzam's sides and asked him to go through.

His ears flattened right back. His entire body tensed, ready to buck. Evie felt him decide to let her stay aboard. It had been a warning she should heed.

But should she let her horse make all the decisions? The finish line was within their grasp. There was no time left to wait. They were one horse-length behind the three front-runners, there was a space between LaLaLady and Thymetofly, and Kazzam had lots of speed left to use. It was now or never. It was right in front of them! *We must make a move!* Evie's insides screamed. *Now! Right now!*

Against her better judgment, she forced herself to wait.

In his next two strides, Thymetofly moved inches to his right, toward LaLaLady. Kazzam gathered his tremendous reserves of power, then grabbed the bit with his teeth. He stormed through the narrowest of windows, right between Thymetofly and Pirate's Dream, and outraced them all.

They won by a cherry.

🌿 27 🌿

The Winner's Circle

Is it possible? wondered Evie. She looked back at the horses still crossing the finish line. Did they really win?

Yes! They'd won the Queen's Plate! *Yes!* Evie pumped her fist in the air, then reached down and hugged Kazzam's neck tightly as he slowed to a stop. *Yes!*

Before she'd even had a chance to think, a pretty brunette rode up beside her on a chestnut quarter horse. The woman smiled brightly and said into the mic, "I'm Renee Keirans, and I'm speaking to Evie Gibb, riding No Justice. Or Molly Peebles, riding Kazzam. Whoever you are and whatever your horse's name, you are both amazing. Congratulations on your ride. You must be so excited!" She stuck the fuzzy microphone in front of Evie's face.

But Evie needed to catch her breath. She was overcome. She felt delirious and didn't want to say anything stupid.

Renee brought the mic back to her own face and continued, "You rode a daring race, Evie. You got past Phil's Pholly and avoided the flying rear hooves of LaLaLady. Good call to wait and come between Thymetofly and Pirate's Dream."

That's why Kazzam refused to pass when LaLaLady gave him an opening, Evie thought. *Only a horse would have known what another horse was thinking!*

"Not very talkative, are you?" Renee laughed merrily. "It was a tough race. You beat Thymetofly by a nose, and LaLaLady came in a close third. Tell me, Evie, how do you feel right now?"

"Amazed. Amazed by my horse."

"A true horsewoman, folks. Once again, Evangeline Gibb, congratulations on a great ride!"

"Thank you," said Evie, tongue loosened now. "But it wasn't me who won, it was Kazzam. I mean, No Justice. He made all the decisions except the bad ones."

Renee laughed again. "Thanks, Evie, you ran a great race." She touched her ear, which Evie noticed had an earphone in it, and her brow suddenly furrowed. "Breaking news, folks. Word is, an inquiry has been lodged. More from Kathy Easton at Woodbine Entertainment."

"Inquiry? What about?" asked Evie, but Renee and her horse had trotted away.

That's when she realized that she was alone on the track. All the others had ridden back and were dismounting. Evie had just turned Kazzam to join them when Jerry, Mary, and Yolanda came running toward her on foot.

Aunt Mary called, "Unbelievable! Bravo, Evie!"

Jerry skipped and punched out his fists. He was too pumped up to say anything except "I'm rich!" and "We won!"

Yolanda had tears running down her face, blending crazily with black mascara. She jumped and hooted with joy. "He did it! You did it! We did it! We won!"

Aunt Mary was the only one who could speak coherently. "Let's get to the Winner's Circle, Evie! For the presentation!"

Evie took her feet out of the stirrups and began to slide down, but Mary stopped her. "No. Stay up. We go just the way we are."

After that, Evie stopped thinking and let Aunt Mary take control. She'd done what she'd set out to do. The whole day was a dream, anyway, with outrageous, unnaturally brilliant colours and way too much adrenalin.

The Winner's Circle was in front of the Royal Box and crowded with people. It was decorated with enormous garlands of flowers, blue and gold satin ribbons, and immaculately trimmed greenery. It all seemed to blend together, Evie thought, but overall it sure was beautiful. Nothing in the world could ruin their triumph.

Nothing in the world but the scene that unfolded.

"Foul! I demand an appeal!" Grayson Gibb bellowed in his strange high voice. It appeared that he'd lost his cool entirely and wasn't bothering to mask his rage with smiles or charm or pleasantries. "I challenge the validity of this horse and this jockey. They should *not* have been allowed to race!"

Evie's heart sank.

Beside him stood Les Merton, his trainer. The man's lips were pressed together tightly and his posture was ramrod straight. He looked very uncomfortable to Evie, but was being loyal to his boss.

"A fraud has been perpetrated," ranted Gibb. "The legitimate winner of the race is Thymetofly!"

Murray Planno, flanked by the two other stewards, had been ready to present the golden, foot-high cup and to drape the flower blanket over No Justice. Now, they stood frozen with indecision as reporters flocked around Grayson Gibb like hyenas to carrion.

Her father's words became obscured by conversations

all around her, as people asked one another what was going on.

Aunt Mary grabbed Evie's foot. "Look over there, dear. To the right, beside the hedge."

Evie looked. "What?"

"Your stepmother, Paulina, and Beatrice and Jordie. Over there." She pointed, and Evie saw the kids waving and jumping to get her attention. Jordie could hardly contain himself as he did a wild victory dance, and Beatrice looked as happy as Evie had ever seen her. Evie felt a sudden rush of love. She waved back and blew them kisses, which they returned tenfold. And there was Sella! She was with them, waving too, which made Evie very glad.

Paulina's boyfriend, Kerry Goodham, stood a little behind them, smiling handsomely. He would be much nicer to the kids than their own father, Evie figured, and with Sella rehired, things were likely to work out just fine, not "agaga." Evie made a wish for that to come true. She blew a special kiss to Jordie and vowed to stay close.

"Oh, my goodness," murmured Aunt Mary. "Evie. At the trophy table. Look at the lovely woman in the blue, wide-brimmed hat and sunglasses."

Evie saw the blue hat and the sunglasses. "Okay, but am I supposed to —" She stopped abruptly. "Is that … my mother?"

Angela Parson Gibb looked almost transformed. She was dressed in a beautiful, periwinkle-blue suit and pink blouse — her racing colours. Her hat, which covered her wound, matched the blue of the suit, and her wild red hair was tamed into a chignon at the nape of her neck. Angela's too-thin legs were enhanced by the mid-length, slightly flared skirt and new black pumps. She carried a black, patent-leather clutch purse at her side. Her teeth had been bleached. Even her fingernails had been manicured and painted the same pink as in her silks! Evie stared admiringly. Nice change from the street-person look, she thought.

Angela had told Evie that she wanted to be there, but Evie had never for a moment dared to hope that she could get herself together and actually come.

"I can't believe it," said Evie.

"I can," said Mary. "She's a very strong person, has been since the day she was born. I'm very proud of my daughter."

Your daughter? Evie shook her head. Aunt Mary must have misspoken, or maybe with all the noise, Evie hadn't heard properly. "You said 'daughter.' Don't you mean your niece, Aunt Mary?"

Mary looked up at Evie with a serene expression. "No, I'm her mother. My older brother and his wife desperately wanted children and couldn't have them. I got pregnant and was too young to raise a child properly. It was the perfect solution for everyone."

"But, why ... why tell now?"

"Why not? Today's a new start. For everybody."

On this day of crazy surprises, the news that Aunt Mary was actually her grandmother seemed exactly right. "Is she coming home with us?"

"Yes." Mary nodded. "Today. Dr. Graham okayed it."

"I guess I call you Granny now? Or Gran Mary?"

"Gran Mary? I like it." Aunt Mary squeezed her foot again. "But look who's there with Angela. The dear boy."

Mark Sellers stepped from behind and appeared at Angela's side with a chair, then held her arm to steady her. He looked a little shy. Evie waved. He waved back proudly. Evie was so glad he was there that her chest actually hurt. And she was deeply pleased that he was looking after Angela.

In fact, she wondered fleetingly, did Mark have anything to do with her mother getting here?

Because her mother had everything to do with Evie getting here, to the Winner's Circle, sitting on Kazzam, her mother's horse. Evie was filled with gratitude to this woman, who remained a big mystery to her. She tried to catch her eye to signal her thanks, but Angela was intent on every word coming out of Grayson Gibb's mouth.

Over at the edge of the crowd stood a small group of jockeys. Had they come to offer support? wondered Evie. Or to see what was going on? Imogene Wilson was among them, and still grimy from her ride on LaLaLady, she wiggled her fingers at Evie.

Evie waved back and pointed to her borrowed saddle. "Lucky saddle!" she yelled. "Thank you!"

Imogene held two thumbs up.

Another familiar face emerged from the sea of strangers. Chet Reynolds held a microphone to Grayson Gibb's mouth to catch every last utterance. He must have felt Evie looking at him, for he grinned at her with raised eyebrows and a nod. He'd wanted a story, and today he was getting one.

Murray Planno was on the stage, trying hard to get things under control. "Hello? Folks? Attention!"

The reporters were finished with Grayson. They moved en masse to the stage, ready to feast on more news and, with luck, more scandal. Cameras and microphones focused on Murray Planno, dressed in his finest mixture of plaids and stripes. He looked very unhappy.

"The stewards cannot make a final decision. We will convene a meeting to review the rightful ownership of No Justice, the winning horse. For the first time in history, the Queen's Plate —"

"Mr. Planno!" Angela interrupted him in a shaky but penetrating voice. She stood beside the large golden trophy, while Mark stood guard at her side. She wobbled. He grabbed an elbow and held her steady.

Most people had no idea who she was, but all heads swivelled toward her, waiting to hear what she had to say. Evie hoped fervently that her mother could pull this off.

"My name is Angela Parson Gibb." Her voice wavered. She cleared her throat and coughed. Mark silently urged her on. "I am the owner of No Justice."

There was an audible gasp in the crowd. "I have legal documentation to prove it." With trembling hands she opened her purse and produced a sheaf of papers. They shook wildly in her hand, but she held her head high and retained an air of quiet dignity.

"Thank you." Murray Planno reached down and took them. "I ask for your patience, ladies and gentlemen."

Mark grabbed the chair and sat Angela down in it while the three stewards bent over the papers, giving them their complete concentration. They conferred among themselves.

Grayson Gibb could not keep quiet. "This is unbelievable! I am an institution. My word should overrule the rantings of a ... a derelict ... a street person!"

The crowd booed him. Evie recognized hurt on her mother's face. Mark squeezed her shoulder in support.

Murray Planno stared Grayson down. "Mr. Gibb, you're out of order. These are valid, authorized, legal papers."

"Have a decent lawyer look at them!"

"That will not be necessary. We have our winner."

"I object! Thymetofly is the winner! Look at the race tapes! No Justice bumped into Phil's Pholly! I'll lodge a complaint against him!"

At the mention of Phil's Pholly, the jockeys got agitated. Imogene Watson stepped up. "Yes, please! Look at the tapes. Phil's Pholly bumped into No Justice. And before him, Roustabout. And then Passenger Pigeon. And —"

"That's bunk!" screamed Grayson.

The jockeys glared at him and looked ready for a fight.

Murray lifted his chin and nodded curtly. Two police officers appeared. They strode through the crowd, parting the onlookers like a boat on the water, coming to a stop at either side of Grayson Gibb.

The officer on his right said, "Mr. Gibb, we're taking you down to the station. You are under arrest for conspiracy to commit fraud and to commit cruelty against animals, causing harm."

People gasped and then a murmur rose from the crowd.

It suddenly became very clear to Evie. The attack on No Justice. It had been her father. He'd ordered it. Aunt Mary was right. He *was* a scorpion and he did what scorpions do. He'd never change. The letter was a fraud. He'd never cared about her. A part of her had known this all along.

The policemen read Grayson his rights, then escorted him out. Grayson yelled hoarsely, making it known that this was a grave miscarriage of justice and that he, Grayson Gibb, would see them all in court.

Then her father was gone. A calm fell over Evie. She cleared her head of everything except her horse. She inhaled the lovely June air and basked in the small black horse's accomplishment. She stroked his smooth, powerful neck. "Thank you, Kazzam. You are the fastest of them all. Today, everybody knows it."

Murray took out a handkerchief and mopped his brow.

He spoke into the microphone. "Let's begin again, folks, shall we?" He smiled, and the crowd applauded. When the applause subsided, he continued, "I hereby declare that No Justice is the winner of this year's running of the Gallop for the Guineas — the Queen's Plate!"

Gallantly and with great ceremony, he handed Angela Parson Gibb the Queen's Plate trophy, polished to a golden glow. She almost dropped it, but Mark caught it in time.

As people cheered and applauded again, Angela searched for and found Evie. Immediately, she began to make her way toward her daughter and No Justice. Her progress was marked by the golden trophy she held.

Mark elbowed her through the crush of people with the assistance of Mary, Jerry, and Yolanda. When they finally got through, Angela passed the trophy up to her daughter, arms shaking and her face wet with tears.

Evie took it. It was warm from the sun, and heavy. Very heavy. She imagined all the years of races and winners that it had seen.

"We did it for you, Mom. I love you."

The loudest cheer of all echoed throughout the stands.

As cameras rolled, Evie held the treasured object high in the air, sitting proudly astride her much maligned little horse, grinning from ear to ear.

Evie had just handed the trophy down to Murray when Kazzam reared up and whinnied so loudly that Murray and several others jumped away. He pawed the air in a show of triumph and then dropped his front hooves down lightly with a great toss of his head and a series of nickers and snorts.

Angela reached over and held Evie's calf, smiling up at her. Her eyes shone with happy tears. "Beautiful ride, Jockey Girl."

Evie felt a lump of gratitude in her throat. "Thank you, Mom. But it's you who's beautiful today."

"Credit goes to Mark and Mary. Mark found me Friday afternoon and drove me up to his mother's lovely new spa."

So that was the errand that Mark had to do on Friday afternoon!

"And Mary took me to her lawyer to get the power of attorney legally changed. Oh … And these are Mary's clothes," she continued, indicating her blue suit and hat. "They've all taken good care of me, Evie. Just look at my nails! Yesterday, they made me spend the whole gosh-darn day soaking!"

28

The Awful Secret

It was Wednesday morning around ten. The chores were done and there was a little lull in activity, perfect for a coffee break. Yolanda was soaking up the sun on the side patio, catching up on her rest and very happy with her cozy apartment over the garage. Mary was inside, working on her next novel.

Evie and Angela sat together on the wicker lawn chairs in the kitchen garden under the birch trees, while Magpie rested under Evie's chair. She leaned down to give the dog a good scratch behind the ears, and smiled at Magpie's complete contentment.

Sunlight sparkled on the dewy grass. Birds were busy with their full nests, and all around them the world of insects was buzzing about its business. The fresh aromas of rosemary, oregano, and parsley hung in the air.

Angela had moved into Parson's Bridge the evening of the victory, waiting for her place in a private rehabilitation facility. Mary had been put in charge of making sure that Angela followed Dr. Graham's orders to the letter before being admitted. She was to be watched at all times so she didn't leave or consume something harmful.

This morning Angela wore Aunt Mary's faded jeans and tangerine blouse, and her feet were bare. She stretched her legs and stubbed out a cigarette, then took a sip of her coffee. Her hands were shaky and she took care not to spill.

Evie had noticed how her mother rarely looked people in the eye. She was in constant motion and never really relaxed. Sometimes she would chew her nails hungrily and make odd facial movements. Tics, really. And scratch at her skin.

She didn't really know this woman, Evie realized. Had trouble thinking of her as her mother. She hoped that as time went by and as Angela got better, that would change.

"I'm glad you're here, Mom. I was a little worried."

"About me coming to Parson's Bridge?"

"Yes. I guess I didn't understand about … you know, addiction. And what it meant, like what could happen."

"I understand."

"It's all so new to me."

"I'm sorry, Evie."

"I … I didn't mean…. I only…."

"Please. Don't worry. It's a new beginning. With lots of new knowledge. Aunt Mary is now my mother, for one."

Evie nodded. "Surprised the heck out of me. She's Gran Mary to me now."

Angela chuckled, coughed, and then said, "My parents were wonderful people. After they died, Aunt Mary was my only family. So really, whether she's my aunt or my mother, it's almost the same." She dug at a mosquito bite with a fingernail as she spoke.

Evie nodded. "I know. She's the same person to me, too, whether she's my great-aunt or my grandmother."

"She's a wonderful lady." Angela's toes twitched in their own rhythm on the grass.

"She sure is. She took me in. And Magpie and Kazzam. Without one question or any conditions."

Angela nodded vaguely and stared into the sky, making Evie wonder if she'd heard what she'd said.

"I'm going into rehab tomorrow. I want to get better. It's the right time for me. If Mary hadn't been there for me, I don't think I'd be here right now, to see this day. In fact, I know it."

Evie shivered, in spite of the sun's warmth. "I'm glad you're here." Her emotions about her mother had been a roller coaster, but it was true. She *was* glad. Sitting outside in the garden with Angela was something she'd thought would never happen.

Angela coughed again. She reached into her bag, pulled out another cigarette, and lit it. Evie hated that she smoked, and so heavily. But Dr. Graham had told them not to expect Angela to break all her bad habits at the same time.

Angela fidgeted with her cigarette and changed the subject. "I'm happy I saw you win the Plate. It was my life's dream, but you did it." She patted Evie's arm.

"Thank you." Evie still had trouble believing it was true. She looked over to the field where Kazzam was grazing with Christieloo. *He's so gorgeous,* she thought. She could watch him all day, admiring his classic lines and gleaming ebony coat.

"Your boyfriend Mark is quite a guy," said Angela. "He wouldn't take no for an answer."

Evie grinned. "He kidnapped you, didn't he. And took you to his mom's spa. I didn't know anything about it until I saw you at the Winner's Circle."

"Is he a keeper?" Angela asked coyly, inhaling on her cigarette. She coughed again and recrossed her legs.

Evie hoped so. Mark had been great throughout the

whole adventure, and she loved spending time with him more than anybody else, but she didn't want to jinx it. "For now he is. I guess we'll see."

Angela nodded. "He's lovely. He took me at face value when I was far from presentable. That's rare."

Evie could imagine how much that might mean to her.

Angela leaned closer and spoke quietly. "I need to explain why I left you all those years ago." She wiped her mouth with a quick motion. "It's my awful secret."

Evie didn't move. Something about her mother's voice alerted her to pay close attention.

Angela stared absently at her cigarette. "When I tell you, you might decide I'm unworthy. I wouldn't blame you." She shrugged. "It's how I've judged myself all this time."

Evie felt herself getting gooseflesh. "I'm ready, Mom. I want to know the truth, whatever it is."

Angela took one last puff and ground the cigarette into the ashtray. Evie noticed that there were already six butts.

"You've heard about my accident at the track and my injuries, and how I needed pain medication?"

"Yes. Aunt ... Gran Mary told me all about that."

"I was in considerable pain. But even after the pain became bearable, I kept taking the pills. I knew that my mind wasn't totally clear, but I didn't blame it on the drugs, really. The truth was, I didn't want to stop."

Angela brought her knees up to her chin, and her manicured toes hung over the seat of the wicker chair. Evie had noticed earlier how much better she looked after a few days of healthy eating and sunshine. But now her brow was furrowed and her jaw was clenching as she chewed hard on a fingernail and stared at her feet.

"Grayson told me. He kept telling me, nagging at me, to get off the pills. I lied. I told him I'd quit and started to hide them. I thought he couldn't possibly know."

Evie sat still and waited for her mother to continue.

"Then things began to fall apart. I didn't know it, though. I got mad when people thought I needed help. Then, when … this thing … happened, I couldn't fool myself any longer." She paused, looking at something distant.

She put her feet back down and twisted her hands together. Her head dropped and her shoulders began to bob as she fought tears.

"You can tell me another time," Evie said quietly. "If it's too hard —"

"No. I need to tell you now. I'm leaving tomorrow." Angela wiped her face with her napkin and fumbled for another cigarette. She spoke in a halting way. "You were three. A healthy, beautiful little girl. All you wanted to do in the summer was get in the pool and splash and play."

Evie was shocked. "Me? In the water?"

"Yes. You loved it almost as much as horses. Which was a whole lot. When you weren't in the barn, I couldn't keep you out of the water." Angela got the cigarette lit and inhaled hungrily.

The idea that she'd ever liked to be in water was hard to believe, and Evie wondered if Angela remembered correctly. "Go on. Please."

"We were at the pool and you were playing. The sun was warm and I nodded off. I don't remember anything until the moment when I saw your father's soaking clothes and your limp body. He stood there shouting at me, screaming for help. Then he turned you over and out came a lot of water. More water than I thought could fit into your tiny body."

Angela cleared her throat and sank deeper into the chair. She still did not look at Evie. Her lips quivered. "I thought you were dead. He gave you mouth-to-mouth and pressed on your chest until you made a choking sound and began to cry. It was the most wonderful sound I've ever heard."

Evie's eyes blurred. She realized that her arms were wrapped around her chest and her legs were wound around each other. *This* was the reason she got a panicky feeling around water.

"You see, Evie? I couldn't look after you. That's when I knew you were better off with your father." Angela rocked in her chair and clenched her hands into fists.

Evie tried hard to comprehend.

"Grayson's lawyer came within the hour. They drew up the papers and I signed them. I didn't read them. I was ashamed. I went away."

Evie was totally numb, but she asked, "Where?"

"To a hotel."

"What did you do?"

"I went to walk-in clinics and doctor's offices to get more prescriptions. It's hard work being an addict."

Evie sat silently. She pictured her mother wandering around, scrounging for OxyContin.

"When I ran out of sources, I went to Toronto and found a hostel. I looked for a job." Her voice became weary. "I went to emergency rooms and more walk-in clinics and more doctor's offices. If you want to know more, I'll tell you all about it. I have no secrets anymore."

"Did Gran Mary know any of this?" Evie croaked.

"I didn't want anyone to know, least of all Mary."

"Does she know now?"

"Yes. As I said, I have no secrets anymore."

"But didn't you ever want to get me back?" Evie found herself almost begging.

"Yes!" Angela grabbed her daughter's hand and squeezed it, startling Evie. "Every time I cleaned up and got a paying job, I wanted to come back to get you."

"So why didn't you?"

Angela released Evie's hand. "Because Grayson threatened to charge me with neglect and being an unfit mother. He'd end up keeping you anyway. I'd slink away again. Ashamed."

"But why did he want me with him? He never even liked me." Evie almost choked on her words, but they were audible.

"He has a hard time with emotion, Evie. You know that. But there was a different reason. With you came the stables and the lifestyle. I'd signed away my inheritance to him so that he could raise you and never have to worry about money. But it made him resent you."

"I wish I'd known."

"I wish I'd been stronger."

Mother and daughter reached for each other at the same moment. Under the birch trees in the kitchen garden, they cried for the lost years and the anguish suffered.

There was much more that Evie wanted to say and much more she wanted to know, but for now, her mother's tearful confession and her own sense of finding something long-lost was enough.

They heard a rap from the kitchen window. Startled, they both looked up to see Mary's concerned face.

Angela waved. "Come on out."

Mary emerged from the house. "I don't want to interrupt you, and I'm sorry if I did, but Jerry called and I've got news."

Angela sniffed back her last tear. She kept an arm around Evie's shoulder and said, "We're finished for now." She looked at Evie and gave a wobbly smile. "Right?"

"Right." Evie nodded. Angela had finally made eye contact. She smiled back at her mother, then looked at Mary, who was bursting to tell her news.

"Grayson's been deemed a flight risk, so there's no bail, and he'll be detained until his trial. He's been formally charged with conspiracy to commit an indictable offence."

Evie was riveted. "Is there proof?"

"There was a cheque for five thousand dollars in the pocket of the bribed security guard."

"Signed by Grayson?" guessed Angela.

Mary nodded. "Yes, but he denies it. The guard, Neil Childs, has been very helpful in exchange for a deal. He said he was to get five thousand dollars more when the job was done. He claims Grayson hired him to put No Justice down."

Evie gasped. "To kill him?"

"That's what Neil claims and what the court battle will be about, I'm sure. Grayson denies everything, but the facts add up to insurance fraud."

Evie whistled. That's what she'd been afraid of since the night she hid in Kazzam's stall and overheard Grayson tell Jerry to get rid of him. *He must've thought that Angela couldn't prove ownership.* Otherwise, *she* would've gotten the insurance money.

Angela became quiet. She coughed and got another cigarette out of her bag. "This is good, in one way at least. I'll redeem my horses and my family inheritance. I want my life back." Angela inhaled deeply and nodded. "I can concentrate on my treatment knowing I have something to come back to."

Evie watched her mother's hands shake as she lit the cigarette and hoped she'd have the strength to make that dream come true.

Mary put her hand on Angela's shoulder. "I expect you won't have any trouble getting your life back, especially now that Grayson has abdicated the position."

Evie considered Grayson's incarceration. He was all alone. Paulina, Beatrice, and Jordie had left him, to start a new life in Newmarket with Kerry. It was sad, but he'd caused it himself, by his own actions. He had also besmirched his name in the racing industry.

The thing Evie would never get past was that her father had tried to destroy her greatest aspiration and, more importantly to her, the horse she loved. For what? To win? He chose his own success over hers every time, always had, but Evie wondered how much of this was to punish her for disobeying his orders. In spite of that letter he'd left at the door in the rain. He must have written it as he was organizing the hit on Kazzam.

But something nagged at her.

Then the realization hit. "He saved my life." She sat back down. "My father pulled me out of the water when I was drowning. He did care about me. Once. At least enough to save me. I wish I'd known that."

Mary tried to soothe her. "You know now. That's what's important."

Evie found herself choked up. Her father had made her feel unwelcome and unworthy in his house. Useless. A nuisance. Nothing in their history had prepared her for this revelation. It was a new reality.

Why had he never told her about saving her life? she wondered. He could have made himself the hero. But he hadn't. Ever. In this one instance, he'd been a gentleman. She'd found one thing to like about her father, and that was very important to her.

Kazzam whinnied loudly, disturbing her thoughts. Evie looked over to his field. Her beautiful, tough, brave little horse stood at the fence, staring at her. His heart-shaped star glowed white against his shiny black face. He raised his front right leg and tapped his hoof against the boards, then whinnied again.

Evie rose from her chair and crossed the sloping lawn toward him. Magpie followed closely on her heels.

No one could see the tears rolling down her face. Not Mary, who had opened her heart and home to her when she ran away. Not Angela, who was back in Evie's life for better and for worse. Not Yolanda, who was fast asleep in the sun. And not Mark, who was coming over that afternoon for a ride on Christieloo.

And if they had, they might not understand that these tears were tears of complete and utter joy. Tears that fell from an overflowing heart.

Evangeline Gibb stroked the soft nose of the most celebrated racehorse in Canada. She looked up into the blue sky and whispered, "Thank you, Lord of creatures great and small."

Epilogue

The headlines the day after the race had been predictable. "Jockey Girl and her Little Black Horse" was written up in the *Globe and Mail*. The *Toronto Sun* proclaimed, "Upset by Upstart!" and the *Toronto Star* boldly stated, "Conflict When Dark Horse Wins by a Nose!"

The definitive piece had been written by Chet Reynolds, of the *Orangeville Banner*. He'd titled it "Justice for No Justice," just like Evie had suggested. Now he had the whole story. Angela had talked to him openly. Mary had revealed pertinent details. He'd interviewed Beatrice, Jordie, Yolanda, and Jerry. He'd pieced together Evie's adventures, from winning the Caledon Horse Race to running away, to finding her mother, to the night she'd spent in a Woodbine stall, to becoming the winner of the Queen's Plate. Chet was offered well-paid positions at big newspapers. By Tuesday he'd received three offers to write a book and two to make a film.

With its million-dollar purse, the Queen's Plate is the richest race in Canada for Canadian-bred Thoroughbreds. The million dollars breaks down this way: sixty percent to the first-place owner, twenty percent to second place, eleven percent to third, six percent to fourth, and three percent to the fifth-place owner. That meant that Angela received $600,000, and Evie as the jockey took her ten percent from that, which is $60,000, as did Jerry, the trainer. The valet and groom shared $3,000.

As well as his ten percent, Jerry made a fortune betting all his money on No Justice, the long shot, and now was in great demand after training a Plate winner.

Grayson Gibb remains in jail after the jury decided unanimously that he was guilty as charged. He's appealing the decision, but Evie believes he'll lose.

Since winning the Queen's Plate, No Justice has become a legend. People come to stroke his nose over the fence at Parson's Bridge and to take his picture. He loves it. He feels he's earned his fame, and has many more races to run. Talk is that he'll be entered in the Prince of Wales Stakes in July, and then, if Jerry has his way, the Breeders' Stakes in August. If Kazzam wins those two races, he'll have won Canada's Triple Crown, joining a very elite club of only seven winners since its origin: New Providence, Canebora, With Approval, Izvestia, Dance Smartly, Peteski, and Wando.

Keep an eye on Chet Reynolds's columns for updates. He's all over it.

AUTHOR'S NOTE

My first horse was named Napoleon. He was a small black Thoroughbred gelding with a big white heart on his forehead and an attitude that kept normal people as far away as possible. Luckily for him, I was a horse-crazy fourteen-year-old who'd begged for riding lessons from the age of five.

My father was a developer. On a property he'd purchased to create a subdivision in London, Ontario, stood an old barn. Hiding in a dark corner of a filthy stall, starved, beaten, and neglected, was a young racehorse who'd been used in chariot races — the meanest, toughest racing of all. Illegal and unregulated, horses are tied to anything with two wheels and forced to run as fast as possible on a country road when a gun is fired.

Napoleon was left in the barn because the owner was too afraid of him to let him out. He came with the property, and was given to me as an alternative to being destroyed. He taught me lessons about horse psychology that I would never forget. I have written this book in his memory.

ACKNOWLEDGEMENTS

There are many people to thank when a book is created, and this small mention is barely sufficient.

I needed experts to teach me about Thoroughbred racing to ensure I got the details right. I found them in Fox Ridge manager Chris Higgins; jockey Emma-Jayne Wilson; her long-time agent Mike Luider; his wife, announcer Renee Keirans; and my friend Frank Merrill, of Tallyho Racing. I cannot thank you enough for the time you spent with me on the track and in conference.

Gordon Mack Scott, of Strategic Improvement Company, helped me plumb the mysteries of living with drug addiction. My sister Deb Matthews was minister of health in the Ontario government, and she opened my eyes to street life and its denizens.

My family has played a huge role in every book I've written, and this one is no exception. My husband, David, was the first reader. My mother, Joyce Matthews, was the second. My children, Chloe Dirksen, Ben, and Adam Peterson, had many valuable insights. To my sisters, Carole, Dona, and Deb Matthews, and Virginia Lato, I give a huge bouquet of hugs.

I thank Linda Pruessen and Robin Spano for their professional assistance, and my agent, Amy Tompkins of Transatlantic Agency, for finding this novel a good home with the Dundurn family.